Zoë Miller was born in Dublin, where she now lives with her husband. She began writing stories at an early age. Her writing career has also included freelance journalism and prize-winning short fiction. She has two daughters and a son.

www.zoemillerauthor.com
@zoemillerauthor
Facebook.com/zoemillerauthor

PREVIOUSLY BY ZOË MILLER

A House Full of Secrets
Someone New
A Question of Betrayal
A Husband's Confession
The Compromise
A Family Scandal
Rival Passions
Sinful Deceptions
Guilty Secrets

THE
VISITOR

ZOË
MILLER

HACHETTE
BOOKS
IRELAND

First published in Ireland in 2018 by
HACHETTE BOOKS IRELAND

1

Cataloguing in Publication Data is available from the British Library

ISBN 9781473664661

Typeset in Arno Pro by Bookends Publishing Services, Dublin

Printed and bound in Great Britain by Clays Ltd, Elcograf S.p.A.

Hachette Books Ireland policy is to use papers that are natural, renewable and
recyclable products and made from wood grown in sustainable forests.
The logging and manufacturing processes are expected to conform to the
environmental regulations of the country of origin.

Hachette Books Ireland
8 Castlecourt Centre
Castleknock
Dublin 15, Ireland

A division of Hachette UK Ltd
Carmelite House, 50 Victoria Embankment, EC4Y 0DZ

www.hachettebooksireland.ie

Dedicated to the memory of my beloved parents, Lockie and Olive
And to the beautiful little ones who carry their spark –
Cruz, Tom, Lexi, J.P., Sophia
Milo and Rosie
Sophie and Harry

THURSDAY,
21 DECEMBER

PROLOGUE

The airport tannoy grated on his nerves. He told himself to stay chilled. The next few hours were critical in his plan to recover what Sam Mallon had robbed from him and he needed a clear head.

The weather had played right into his hands. Severe polar conditions had brought snow and ice blanketing down across Western Europe, disrupting travel severely at one of the busiest times of the year.

He stood at the edge of the food hall, sipping watery coffee, checking the electronic display board, carefully noting the various flights that had been diverted from other airports into Dublin. The passengers flooding in through the festively decorated arrival gates fell into two categories:

ecstatic that they'd made it home despite the worsening weather conditions or shell-shocked that their flights had been redirected to Dublin, throwing their Christmas travel plans into disarray. Now the snow was sweeping into Ireland and presently an announcement came across the tannoy. The runways were being shut to allow for snow-clearing and de-icing. A collective gasp of desperation rippled around the packed crowd at this fresh outrage.

Perfect. For him, the snow was a beautiful bonus. To all appearances, he was nothing more than one of the stranded thousands, stuck in the wrong airport, where a seat on a flight out between now and Christmas Day was the equivalent of gold dust.

He'd had a couple of scenarios ready. Losing his passport had been one; being turned back at immigration had been another plausible excuse; and with overbooked flights at Christmas and a delay in his paperwork, either of those pretexts would have given him four or five days. He didn't need them now. Stranded at Christmas was the perfect cover. Still, he wasn't taking any chances. He didn't have to be there, but he'd checked out of his city-centre hotel and come out to the chaotic airport because he knew that experiencing the bedlam at first hand would lend him credibility. He checked his phone. Thanks to the software he'd installed on hers, he knew her every move and communication. Izzie Mallon was still in the office, so he had to hang loose for a while. As soon as she left for home, it would be his cue to get out of this wretched place and make his way to her place on Henrietta Square, arriving suitably travel-worn and dishevelled. Thanks to the information coming through to his phone, he knew she'd be there from this afternoon, burrowed away for Christmas. She sure as hell wasn't going to family, never mind anywhere else.

He focused his mind by staring at his luggage label, imprinting the name on his brain: Eli Sanders. He daren't forget, not for a moment.

CHAPTER ONE

'What part of the country are you off to, Izzie?' Gemma asked.

Izzie took a slow breath and nailed a neutral expression on her face before she looked up at Gemma. The younger woman stood beside her desk, her halo of blonde curls framed by the forest of Christmas tinsel, glittering baubles and cheap and cheerful festive bling that festooned the office.

Sensitive to her situation, they'd asked Izzie if it was okay to put up decorations. She'd told them to feel free. After all, it was just a meaningless heap of gaudy glitter, tawdry and tasteless. Although she never used to have that cynical view of Christmas. She used to love this time of year, even the bling, for its essential message of joy, love and peace. This year was different. This year she was blanking it all out. Like everything else.

'I'm off to the Blackwater Valley,' she told Gemma.

'Sounds like a lovely part of the country,' Gemma said, turning to look out the window. 'Although I think you'll be lucky to get going anywhere in this weather, never mind the depths of Munster.'

Izzie followed her gaze. Outside on Baggot Street, beyond the first-floor window of O'Sullivan Pearse Auctioneers, the sky resembled a dense, murky cloak pressing down on Dublin city centre. Underneath that, a cloud of spinning snowflakes eddied and bumped against each other in a thick cascade. The snow had started falling earlier that morning – she'd awoken to a world dusted in white, but now it was getting heavier. A dense layer of snow covered the paths and the road outside, gouged sporadically with footprints and tyre tracks from slow-moving traffic. Small hillocks of slush were piling against the kerb.

Sam would have loved the snow. He'd missed it by almost twelve weeks. Eleven weeks and five days to be exact.

She was still counting in days and weeks. Soon it would be months. 'My mum says it reminds her of the Christmas freeze of 2010,' Gemma continued, her overly chatty tone telling Izzie that her young mentee had sensed her pang of sadness and was doing her best to keep things light for Izzie's sake. 'I didn't take too much notice at the time – I was fifteen and indulging in a major wallow of self-pity over my first painful breakup.' Gemma rolled her eyes. 'He went off with one of my so-called friends. You should have seen me, Izzie, talk about tragedy queen. I spent most of that Christmas holed up in my bedroom, writing crap poetry and planning horrible revenge.'

Izzie felt a small smile curving her mouth at the image Gemma conjured up. 'Poetry is never crap,' she said.

Seven years since the last big Christmas freeze. Izzie had been twenty-five and had enjoyed the novelty of it all. She lifted her chin. 'I'm not going to let a bit of snow stop me,' she said. At least things were still moving in the city centre – albeit at a snail's pace – but if the snow continued like this into the afternoon or evening, everything could grind to a halt.

'A *bit*! Yeah, right. You're so funny, Izzie.' Gemma's brow wrinkled. 'So long as you don't get stranded somewhere. Could easily happen, you know, according to the forecast. Please stay safe.'

'I'll be fine. I'm out of here by lunchtime, and I'll be halfway there before it gets any worse.' She didn't bother crossing her fingers at the lie.

Gemma's eyes glinted merrily. 'I'll think of you forcing down cabbage soup when I'm tucking into my yummy turkey and ham.'

'Less of the cabbage soup,' Izzie said. 'It's a holistic retreat and we'll get fed, healthily and nutritiously. I'm not that much of a martyr.'

'Anybody who turns down Christmas and all the trimmings in favour of a country yoga retreat has to be a saint of some description. I'd sooner die than pass up a Christmas dinner. Ohhh—'

Izzie watched the dawning realisation ripple across Gemma's face as her hand went up to her mouth and knew exactly what was coming next. She could manage this. She *could*.

'Jeez, Izzie, I'm awful sorry. I forgot for a moment …'

Gemma said, speaking through her fingers as though the flimsy barrier might prevent a further faux pas from breaking free, the effect lessened by the flashing knuckleduster Rudolf ring she was wearing.

Izzie twirled a pencil between her slim fingers. 'It's okay. I'm glad you forgot – I'd far prefer that. Life goes on, as they say.'

She was glad Gemma hadn't been around when the bottom had dropped out of her world. Gemma had only begun her internship shortly before Izzie had returned to her job in the head office of O'Sullivan Pearse in mid-November, after six weeks' leave of absence, and Izzie knew full well that she'd been quietly advised as to her mentor's delicate circumstances, lest she put her foot in it. She was glad that Gemma occasionally forgot to walk on eggshells around her. It meant she saw Izzie as a normal person and not a dysfunctional wreck.

Gemma slapped her own forehead. 'Shut me up, please. I'm not usually this stupid. I was out with my mates last night – too late.'

'You're forgiven,' Izzie said. 'And you're doing exactly what you should be doing – having plenty of late nights and fun.'

'Is there anything I can do to help you finish up?' Gemma asked. 'The sooner you get going the better.'

Izzie stared unseeingly at the icons on her desktop and shook her head. 'There'll be nothing much happening the rest of today,' she said. 'Anything that could be signed and sealed is wrapped up.'

'Even the Conways?' Gemma asked, her face brightening.

'Nah, unfortunately they won't be getting sorted until after Christmas.'

Gemma's face dropped. 'I don't believe you. That's *so* disappointing. They were really keen to be in their new home for the big day, with the baby and all …'

'They won't be now.' Izzie had a mental image of the young couple and their month-old baby, bubbling with enthusiasm over the house of their dreams. What had seemed like a straightforward purchase had been beset by unexpected red tape, right up to the end.

'What went wrong?' Gemma asked.

'Their solicitor caused hold-ups because the right boxes weren't ticked on time, and at the last minute it was discovered that he'd forgotten to get the vendor's signature on one vital document. The vendor who left for the Canaries three days ago and won't return until mid-January. Then the solicitor made the biggest mistake of his career by deciding he'd do everyone a favour and fake the vendor's signature on the document. He was desperate to meet his targets before the end of this financial year.'

'Wow – what'll happen now?'

'There's a good chance the solicitor will be struck off. The case has been passed to one of his colleagues and the Conways will have their keys in the new year.'

It wasn't the worst thing that could happen. At least they had each other. *And* their baby. Something twisted in Izzie's gut and she took a deep breath. 'I'm just as annoyed as you are,' she said, 'but at least they'll have something to look forward to – and it's not exactly moving house weather, is it?'

'It certainly isn't,' Gemma said.

'Right, I'm officially out of here,' Izzie said, clicking on a tab and typing in her 'out-of-office' message. 'You can head off as soon as you like – get home before the weather is too bad in case the buses stop running.'

'I can walk home from here, it's no problem, and I'm staying on for the cheese and wine,' Gemma said. 'It's my first time at an office Christmas party.'

'The first of many Christmas office parties. Enjoy,' Izzie said, feeling a moment of fondness for the young woman. Oh, to be starting out in life again, a glittering ball of enthusiasm and innocent of the rotten tricks life could play. 'You don't need to come in tomorrow,' she went on. 'There won't be much happening.' It was only going to be minimal staff and the office was closing at lunch hour. Izzie was bowing out a day early to avoid the worst of the last-minute Christmas extravaganza of hugging, kissing and well-wishing.

'I'll see how my head is in the morning,' Gemma said. 'At least let me look after that,' she said, indicating the last of the paperwork on Izzie's desk.

'No bother, it'll only take me a minute. But while you're here …' Izzie took a small gift-wrapped package out of her top drawer and handed it to Gemma.

'What's this?' Gemma asked, her eyes widening in surprise.

'It's to say thank you,' Izzie said. 'I appreciate all the help you've given me since … in the last few weeks.' She swallowed hard, feeling a crack in her voice but determined to finish what she wanted to say. 'You've been a great support.'

Gemma shook her head. 'Not at all, it's been a pleasure. You didn't have to do this, Izzie, but thank you so much.' She leaned over and gave her a hug that was unexpectedly tender.

*

Izzie went through the half-dozen documents on her desk and filed them away in the cabinet. She shoved pens, notebooks and Post-its into a pile before closing down her computer. She eased off her stilettos and put them in a bag in the bottom drawer of her desk. Then she pulled on a pair of woollen socks and thick-soled walking boots.

'You're all set,' Gemma said, smiling across at her from the next workstation. 'I hope you have a peaceful break and a good chill out.'

'Oh, I will, that's for sure.' Izzie checked her bag for her house keys, emptying half the contents out across her desk. She finally located them. Over by the coat stand, she pulled on her scarf and coat, tucking her keys into the zipped pocket to keep them safe. One of the things she hadn't expected in the aftermath of loss was her silly carelessness. She'd mislaid her phone when she was out to lunch once – luckily it had been found the next day. She'd also left her handbag behind in a supermarket – thankfully it had turned up later, minus the cash in her purse.

She threaded her way through desks decorated with tinsel and streamers, relieved that, apart from Gemma, the office was deserted. Most of her colleagues were either taking an extended morning break or had gone on an early lunch.

When she stepped out of the building onto Baggot Street, the icy cold took her breath away. Thick snowflakes whirling down from a smudged-grey sky stung her face. People scurried by on the slushy pavement, heads bent, clutching shopping bags. She saw her reflection in a shop window. With her coat already covered in a layer of snow, she looked exactly like how she'd felt inside for the last eleven weeks and five days – frozen.

Thanks to her carefully laid plans, the Christmas break would give her some precious down time to mope in perfect privacy and wallow all she wanted in a grief-laden binge. Surely by the new year the worst would be over and she'd find a reason for living again.

CHAPTER TWO

Gemma looked down onto the street and watched Izzie's hooded figure make its way up towards the canal, the shoulders of her padded coat gradually dusting over with a thin film of snow. When she disappeared from sight, swallowed up by the whirling flakes, Gemma took a carrier bag from under her workstation and went out to the ladies'. In one of the cubicles, she took off the black jumper and trousers she'd worn to the office that morning, changing into sequinned jeans and a cherry-red Santa Claus sweater. Outside, in front of the mirror, she redid her make-up so that her blue eyes appeared larger and smokier. There was little she could do with her mop of curly blonde hair, save for scrunching it up here and there with some gel, giving it more of an edge. She put on flashing holly-shaped earrings and wrapped strands of tinsel around her neck. Lastly, she put on her reindeer-antler hairband.

She'd planned to arrive in that morning dressed in her Christmas bling, but just before she'd left home she'd realised that it wouldn't feel right in front of Izzie, so she'd changed back into normal work clothes – forgetting about her sparkly ring: *duh* – and now she was party ready.

Back in the office, she went across to the cabinet and, having taken note of the cases Izzie had been working on that morning, plucked out the files. As she'd guessed, Izzie had incorrectly filed some of the documents, so she fixed that, assigning the paperwork to the right files before putting them away again. Izzie's computer was showing the restart option, so she clicked on shut-down, powering it off completely, as they'd been instructed to do for the holiday period. She opened the bottom drawer in Izzie's desk and took out the cotton bags containing her shoes, pulling them out and matching up the pairs correctly. Izzie kept three different pairs of stilettos in the office, and if anyone had noticed that she'd been going around that morning wearing one plain black and one patent leather shoe, they had wisely stayed silent.

Gemma shook her head at the sight of Izzie's bulging yoga bag, tucked into the far corner underneath her workstation, a rolled-up mat poking out of it. In all the time Gemma had worked here, it hadn't been disturbed. So much for Izzie's yoga retreat. She'd been quite vague about it, so this was confirmation to Gemma that she had other plans.

She picked up Izzie's favourite fountain pen, the one she used for all her significant signatures. It had been abandoned on the desk, and she replaced the cap, tucking it away safely in the top drawer. She made a neat pile of Izzie's assortment notebooks and yellow Post-its, tucking them beside the monitor. Izzie's desk calendar was still turned to the month of September, an image of Glencar Lake in County Sligo above the rows of dates. After late September, right through to December, all the dates were blank. Just, Gemma guessed, like Izzie's life right now.

Looking after Izzie in this way hadn't been something she'd expected when she'd been lucky enough to be offered a six-month paid internship in the O'Sullivan Pearse group, one of Ireland's largest property firms – not forgetting auctioneers, estate agents, lettings and financial advisors, as her mum loved to point out when she was boasting to the neighbours about Gemma's brilliant job. It had been a mega opportunity, coming just as she'd graduated from college. Not bad for someone from St Finnian's Gardens. Nearly like winning the Lotto.

'You'll be on Izzie Mallon's team,' Rachel, one of the senior managers, had told a breathless Gemma in a follow-up chat after she'd been offered the job.

'Izzie ... sounds good,' she'd said, embarrassed that she couldn't think of a more intelligent remark. A real job, being part of a team, and Izzie – with a name like that she already sounded nice and approachable, certainly not domineering or bossy, or someone who might look down her nose at Gemma.

For her, even getting to college had been an achievement in itself. Less than a third of her school contemporaries had managed that leap, and fewer again of the young residents of the north-inner-city-council apartment complex where she lived. Still, Gemma had had her older sister, Janet, encouraging her all the way, blazing a trail for her to follow, and now her younger sister, Amy, was coming up behind her. Janet was carving out a great career in the Dublin hub of an American multinational. As far as Gemma was concerned, O'Sullivan Pearse was just her first rung on the ladder. Her mother was bursting with pride. Anne Nugent had raised her three daughters single-handedly as well as holding down two part-time jobs when their uncaring father had absconded to England with a young one half his age. She'd sacrificed a lot to help get Janet and Gemma where they were.

'Izzie's actually out at the moment,' Rachel had said, a little delicately.

'Oh.'

'She's on special leave. Due to family circumstances. We're not sure when she'll be back. We need someone in there to answer the phone, check general business emails, know when and how to refer the queries and escalate any issues. Katy will take you through the ropes for the first few days and be your go-to person, and then when Izzie comes back, you'll be a support to her.'

Then three days into the job, she'd been finding her feet in this busy, fast-moving office when she discovered during coffee break with Katy exactly what Izzie's family circumstances entailed and why she'd been on special leave.

Izzie's husband, Sam, had died unexpectedly.

'Hold on, did you say her husband *died*?'

'Yes, it was a terrible tragedy. We were shocked.'

'How long were they married?'

'About six months,' Katy had said.

Gemma had been afraid to ask what kind of tragedy.

Izzie had a big corner workstation by the window, as

befitted her senior mortgage advisor status, and there was a photograph on the desk that Gemma had secretly admired. It had been taken on Izzie's wedding day, in a garden somewhere: a happy, joyous photograph of her in a fitted, Grecian-style, cream lace wedding dress that skimmed her ankles. She had a wreath of flowers in her dark hair and her face was alight with love, her body angled as she smiled up at a guy in his mid-thirties whose hand was holding hers aloft, their fingers interlinked. The photograph spilled over with love and happiness and oodles of promise for a wonderful life ahead. Looking at the image, Gemma had known that in the fullness of time – after she'd spread her wings and done a whole lot of partying and fun living and travel, of course – she wanted a guy to look at her like that. As though he adored her. Now her stomach clenched, horrified that this lovely guy wasn't around anymore to look at Izzie like that. Jes*us* – how could he be gone? What kind of a shit thing to happen was that? Of all the crap that life could bring, this was off the scale.

It was tough enough getting to grips with a new job and all its serious responsibilities – now she'd be terrified of saying the wrong thing.

Then less than two weeks after she'd started, Rachel had called her into her office. Izzie was coming back to work. Next week.

'I don't think I'm up to supporting her,' she'd had to admit to Rachel, even though it embarrassed her.

'Yes, you are,' Rachel had said. 'We have every confidence in you. You're bright and bubbly, and having you shadowing her will keep Izzie occupied. She said she wants to be kept as busy as possible.'

The Friday before Izzie returned, Katy had put the photograph away.

'Izzie messaged me and asked me to take it down,' Katy had explained. 'I expect she wants no reminders staring her in the face.'

Gemma had looked at the gap on Izzie's desk, trying not to visualise the horrible gap in her life. How on earth would she be able to support her? Her first work placement was going to go down the tubes. So much for all the grand plans. Then she'd remembered the time, five years ago, when her mother had fought and won a cancer battle. Gemma and her sisters had rallied around. Her mother hadn't wanted any fuss or to be treated as a victim, but they had made life easier for her by looking after the practical realities of everything and by making sure little treats were a regular part of her everyday life. So first up, Gemma had filled the space on Izzie's desk where the photograph had been by nipping out to Marks and Spencer's early on the Monday morning and buying her a small vase and some fresh flowers. She'd bought small chocolates for coffee break and a beautiful china mug for Izzie's coffee.

The slim woman with the thin, drawn face who had arrived into the office soon after ten o'clock on that Monday morning bore little resemblance to the joyful bride in the photograph. She had huge, haunting dark eyes, an aura of vulnerability and a delicate, ethereal presence. She made Gemma think of a finely spun, diamond-cut crystal glass, intrinsically strong, yet liable to shatter at any moment. Izzie had already sent word that she didn't want to talk about what had happened and she hoped her colleagues would respect her privacy. Neither did she want anyone's sympathy. She just wanted to get on with the job in hand. Gemma found herself supporting her in ways she hadn't expected, picking up on her small mistakes, generally easing her day-to-day tasks, fixing daily incidentals with as much discretion as possible. And every Monday morning, she put fresh flowers in the vase so that Izzie's desk was brightened with colour and the air around her infused with scent.

She finished tidying Izzie's desk, and that's when she saw it tucked underneath the keyboard: a small purse with a glittery butterfly motif, like something a child might own. She guessed the purse had slid under the keyboard when Izzie had emptied the contents of her bag across the desk in her rummage for her house keys. She recalled Izzie's frantic face the previous week when she'd thought she'd mislaid the small purse during her lunch hour, and her relief when she'd found it in a side pocket of her bag.

Whatever it was, it was important to Izzie.

Gemma opened the zip and peeked inside. Stuck between a seashell and a small beach pebble was a USB memory stick. It could be Izzie's back-up for all her work files, but more likely it was for personal stuff if she kept it in her bag, and Gemma wondered if she'd need it during the Christmas break. Probably not if she was 'off to a yoga retreat', which is where Gemma and everyone else was supposed to think she was going. Best thing to do, Gemma decided, was to text her to say she'd come across it on her desk and would lock it away in the cabinet until Izzie's return in the new year. She went over to her desk and picked up her phone.

'Hey,' she heard a voice calling. 'What's keeping you? We're almost ready to start the party, but we need your sparkling fun.'

Kian Casey, one of the letting agents, strode across the floor holding two glasses and a bottle of Prosecco in his hands. She turned around to see who he was talking to, the person he declared to be such sparkling fun, but the desks behind her were empty. He scarcely meant her, did he?

Sparkling fun. She'd never been called that before.

'Is it starting now?' she asked. 'I thought it was this afternoon.' She knew her voice sounded tinny and her face was reddening to match her jumper. Kian was gorgeous – not only gorgeous, but seriously hot – and someone she'd fancied since her first day, when she'd spotted him in the canteen. He looked different with his tie off and his white shirt open at the neck – more relaxed and casual. She was used to seeing him perfectly groomed, buzzing around the reception area with clients, a phone in one hand and a briefcase in the other. She didn't think he'd taken any notice of her. Not with the likes of the other female staff who worked here: the clever Katy and the lovely Andrea and Sabrina. To her amazement, he smiled warmly at her.

'Gemma! Welcome to the world of corporate entertainment,' he said. 'Is this your first Christmas in the exciting business world?'

'Well, yeah, I guess so,' she said, unwilling to anoint herself with novice status, but unable to tell a lie. He had to have known she'd come straight from college.

'Great. You're going to enjoy it, but you've a lot to learn. First up,' he leaned in closer and said conspiratorially, 'we're not waiting until after lunch. Tough on those who went out, thinking they're starting the party out there – we're starting it in here. Right now. Grab your bag and come down to the boardroom. Katy and Sabrina have been busy getting organised and it's time to open the fizz. That's an order,' he went on, winking at her. 'Has Izzie left?'

'She has.'

'Well then, in her absence, I'm putting myself in charge of you.'

'Oh, gosh …' Her voice faded away. With Izzie gone she could relax a little, couldn't she? Let go of the thread of anxiety she'd been carrying around since she'd heard of her circumstances, and the way she'd been on her guard every day since Izzie had returned. The O'Sullivan Pearse Christmas party was starting now and she'd be at it. In a glow of delight mixed with a tingle of apprehension, she picked up her bag and tucked away her phone and Izzie's small purse. She'd look after that later.

'All set?' Kian said.

'All set.' She nodded, meeting his eyes with a steady gaze of her own, her head dizzy with anticipation.

'I like the Christmas jumper,' he said, his eyes roving slowly across her red sweater with the glittery Santa Claus motif.

'Thanks,' she said, feeling a little faint.

CHAPTER THREE

Izzie arrived at the canal bridge without knowing how she'd got there. She looked down on a world of white towpaths and frozen stretches of water, the skeletons of trees stiff and silent and gilded with snow. The snow tumbling out of the sky had eased off to gentle flurries that eddied to and fro in the slight breeze, although the dark sky told of more to come. She crossed the road at the traffic lights and went into a large Tesco store.

It was thronged, the entrance wet with sludge dropping off boots and umbrellas. Lines of shoppers snaked around the aisles, Christmas music blaring, heightening the frantic atmosphere along with flashing neon lights. She was immune to it all and glad no one took any notice of her when she went to the checkout desk with two litre bottles of gin. Better to buy them in the anonymity of this store rather than her local mini-market. The alternative to cabbage soup, and far more effective for her body and soul. She tucked them into her tote bag and took the weight easily on her shoulders, going back out to the canal to walk down as far as the turn off for home.

Fifteen minutes after leaving the supermarket, she arrived at Henrietta Square. It had a park in the centre, surrounded on four sides by two- and three-storey Georgian terraced houses. Some of the houses had been renovated and brought back to their former glory, others were in the process of having a facelift and a few still bore the scars of years of life and living. The square came into its own at Christmas. The Georgian frontages seemed specially designed for holly wreaths on doors, fanlights glowed with the reflection of twinkly fairy lights adorning hallways and decorated Christmas trees glittered from long sash windows. Now with the covering of snow, Henrietta Square resembled a heart-warming, old-world scene from a picture-perfect Christmas card.

Izzie went through the gate into the railings-enclosed park. Even with the low skies, this too was beautiful: tree branches as delicate as white filigree lace, shrubbery and pathways festooned in white finery. In the middle of the park, children clad in bright, puffy coats, hats and gloves were swarming around, rolling large chunks of snow and building snowmen and other misshapen figures.

'Izzie!'

She whirled around, unable to discern who was calling her name in among the colourful knot of children.

'Izzie! Over here!' A gloved hand waved against the stark

white snow, the hood of a red jacket pulled tight around a pale oval face that was split with a huge, toothy grin.

'Noah?' she ventured. Noah Brady, the young boy who lived with his father, Tom, on the floor below her. He was ten. She recalled him proudly announcing his move into double digits when she'd bumped into him and his father in the hallway of the house a couple of months ago, Tom ushering him swiftly past Izzie, correctly guessing she was in no humour for chit-chat, although she would have made an exception for Noah.

'Isn't this *brill*!' he shouted. 'We're off school now for *ages*.'

'Good for you,' she said.

'I can't believe we have this much snow.'

'It's wonderful,' she said.

'See ya later,' he called out.

She crossed the park and went through the gate set into the railings on the far side, standing opposite number sixteen for a few moments. A neat Christmas tree shone from the window of the ground-floor apartment; Florence, the occupant, had put it up a couple of days ago. In the first-floor window, the apartment Noah lived in, a larger tree beamed out, branches hanging down with an assorted army of ornaments.

Izzie found it surreal that, on the surface, life went on much as normal and the world continued to turn after Sam had left it. The days slipped past, sneaking up on her and beyond her, the seasons changing from glorious autumn to winter almost by stealth. Not that she was engaging with them. From the top-floor windows, far from the beautiful Christmas tree she'd visualised when she'd stood here with Sam on a bright spring day prior to moving in, there was nothing whatsoever to indicate anyone even lived there. She stared at windows that were darkly blank compared to everyone else's. This would be her haven for the next few days; her safe and solitary hidey-hole in the middle of a life turned to solid, unmoving ice. She'd curl up and obliterate the pain of losing Sam bolstered with as much booze-soaked comfort as possible before she faced into the world again, and into a brand new year.

CHAPTER FOUR

In the bedroom of her ground-floor apartment in 16 Henrietta Square, Florence Hawkins smoothed her black leather jeans up over her hips. Zara, in a Black Friday sale. She turned sideways, striking a warrior pose in front of the mirror. They'd do nicely. She turned, full face to the mirror again, and stood, arms akimbo, examining her naked top half.

'Come on, Girl Power, let's be having you,' she said to her reflection, glad there was no one to overhear her, let alone see her.

She shimmied into a black sleeveless vest and lacy top. She had several dressy tops, accumulated over the years from Christmases past and January sales, and she rotated them according to the degree of bling necessary for the occasion. The more bling the merrier for Christmas Day, even though she'd spend a lot of the day engulfed in a huge Mrs Claus apron. At some stage she'd be whipping the apron off and wanted to look her best.

That's if she got there.

The window of her bedroom was shielded by a net curtain and it looked out onto the rear of the square. There wasn't much to see apart from a private, narrow laneway leading to the next street and a mews building to the side of that. Today, the world outside was smothered in several inches of snow, making it impossible to see the kerbside, and flurries were falling steadily from a smudged-grey sky, challenging any kind of trip outside. Christmas 2010 all over again.

She'd beaten the snow then; she'd beat it now.

She took off her Christmas clothes and folded them away. She pulled on jeans and a T-shirt and, over that, a crimson jumper with a Christmas tree motif. Then she remembered her glittery Christmas headband – it would be perfect for the day – so she rummaged in her bag of spare Christmas decorations and found it, putting it on as well. This time, she made a face when she studied her reflection in the mirror. The jumper and the headband kind of clashed with her freshly coloured hair. She'd thought the red shade would be perfect for Christmas, but she would have been better sticking to her usual pink or purple streaks. Still, she cheered up, it would contrast well with her black attire on the big day.

In her living room, she picked up her phone, selecting her Just Seventeen WhatsApp group: 'Hey, what's with the snow? Hope we're okay for 25th – how are you both doing?'

Jean replied immediately: 'It'll take a lot more than this

powdery stuff to keep me away. I've dug out my snow grips, so I'm all set.'

Wendy's reply came a few minutes later: 'People are depending on us so I'll be there, one way or another, even if I have to come flying in on my grandson's toboggan.'

Florence replied, adding their mantra on at the end. 'Good for us, we'll do this. Girl Power!'

The radio was on in the background, and a festive staple came on, something about being lonely at Christmas.

'I'm not listening to any of this lonely shit,' Florence said aloud, immediately switching stations until she came to a cheerful reindeer song. Much better. That was the good thing about living alone. She could listen to whatever she liked, look at crap television until three in the morning, stay in bed until lunchtime, have crisp sandwiches for her dinner or even her breakfast without anyone raising an eyebrow; and in the comfort of her own home, she could speak her mind out loud and clear without fear of being overheard or people thinking she had lost it, now she was of advancing years.

Advancing years? She caught the tail end of that evil thought immediately. Whoa – or WTAF, as Wendy would say. She turned it around and fired it back to where it came from. How dare it have the utter cheek to drift across her consciousness. You might deduce from her birth certificate that she'd been on this planet for a grand total of seventy-two years. But that didn't mean she felt any one of them. In her heart and spirit she knew the figures were way out. Wendy and Jean were of the same vintage as her. They'd all hit seventy within a year of each other and had duly celebrated with big birthday *festivals*, no less – no puny parties for them.

They'd also agreed that seventy could quite easily sound like seventeen.

On a good day she was seventeen on the inside. Like the song. But not the Frank Sinatra song, proclaiming it was a very good year – that was all about him. Rather the Beatles song, where the lyrics were all about being just seventeen and you know what I mean … woo hoo! They'd agreed a pact, her, Jean and Wendy – that was the age they all felt and were going to stick to, no matter what lay ahead. If things worked out on Christmas Day, they'd sing the Beatles song to the homeless group after they'd served the first setting for dinner, accompanied by Des on the piano. They'd make a great fist of it, even though Wendy would be way out of tune and sometimes Jean forgot the words.

Thinking of it now, with the song going through her head, she rehearsed a few bars as she jigged across the living room – something else she was free to do whenever she took the notion, especially if she couldn't get out for a walk – and spun over to the window, which looked out onto the front of the square. She caught her breath for a moment at the sight of the snow-covered park. In the middle of the picture-postcard loveliness of it all, she saw young Noah in the scramble of children playing in the snow.

Noah. The grandson she'd never had. And a pang of regret that she instantly squashed. Having the child living on the floor above her was a gift she hadn't expected. She was lucky he was part of her life. He and his father, Tom, had moved in over two years ago, and once the curious chatterbox Noah had discovered she was a retired teacher, he often found his way down to her with his Irish homework and she loved that. He was also her chief tasting officer and quality control assistant when it came to her baking efforts. On the rare occasions that Tom was delayed at work, Florence was there to keep an eye on Noah and she knew Tom appreciated that.

Then she saw Izzie standing across the road, and her heart stalled. If Noah was the grandson she'd never had, then Izzie was the daughter she'd never had the opportunity to love. A much bigger pang of regret that she took longer to recover from.

Izzie might be putting up a bold, brave front, but the cold, hard look in her eyes made Florence catch her breath. And there was nothing at all she could do to help. That was one of the hardest lessons she'd had to learn in life: sometimes you were totally helpless in the face of other people's distress. Even with the best support from family and friends, no one could climb into a body and make it feel better. She shrank back from the window lest the young woman spot her staring at her. Izzie had enough to cope with besides being watched by her nosy neighbour.

Not that she was nosy, at least she hoped not, but in Izzie's frame of mind anything at all could be seen as interference. She'd hesitated to ask her what she was doing for Christmas, and then the words had popped out of their own accord one evening last week when Izzie had been coming through the hall.

'I'm not doing anything,' Izzie had said, both her face and voice as wooden as each other.

'And your family?' Florence had asked as gently as she could. She knew Izzie had a mother and brother. She'd already met them, coming through Henrietta Square at the time of Sam's funeral. Izzie's mother still lived in the family home in the south County Wicklow valley where Izzie had grown up, her brother and his family lived nearby, and after Sam's death, Izzie had spent several weekends there. Florence had assumed she'd be spending Christmas with them.

'I'm not seeing them,' Izzie had said, stalking by. Then she'd stopped abruptly at the bottom of the stairs. 'Florence?'

'Yes, dear?'

Izzie had locked eyes with her. 'I'm not expecting them, but if by any chance my family happen to drop by here, I'm not in. I'm not here at all. I'm gone off to a yoga retreat, right?'

'Right,' Florence had said, slightly mystified. Did Izzie mean she wasn't going to be upstairs at all, thanks to this retreat stuff, or was she just not in for her family? She knew people did alternative things to get away from the mania of Christmas, but it sounded to her like the latter. How awful. Surely Izzie shouldn't be left alone, this Christmas above all? She shouldn't allow herself to become isolated in her pain or shut herself away.

Like I had, she reminded herself. So who was she to talk or give advice? On another level, she could understand Izzie. Families could be brilliant; to have one surrounding you with love and care could be the best thing in the world. But there were times when even the best family could be too close for comfort, too smothering, too in your face, especially if you just wanted to crawl into a dark corner and lick your wounds in peace and silence, and she knew all about that too.

And if she had her life to live over ...

Oh, God, the things she would do.

Correction: the things she would *not* do...

She closed down that train of thought, increased the volume on the radio and jigged back across the room.

CHAPTER FIVE

Tom Brady heard the slight creak of Izzie's footsteps overhead. The noise was faint because the house was solidly built, but there was no mistaking the fact that she was home. He went out to check the landing and staircase and, right enough, she'd dropped something. He picked up Izzie's scarf from the floor of the return. Pale blue, the texture was soft and smooth in his hands. He went up to the second floor and checked her door – all fine, no keys dangling from the lock this time.

He'd learned to watch for Izzie any time he heard the heavy door to the house closing, followed by the sound of her moving around upstairs. She'd left keys in her apartment door too often for his liking. She'd even left her handbag outside her door on one occasion. Her shopping another time. Not that anyone could breach the stout entrance door to number sixteen all that easily, which was some level of security. And Florence was more vigilant than any guard dog, but she wasn't always around.

He knocked softly on Izzie's door, waited a moment or two and knocked again, slightly louder. He was just about to drape the scarf over her door handle and go back downstairs when she pulled it open.

She stared at him, her dark eyes impenetrable. She tilted her head a little as if she didn't know who he was, a fragile ghost of the person who used to move through the hallways of number sixteen like a woman who was deeply and happily in love.

He held out her scarf. 'I think this is yours, Izzie.'

'It is, thank you.' Her voice was wooden.

'Is there anything – do you need anything at all?' He heard the words coming out of his mouth, stock words, and the sheer banality of them made him feel helpless in the face of her pain. *I know how it hurts,* he wanted to say. *You won't believe me now but in time you will pass through this and come out the other end; changed, yes, altered beyond recognition, a different person, more resilient, softer and harder all at once.*

But for now, it's just a thick, black cave. I know. I've sat in it.

'No, thanks,' she said.

He blinked. For a nano-second he imagined he'd spoken aloud.

'I don't need a thing,' she went on. 'I'm perfectly fine.'

'Good. Great. Well, you know where I am if you do. Need

anything, that is. I've finished up in the office for the holidays and I'll be here until Christmas Day morning.'

Yeah, Tom, that's right, well done, remind her that it's Christmas, why don't you? He could have bitten his tongue.

He waited while she closed the door, still looking through him with those blank eyes until the sight of her gradually disappeared in the narrowing gap. When he went downstairs to his apartment, he picked up the framed photo of himself, Cathy and Noah that sat on the sideboard. It had been taken on Noah's fourth birthday. A few months later, Cathy was gone from their lives, dying suddenly of an aggressive cancer, breaking their hearts in the process. Even though it had been six years ago, he knew only too well the kind of frozen, absent-minded fog Izzie was drifting around in because he'd been there himself.

Childhood sweethearts, he and Cathy had met at school in Cork. He'd been seventeen to her sixteen. Their close friendship had developed and deepened through college years and beyond into warm and tender love and commitment, an engagement ring followed by a wedding. When he'd been successful in securing a job as a senior engineer in Dublin City Council, they'd settled in a spacious family home just outside Clane in County Kildare. Tom commuted by train and Cathy worked locally, teaching in a village national school. In time, there had been the wonderful joy of Noah and they had hopes and expectations of more children to add to his and Cathy's joy, their love deepening year on year, their careers going from strength to strength.

They were so happy he thought at times he was going to burst with it. They had never expected their lives to implode the way they had, Cathy's illness and death smashing their dreams into smithereens. He'd turned forty two months ago, and in those early years of marriage, he'd never envisaged living a totally different life by the time he reached that milestone. When he'd climbed out of the worst of his grief, in an effort to make a fresh start and leave the heartache behind, he'd sold up in Clane and moved to Henrietta Square. It was a pleasant change and he was glad to be close to the thrum of the lively city centre instead of rattling around a quiet house that was too big for the two of them and echoed with memories of shattered lives. It also meant he was far closer to his job and around more for Noah.

Last Easter, when he and Noah had arrived back in Henrietta Square having spent the holiday break in west Cork with his father, Florence had told him about the new couple who had just moved into the apartment upstairs.

'They married recently,' she'd said, looking delighted to be the bearer of good news. 'He's American but she's from Wicklow – Izzie and Sam Mallon.'

He'd met Sam first, in the hallway that Saturday, liking the clean, fresh look of the guy with the slim build. Then the following week, he'd seen a woman juggling bags of groceries as she tried to lock the hall door. She was dressed in a navy suit and he guessed she was on her way home from the office.

'Let me give you a hand,' he'd said. She had dark hair and eyes and gave off an aura of warmth and happiness that was contagious.

'Oh, thanks,' she'd said, laughing softly. 'I bought more than I meant to.'

'Grocery stores are designed that way on purpose. I'm

Tom,' he'd said, taking her bags. 'Tom Brady.'

'Izzie Mallon,' she'd said. 'Sam and I moved in a couple of weeks ago. We love it. It's so central. You must be Noah's dad.'

'I am, yes,' he'd said. 'I take it you've met him already?'

'We both have.'

'I hope he wasn't annoying you.'

'Not at all, he's a lovely young fella. Sam was quite taken with him. So am I.'

They'd walked up the staircase together, seeing their reflections in the big mirror on the landing at the same time and smiling in unison.

'His mother – my wife – died a few years ago so it's just the two of us.' He didn't always volunteer this information, but for some reason he wanted her to know. Thanks to the passage of time and the way his heartache had softened, he found it a lot easier to articulate those words now, compared to a few years ago.

'Oh. I'm very sorry to hear that,' she'd said. They'd reached the door of her apartment and her eyes were soft and kind as she'd looked at him.

Soon after that, he'd been invited up to their apartment for a drink, along with Noah. Izzie had asked him some practical questions, checking the finer details about refuse collections and parking permits, while Sam and Noah had bonded over a mutual love of *Star Wars*, Noah proudly wearing his new Chewbacca T-shirt.

After that, they often met in the hallway because they usually arrived home from their respective city-centre offices around the same time. Occasionally at the weekends he saw her and Sam together, sometimes coming through the small park hand in hand, another time buying wine in the local mini-market, and she had joked about them having an all-night party and disturbing the neighbours.

It was clear she was a woman in love – it radiated from her like a warm glow and softened every movement in her body. One evening he saw Izzie and Sam in the Italian café around the corner, sitting opposite each other in a quiet nook, hands linked across the table, engaged in deep conversation, looking like lovers do all the world over, and he felt alone in a way he never had before.

There had never been another woman in his life after Cathy, even though he'd had plenty of offers. Apart from not being interested, there was Noah to consider.

Noah, who had lost his mother at a tender age. Noah, who still spoke to his mother on a daily basis and who lately seemed to be spending more time than ever in front of the framed photograph on the sideboard. Noah, who still carefully placed his intricate Lego creations alongside that photo, as if Cathy could somehow see and admire them. How could Tom ever introduce another woman into their lives? Besides, coming up to the awkward pre-adolescence stage, Noah would never talk to him again if he thought Tom was considering a replacement for his beloved mum.

Tom put the photograph back on the sideboard and went over to the kitchen. Apart from anything else, love sucked, didn't it? That was another reason why he'd locked his heart away somewhere unreachable and had vowed to never go down that road again. Now Sam was gone, the victim of a senseless accident. Florence had told him the shocking news.

He'd been away in France, at a cousin's wedding with his father and Noah, and by the time he was back in Henrietta Square it was all over, and Izzie was spending a couple of weeks with her family. He knew she was going around with every stitch of her life unravelled and every dream imploded because he too had been like that once.

CHAPTER SIX

Why on earth had she been so rude to Tom, closing the door in his face? He'd been doing her a favour, returning her scarf. He'd been perfectly polite and friendly, even though he too had lost his partner and was facing another Christmas without her. And it wasn't the first time he'd picked up things she'd been careless with. Partly the reason she felt safe in Henrietta Square was his presence on the middle floor.

Izzie went back into the living-room-cum-kitchen. She wasn't long in the door and already her private haven seemed flat and lifeless. The spacious room ran the length of the front of the house, with a compact kitchen at one end and two long sash windows facing out over the park. Izzie walked across the floor, the children playing in the park coming into view.

No echo of their laughter carried into this room because the windows were triple glazed. She watched the scramble of small bodies, colourful against the starkness of the snow, and it could have been a silent movie. In the early afternoon, the light outside was already beginning to fade, thanks to the sullen grey skies.

Her phone rang, the sound unnaturally loud and disturbing. Audrey, her sister-in-law.

'Hiya, Izzie, how are you?'

'I'm fine,' she said, forcing a light tone into her voice.

'You haven't left for your yoga retreat yet?'

'No, I'll be on my way soon.'

'I hope you make it all right, but in case you've changed your mind it's not too late to join us in Wicklow.'

'Thanks, Audrey, I appreciate it, but I haven't changed my mind,' Izzie said.

'Well, if you do, feel free to join us anytime, but sooner rather than later – the side roads are looking a bit grim.'

'Thanks. I hope you all have a lovely few days,' Izzie said.

'You too,' Audrey said. 'I hope it'll turn out to be perfectly peaceful,' she went on. Her sympathetic voice wobbled a little, hardening Izzie's resolve to spend Christmas alone.

'Thanks, Audrey,' Izzie said. 'I'll be fine. I'm looking forward to peace and a total recharge.'

'Your mum wants to have a few words.'

There was the sound of Audrey's phone being passed to someone else, a hurried whisper and then Izzie's mother, Marian Gray, was on the line.

'Darling! I hope you're okay. I've already arrived in Paul and Audrey's.' She went on without taking a break, 'I don't like the look of this weather so Paul insisted I get here early.

We're all very comfortable – aren't we, Audrey? Paul has the fire blazing and Audrey has already insisted on pouring me a rather large glass of mulled wine. I'd prefer if you were here too but I *totally* understand your decision. And I'd never interfere with what you want to do – you know that, darling, don't you?'

Finally Izzie got a word in. 'Yes, Mum.'

'You're getting the bus down to this retreat place, aren't you? I think the main roads are still passable and you're wise to let someone else do the driving. But as Audrey said, if you do by any chance happen to change your mind, the snow is quite deep outside but we'd get you here somehow … even by tractor. The farmer next door is lovely – I saw him ferrying some people down the laneway already.'

Izzie didn't respond.

'Don't mind me,' her mother said, sounding disappointed. 'It was just a casual suggestion. I understand how you might be feeling. Make sure you text us when you arrive. I want to know you're safe and sound.'

'I will,' Izzie said, hot and cold at the lie. 'We have to hand up our phones as soon as we get there so I'll be silent after that.'

'Well … we'll be thinking of you all the time, we all send our love.'

'Thanks, Mum. I'll be grand, honestly – I need some chillout time. You enjoy being spoiled and have a great Christmas. I'll talk to you as soon as I'm back.'

Izzie ended the call and looked at the litre bottles of gin lined up on her kitchen counter, which she'd added to the dozen bottles of wine already there. More than enough to ensure oblivion right through to the new year.

Her family were good, *too* good. They meant well. They'd been handling her with kid gloves since Sam had died, which was one of the reasons why she had no intention of inflicting herself and her wounded soul on them for Christmas. The chill-out, peace and recharge few days she was looking forward to at a hideaway yoga centre set in the lush countryside of the Blackwater Valley were a total fabrication, designed to give her a cast-iron reason not to spend Christmas in her brother's roomy south County Wicklow home, surrounded by an overabundance of sympathy and carefully selected comments, her mother tiptoeing around her, her sister-in-law casting her sorrowful looks, her brother, sad and quietly furious at the hand fate had dealt her, her beautiful young nieces, Tara and Emily, their Christmas magic soured by the cloud of anxiety hanging over all the adults. Everyone's Christmas celebrations would be tinged with the awkwardness of it all, their love and concern feeling like an onslaught on her senses. Izzie knew that trying to cope with other people's emotions, no matter how well-intentioned, would be exhausting.

The yoga centre did exist, and it *was* holding a retreat for those who wanted to escape all things Christmas – she'd checked out the details. And then, in order to avoid shock and dismay over the phone, she'd emailed both her mother and Audrey, explaining all her reasons why this year she wanted to avoid Christmas altogether and had decided to get away from it completely and experience some total downtime by doing the retreat. 'You've all been great, truly wonderful,' she'd said. 'But I know you'll understand that I just need some quiet space now.'

She'd also sent the email to Paul, so he'd know about it, but she'd added a postscript to tell him the truth: that she was staying put in Henrietta Square. 'Just in case there is a dire emergency,' she'd written, 'I don't want you searching the Blackwater Valley for me.' There were six years between them, Paul being the elder, but the siblings were close and they understood each other. She knew she could trust him to keep her plans to himself. They'd always kept each other informed of their whereabouts since their father had died suddenly while Izzie had been island hopping in Greece five years ago and it had taken Paul two angst-filled days to track her down.

There had been protests, but not too many; no one wanted to upset Izzie unduly. Paul had even said he'd probably opt to do the same and block out the whole Christmas shebang if he were in her shoes.

Izzie went into her bedroom and switched off her phone, putting it on her bedside table. The heating had come on earlier so the apartment was warm and cosy. She took off her office clothes and pulled on a terry robe, then she went into the bathroom and ran a bath, throwing in some relaxing scented oil. When the bath was three-quarters full, she sank into the aromatic water and closed her eyes, sliding down so that just her nose and mouth rose above the surface. Warm water lapped at her skin and she wondered if she could stay like this forever: motionless, barely breathing, most of her body under water, barely alive …

Then her vision filled with an image of Sam, barely alive; he was lying on the ground, his face a putty-coloured blur against the cobblestones where he had fallen, dark crimson liquid blooming from the back of his head, the horror of it all sliced into onlookers' faces. *Noooo.* This wasn't happening. It couldn't be …

Shock gripped her and squeezed her chest and she sat up abruptly, gasping for air, sloshing water out onto the tiled floor. When she caught her breath, she climbed out and dried herself, limbs like jelly, pulling on fresh underwear, fleece PJs and her terry robe, sliding her feet into warm slippers.

Out in the kitchen she poured a glass of white wine, her hand shaking a little as she lifted it to her mouth and drank deeply.

In the living-room area, she sank onto the thick, cushiony sofa and switched on the television, flicking to the news. It was all about the weather: snowstorms blanketing Western Europe – England, Scotland, Wales and Ireland, with England being hit particularly badly. Images showed long tailbacks of traffic halted on snow-blurred motorways as people tried to get home for the long Christmas break before the snow tightened its grip and the roads became impassable. There was footage from Dublin airport: a news correspondent holding a big fluffy microphone issued a warning that the runways were closed so passengers were stranded and had nowhere to go and, at the moment, little prospect of getting home in time for Christmas Day.

Izzie sipped her wine, willing the pictures on the screen to chase away the memories of Sam stalking the back of her mind.

She'd be fine, she'd be okay. She'd got this.

CHAPTER SEVEN

When her intercom pealed in the late afternoon, the first thing Florence did was to glance down at her attire and make sure she was presentable. It wouldn't do to answer the door unless she had her best side out, but her Christmas jumper, even if it clashed with her hair, was perfectly acceptable.

She pressed the intercom button. 'Who is it?' She wasn't expecting anyone but sometimes carol singers rang her bell as it was the bottom one on the panel. They figured they had a better chance of getting a response from the ground-floor occupant than those on the first or second floors. And her Christmas-tree lights by the window were a dead giveaway that she was home.

'Hi, I'm really sorry to bother you, and I know this is an inconvenience.' A gentleman's voice. A different accent, but sounding extremely apologetic and well-mannered. 'I'm looking for Izzie, Izzie Mallon.'

Hmm. Florence never gave out details of the other occupants of the house, not even confirming who lived there. Whoever he was, he had that information already, but clearly he didn't know Izzie well enough to know what floor she lived on.

'I've come from the airport,' he said. 'I really need to see Izzie, I'm an' – a slight pause – 'an old friend of Sam's, from New York,' he went on, his voice a little subdued.

Sam. Florence was shaken by a sense of loss on hearing his name unexpectedly. Sam Mallon had only lived on the top floor for six months, but in that time Florence had grown to love him. How could she not have loved the American man with the smiling eyes and attractive face? Not that she went by outward appearances, but he'd been equally lovely, kind and considerate behind that gorgeous face. He'd made a point of knocking on her door at least once, sometimes twice, a week with an offering of dessert, perhaps some cheesecake or banoffee. He'd told her he'd held down a part-time job in a restaurant while he'd worked his way through college and desserts had been his speciality. He loved making desserts for Izzie but, in his enthusiasm, he often made too much, and Florence would be doing him a big favour if she took some off his hands.

She'd loved the way he'd said 'Florence' in his American accent and had always accepted the treats with pleasure, but to her eternal regret, she had never returned the favour. Never asked him in past the threshold. Never had him and Izzie over for drinks. Never dreaming for one minute Sam would be gone so soon. Life was so full of shite it was ridiculous. The older she got, the less she understood.

'I knew Sam from college and we worked together for years,' the man said, his voice full of respect.

Florence called a halt to the river of memories. She did what she usually did when matters of security and the need to stay safe were paramount. She went to the front window and looked out. All she could see from this vantage point was a side view of this man. He was tall and wrapped in a thick hooded jacket that was dusted with snow.

She went back to the intercom. 'I'm at the window. Please show yourself to me,' she said in her most imperious voice.

'*Show* myself?' A moment's pause. 'Oh. You mean you want to see my face.'

'Of course,' she said. 'What did you think I meant? I'm hardly looking for your naked selfie, I can assure you – not from a stranger, anyhow. Unless you're George Clooney, which I doubt.' She took up position at the window once more until the man leaned out over the railings running up alongside the steps and pulled down his hood. With his clean-shaven face and tightly cropped blond hair, he looked exactly as his voice sounded: gentlemanly and respectful. It might do Izzie good to have an old friend of Sam's calling on her like this. The man was mouthing something to her that she couldn't hear. She stabbed a finger in the direction of the intercom and he finally understood.

'I'm sorry, I've never been in any movies but I promise I'm an upstanding, law-abiding citizen,' he said.

'I'll bet Hannibal Lecter said the same to his victims,' Florence said, partly under her breath.

'Excuse me?'

'I was comparing you to Hannibal Lecter, but just for a moment,' she said. 'Forget what I said. I don't normally do this but, under the circumstances, Izzie's on Floor 2. You can ring the bell for that floor but it's up to her whether she'll let you in or not.'

'So she's there now, is she?'

'I can't possibly confirm that she's in.' He wasn't a family member, so she wasn't bound by Izzie's request to say she wasn't in, that she had gone off to a yoga something, but still …

'Thank you so much.'

Less than two minutes later he was back again. 'Sorry to bother you again but Izzie's not answering her intercom. I fully understand that she mightn't be in the mood for visitors but I know if I got a chance to say hello, let her know that it's me, and that I'm here for her, she'd be glad to see me.'

'How do you know that?'

'Sam and I go back a long way. I'm as cut up as Izzie is after what happened. I'm someone who understands exactly what she's going through right now.'

'Are you?' she said, not bothering to hide the uncertainty in her voice. No one ever knew what was really going on in the depths of someone else's heart. 'Even if you do know exactly what she's going through, how will that help Izzie?'

'I don't know,' he admitted. 'But it's worth a try. I owe Sam a big favour and if I could help Izzie at all …'

Florence thought of Izzie's drawn face, of the stony look in her eyes, so at odds with the soft, smiling woman, head over heels in love, that she'd met when she and Sam had moved in earlier that year. If there was anything anyone could do …

and surely an old friend of Sam's *could* help Izzie in some way?

'I'm a bit stranded as well,' he said.

'Stranded?'

'My flight was diverted to Dublin instead of Heathrow and I missed my connection to New York, and now the airport has closed.'

Stranded at Christmas. Surely in this case a little act of kindness was called for? 'Seeing as it's the season of goodwill,' Florence said, 'I'll give you the benefit of the doubt. I'll buzz you in to the house but I don't want to hear from you a third time if Izzie won't open her door.'

'Agreed, and thank you so much.'

She closed her eyes for a moment and hoped her act of kindness was in everyone's best interests. She pressed the door release and heard him coming into the hall, the ponderous tread of his footsteps on the tiled floor, then the clang of the heavy hall door as it shut behind him.

CHAPTER EIGHT

Out in the park, Noah's hands were freezing and he couldn't feel his toes. Snow had trickled in over the tops of his wellies, and every time he took a step, his feet squelched thanks to his sodden socks. A lot of his mates had gone home but he was still here with Tigi, the twelve-year-old girl from two doors down, and it was the best fun they'd had in ages. No school for three whole weeks, Christmas Eve only three days away and *gangs* of snow. Enough snow for him to make an R2-D2. This was going to be the best Christmas ever.

Well ... since the Christmas he'd been four, his last Christmas with Mum.

He'd heard lots of talk about the previous time there had been huge snows at Christmas, but he didn't remember much of that. He'd only been three years of age but he knew it had been massive. There were photos of him in the album in the sideboard taken during that snow, but he rarely looked at them. Photos of him so well muffled in a big, fat yellow coat that you couldn't see his face. Standing beside his mum, who was on her hunkers so they were almost the same height, her arm around him, and on his other side, the crocked-looking snowman they'd made, with the lopsided face and carrot for a nose. In the snow-filled back garden of their house in Clane. Where they'd lived when there had been the three of them. In the photograph you could see the dents they'd made in the snow where they'd rolled big balls together for the head and the body. You could see the huge drifts of it in front of the shed, how it piled in heaps on top of the garden furniture and almost two feet of it on top of the green bin.

You could see the criss-cross of two sets of footprints through the garden, small ones and medium ones; you could see lots of things, but not his mother's face. She'd been wearing a dark-blue coat with the furry hood hiding most of it. Looking at the footprints she'd made in the snow had given him a funny feeling. As though they were a real sign that she'd been alive, an actual physical presence, and that she'd walked around that garden and tramped in the snow.

He didn't want to remember other things – things like how much she must have loved him, and how much she must have loved his dad, because all you could see of her face in the photo was her big huge smile, and she must have been smiling at Dad. It was kind of sore to remember, but the problem was, he knew he was forgetting her. Bit by bit. Birthday by birthday.

And it was extra sore this year, because he'd betrayed her. Big time.

'I'm nearly done, Noah,' Tigi said, clapping her gloved hands together to warm up. She'd made a big rocket shape with the snow and it was cool.

'Okay, I'm going in soon as well.'

He looked over at number sixteen. A man was standing outside the hall door, a big man with a case and a backpack. As Noah watched, the hall door opened and he went in. Someone had let him in. Someone had been expecting him.

Not his dad – he'd have told him. Besides, they rarely had visitors. Not Florence – he'd talked to her on his way out to the snow, and she'd said that, while she'd have loved to go outside and make a snowman with him, she needed to start baking some cakes for Christmas Day. She'd said nothing about expecting a visitor. So the visitor had to be for Izzie. His heart sank. All his hopes would be ruined. Still, it served him right after what he'd wished for and the dreadful thing that had happened.

Because the first time he'd met Izzie, he knew she'd be perfect for his dad and he'd wished Sam wasn't in her life. He knew by Izzie's soft face and the way she spoke that she was kind and gentle, and liked a laugh and a bit of fun as well. He'd imagined what it would be like if Sam was out of the way and Izzie and his dad got together. Problem was, he'd loved Sam too, almost as much as he loved Izzie. He was ace and he knew all about *Star Wars*, more than Noah did – he'd even invited Noah into their apartment to watch some of his original DVDs, and then he'd actually *loaned* them to him, and no grown-up had ever trusted him with anything like that before. So Sam was a legend. Then Izzie had offered to bring him to the movies one summer evening. Sam had gone back to New York for a few days so Izzie was on her own.

'I'm stealing you away,' she'd said. 'You like movies, don't you? I want to see *Wonder Woman* myself so it's a good excuse to go with you. I hope your dad doesn't mind. I'd better check with him first – it has a 12A rating.'

Dad had said that Izzie was very kind to offer to bring Noah to the movies. *Wonder Woman* had been good, for a girl's movie. Izzie was fun and she bought popcorn and ice-cream and kept cracking jokes, and he thought she even looked a bit like the Wonder Woman girl, with her eyes and her hair, which was way cool.

That evening he'd pretended that Sam had gone back to New York for good, and even when Izzie had delivered him safely home to his dad, he'd pictured how lovely it would be if she came in with him instead of going on up to the second floor. He'd pictured them being a proper family and his dad being really happy, not just pretend happy. Noah knew he'd be mega-happy too, with Izzie as his sort-of mum, instead of having this constant feeling that there was a dark spot in his head, and instead of putting up with the odd looks of some of his schoolmates when they found out he'd no mother, because he was different to them and they couldn't imagine not having a mother.

And after all his wishing, what had happened? Sam was out of the way all right, and he was never coming back. He'd gone to Galway with Izzie one weekend and had died in an accident. A lot of the time, Noah wondered if he was to blame for that, as if his bold wishes had somehow gone up to a satellite in outer space and pinged back down, taking Sam away, like Darth Vader taking out Obi Wan Kenobi with his light sabre. His heart already heavy because he knew he was betraying his mum in some way by wanting Izzie to take her place, this was tummy-churning guilt.

And no way could he say any of this to his dad.

His dad had told him that his mum's love would always surround him, that she would always be looking down on them, cheering them through life, making sure they enjoyed it as best they could. He wasn't sure where she was looking down from – his dad said she was like a far-off star in the night sky, beaming and sparkling, you couldn't see her but you knew she was there, so he could talk to her whenever he liked. Noah also had the wicker chair in his bedroom that used to be in his nursery in Clane. His mum had sat in that when she was feeding him, so Dad had replaced the baby-blue cushion with a *Star Wars* cushion and told him that whenever he sat in it he would be able to feel his mum around him like a big hug.

He was afraid to tell Dad he didn't actually *feel* anything except a bit uncomfortable.

But he knew he'd messed it up big time, wanting Sam out of the way. He could see how unhappy Izzie was. It reminded him a little of his dad: he had a dim memory of the house being hushed and quiet, his grandfather Sean forcing a smile, pretending things were okay, bringing a young Noah out of the house as much as he could, to the Zoo and McDonald's and for walks in the park and on the beach.

Even worse, now that Sam was out of the way and Izzie was all alone, there was no sign of her getting together with his dad. When they met in the hallway or on the stairs, they were like robots. And Izzie looked terrible. She'd got her hair cut short and choppy, so it still looked cool, but it was the rest of her. Her face was like a pale-yellow mask, her eyes were like fish eyes – you wouldn't think they could actually see anything – her voice flat, so whatever chance he might have had of bringing them together beforehand, it would be harder than ever now.

Then two weeks ago, he had the idea of the choir. The night before Christmas Eve, his school choir was singing at a charity carol service in the local parish church, and Noah had been chosen to sing solo on one of his favourite Christmas songs, 'Walking in the Air'. He was going to ask Izzie to come along. He'd imagined the three of them going around together, wrapped up in boots and hats and scarves, almost like a family. He'd imagined how nice it would be, Izzie and his dad sitting side by side in the candlelit church, listening to Christmas carols, talking to each other in the interval.

He'd even stood in front of the framed photograph on the sideboard and silently told his mum what he'd planned, hoping she wouldn't mind.

Only now all that was spoiled. A visitor had arrived and he was sure the man was here to see Izzie. *And* he was lugging a case and a backpack, which looked like he planned on staying. Still, it served him right for having bad thoughts about Sam, never mind wanting Izzie to take his mum's place. Noah aimed a kick at his snow R2-D2 but he couldn't follow it through. He kicked at a drift of snow instead and in his head he shouted the bad language his dad had forbidden.

Bollocks.

CHAPTER NINE

Izzie was pleasantly woozy by late afternoon. It would be perfect if she could just stay for a while in that cosy buffer zone between being stone cold sober and blind drunk, but alcohol didn't work that way. She'd need to keep topping up the levels to hold onto the effect, and it would end up giving her the hangover from hell.

Her intercom buzzed and she was startled out of her lethargy. No worries, it couldn't be for her – even if family or friends were coming to visit, they never dropped in unannounced. Someone had obviously pressed the wrong button. All she had to do was sit tight and ignore it. When she heard a tapping on her apartment door a few minutes later, she jumped. Once again she ignored it, hoping whoever it was would go away. But the knocking came again, more forceful. Maybe it was Tom, back again. Shite. He'd smell the wine off her breath and see that she was in her pyjamas. She gathered her robe around her and marched out into the hall, and, without checking the spy hole, she unlocked the door and flung it open.

It wasn't Tom. It was a man she'd never seen before. He was tall and broad, his figure bulked out further by the thickly padded jacket he was wearing. Her eyes were on a level with his chest and she noticed the jacket was damp in places with melting particles of snow. Most likely he was a friend of Tom's who'd come up to the wrong floor.

'What is it? Who are you looking for?' she asked waspishly, her peculiar sense of invasion mixed with relief that the caller couldn't be for her.

'Hey!' He raised a big gloved hand as if in self-defence.

'You must have come to the wrong floor,' she said.

His next words shocked her. 'Izzie? Izzie Mallon? It is you, isn't it? I recognise you from your photograph.'

He knew her name. It was a further intrusion and it threw her off balance, especially because she didn't know who he was. He wouldn't have been out of place marching off a marauding Viking ship. Then she registered that he'd spoken in an American accent and a shiver slid down her spine.

'What do you want?' she asked, gripped by a sudden foreboding.

His intense light-blue eyes held her transfixed. 'I'm sorry for disturbing you and calling out of the blue like this, but I'm in trouble.'

'What kind of trouble?' Her head was swimming. He had a case by his feet and a rucksack sitting on top of it. Her brain frantically clawed at disparate thoughts. How could she get rid of him? How fast could she do it in a city that was experiencing a transport meltdown? Who the hell *was* he?

He shrugged his shoulders, put out his hands in a gesture of supplication and grinned disarmingly. He spoke again in that American accent that made her nauseous. 'I'm stranded,' he said. 'Stuck. No room at the inn.'

Her fogged-up brain slowly made connections. He knew her name. He recognised her from a *photograph*. He knew where she lived.

'Who are you?' Her voice was a whisper, blurry from wine.

He looked at her quizzically. 'Hey, don't you recognise me?' Then his face cleared and he smiled warmly. 'Although you probably don't,' he said gently. 'How could you? I look quite different to what you would have expected. That's what traipsing around the world does for you. I've got rid of the beard and had the hair cut ridiculously short. We've never met,' he went on, sounding respectful. 'Even though I've heard all about you. You might have heard even a little bit about me?' A pause, while he allowed his words to sink in.

'If we've never met, how could I have heard about you?' she countered.

'Oh, I'd say you have – we've even exchanged emails,' he said, as gently as if he were talking to a six-year-old. 'Izzie, it's lovely to meet you at last. I'm Eli. Eli Sanders.'

The name slammed into her head, an echo bouncing back from her aching, bitter-sweet, recent past. From the precious place that was banished behind a wall of ice, the place where Sam had lived and laughed and loved her.

CHAPTER TEN

New York,
fourteen months ago

We're sitting outside a coffee shop on a sidewalk close to Central Park. It's an October afternoon of clear blue skies, with honey-coloured sunlight fizzing through russet and flame shaded trees. I think autumn is the best time to visit New York. The humidity of the summer has subsided, and there are days when the beauty of blazing leaves set against a blue sky rimmed with a medley of light-reflecting skyscrapers makes you feel you could soar.

But this is a golden afternoon because you're sitting opposite me, alive and breathing. It's been five weeks and three days since we met, or rather seventeen days if I count the actual days we've been able to spend together. The days and hours are irrelevant in the rhythm of time; in my heart I've known the essence of you for all the hundreds and thousands of hours I have ever lived.

'Hey, Sam, you're holding out on me,' I say.

'How?' you ask.

'There are still a few details missing from your bio,' I say, walking my fingers across the small table until they interlace with yours.

'So what?' You catch my hand and hold it against your chest. 'You know all the important things, don't you?'

I nod, my throat constricting a little.

You made sure I knew the most important thing about you from almost the beginning. You're wearing a navy sweater and I imagine the tips of my fingers picking up the thrum of your heartbeat from inside your chest and I soak up the feel of it and will it to keep on thrumming for as long as possible.

'I've told you about my family,' you say. 'You know where I work, you've seen me butt naked, eating hot dogs off a stand, strumming air guitar along with the best artists in the world, playing love songs to you …'

I'm happy to go along with you and focus on the inconsequential instead of the big, dark elephant sitting between us. 'I don't remember you being butt naked when you ate hot dogs off a stand …'

'Don't you? I saw you, as naked as the day you were born, trying to lick the juice off your chin.'

'You didn't.'

'I did, in my mind's eye,' you say. 'I thought of what you looked like under your jeans and I said to myself, I know, I *know* what this beautiful lady looks like, I *know* the lovely curve of her butt, how soft it feels under my hand when I tickle it, how perfect it feels against my body when I—'

'Very clever, but you needn't think you can change the subject that easily. I know all about where you are now – I've seen your profile details online.'

'You googled me.'

'Of course I did, the day after we met.'

'So what else do you want to know?'

'There's a gap. Of six months, just over three years ago, before you started working for Stanley Trust.'

'What makes you think it could be anything interesting?'

'I'm nosy. Plus the fact that you've never mentioned it to me. Even now you're holding out. I mean, six months. Did you feel the need to go off and find yourself on a Buddhist retreat?'

'Not exactly,' you say. 'That's the time I was in Zambia with Eli.'

'Eli – the guy I haven't met. The roving adventurer.'

'Yup, he's that all right.'

You've already told me about your best mate, whom you met on your first day in college. There are photographs on your phone, a tall, burly man with shaggy shoulder-length hair and a bandana caught around his forehead, white teeth grinning broadly below a pair of wraparound sunglasses; another one with Eli wearing full mountaineering gear. In the first photograph he'd been embarking on a hike through India; in the second, he'd been about to climb Mount Kilimanjaro. He's travelling the world and you've told me you haven't seen him in about a year.

'What were you doing in Zambia?'

'This and that.'

'Come on,' I say, 'tell me more. I sense a story here from the sound of your voice. *And* reluctance to elaborate.'

'As you insist … I was between jobs at that time. Eli was already working for Stanley Trust, but his parents had just died in an automobile pile-up on the interstate and he needed time out to get his head straight so he took a sabbatical. We went to Zambia as volunteers. We spent six months helping to renovate schools and community centres.'

'Oh wow. Fair dues to you both. That was some project. Some commitment as well.'

'It helped Eli sort himself out. As well as that, we'd been earning pretty good bucks and were happy to give something back. It was one of the most rewarding experiences in both our lives. The kids swarmed all over us, they were wonderful: spontaneous, warm and loving. They were central to the work we did, and made it so worthwhile.'

'Wow. And I bet you'd never have said anything to me about your volunteering efforts only I asked.'

'Didn't you sense it about me?' he teases.

'Of course I did, you show-off. How come Eli went off again? Is he still saving the world?'

'Not quite. That's another story, one I was going to tell you because you need to know, just in case …'

'In case what?'

'In case you meet him later,' you say.

I don't reply. I know what 'later' means. It's not good. I press my index finger to the muffin crumbs remaining on my plate and I lick them off my finger, the sugar sweetness exploding on my taste buds.

The blast of an ambulance siren cuts through the mellow afternoon like a harbinger of doom and you wait until it passes before you continue. You lean closer across the table. 'When we arrived back in New York,' you say, 'an opportunity opened up for me in the IT security area in Stanley Trust and I took it.'

'Working with Eli?'

'Yep. It was like being back in college again. We provide IT security expertise to the children's charity Share a Wish Foundation, based here in New York, and last year they had cyber attacks coming in below the radar. Eli and I worked on a project to strengthen all the firewalls, and we fixed a couple of kinks in the interfacing with their accountancy partners. Then Eli was kinda intimidated.'

'How?' I ask.

'His car was damaged, his apartment broken into, he was jumped on one night by a couple of guys in the subway who roughed him up. Seemingly random events, with nothing to link anything to anyone.'

'Was it something to do with his work?'

'He wasn't sure. He couldn't prove anything and it came at a bad time. His parents' financial affairs had finally been settled, they'd sold the family home and it brought the loss of them back to him. He decided he was outta here and he's been travelling the world ever since. I get occasional emails from him and I think right now he's on an expedition into the deepest Amazon basin or something like that.' You lean forward and hold my hand a little tighter. 'Izzie,' you say to me gently, 'Eli doesn't know about me ...'

I swallow and nod.

'But I wanted to fill you in on his background in case he ever comes to visit you later on.'

Later ... that horrible word again.

I look at you steadily. Everything slows down until the moment sharpens into crystal clear pixels. From a nearby tree, a burnt-orange leaf loses its tenuous hold on life and I watch its inevitable fall as it spins gently in the air and floats down helplessly until it comes to rest on the kerbside. I hear an alarm bell, like faint thunder in the far-off distance. I push it away and empty my mind, then I fill all the spaces in it with you and this moment, wishing I could stay in it forever.

CHAPTER ELEVEN

Izzie had to make a monumental effort to step away from the memories fizzing in her head and come back to her apartment door. A sudden up-draught of chilly air rose from the stairwell and signalled that, down in the hall, the main door had opened. She heard Noah's young voice as he spoke to Florence and it grounded her a little. She stared at the man standing in front of her, trying to equate him with the photographs Sam had shown her. This man had the same big, burly figure and blast of white teeth, but he was clean-shaven, and his dark blond hair was cropped tight.

'*Eli?*'

'Yes, it's me,' he said. 'I might look a bit different from

the photos I'm sure Sam has shown you. I've come back to civilisation and cleaned up my act a bit.'

Izzie stared at him, her mind whirling.

He backed away. 'I'm sorry. I've given you a shock. Forget I ever knocked on your door. It's entirely my fault I'm stranded. I shouldn't have intruded.' He turned to leave, picking up his rucksack, and was on the point of swinging it up to his shoulder when she spoke.

'What do you mean, stranded?' Her voice was hoarse.

'Don't worry about me,' he said. 'Don't even give me a thought. I'm sure you have plans for Christmas. I'll be fine … I'll grab a bench in the airport or a corner of the floor or something …' He gave her a soft, lopsided smile.

'Wait!'

She'd forgotten momentarily that it was Christmas, caught up in the memories of New York City fourteen months previously. The news footage of discommoded passengers and a chaotic airport had scarcely registered with her as it drifted through her apartment from the safe remove of the screen. Now it came to life in front of her. How could she turn him away? Still, something rose inside her, a peculiar sense of unease. She'd never actually met Eli – that was surely why her gut instinct was one of disquiet. 'How do I know you are who you say you are?' she asked.

'I don't blame you for checking me out,' he said politely. 'I can give you a potted history. I met Sam in college in Albany, back in 2000, and we both studied IT security. He was nuts about John Lennon and learned to play the guitar in his teens. We started our careers in different New York firms but kept in touch. I'm six months older than Sam – his birthday was the first of December, mine the first of June. The year my parents died, and to get out of my own head, I went to Zambia for six months. Sam came with me, and when we arrived home, he joined me in the security division of Stanley Trust. He preferred beer to wine and hated the gym, but loved running. He did the New York City Marathon twice, in his late twenties. About two years ago, I left Stanley Trust to travel the world. Then last September, Sam met you in New York, you got married here in Ireland last March and I know you were the absolute love of his life. And then, this September ...' His voice softened.

'Okay,' she said, knowing what was coming next, 'I've heard enough.'

'Are you sure?' he said. 'I didn't intend to turn up like this, out of the blue. As I said in my email, I'd hoped to come to Dublin to visit you next spring, then my plans changed and ... here I am.' He dropped his backpack to the floor and began to rummage around. 'I can do a dig around here for my passport if you like. It's here, somewhere.'

'I said it's okay.' She'd had lots of emails in the last three months, and more in the last couple of weeks as Christmas approached, some quite supportive, others full of an outpouring of sympathy in view of the time of year, most of which she'd barely scanned. Eli had sent her a lovely email after Sam had died and she'd read every word of it. Sam had been a true friend to him, he'd said, one of the best, and although he'd never met Izzie, he knew from what Sam had told him that she'd been the best thing to ever happen to him. As soon as he was back in her corner of the world, perhaps next spring, he'd arrange to pay her a visit. He'd offered to call her for a chat, asking for her phone number, but she hadn't replied.

Sam's best buddy, stranded at Christmas. What would Sam have done? She knew exactly what he would have done. 'At least,' she heard herself say, 'while you're here, come in and have something to drink.'

'I don't want to impose,' he said. 'And I don't, especially, want to be a burden at what I'm sure is a difficult time of the year for you.' His voice was full of careful respect, not dripping with sympathy or pity nor patronising, as though he saw her as a fully functioning human being and not a broken piece of humanity.

She sighed. Her gut instinct was to tell him to go. Sam's best mate or not, she really didn't owe him anything and, anyway, it wasn't convenient – hey, she had plans for the next few days that she'd carefully laid. But her innate manners took over.

'One drink is hardly going to burden me,' she said, opening the door wider and inviting him in.

CHAPTER TWELVE

He stepped across the threshold. He was in.

He'd been right to bide his time. It had just been a question of watching and waiting for the best opportunity. He dropped his case in the hall and followed her down a short corridor, noting that there were three doors to his right leading to rooms and one to his left. Carrying his backpack, he followed her in through the door on the left.

'What am I thinking?' she said, wheeling around and catching him unawares so that he struggled to hide the triumph that was surely blazing from his eyes.

'Take off your jacket,' she ordered, holding out her hands. 'I'll leave it near the radiator in the hall. I don't normally do this with damp clothes but it might help to dry it out.'

He took his phone out of his pocket and shrugged out of his jacket, handing it to her. She was a little different to what he'd expected. Then again, the photos he'd studied had been taken months ago. The woman he'd examined had been in her prime: medium height with a curvy figure, she'd been some looker. No wonder Sam had fallen hard for her, letting his dick rule his head. She hadn't been active on social media in the last three months but no surprises there. Now, her face was thinner, with dark circles underneath her eyes, and her figure was encased in a shapeless cream robe. When she went back out into the hall with his jacket, it gave him the opportunity to do a quick surveillance of the room. It was a long room, with sash windows overlooking the park, a galley kitchen to his left, a table and chairs dividing the compact kitchen area from the main living area. He went across to the windows. They were triple glazed and locked. There had to be a key somewhere, although there was too long a drop from the windows to allow her a safe escape if it came to that. He turned back into the room, assessing it. The kitchen was lit by recessed lighting in the ceiling, and a triple copper pendant light hung down over the table.

The living area held two big sofas, and along the wall opposite the windows a low cupboard held a record player and a flat screen television showing a children's cartoon, the sound muted. Underneath were cubbyholes for storage. There were bookshelves and a coffee table and original paintings hung on the walls. There was also a restored fireplace, with a large mirror over it, reflecting the chandelier set into the ceiling rose. A cosy little love nest for this bitch and her asshole husband Sam, and the last place on earth she'd see if things didn't go his way …

She came back into the room. 'Tea or coffee?' she asked. 'Or would you like something stronger?'

He'd already spotted the opened white wine and the bottles of red wine lined up on the kitchen counter alongside two litre bottles of gin. Perfect for an alcohol and drug overdose if she proved to be too awkward. Sam Mallon had robbed his future and put his life in danger. He'd have no problem taking out his bitch of a wife if she didn't co-operate.

'A glass of white wine would be lovely, thanks,' he said. 'I really appreciate this – it's been a long day.' He tried to hit a note between humour and exhaustion.

He didn't like wine, but it was better to drink along with her. It might encourage her to down more because she wouldn't realise exactly how much she was knocking back.

She looked at him warily, as though she was figuring out exactly how he'd got there. She took a glass out of the cupboard, poured in some wine, then refilled her own glass. 'Sit down,' she said. 'Make yourself comfortable.'

'Thank you,' he said, smiling at her with the most disarming smile he could muster. 'You're so kind.'

She sat down on a sofa and he sat at right angles to her. He took a sip of the wine, hiding his distaste. 'It's good to feel human again. Airport coffee wasn't doing it for me.'

'You've come straight from the airport?' she said.

'The airport? More like the corridors of hell,' he said, shaking his head, allowing a smile to play around his lips as though he was making light of it. 'It's total chaos. I thought I would have been almost home in New York by now.'

'Flight delayed?'

'More than that.' He shrugged. 'I was en route home from Johannesburg via Zurich and Heathrow, with a connection from there on to JFK, but got diverted to Dublin when Heathrow closed. So, no connection to JFK. Now Dublin is closed until tomorrow. So many flights have been disrupted that almost fifty thousand people have had their travel plans thrown in the air. How about you? You must have plans for the vacation ...'

He saw by her surprised face that he'd caught her on the hop. She swallowed, recovered some equilibrium.

'I have plans all right,' she said. 'I'm off to a yoga retreat.'

'A yoga retreat?' Was she now? He'd been sure it was nothing but an excuse to avoid her family at this time of the year. She'd even told her brother she was staying put. She'd hardly changed her mind since she'd sent that email. There had been no activity on her phone to indicate she had actually booked a place. He allowed himself to scan her attire for an infinitesimal moment and an element of surprise to show on his face. He saw by the flicker of her eyes that his hunch was correct. She was lying.

She raised her chin a fraction. 'Yeah, tomorrow. I figured it was a far more relaxing way to spend the season of over-indulgence.'

'Absolutely. Far kinder to the body and soul. However, they are warning people to avoid unnecessary travel. You'd want to be careful on the roads.'

'I'm not driving,' she said. 'There's an expressway bus from the city centre that will bring me most of the way there.'

'Good for you,' he said, knowing it was best to play along with her for now. 'I'm still determined to get to New York in time for Christmas.'

She sat back against the cushions, studying him through half-closed eyes. 'The last I heard of you, you'd left the Amazon and were on safari somewhere in deepest Africa.'

'I was. I had planned on travelling home next spring and coming through Dublin to meet you.'

'So what happened?'

'Sam happened.'

He saw her grip her glass so firmly that her drink slopped slightly.

'What I mean is,' he said, forcing himself to adopt a softer tone, the better to get her onside, the easier to get what he came for. 'I was thinking about him and the importance of love and family, and he was the reason I changed my mind at the last minute and decided to spend Christmas and New Year with my elderly aunts in New York, rather than pitch camp up a tree so I could study the mating habits of elephants. Unfortunately, I told them of my plans and they're expecting me and greatly looking forward to my visit. Now there's a chance I won't get there in time. There's a huge backlog of passengers as it is, which will get worse if the weather doesn't clear soon.'

'Fingers crossed,' she said, looking at him over the rim of her glass.

He allowed silence to fall between them for a long moment and watched her take two big gulps of her drink. Then he sat forward, as though he was inviting a confidence, looking at her with all the kindness he could summon.

'I won't talk about it if you don't want to,' he said gently. 'But as I said in my email, I couldn't believe it when I heard about Sam.'

She watched him guardedly, the way a small animal might size you up, sensing a disquiet of sorts but not enough to cause any major upset. She hugged herself with her arms and still managed to tilt her glass towards her mouth for another long gulp as though it was a manoeuvre she was used to doing.

'Sometimes life is crap,' he said. 'But losing Sam was the worst form of crap I've ever heard. You must be rightly pissed off about the way he died, in such a silly, senseless accident.'

'You're right,' she said. She rose to her feet and he watched her go across to the kitchen and empty the last of the white wine into her glass. She opened the fridge and took out a fresh bottle, filling her glass to the brim. 'More?' She waved it in his direction, not noticing that he'd barely sipped his.

'Sure, thanks,' he said, knowing it was best to appear to be joining in.

She padded across the room and slopped some into his glass, slightly unsteadily. She left the bottle down on the coffee table, forgetting to bother with the cooler.

'I'm right?' he said encouragingly.

'Yep. I'm rightly pissed off and I can't bear to think about that accident.' Her face was shuttered. She wasn't exactly going to be a pushover.

Far from the emotional, weeping woman he'd expected, her loss magnified by the sentimentality of the Christmas season, this bitch had her defences up any time he mentioned Sam. He'd find a way to get around them if he had to. Nothing like having a few Mafia sharks chasing him for money to sharpen his wits. His life depended on getting back what Sam had robbed from him.

'I don't want to inconvenience you any longer than I have to,' he said. 'It might be an idea for me to check the news and see what's happening in the airport.'

She picked up the remote and pointed it at the television,

flicking through menus. 'Sure. We'll have news on soon, but why don't you check your phone? Sometimes Twitter is more up to date.'

'I can't, actually,' he said. 'My cell phone is not compatible in this country.'

She looked at him a little unhappily and then she sighed. 'I'll get mine so.' She went outside and he heard her going into her bedroom. She had put her phone away, which suggested she didn't want to be disturbed, and adding that to the drink she had lined up, he guessed she'd intended staying home alone with nothing but a few bottles for company. She'd scarcely planned on holding a wild Christmas party – there had been no activity on her phone to suggest that either.

While he was alone in the room, he did another quick scan until he found what he was looking for. Two laptops, one sitting on top of the other, tucked onto a shelf at the bottom of the bookcase.

Two. One of them had to be Sam's. Hardly the one on top, with the purple lid.

Good. He didn't have to go looking for it, which might make things a little easier.

CHAPTER THIRTEEN

'Enjoying the party, Gemma?' Rachel asked.

Rachel, in her corporate persona, was always groomed to perfection, exuding a mixture of confidence and brilliance, and so scarily capable that Gemma knew she was someone to emulate as she climbed the ladder of success. This evening Rachel's face was slightly flushed and her Christmas hat askew. It made Gemma's lofty and remote superior colleague seem more approachable.

'It's amazing,' Gemma said. 'The best way ever to kick off the festivities.' She looked about her, seeing everything through a hazy blur of wine-coloured contentment.

The boardroom had been transformed into a Christmas wonderland, with tinsel, baubles and glittery streamers decorating every possible surface. However, the fake snow that had been sprayed on to embellish the floor-to-ceiling windows was no match for the real deal outside. Someone had hooked up a laptop to the sound system and Christmas songs were streaming around – ones that Gemma might have dissed in years gone by as being too schmaltzy, but this year was different. Thanks to the vibe of her first official office party, and Kian's welcome attention, she was seeing Christmas in a different light. Everything was glitterier and shinier, the Christmas music more fun; the boardroom and the office seemed lovely spaces to drift around in, and miles removed from the formal place where she was always on edge and acutely self-conscious of every word out of her mouth, never mind every outfit she wore. Not having to worry about saying the wrong thing to Izzie was even a bit of a relief. Everything combined to make her feel on a high and she wondered why life couldn't always be just as good as this.

'You deserve to let your hair down a little,' Rachel said. 'You've been great with Izzie over the last few weeks.'

'Oh, gosh …' Gemma wasn't sure what to say. Once again, an intelligent response evaded her. A lot of the time she'd felt she was floundering around Izzie, like an elephant around an injured gazelle. How had Rachel noticed? Was she being observed? Still, Rachel had said she'd been great, which meant everything was fine. She hadn't been found wanting.

'So don't be shy,' Rachel said. 'Help yourself to everything. There are some hot nibbles arriving in shortly from the pub down the road, so make sure you have some of those too.'

'I'll take care of that,' Kian said, overhearing. He picked up a bottle of wine and filled Gemma's glass. She felt Rachel was about to make a comment but thought the better of it.

Instead the older woman gave Kian a look before smiling at Gemma. 'Don't take him too seriously,' she said. 'He can be a bad influence.'

'What – me?' Kian asked in exaggerated horror. 'No way. I've taken Gemma under my wing and I'm looking after her very well, aren't I, Gemma?'

'Hmm, I'm not sure about that yet,' Gemma said, feeling suddenly powerful. His attention was going to her head. This was Gemma Nugent, forging her own path in this new corporate world. Throughout her school years, she'd compared herself to the pretty, talented and clever Janet – she had been a hard act to follow for tall, rather plumpish Gemma, even though Janet had encouraged her all the way and the sisters got on like a house on fire. Then the music changed to an upbeat Emeli Sandé track and Gemma's spirits soared even further.

This, now, was the rest of her life unfolding in front of her. All those years at St Finnian's, buoyed by Janet and Mum as she'd run the gauntlet of the jeering gangs who couldn't care less and mocked her for working steadily, had paid off. College had been easier, Mum and Janet insisting that the world would be her oyster once she had her degree under her belt, and here she was, launching herself out there at last.

After the hot finger food, it was time for the Kris Kindle. The gift-wrapped presents were tipped onto the table and Katy distributed them. It had been an anonymous draw, everyone pulling a name from a hat, and she'd been slightly mortified to draw Rachel's name, buying her a scented candle that came in way over the ten euro limit per gift. But a lot of the token gifts were naughty as opposed to nice, and Gemma's heart thumped when she was handed a well-sealed package and everyone started a countdown while she unwrapped the various layers of glittery wrapping. To her embarrassment, she revealed a cheap and tacky bondage kit, including an eye mask, a small plastic whip and aluminium handcuffs, complete with key. A wave of heat engulfed her, relieved only slightly when she realised that everyone was cheering and whooping and she was being hailed as good fun for taking it in her stride. She forced laughter, the blood roaring in her ears.

'I should have warned you,' Katy said. 'Sometimes the newbie is landed with a bit of smut.'

'Someone must have lust-filled ideas about you,' Kian said, with a glint in his eye. 'I wonder who that could be.'

'I wonder too,' Gemma said, emboldened. 'Whoever it is, they're very naughty and I might need to handcuff them.'

'Sounds promising,' Kian said in a low murmur that was just for her ears. He refilled her glass.

Gemma took a few more sips, her head in a swirl of excitement.

She was in even more of a tizzy when a few of them decided to take the party to the pub, and she was invited. The sensible ones were heading home in view of the weather but the real party was only beginning and she was part of it. When she went back up to her workstation to collect her coat, she had a vague recollection of something she'd been supposed to do, something she thought might be important. But it slipped her mind, and anyway, what could be more important than Kian smiling at her as he slowly unwrapped her tinsel scarf from around her neck and tucked her woollen scarf in place before helping her into her coat.

Her first office Christmas party. She was twenty-two and her wonderful life was all ahead of her. Welcome, Gemma, to the real, important, dynamic, exciting world.

CHAPTER FOURTEEN

In the privacy of her bedroom, Izzie clicked on a lamp and pulled the drapes against the grey-white world outside. She took a few deeps breaths, centring herself and her already woozy head by focusing on the room around her. The bedroom she had once shared with Sam was calming and relaxed and decorated in neutral shades of silver and grey with pops of colour here and there, thanks to a cobalt-blue vase and scented candles on a chest of drawers, matching cushions across the bed and beautiful prints of both New York and the Wicklow hills on the walls, courtesy of both their birthplaces.

What did she think was she doing? She gave herself a mental shake as she picked up her phone. One: she'd invited a man she'd never met before into her apartment and right at this moment he was sitting on her sofa drinking wine. His snow-soaked jacket was drying in her hall. Two: she was switching on a phone she'd had no intention of engaging with for the next few days.

And all her plans for a peaceful and reclusive, booze-fuelled Christmas were teetering on the edge.

No, they weren't. She straightened up and exhaled long and sharply. Eli Sanders would be on his way as soon as he'd thawed out a bit. He was due in New York for Christmas. He wanted to be home. With his elderly aunts. She was just being hospitable to an old friend of Sam's for an hour or two. She might be feeling removed at one level from life going on around her, but she would have been some kind of monster to have turned him away in this weather.

When she went back into the living room, Eli was watching the news on the television, his face creased with annoyance. The news correspondent, muffled in a thick jacket and a hood, was standing at the entrance to the airport terminal. The picture shifted to inside the building, the camera scanning endless queues of dejected-looking travellers waiting in line as airport staff handed out piles of blankets.

'No need to check your phone,' Eli said. 'They've already confirmed that the airport has closed until tomorrow morning.'

'So no flights out this evening,' she said.

'Nuh-uh.' He shook his head. 'But it might be best to head back out and take my chances. I've got my name on a standby list. I want to make sure it stays there and doesn't get pushed further down.'

'Standby? Looking at that crowd you have some hope.'

'It's all I've got. All scheduled flights for the next few days are overbooked, and more have now been cancelled. I'll camp out and throw myself at the mercy of the flight attendants. It all depends on what additional flights they manage to put on as soon as the runway is cleared.'

'Why camp out in the airport?'

He looked at her, a hopeful expression on his face.

'Aren't there a couple of hotels close by?' she said. 'At least you'd be somewhere convenient for when flights get going again.'

'There are, and I would, but unfortunately every hotel in Dublin is booked solid. I went to the accommodation desk in the airport to try and book something, but I had no luck. Between the snow, diverted passengers and office parties on tonight, there's not a bed to be had in the city.'

'So you came here.'

'I'm not looking for a bed – I wouldn't dream of imposing.' He leaned forward. 'I know this will sound corny, but it seemed like fate when I heard my flight was being diverted to Dublin. Even though my arrival was unexpected and I guessed I'd take you by surprise, I thought it would be a good opportunity to see you. It's a pleasant break from the airport, and a change from the crap coffee and plastic sandwiches.'

'What am I thinking of?' Izzie said, suddenly realising she'd been less than hospitable. 'You must be hungry.' She tried to recall the contents of her fridge. Not that there was much. She hadn't planned on having an appetite over the next few days.

'I'm fine for now,' Eli said. 'And I'd bet you've allowed your supplies to run down if you're heading away for a few days.'

'You're right, I have,' she said, relieved to jump on the excuse.

'So, please, just relax,' he said soothingly. 'Do what you'd normally be doing if I wasn't here. I'm grateful to simply thaw out and then make my way back to the airport. Even though it's like Armageddon out there, I reckon it's the best way to give myself a fighting chance of getting home in time for Christmas.'

She poured more wine. To hell with it. So what if he thought she was knocking it back? She wasn't going to let Eli Sanders make her change her plans.

'At least we can have a snack of sorts,' she said. She got up and searched the kitchen press and found a big packet of crisps that she upended into a bowl. She opened the luxury chocolates the girls in the office had given her, putting everything on the coffee table.

'Our own little party.' He smiled and looked around the room. 'Your apartment is a delight,' he said. 'Such graceful proportions, the sash windows and the wooden recesses ... and is that the original fireplace?'

'It is,' she said. 'We' – her voice choked on the word – 'moved in in March. And' – she swallowed hard – 'there was little to do. It had all been restored and brought back to a lot of its former glory.' She watched his eyes rove around, taking in the corniced ceiling with the chandelier, the elegantly carved fireplace, classical and strictly in proportion, until his gaze returned to her.

'Beautiful,' he said. 'Absolutely beautiful.' He seemed to be staring at her, however, as though she was the focus of his words. Was he trying to come on to her? Unsettle her?

Yeah, right. She was imagining it. She'd had too much wine. 'Where have you been?' she asked, turning the focus to him.

'Dublin airport, before that Zurich, before that Johannesburg.'

'That's not quite what I meant,' she said. 'But why didn't you get a direct flight to New York from Johannesburg? Or even from Zurich?'

He gave a wry laugh. 'That would have solved all my problems,' he said. 'As in, I wouldn't be sitting here now, I'd be home. It was a late decision and, unfortunately, by the time I went to book my flights they were all full. Christmas is a crazy time of the year to be travelling anywhere. There were a few seats available going through Zurich and London, on to JFK. I figured the journey would be worth it.'

'And what were you doing in deepest Africa besides checking out the elephants?'

'I was helping out on an endangered wildlife programme. I'm not just a philandering adventurer.'

'I wouldn't dream of calling you that.'

'I'm not sure how much you know about me …' He looked at her with a soft smile.

Izzie stared back at him, making no reply, not sure where this was leading.

'Or why I went off around the world not once, but twice.' His eyebrow was cocked, inviting her comments.

'I have an idea,' she said.

'Not that I would dream, in a million years, of suggesting there was anything similar in both of our experiences,' he continued. 'I'm just letting you know that I've also experienced loss.'

In spite of the buffer of alcohol, a sudden stab of pain caught her by surprise.

He must have noticed her reaction because he went on,

his voice gentle, 'I won't talk about it after this, but are the authorities happy Sam's death was a genuine accident? There was nothing to indicate anything suspicious?'

'Suspicious? Like what?'

He shrugged. 'I dunno. You were there at the time, I wasn't. It's so hard to believe he's gone, it's just … Hell.' He looked away, swallowed hard, then looked back at her, his face creased with unhappiness. 'I still see Sam wearing his big grin the first day I met him in college. He was three months short of his twentieth birthday, it was the year of the millennium and we were young, invincible, full of hopes and dreams and ready to take on the world.'

Izzie's head filled with images of a Sam she'd never known – a younger Sam, a carefree student moving around an American college campus as if the whole world was in the palm of his hand.

'We were best buddies,' Eli went on. 'Man, the stories I could tell you about him.' He smiled ruefully and shook his head. 'I'd been looking forward to seeing you next spring, to share some of my funny memories.'

'You knew him a long time,' she said. She'd only known Sam for one short, precious year.

'I did,' Eli said. 'I'm not sure if you're happy talking about him, but I'd like to put it on record that over all the years we've been buddies, I never knew him to be as happy as he was with you. He loved you more than he'd ever loved anyone in his life. He thought you were the most beautiful woman, arriving into his life when you did. I wasn't surprised when you guys married barely six months after you'd met.'

His eyes watched her intently and, despite her slight sense of discomfort, she was oddly transfixed.

There was a soft knock on the apartment door.

'Expecting any visitors?' Eli asked.

'No, I'm not,' Izzie said. 'And no one has buzzed to come up.'

'I'll go,' Eli offered.

'No, it's fine,' Izzie said, reluctant for him to take charge. She gathered herself together, getting up off the sofa, pulling the sash of her terry robe tighter, pushing her feet into her mules.

She went out into the small hallway. There was another knock as she looked through the spyhole and when she saw who was waiting outside, she opened the door immediately. If there was anyone in her life right now who was totally non-threatening and the least annoying person to be around, and therefore welcome at all times, it was this young boy.

'Noah? Is everything okay?'

CHAPTER FIFTEEN

Earlier, when he'd come in from the park, Noah had seen Florence in the hall and she'd said that, yes, a lovely American man had called to see Izzie. Noah had trudged upstairs, and not only could he scarcely feel his feet and hands because they were so wet and freezing, his whole body was cold too.

His dad had told him to get into a bath immediately and when he came out, slightly warmed up, a bowl of soup was waiting for him. 'Dinner will be another hour,' his dad had said.

'Great, thanks,' Noah had answered. The soup warmed him up even more, but even better again was the idea he got just as he finished the bowl. He still had *Star Wars* DVDs belonging to Sam that he'd never returned. He'd tried to, a couple of times, but whenever he'd met Izzie on the stairs she'd told him not to worry about them. She'd had that blank look on her face, the one that said she didn't really hear him. Returning the DVDs would be a great excuse to knock on Izzie's door and find out what was going on with her visitor. If she looked happy with him, like the way she'd looked when Sam had been around, it could mean there wasn't a skinny chance she'd come to the concert with him and his dad. That would scupper his plans to get them together. It was bad enough that his dad seemed to have no interest in Izzie whatsoever.

'I'm going up to Izzie for a minute,' Noah had said.

'Izzie?' When he looked up from his laptop, his dad's face had been as blank as his voice had sounded.

Not good.

'Yeah. The lady who lives upstairs. Remember?'

'What are you going up to her for?'

'I'm bringing back some DVDs. Sam lent them to me ages ago. I still have them.'

'Why now?'

Noah had shrugged. 'I know she's in.'

'Oh. Okay.' His dad had returned to his laptop.

No interest whatsoever. He could have been talking about cabbage or Brussels sprouts, Noah's two least favourite foods. So much for his Christmas wish. His legs felt heavy as he went upstairs. And his hands were hot on the DVDs. He hoped they wouldn't be sweaty when he handed them over.

Izzie opened the door. If she asked him in, it was a good sign. If she didn't ask him in, it meant she was too wrapped up in her visitor and his plans for her and his dad were toast.

'Noah? Is everything okay?'

'I thought it was about time I gave these back,' he said, holding out his small bundle.

'Come in,' she said.

Result. A good sign. And her face didn't look all glowy like it used to when Sam was around. Another good sign. But when he went into the living room, the visitor was relaxing back on a sofa, his jean-clad legs outstretched as if he lived there all the time. Bad.

Izzie said, 'Noah, this is Eli. Eli, this is Noah from the floor below.' Funnily enough her voice was as blank as his dad's had been. Nonetheless, he stood there awkwardly, unsure of what to do next. As did Izzie.

She picked up a bowl of crisps and thrust it in front of him. 'Here, have some.'

He couldn't help himself to the crisps because his hands were full. 'I came to give you back these,' he said again, holding out the DVDs.

'What are they?' One look at them would have told Izzie what they were. She just wasn't registering it.

'*Star Wars* DVDs. I had a loan of them from Sam. They're his special collection – you should have them back.'

Izzie backed slightly away, as though the DVDs were about to detonate. Bad sign. Noah hurriedly put them down on the low coffee table.

'I don't think—' Izzie began, frowning at them. 'Actually, Noah,' she said, shoving a tendril of hair behind her ear, 'I'm happy for you to keep them. I'm sure Sam would have liked you to have them, all the more if they were his special collection. Isn't that right, Eli? Eli is an old friend of Sam's.'

'Sure,' Eli said.

'You're Sam's mate Eli?' Noah asked him. '*The* Eli?'

'Yeah, why, did Sam talk about me?'

''Course. Loads of times. He said you were great mates and a big fan of *Star Wars* like him.'

'That's right,' Eli said.

'We had some brill talks. Sam was way cool.' As far as Noah was concerned, Eli didn't look as though he was any way cool. For starters, his eyes weren't friendly and he didn't look like he'd be interested in chatting with him the way Sam used to.

'Sit down, Noah,' Izzie said. She picked up a box of chocolates. 'Help yourself. Eli's stranded with the weather,' she went on.

'Oh.' Noah took a chocolate and sat down on the edge of the sofa furthest away from Eli.

'His flight was diverted to Dublin instead of landing in Heathrow,' Izzie said. 'Now both airports are closed for the time being.'

'You could be stuck here for Christmas,' Noah said, his temporary joy that Eli was an unexpected visitor giving way to the alarming prospect of him having to stay with Izzie all over Christmas. Because from what Sam had said of his great mate, he'd be a perfect replacement for him. It would nearly be like having Sam back again.

'I could indeed,' Eli agreed. 'But I hope not. I'd far rather be at home in New York with my aunts, instead of sitting on a bench in the airport, hoping for a standby seat. The snow has disrupted everyone's travel plans, so I'm not alone.'

'At least Santa Claus won't be stranded,' Izzie said, winking at Noah. 'He's used to travelling through thick snow.'

'Santa!' Eli said, shaking his head. 'At a guess, son, I'd say you're far too old to believe in any of that mumbo jumbo.'

'I disagree, Eli,' Izzie said quietly. 'No one is ever too old to believe in the magic of Santa.'

Eli looked at her as though he wasn't entirely happy. 'We'll have to agree to disagree in that case. You okay with that, son? I hope haven't said anything to upset you?'

'No.' Noah shook his head. Deffo not. He was delighted Izzie saw a reason to disagree with Eli. He knew Sam would have sided with her on this. He realised something: he didn't like Eli, not one bit. He didn't like the way he called him 'son'. And he seemed to be nothing like Sam, even though he'd been his good friend. He hoped Izzie realised this too. He hoped she realised his dad was far more like kind and thoughtful Sam than this dude sitting here. If she was ever looking for a replacement.

'But my dad would agree with Izzie,' Noah spoke up, annoyed that his voice sounded a little squeaky.

'Your dad …? Good for him,' Eli said, sounding bored to Noah's ears.

'Dad's on his own, like Izzie,' Noah said, emboldened enough to put them in the same category.

'Not quite on his own, if he has you looking out for him,' Eli pointed out.

'I look out for Izzie as well,' Noah said. He took out her rubbish whenever he could, he opened the hall door for her if he happened to see her approaching it – except for today, when he'd been too busy with the snow. And a couple of times when he'd seen her in the local store he'd carried her bags home.

'Seems you're in capable hands all round,' Eli said, looking at Izzie.

Izzie's mouth stretched in a tight smile, but her eyes were empty. Noah remembered his dad being like that for a long while, until he was seven or eight, and the sick feeling it used to give him. It gave him the same sick feeling to see Izzie like that now.

'Would you like some hot chocolate?' she asked him.

'No, thank you,' Noah said, as mannerly as possible. He loved hot chocolate, especially when his dad put mini marshmallows into it, but he didn't want to be stuck talking to Eli while Izzie went down to her kitchen to make it.

Izzie got up. 'Come on, of course you'd like some. It'll only take a minute.'

He went over to the kitchen area with her, feeling Eli's eyes boring into his back.

'What are you and your dad doing for Christmas?' Izzie asked, pouring milk into a cup and putting it into the microwave.

'We're going to Granny O'Connor on Christmas Day and then on down to Grandad Brady after that.'

'That'll be nice,' Izzie said. 'So long as the weather doesn't stop you.'

'Do you think it might?'

'I dunno.'

He wouldn't have minded giving Granny O'Connor a miss, even though that sounded terrible. She always made him sad with her sorrowful looks. She squeezed him too tight when she hugged him and she had hundreds of photographs of his mother around the house. He knew they would make him feel awful guilty, with the way he was forgetting her bit by bit. He didn't want to miss out on a visit to Grandad Brady, though. He was brill and Noah loved spending time with him in his house in west Cork. Still, if they couldn't get to Granny O'Connor in Kilkenny, they'd never make it to Grandad's.

He was afraid to ask Izzie what she was doing. Especially for her first Christmas without Sam. With no Christmas decorations, her apartment seemed bare and empty. And even though Eli talked of getting a flight home, he looked too comfortable, as though he could see himself settling in for a few days. The only thing that cheered Noah a little was that Izzie didn't seem to be seeing him as a replacement for Sam. There was still hope for a Christmas miracle.

The microwave pinged and Izzie took out the warmed milk. She opened an overhead press, taking out a jar of instant coffee. Without realising her mistake, she poured a generous spoonful into the hot milk, stirred it around, and handed it to him with a smile on her face. 'There you go, Noah,' she said. 'Hope you enjoy that. Sorry I've no marshmallows or chocolate toppings.'

He hated coffee. He hated the taste. But he hated most of all the look on Izzie's face, as though it was going to crack with the effort of her smile. He brought the cup over to the living area and sat down once again as far away as possible from Eli. He was glad when Izzie sat opposite him, and as they chatted about the snow, he sipped the coffee until it was all gone. He didn't want to leave even a trace, in case Izzie realised her mistake and it embarrassed her.

'I'd better be getting back,' he said, going over to the sink with his cup and giving it a rinse before she could stop him. Then he congratulated himself for thinking up a great excuse to bring Izzie and his dad face to face. 'If you need anything, Izzie, from the shops, and you don't want to go out into the snow, I'll get it for you. Just knock down. Dad's off work from now as well.'

'Thanks, Noah, you're very thoughtful. I'll let you know. Don't forget the DVDs – I know you'll appreciate them. They can be a Christmas gift,' she went on, as though she was happy with the idea. 'I didn't do much shopping … although by rights I should have wrapped them and put them under your tree.'

'Well,' Noah began, in a small voice, 'if you like, you can still do that.' He pictured his dad and Izzie, standing together as she put the wrapped gift under their tree. Even that would be a start.

'C'mon, son,' Eli interjected. 'Why put Izzie to that trouble? You can't expect her to celebrate Christmas under the circumstances.'

Eli was right. Noah's tummy began to ache. He'd asked for too much.

'Maybe I'm not celebrating it, but that doesn't mean others can't,' Izzie said. 'Leave them, Noah, and I'll organise that. I'm far from being anti-Christmas, the opposite in fact, we – I always loved it, and it's the least I can do.'

'Wow, thanks Izzie!' Noah wanted to give her a hug but he held back. 'Better go down now, Dad's cooking the dinner. He's a brilliant cook.'

Well, actually, his dad was taking something out of the freezer for this evening's dinner. He usually cooked, and was good at it, and was showing Noah the ropes as well. He said it was important for everyone to be able to look after themselves and take responsibility for their wellbeing. His dad was big into that, so Noah was also a dab hand with the dishwasher and the washing machine. He knew that Sam had often cooked as well, but Eli looked like he wouldn't know one end of a wooden spoon from another, and although he didn't like leaving Izzie alone with this dude, Noah was going to quit while he was ahead.

'I'll see you out,' Izzie said, getting to her feet.

CHAPTER SIXTEEN

Tom had taken a double portion of chicken casserole out of the freezer for dinner and it was heating in the oven, the appetising aroma drifting around the apartment. Noah was upstairs with Izzie, finally out of the snow. Even though his fingers and toes had been freezing, Noah was in seventh heaven with the weather, and Tom was glad there was something to keep him distracted from missing his mother at Christmas.

After some warming soup, Noah had mumbled something to Tom about DVDs and Izzie before he'd disappeared upstairs. When Sam was alive, Noah had been in the habit of popping up to him every so often once he'd discovered that Sam had been a *Star Wars* fanatic. Sam was someone else

Noah was bound to be missing, so chatting to Izzie was the next best thing, so long as he wasn't making a nuisance of himself.

Before he set the table for dinner, Tom finished his Christmas gift-wrapping. While Noah had been playing out in the snow, he'd already wrapped Santa Claus presents for him, hiding them under his bed, ready to be placed under the tree late on Christmas Eve when Noah would be asleep. He reminded himself to drop down to Florence with wine and chocolates. He'd tried before to give her a more expensive gift as a way of saying thank you for keeping an eye on Noah on the few occasions he'd been home late from the office, and for all the times Noah disappeared down to her with his homework, but she'd been so highly insulted that she'd sent him away with a ginormous flea in his ear and he'd never attempted it again.

He shook out a fresh roll of gift wrap, wrapping perfume and a scarf for Cathy's mother, Deirdre. She'd moved from Cork and was now living close to her son in Kilkenny, where they were all gathering for dinner on Christmas Day. Tom knew it would be a strained occasion thanks to the huge gap left by Cathy, but now, six years down the line, he was determined to try and soften Deirdre's ache by putting more emphasis on celebrating Cathy's life and legacy of love rather than mourning her absence.

For Sean, his father, he wrapped photography books and vinyl records. They were due to spend a few days with him in west Cork, travelling down on Stephen's Day, and he hoped the snow would ease up soon. The television was on, and a further update on the weather situation and emergency services available throughout the country was due shortly from the National Emergency Coordination Group.

Tom put the wrapped gifts under the tree and then set the table for dinner, which was just ready. There was no sign of Noah, and he decided he'd better go rescue Izzie from his chatterbox son. He could text her and ask her to send him down – he'd made sure they'd exchanged phone numbers after Sam's death just in case she needed anything – but today, a text might be a bit impersonal. Better to show his face and it would be another opportunity to see how she was bearing up – her first Christmas without Sam was bound to be difficult.

Just as he raised his hand to knock at her door, it opened on Noah and Izzie. Noah looked slightly glum and Izzie appeared to be dressed for bed: she was wearing a white robe over a pair of pyjamas, her choppy dark hair forming loose tendrils around her taut face, emphasising her cheekbones and soft brown eyes. In spite of being cocooned in the comfort of her thick robe, she reeked of jagged fragility and it unsettled Tom.

'Good timing,' he said, wishing he could say something to lift her spirits, even slightly.

'Is the dinner ready, Dad?' Noah asked, his face brightening a little.

'Just about,' he said.

He was more unsettled when Noah turned to Izzie and said, 'Great. Knowing Dad, I bet it's five-star yummy. Can't wait to tuck in.'

Izzie smiled faintly at Noah.

Suddenly conscious of Izzie's lone status set against the picture Noah was painting of a delicious family meal – which Tom considered was over-the-top boastful and out of order for the usually sensitive Noah – he found himself swiftly calculating that with the addition of a mixed salad and some crusty bread he could make the casserole stretch to three, and he heard himself saying, the words sliding out of their own accord, 'You're more than welcome to join us, Izzie.'

Noah's face flashed with surprise.

As did Izzie's eyes.

Tom hoped she'd take him up on the offer. It would be good for her to be with company. He saw himself opening the bottle of fine wine he'd planned to bring to west Cork, pouring her a glass and talking to her about Sam, if she wanted. He could at least empathise with her about the sheer craziness of life. He might even manage to bring a smile to her face.

She wrapped her arms around herself, gathering her robe a little more snugly. 'Thank you, but it doesn't suit.' She shook her head, her voice low. Casting a swift glance behind her, she continued, 'I have a visitor.'

'A visitor?' Tom echoed. Then he spotted what he'd missed earlier – a great big hulking jacket spread across the radiator in the hallway. His eyes automatically went to the living-room door, which was ajar. He saw a shadow loom against the spill of light falling from a lamp, and he had the instinctive sense that Izzie's visitor, whoever it was, had moved closer to the opened door and was skulking there, the better to overhear the conversation in the hallway.

'Yes, he's a friend of Sam's,' she said, her voice soft.

He. A friend of Sam's. Visiting Izzie. And she was obviously very much at home with this friend, clad as she was in her robe and slippers.

'That's great,' Tom said shortly, backing away from the door.

CHAPTER SEVENTEEN

Florence's apartment was slightly smaller than Tom's or Izzie's. Her living room led straight out onto the ground-floor hallway in Henrietta Square, and sounds from the hallway carried into her living room. Now, she could hear Noah outside messing with a ball, even though it was late in the evening and Tom had forbidden this activity indoors.

Sometimes this was Noah's way of getting her attention. Sometimes he liked being asked in for a small treat, and she was more than pleased about this. Sure enough, within a minute, there was a soft knock on her door.

'Sorry for the noise,' he said. 'I hope it didn't disturb you. I thought I'd lost this,' he went on, holding up a hurling ball, 'But it was underneath the hall table.'

'Come in, Noah,' she said, knowing by the appealing look in his eyes that this was what he was really after.

As he took in her appearance, staring up at her hair, his forehead crinkled. 'Are you going out to a party?'

'A party?' She put her hand on top of her hair and realised she was still wearing her glittery Christmas headband with the flashing lights. Had she been wearing it since earlier that day? Even when she'd spoken to Izzie's American visitor? God.

'No, not this evening,' she said. 'I just put it on to feel Christmassy. While you're here, I need you to sample some of my festive cupcakes, if you don't mind. I'm not sure if I got the recipe right. I need them tested before I bake more.'

'Sure.'

It took three cupcakes and two glasses of lemon cordial for Noah, and one cupcake along with some tea for her, before he got to the point.

'Did you meet Izzie's friend?' he asked.

'What friend?' She pretended ignorance.

'That guy who arrived this afternoon.'

'Not exactly,' Florence answered. 'I saw him at the door. And I spoke to him on the intercom. He seemed nice.'

'Did you think so?'

'Why, didn't you?'

'No,' Noah said, crumpling up the paper from his cupcake. 'I didn't like him. I met him up in Izzie's. He said I was far too old to believe in Santa, that it was all mumbo jumbo.'

'Did he now?' Florence swallowed a spark of vexation.

'Not even my dad would ever say such a thing. And even Izzie looked a bit annoyed. She said she still believes in the magic of Santa, even though she's without Sam.'

'Of course she does. Even I do, still, and I'm around a lot longer than Izzie.'

'Good. 'Cos I'm hoping for something really special this year …'

'Are you, Noah?'

'Yeah. I'd really love – do you think it's okay to ask this? I don't care if there's nothing at all under the tree, but I'd love for my dad and Izzie to be friends and get together. It would make it a perfect Christmas.'

'Oh, Noah.'

He was so caught up in spilling out the words about his dad and Izzie, now that he had started, that he didn't notice the expression on her face.

'That's why I don't like this guy – Eli,' he said. 'Why did he have to turn up now? He said he was stranded. I think he wanted to be stranded 'cos he looks happy to be in Izzie's, and what's the betting he won't get going anywhere until after Christmas? He's spoiling everything and getting in the way of my plans.'

'What plans?'

'My concert plans. I'm singing in the parish carol concert on Saturday night and I was going to ask Izzie if she'd like to come. That way, my dad would have to talk to her.'

'I see.' Oh dear. Noah had thought this through with all the naiveté of a ten-year-old boy. Florence didn't want to be the one to burst his bubble.

'I really like Izzie,' Noah said. 'I don't want her to be so sad. And Dad's on his own a lot. That's sad too. I know you're on your own as well, but it's different for you …'

'How come?'

He put his head to one side and looked at her trustingly.

'Even though you're old, you seem really happy and cheery. *All* the time. Like my grandad.'

'That's because I might look a bit battered on the outside, but on the inside I still think I'm seventeen. Sometimes, anyway. And that's where it counts the most.'

Still, in the face of his innocent words, Florence was consumed with the unwelcome realisation that her body *was* getting older. The funny thing about advancing years and their effects on her body was that her skin might look a little wrinkled and worn out, her once lustrous hair was fragile and weak and the doctor had cautioned her several times about her liver function, but her capacity to feel hadn't diminished in any way and her heart still squeezed and melted and contracted as strongly as it ever had, sometimes more powerfully than ever.

Now it melted on Noah's behalf. His mother was gone so long now, he had surely only a dim memory of her. She wondered, not for the first time, how come the perfectly eligible Tom was still unattached. He had the looks – he reminded her of that Irish actor, the lead guy in *Poldark*, the one that she and Wendy and Jean agreed was more than a bit of all right. But in person Tom was far kinder and all round lovelier than his screen character. It surely wasn't for the want of women throwing themselves at him. If she'd been any younger – make that a lot younger. If she'd been thirty years younger ... Thirty years had gone by in the blink of an eye.

Happy and cheery, Noah said. A lot of the time it was a front, put on to humour herself and satisfy everyone else. Sometimes her cheery face was as heavy as a cast-iron shield. She pulled off her hairband and wondered if there was ever a time when you learned to accept the vicissitudes of life and grow old with dignity and grace. Or was she always going to rage against fate in the depths of her heart? A fate that had seen her born onto this planet and into this country about two decades too soon. Her life would have been different had she been born into a more modern, enlightened Ireland where women had equal status. Although, even now true equality between the sexes still had a long way to go.

Still, she told herself, there were other fates that were far, far worse. She only had to read the papers or look at the television to appreciate that, and it made her feel tired and weary of the human race as a whole. In the meantime, this ten-year-old boy was looking at her as though she had all the answers to the vagaries of the universe.

She could see exactly why getting Izzie and Tom together seemed to be the ideal solution to Noah. In his head, it was all so simple. And wonderful, also, that the child would have welcomed Izzie as a sort of replacement for his own beloved mum. But Christmas magic or no magic, she sensed it wasn't going to happen. Izzie had a long way to go before she was ready to look at another man in that way again. If she ever did. As for Tom, he had come through so much himself he needed someone who wasn't nursing a grief of her own. How could she let Noah down gently?

'Noah,' she began softly, 'it's good to hope in the magic of Christmas and Santa—'

'But? I know there's a "but" when you talk like that.'

'Well, Izzie is still very bruised, and you know sometimes if you have a bad wound, or something major like a broken leg, it needs time to heal before you're able to go about your normal life again. You need to rest up and mind yourself. If not, you'll end up having worse trouble. Imagine if you started running on an injured leg before it was properly mended? Izzie is a bit like that at the moment – her heart is sore. She needs plenty of time to make sure that part of her feels better before she picks up a normal life again.'

As if. Florence hid her cynicism. There was no putting a Band-Aid, never mind a splint, on Izzie's pulverised heart and expecting it to recover.

'Yeah, but someone like Dad could help her, couldn't he?' Noah said beseechingly. 'He's been through it all already, when Mum—' He swallowed. 'He should know more than anyone how to talk to her.'

'That's what I'm trying to explain.' Florence desperately searched for words. Her friends would be better at this than she was, already having grandchildren of their own. 'There are people out there to help you, trained and experienced, if you want that kind of help. But when men and women come together in a relationship, like the sort you're talking about, it's much better for both of them and the relationship if they're already feeling good about life and themselves, so to speak. Have you said anything to your father?'

'How can I?' Noah looked at her imploringly. 'That's the other major problem. He might think I'm trying to replace Mum, that I've forgotten all about her, that I don't love her anymore. But it's not that.'

She dared to reach out and ruffle his hair and he didn't back away. 'Of course it's not that,' she said. 'Thing is, Noah, we don't always get what we want in this life, even at Christmas. Well-meaning people might tell you that you can have anything you want or be anyone you want to be, but that doesn't always happen.'

Noah nodded. 'So my dad tells me. He says sometimes life sucks for no reason at all, but he would say that, wouldn't he?'

'I guess he would.'

'I think *he* sucks,' Noah said.

'Who sucks?'

'That guy, Eli.' He folded his arms and looked at her stubbornly. 'I don't want him getting in with Izzie. I'm sure if Izzie could just see my dad and Eli together, she'd see the difference between them,' Noah said.

'And how would you do that?'

'Do you think I could ask Dad to have a party? Wouldn't that be a good idea?'

'Noah—'

He gabbled on as though he hadn't heard her. 'Like, because of the snow … If I get Eli in the same room as my dad, Izzie will see that my dad's much better for her. We even have lots of Christmas stuff out from when I was small. Dad puts out the same things every year, even though I'm not four or five anymore. I kinda like it. I think Izzie would like it too.'

A party. Florence had never been up to Tom's apartment at Christmas time, although she'd been invited. He usually invited her up for a festive glass, but she'd never gone because it would have meant returning the favour and she wasn't prepared to do that. She was good at getting out there, helping at community functions, where she'd met Jean and Wendy, going to bridge, aqua aerobics, the library, having the occasional weekend away with her friends. Outside Henrietta Square, it was easy to put her best face forward.

Here, on home territory, it was different.

Ten years ago, when her cherished hopes and dreams had imploded around her, it had been the catalyst for streamlining her life. She'd retired from teaching and sold her small house in Marino, having decluttered all her possessions with a ruthless rage. Then she'd relocated across the city to the sanctuary of Henrietta Square, bringing nothing but the essentials. However, she might have excised every part of her old life physically, but not emotionally, as she discovered.

Letting Noah in had been fine – the lovely young boy was no threat whatsoever to her sanctuary – but people she didn't really know all that well, other adults, would sense a life stripped bare reflected in her uncluttered surroundings, the absence of any photographs, the dearth of memorabilia, the lack of references to family, the all-too-clean and spartan furnishings, untouched by visitors' or small children's fingerprints, the absence of a soft toy, a stray child's sock. She didn't want perceptive adults getting close enough to sense the big gap in her life, a gap that should, if she'd lived at a different time, have been filled to the brim with the beautiful imprints of family life.

'Noah, Izzie might not want to be reminded that it's Christmas,' Florence said gently. 'She might be giving it a miss this year because it would make her sad that Sam's not around to share it with her.'

Noah fell silent, his face glum.

Izzie was probably not even computing that it was Christmas, and Tom was no doubt missing his lovely wife. But what was she, Florence Hawkins, who was of sound mind and body, and just seventeen on the inside, with a Girl Power mantra, doing about all this? What was she doing to spread a little kindness and support the people who lived around her? Shame on her.

To her surprise, she found herself breaking a strict, self-imposed rule and saying, without knowing how the words got there, 'Look, instead of bothering your dad, why don't I do something? Have a small get-together just for us? Maybe tomorrow evening if we're still snowed in?'

'Are you sure?'

''Course I'm sure,' Florence said, privately quailing at taking such a giant step out of her comfort zone. 'I could ask your dad and Izzie and Eli, if he's still around.'

'He will be, I bet.' Noah glowered. 'He was sitting on Izzie's sofa as if he owned the place.'

'It might be easier for Izzie to come if she has a friend with her. And if Izzie refuses to come, you won't be disappointed?'

'At least we'll have tried.'

'And she'll be saying "no" to me and not your dad,' Florence pointed out.

'Yeah, good idea. Does that mean you agree with me? About Dad and Izzie? Even a little bit?'

Florence chose her words carefully. 'I think your dad is a lovely man. He's my kind of man, the kind I'd have married myself if he'd been around when I was much younger. I think Izzie is a lovely woman; she's soft and caring. They both deserve happiness, but it's far too soon to say if they could find happiness together. However,' she paused, 'it would be good for Izzie to know that the people who live here, that means me, and you, and your dad, are around for her, so showing her that would be a start.'

'Thanks, Florence.'

'That's settled, then,' she said. 'But I won't call it a Christmas

109

party – it'll be more like a snow-survival get-together. I can even bake some snow-iced cakes. And make shapes with ice. Or anything else I can think of that's snow-themed. Snowy lemonade – how about that?'

She had a sudden memory of Snowballs – a drink, in a green bottle, practically zero alcohol, her mother sipping it suspiciously when it was thrust into her hand by a neighbour at Christmas. A sour memory of another era.

Noah rescued her from falling down that particular rabbit hole.

'Thanks, Florence, that sounds ace,' he said, his eyes bright.

'Leave it to me, so,' Florence said. Planning a snow party would keep her far too occupied to dwell on what might have been, thoughts that were always too close to the surface at this emotional time of the year.

CHAPTER EIGHTEEN

They were watching Sky News, Izzie barely noticing when she'd opened the next bottle of wine but, bizarrely enough, noticing how small and flimsy the wine glass seemed in Eli's hand. One small squeeze and the glass would surely shatter in that grip. She only realised how wobbly she was on her feet when she went over to the kitchen to get a glass of water and began to tilt sideways. Not good.

'Would you like some water?' she asked Eli.

'Yes, thank you,' he said. 'Allow me,' he went on, getting to his feet.

'Stay where you are,' Izzie said, a little shriller than she'd intended, not wanting the bulk of him to crowd her in the compact kitchen. She had to concentrate hard on getting back to the coffee table without spilling anything.

Eli took a long gulp of water. 'So who exactly is resident here?' he asked. 'I've met the lady on the ground floor – she let me in when you didn't answer your buzzer.'

'You mean Florence,' Izzie said. 'She lives alone, then there's Noah with his father, Tom, on the first floor.'

'That's it?'

'Yep. That's about it. I'm lucky with my neighbours – they're all lovely, no disturbances or wild parties. But what was all that about with Noah earlier?' Izzie asked.

'What do you mean?'

'He thought he was doing me a big favour, bringing back the DVDs, but you seemed a little unfriendly to him.'

She didn't like the way his pale eyes scanned her face. 'I thought he might be annoying you,' he said after a while. 'I apologise if I upset anyone.'

'Noah's just a child.'

He smiled ruefully. 'Maybe I'm not that good around young kids.'

'Noah got on great with Sam,' she said, her voice cracking slightly.

'Everyone got on great with Sam. He was very popular. Everyone loved him. I'd love to know how he was these last couple of years. I wasn't good at keeping in regular contact. Sporadic emails don't tell you much, but then again I was a bit challenged when I was in the heart of the Amazon basin.'

'I'd say you were,' Izzie said, finding the way he was looking at her a little intense. She got up and went over to the window. Outside, the evening had folded into the night; the square was silent and deserted and bathed in the yellowy glow of the ornate street lamps. Snow was still falling, beautifully and gracefully, the flakes gilded saffron-white in the glow of the lamps.

'It's beautiful, isn't it?'

She jumped. Eli was standing right behind her, so close that the back of her neck prickled uncomfortably. For a man of his size, he moved quietly and economically. 'Like a picture postcard,' he went on in a soft voice. 'Perfect if it's not stopping you from going anywhere.'

A little spooked at the proximity of his burly figure, she ducked away from him and switched on another lamp. Then a wave of tiredness washed over her and she subsided onto the sofa.

Standing over her, Eli handed her her phone. 'I'd appreciate it if you checked for local travel updates so I can make some kind of plan.'

How come he had it? She couldn't remember where she'd left it down. Surely, though, it had been on the coffee table? 'Sure. Sit down and relax,' she said, a little intimidated with the way his body loomed over her. Too much wine, that was her problem. She was all over the place. As soon as he was sitting at the other end of the sofa, she keyed in her PIN, going to her Twitter feed and scrolling through for news and transport information.

'It's not looking too good,' she said eventually. 'All public transport is off for the rest of the evening, driving conditions are hazardous and passengers need to check transport providers in the morning before they attempt to travel.'

'So you mightn't get going after all.'

'Going where?' Her mind was blank for a moment. She fished around in her frozen brain cells.

'Your yoga retreat,' he said.

'Yes, I hadn't forgotten. I just had temporary brain fog,' she said, recovering herself and putting her phone down on the arm of the sofa.

'That's allowed,' he said gently. 'I mightn't get going anywhere either,' he said, so softly he could have been talking to himself. But the words swirled in the air between them and Izzie almost heard her automatic response: you can stay the night. Still, something in her gut urged her to say nothing.

She took a big glug of wine. Outside, nothing was moving. Therefore, this guy sitting beside her was stuck. How could she cast him out into the snowy night?

'Excuse me a minute,' she said, getting up and padding into her bedroom and on into the privacy of her en suite, where she took several deep breaths. How had this really happened? A man she'd never met before was sitting outside on her sofa. Had she been about to ask him to stay the night? After all her plans? But he wasn't just a stranger; Eli had been Sam's best mate. He'd known Sam for years, they'd come up through college and had worked together, he'd known a happier, more carefree version of Sam, a side to Sam that Izzie had never seen and would love to know more about. He was stuck and it was Christmas and she had a spare bedroom. Once he was gone, she'd have the rest of Christmas to hide away in her apartment, a few days of indulgent wallowing before she began to pick up her pieces and face into a new year. She tightened the belt of her robe and went back into the living room.

'Look,' she began, 'we could bounce this around between us for another couple of hours, but there's no point in pretending.'

'Pretending what?'

She was distracted by the sight of her phone on the coffee table. Had it been moved in her absence? In her woozy state, she must be imagining it.

'You're not going anywhere tonight,' she said. 'How can you? There's no transport, nothing's moving out there.'

He looked at her soberly. 'I've realised that,' he said. 'But I know I've put you in an impossible position. I had no intentions of putting you to any trouble, and now it seems I must.'

'It's no trouble, it's the least I can do for Sam's friend. And it would be good to hear about his college days. They're a part of him I never knew.'

'So it's okay to crash out on your sofa for the night?' he asked. 'Hopefully things will be better tomorrow.'

'You don't need to use the sofa,' she said. 'There's a spare bedroom.'

'I appreciate this. At least let me make myself useful,' he went on. 'I could organise some food for us if you point me in the right direction.'

'Food?' she said, trying to think. 'I don't have much …'

'I know, you were expecting to be away. I might be able to get out to a nearby shop and pick up something for us both?'

'There's a local mini-market but I'd guess they're either closed or about to close,' she said. 'There's some pizza in the freezer, if that's okay.'

'Perfect. I can look after that.' He went to get up.

'There's no need,' she objected. 'It'll only take a minute to stick it in the oven and I know where everything is.'

She knew she was definitely sloshed as she half-reeled, half-walked over to the kitchen area. She took out the pizza and checked the best-before date: it was okay – just about. She slid it out of the box, took off the cellophane and stuck it in the oven, realising too late she'd forgotten to preheat it. While she was over there, she poured herself a generous gin and tonic, adding some ice. No lemon and certainly no cucumber – she didn't have any and there was no point in bothering with niceties when the alcohol was all that mattered. 'Would you like a gin?' she asked, waving the bottle at him.

'No, thanks,' he said. 'I might have a beer if that's okay.'

'Beer. I think I'm all out of beer,' she said. She was a little dizzy and needed to grip the counter top to stop herself from falling over.

Sam used to drink chilled beer. Only last month she'd come across some at the bottom of the fridge – the bottles had been there for weeks but hadn't registered with her. She'd taken them out one by one and poured the liquid down the sink, running the tap afterwards until there was no trace of the smell. No trace of him. She saw the shape he'd made as he leaned into the fridge and pulled out a bottle. Flipping open the lid of the bottle with his funny opener, the one that made a noise like a police siren. Tilting his head to take a long gulp. His white teeth grinning at her.

Her throat nearly closed over. *Breathe, Izzie, breathe slowly.* Out and in. Out and in.

A hand touched her waist and she spun around so suddenly she almost fell against the hardness of a male body. Eli. A black tide of anger that it wasn't Sam. It would never be Sam; she'd never be touched by him again. Never be drawn close to him again in a great big hug or rest her head against his shoulder. The pain came, familiar, ready to slice her into two. Oh, Christ.

Stop.

'Don't touch me,' she hissed.

He sprang away, his hands held up defensively. 'Hey, you went so white I thought you were going to faint.'

'I don't faint that easily,' she said, standing back against the counter for some support.

'You go sit down,' he said. 'I'll find plates and check that pizza.'

She sat down, still dazed, aware of him moving about and gathering dishes, and when the pizza was ready Eli came over with it neatly sliced and laid out on two plates.

'Fifty-fifty,' she almost heard Sam say – it had been one of their catchphrases. Eli went back for cutlery and sheets of kitchen roll to act as temporary napkins.

'Not sure if we need these,' he said, putting down knives and forks. 'I think it tastes better off your fingers, don't you?'

'Mmm,' she said. She hadn't tasted food properly in three months. The pizza stuck like cardboard in her throat, just as everything else did, but she made herself swallow it. She knew she needed some soakage. They checked the forecast on the television while they ate their food and Izzie brought up RTÉ just in time for an update from the Coordination Group. Forecasters were predicting that parts of the country were to be hit with blizzard-like conditions overnight. There were reports from farmers unable to get to their flocks, and footage from emergency bed centres set up in the city to help take the homeless off the streets.

'Just as well I found sanctuary,' Eli said.

'Hopefully the east of the country won't be too badly affected,' she said. 'The sooner things get back to normal, the better.'

She needn't have worried about his overnight stay invading her space. He was the perfect guest. She enjoyed hearing him talk about Sam and recounting funny anecdotes about the mad college escapades they'd shared. Then Eli suggested they put on a movie and she was happy to go along with that. She wasn't remotely interested in watching *The Wolf of Wall Street*, but they'd run out of conversation and it was an easy way to pass the time.

'I'm pretty whacked,' Eli said as soon as it was over. 'I'd like to turn in for the night if that's okay with you.'

'That's fine,' she said, switching off the television. 'I'm going to bed as well.'

'You don't need me for anything?'

'Absolutely not,' Izzie answered. She showed him to the spare room, pointing out the bathroom.

'Good night,' he said, standing in the doorway.

She was tired and befuddled herself, and for a brief moment she thought his lips brushed her mouth as he leaned in to give her a quick hug, but when she went back into the living room to switch off the lamps and get another glass of water, she decided she'd been imagining it.

He wouldn't have dared. No one had kissed her like that since Sam.

CHAPTER NINETEEN

New York,
fifteen months ago

There is no formula, no set of circumstances, no particular alignment of the sun, moon and stars that can signal fateful, life-changing moments. Extraordinary things can happen in the ordinary space between the inhale and the exhale of breath. You can be born, you can fall in love and you can die.

Right now, in the space of this moment, I'm falling in love.

'Falling' is aptly put. At the party in this downtown Manhattan apartment, I look like I'm drifting carelessly around with a glass of wine in my hand, smiling at everyone and no one in particular, but, inside, everything I've ever been up to now is falling away, all the everyday pieces that made up my life are blown away like dandelion clocks in the breeze.

Because of you.

You are standing by the balcony door with your back to the light. You're wearing denim jeans and a dark-blue T-shirt. I don't need to get up close to your dark grey eyes or your neat, cropped hair, or even say hello. The minute I see you, and absorb the contained energy in your silhouette, the way you are standing, the calm attention emanating from your eyes, there is a spark of instant recognition and a fresh new vitality leaps inside me.

All my nerve endings fizzing with effervescence, I move around the gathering, say hello and chat with various people, and I'm conscious of your eyes on me like a laser beam, knowing that as sure as the sun rises every morning, you will seek me out.

The moment of introduction feels like I'm meeting a part of myself, something as fundamental as my right arm or my left leg, as though you have always been intrinsic to the reason I live in this world. I want to laugh for sheer, undiluted joy. I want to cry: why now? After a three-week holiday in New York, I'll be going home in four days' time. Although I know already that a continent between us will be irrelevant.

Ruth taps me on the shoulder. Ruth, my good friend and one-time flatmate, who moved to New York last year after a big promotion, with whom I'm staying.

'Hey, Izzie,' she says, steering you across to me, 'I don't think you guys have met.'

But of course we've already met; I know you, in my bones,

in all my capillaries; the knowledge of you has been there since I first took breath.

Ruth's words echo from a distance. 'Izzie, meet Sam – Sam Mallon. He's been waiting to say hello to you.'

You smile and your eyes meet mine and I know that you know already how I feel, and I don't bother to hide it, there is no point.

'Sam, meet Izzie Gray.'

'Hi, Izzie Gray,' you say in a soft American accent that pours through my veins like life-giving blood.

Then as soon as Ruth has moved away, you continue. 'I thought you'd never stop.'

'Stop what?'

'Pretending to ignore me.'

I feign innocence. 'Was I?' How did you know? Can you read me that well?

'Haven't we met already, Izzie Gray?' Your eyes carry a question. They are kind and warm, with a hint of amusement.

If I'd known then what you told me two days later, would I have walked away? This was the point at which I could have changed the conversation and changed the course of our short history by ending it before it had a chance to breathe. But I could no more change anything than I could the turning of the ocean tides. I had to let it all unfold as it was fated to, warmed by the look in your eye and the steely pull I felt towards you.

'You mean you don't remember? How could you have forgotten if you'd met me?' I say, while bubbles of delight rise inside me. Without saying anything further, we move outside onto the balcony, to a small table where we sit on plastic chairs. I don't remember talking to anyone else for the rest of that night. We're giving off sonar waves of some kind that form an invisible layer around us because no one disturbs us.

'Tell me all about you, Izzie Gray.'

I think I sum up the bare bones of my life in about three short sentences: that I love hillwalking, especially in the Wicklow hills where I'd spent a happy childhood and adolescence, and I can do a mean yoga wheel, my favourite holiday destination is the south of France, oh, and my real name is Elizabeth but few people know that, and only the chosen few are allowed to call me by that name. I don't tell you then about the man I'd been seeing for three years up to recently, who was disappointed when I refused to marry him. Gut instinct had told me it wasn't the right thing for me to do, and now I know who my intuition had been saving me for.

You.

You speak about your life in New York, your running club, your love of music, your favourite artist, John Lennon, your iffy guitar playing, but we don't go into details. The words we exchange don't matter. All the important details can be discovered in time because we already know we are reaching something inside of each other that no one has ever touched before. This evening, it is like we are bound together in a wonderful anticipatory moment of gratitude for what fate has delivered up: us meeting here, now, in this crazy continuum of life.

FRIDAY,
22 DECEMBER

CHAPTER TWENTY

Izzie woke up, startled out of sleep. She lay unmoving in the dark, finding the impenetrable blackness swirling around her oddly soothing. It didn't ask anything of her, and she didn't need to paint on a face, much less construct a front to hide that face behind. In the total darkness, life was suspended and she could simply be still.

She'd had so much to drink the previous evening that it had plunged her into an alcohol-induced semi-coma but something had woken her. After a while she scrabbled for her phone and checked the time: half past two. Everything was silent, unusually so. Thanks to the snow, there was no hum of occasional traffic on the laneway behind the square and no voices of passers-by carrying up in the quiet of the early hours.

Then she remembered the man.

She had a man in her apartment who was virtually a stranger to her. What had possessed her? Gripped by a sudden apprehension, she switched on a lamp, pushed the duvet aside and hauled herself out of bed. Her head was swimming and it took her a moment to orient herself. She opened the bedroom door as quietly as she could. In the spill of light funnelling out into the hallway, she saw that the door to the spare bedroom was ajar and there was a crack of light coming from under the living-room door.

She padded down softly and pushed it open.

'What are you doing?' she asked, annoyed that her voice sounded quavery and thin.

Eli looked at her over the lid of Sam's laptop, smiling easily. 'Sorry, did I disturb you?'

'No. I was awake anyhow. What are you doing with that laptop?' She struggled to pull herself together. There was something here she couldn't grasp. It was more than the upset that her privacy had been invaded or that he was taking blatant advantage of her hospitality. What was he doing sitting at her table with the laptop open, in the same way Sam used to? Never mind at this hour of the night? She was annoyed she'd had too much alcohol last night and her head was thick and fuzzy. Eli didn't look like he'd had too much to drink. He was still dressed in a sweater and jeans and it looked like he hadn't gone to bed at all.

'Sorry,' he said in a voice full of apology. 'I should have asked permission but I didn't want to disturb you.'

'How did you know if I was asleep or not?'

'Well, I … weren't you?'

He'd hardly looked into her bedroom – or had he? 'What do you want with that laptop?'

'Oops, did I do something wrong? I did, didn't I? I couldn't sleep, thanks to jet lag across two continents. I was hoping to connect with my aunts and some New York friends, let them know what's happened. Email is convenient because they can pick it up at any time.'

'What about your phone?'

'There's a connectivity issue, as I explained last night.'

'You could have asked to use my phone. You could even have called them.'

'Like I say, I didn't want to inconvenience you. Anyhow, had I waited until the morning it would be the middle of the night in New York. This is a good time.'

'Is it?' Surely the hour of the day didn't make much difference if email could be picked up anytime.

He sat back, his hands clasped behind his head in a nonchalant pose as though he was doing nothing untoward. 'Yeah, it's coming up to ten o'clock over there – a good time to get people when they're home for the evening and before they retire for the night. I want to reassure my aunts that I'm not lying on an airport floor, trying to snatch some sleep while safeguarding my wallet and phone. They're elderly. They worry about me,' he said, an indulgent smile on his face.

Izzie didn't respond. She couldn't find the right words to ask him if he'd been concerned about their worries for him when he'd been gallivanting in remote parts of the world with little or no access to email.

'And I need to send some sensitive emails that require a secure connection. I thought maybe Sam's laptop was the safest and easiest way to do it – we've often shared laptops before, in college and at work in Stanley Trust, and we pretty much use the same software, but now, hey.' He grinned. 'I can't seem to get through. Whatever he has put on this, I can't get into it at all.'

'What makes you think that's Sam's laptop?'

'Isn't it? I guessed it wasn't the one with the purple lid.'

Even this minor calculation seemed overly familiar to her. *And* he'd obviously been snooping around the living room.

'Don't you have a laptop with you?' Izzie asked. Sam had rarely travelled without his.

'I left it behind with the wildlife team,' he said easily. 'It was a bit dated and I figured I'd get me a spanking new one as soon as I hit New York. So. How do I get into this one?'

He sat quietly, unnerving her a little, his figure big and blocky behind the table, and she had to forcibly remind herself that Eli was Sam's best friend. He was clearly waiting for her to supply a password, in answer to his implied request, but even if she was distinctly out of it, she wasn't about to help him on that score. She hadn't switched on Sam's laptop at any stage after he'd gone, finding it an impossible leap. She wasn't about to give Eli access to the contents.

'You'd find getting into Fort Knox easier,' she said. 'I'm sorry, I can't help you.'

'Don't you know his password?'

A silence dropped between them that sounded loud to Izzie's ears. 'There are about three levels of security on that laptop,' she said, not answering his question.

'Jesus. What was he hiding?'

She flinched. Her reaction wasn't lost on him. He pushed down the lid. 'Sorry, what was I thinking? I hope I didn't upset you. I understand the security, I know his work was super sensitive – we networked regularly and had a mutual client.'

'Networked? I thought you worked together in Stanley Trust?' Izzie said.

'That's what I mean,' he said, getting up from the table, fixing her with his eyes and coming around the desk to walk slowly across to her. He was in his stocking feet. Why had he taken off his shoes? The better to move around quietly?

'I keep forgetting he's not around anymore,' he went on, his voice husky. 'I keep expecting him to walk into the room, to be with you, with his quirky smile, to be around you, his emails were so full of you, they told me how much you meant to him … it's all still … so unbelievable. So unbelievable that I forgot for a while and automatically picked up Sam's laptop the way I often did when we worked together, but I can see now that I was way out of line.'

He closed the gap between them and she caught the pungent scent of his aftershave. She ducked sideways and went over to the table, picking up the laptop and putting it back on the shelf. The cheek of him to have helped himself to it.

'I've put my foot in it. I didn't mean to annoy you. I'm sorry for taking advantage of your hospitality. It was wrong of me, considering the circumstances.'

She looked at him and saw the sincerity in his face. But her gut reaction was that, just like his words, it was all a bit false.

'It's still snowing out,' he said in a warm murmur, the tone of voice you'd use if you were talking affectionately about a sleeping baby.

'Imagine that,' she said, not caring if she sounded sarcastic. 'It's not exactly something to celebrate.'

'Hopefully there'll be better news tomorrow,' he said. 'Who knows, I might even make it home for Christmas. There's still time and there'll be internet facilities in the airport. I'll do my best to get to the top of that queue.'

She stood there silently as he padded out of the room, head held high as though he didn't give a shit. She waited until she heard the soft click of his bedroom door closing before she switched off the lamps. He might have been Sam's friend but she realised she didn't particularly like Eli Sanders. There was something about him that struck a raw nerve, apart from his rude assumption that he could use Sam's laptop without her permission.

She'd no intention of giving him access to it, considering the critical files it contained, files that were Sam's precious work and daren't get into the wrong hands. Pity about his emails but she wasn't about to take any chances with Sam's confidential files, even though coming back from Africa, they were hardly of any relevance to Eli. She tried to dismiss the disquieting idea that he might have been after them for some covert reason of his own, but it rattled her so much that she wanted him gone.

CHAPTER TWENTY-ONE

Gemma became aware of the sound of something hammering away at the top of her head. Through a dim haze, she gradually realised she was in bed. Either the neighbours had the bulldozers in or her ever-enthusiastic mum was up to some of her inexpert DIY. Most likely the neighbours, she thought vaguely, because the noise reverberating through her head sounded like a huge machine at work. She thought it must be coming through the wall, but when she tried to lift her head off the pillow and get away from the noise, everything bounced around her as though she was being tossed helplessly on a stormy sea. She made an attempt at opening her eyes, but it was so difficult there could have been concrete bricks sitting on her eyelids. Very gradually, from the feel of the mattress beneath her and the duvet twisted around her, she grasped two things: she wasn't in her bed at home, and instead of wearing her velour pyjamas, she was in her underwear.

Make that three things: she was not alone.

The sound of low, rhythmic snores came from something warm beside her. Another body. She was in bed with someone. Very gently, mindful of her throbbing head, she managed to open her eyes to a tiny slit and turn around to see who it was. A man. Also lying on his back, the duvet drawn up to his chest.

She realised it was Kian. Hot Kian. O'Sullivan Pearse Kian. Something hard and painful crashed through her head.

Slowly, as though she was struggling through a misty landscape, some of the events of the last twenty-four hours came back to her. She tried to piece together what had happened and how she'd got here, but it was like trying to hold on to snowflakes in the palm of her hand – they just melted away.

There had been a pub. Faces sliding in front of her like a disjointed videotape.

There had been food, of sorts. She had a dim vision of platters going around, fingers reaching across the table. She saw gin being poured over a mountain of ice cubes in huge balloon glasses. Someone fishing out slices of cucumber and sticking them to their eyes. Hoots of laughter that pained her tummy. Had *she* done that?

The moment when she knew her heady, charged-with-excitement feeling had changed, had tipped over into something else. Something that was careening away, out of her control. Voices asking if she was all right. The sound of her laughter. Her slurry voice – she was absolutely fine, not a bother on her.

Had that been before the cocktails or after the shots?

Shots.

Shots?

'You can come home with me if you like.' Katy's voice, like an echo in her head. 'I'm leaving now. The buses will soon be off the road.'

'I don't need a bus, I can walk home.'

'I'll look after her.' Kian's voice. His warm smile. That glow it gave her on the inside, even if everything was reeling away in front of her.

This was her wonderful new life. The exciting corporate world. And hotshot Kian fussing over her …

'Gemma? Are you sure you're okay with that? Staying on here with Kian?'

They were still in the pub, in the ladies'. There was a smell of cheap disinfectant and the mirrored walls were spinning around her, like the toy she'd had one Christmas, a spinning top, with the colours bleeding into each other the faster it went.

'Izzie, I have to do something for Izzie,' she heard herself say as she lurched against a basin. 'It's important.'

'Izzie left the office hours ago.' The words came from far away.

'Hours ago? What time is it now?'

Drifting outside, and Kian was there, smiling.

Holy crap, what had she *done*? Then everything blanked like a television screen switching off and Gemma drifted into sleep again, sinking beneath a dark wave, allowing it to roll over her.

CHAPTER TWENTY-TWO

By the time Izzie went into her living room early that morning, showered and dressed in a red fleece and black jeans, Eli was up already. He was standing by the window, framed in the glare of a Henrietta Square blanketed under an expanse of snow. He heard her coming and turned around, smiling easily as though nothing out of the ordinary had happened in the middle of the night.

'Hi,' he said. 'Hope you slept okay? Can I make you some coffee?'

'No, thanks,' she said, going across to the other window, looking out at the silent, hypnotic fall of the thick white curls drifting down from the sky. The outline of the four shallow steps outside the hall door was barely distinguishable. Even the square was barely recognisable, everything obliterated by a thick white coating, including the tracks the children had made yesterday. The shrubs in the park were misshapen white stumps, only recognisable by odd branches poking out at angles like thin stick insects, starkly black against the white drift.

She took a carton of orange juice out of the fridge and poured a glass. Her head throbbed but it was beyond a hangover, more a thick kind of dizziness. She glanced at the bottles lined up on her counter, wine and gin, trying to work out how much she had drunk the night before. Almost two bottles of wine gone, with Eli drinking some of that, and at least two decent glasses of gin.

'Thanks for letting me stay over,' Eli said, 'and sorry again for disturbing you during the night.' He looked at her quizzically as though he was trying to figure out if he was forgiven or not.

'*Disturbing me?*' she said, hoping her cold tone of voice would tell him that she wasn't about to ignore the way he'd overstepped the mark in slyly trying to access Sam's laptop. 'What was that all about?'

He put his hands up in surrender. 'I know, I know I should have asked first. It was a dumb thing to do. Sam and I were just such good buddies that we took each other and our possessions for granted.'

When she didn't respond, he went on. 'Don't look so worried. I'll be out of your space as soon as I organise some transport to the airport.'

'How are you going to do that?' she asked. 'It doesn't look like anything much is moving out there.'

'Not in the square, but I'll head out to a main road, it might be clearer. There's bound to be some traffic moving.'

'I'll check to see if there's any news,' she said, switching on the television in time to hear that an update was due from the Coordination Group in ten minutes.

None of the updates were positive. The airport was hoping to reopen later that day, but early-morning flights had been cancelled, with no additional flights scheduled, putting pressure on any that might get out on what was traditionally the busiest day of the Christmas season. When the airport reopened, even scheduled services would be dependent on the positioning of the aircraft, given the chaos in all the Irish and UK airports. Footage showed long queues inside the airport and Izzie's heart dropped. The possibility of Eli getting out of Dublin looked remote.

Her annoyance must have shown in her face because Eli said, 'I'm going to go out anyway and take my chances. It was decent of you to put me up last night but I won't get home by staying here.'

The update then switched to the rest of the country and the general consensus that the adverse weather was bringing out the community spirit in some people: neighbours who scarcely knew each other were getting together, clearing paths of snow, ensuring the elderly and mothers of small children were okay for food and warmth. Stories of particular acts of heroism were referred to: in hospitals, doctors and nurses were sleeping on mattresses on the floors to ensure they were there to provide a service. Izzie didn't feel particularly kind or heroic. She'd done her bit for the snow effort by allowing Eli to stay last night, only he'd taken advantage of that.

'Do you think you'll get going yourself?' he asked.

She had to think for a minute before she realised what

he was referring to. 'I'll leave it for today and try to travel tomorrow,' she said. 'The snow can't go on forever.'

'I agree. Although, if you don't mind me saying, there's not much in your fridge. I could go out and fetch some milk and groceries to keep you going until then. That would also give me a chance to check out the roads before I start lugging my case anywhere. What do you think?'

'Sure, thanks,' she said. 'I need milk. Hold on until I get my purse.'

'Not at all, I'll take care of this.'

'Have you got euros?'

He stared at her. 'Why are you asking me that?'

She didn't like the unfriendly look flickering in his eyes. A sliver of unease uncoiled inside her.

'Irish currency,' she said. 'I thought – with you coming from Zurich and South Africa that you mightn't have any …'

His face cleared. He smiled. 'Got you. For a minute there I thought you were trying to catch me out. I went to one of those machines in Dublin airport.'

'Why would I want to catch you out?'

There was silence, still as a deep pool, as they stared at each other.

'I'm not thinking straight,' he said smoothly. 'Everything is up in the air and my head is all over the place. Most of all, seeing you like this, in the morning, soft and vulnerable without your make-up, makes me realise how alone you are without Sam. How much you must miss him.' A short pause. His voice as soft as thistledown. 'My brain – I just can't compute it and I don't know if you're really coping, deep inside. I don't know what to say for the best.'

'Then it's best not to say anything,' she said sharply. 'The only thing I need from the outside world is milk. There's a mini-market nearby. The quickest way is to go through the park, turn right and turn left at the junction. You can't miss it. There's a main road up at the next junction – you could have a look there and see if there are any taxis. If you manage to get one, you could come back here in it and collect your bags.'

'Thanks, sounds like a good plan. I'll leave my bags ready in the hall. And I'll get more than a drop of milk for you – you can't live on fresh air.'

Out in the hall, he pulled on his thick jacket.

'Got everything?' she asked.

'Yep,' he said. He patted his pockets. 'Phone, wallet, passport, all the essentials. See you in a short while and hopefully I'll have a taxi in tow.'

She locked the door after him and leaned against it, as weak as a kitten. He'd unsettled her with his reaction when she'd asked him about the euros. A simple question, but she had obviously taken him by surprise. It had shown a different side to Eli Sanders and she knew instinctively he was someone she wouldn't like to cross.

And he'd more than unsettled her with the furtive way he'd waited until two in the morning to try and log on to Sam's laptop. Even though her head was muzzy, she knew he must have been up to no good because, whatever he'd been after, he hadn't wanted her to know.

CHAPTER TWENTY-THREE

Noah was at the hall door, all muffled up in his jacket, scarf and dried-out wellies, when he heard footsteps coming down the stairs behind him, too heavy to be Izzie's. He turned around expecting to see his dad and came face to face with Eli.

The word came into his head – bollocks.

'Out to play, son?'

Son? Bollocks again. *Bollocks, bollocks, bollocks*. Noah didn't know how he managed to keep his face straight. Eli seemed to think he was five years of age.

'No, I'm going to the shop,' he said.

'So am I. Izzie's fridge is empty. I don't know what she was thinking. She needs someone to keep an eye on her.'

Noah wanted to puke. Eli managed to make it sound like they were a couple, even the way he said Izzie's name. He didn't bother to say he was going for milk and eggs. By now he'd opened the door onto the cold, snowy morning. There was an inrush of freezing air, and he could have cried that this dude was sloping alongside him. He'd wanted to be the first to put pristine new footsteps on the snow covering the steps outside the house – his dad was planning on clearing it later that morning. He'd been looking forward to tramping through the drifts of snow pretending he was Luke Skywalker. The sky was full of snow-laden clouds, and he could have imagined the Millennium Falcon was hidden in those clouds, ready to land in the park. Not that it would have fitted.

'Are you allowed to go to the shops all by yourself?' Eli asked.

'Of course I am,' Noah said hotly as he pulled the door closed behind them, the brass ring so frozen it was almost painful to touch, and he hurriedly thrust his hand back into his padded mitten. 'It's not far, and Dad trusts me not to talk to strangers. As if.'

'Glad I don't fall into that category,' Eli said. He laughed shortly, but it irritated Noah, like everything else about Eli irritated him.

'You don't because of Sam,' Noah said. 'He was ace.' He emphasised the word *ace*, hoping Eli would get the message that, while Sam might have been ace, Eli wasn't.

'He sure was,' Eli said. 'He was one of the best.'

'Me and Sam were great buddies,' Noah said as they went into the park. The snow was thick and parts of it were hard and icy, so it took a lot of concentration not to slip and slide. Had he been on his own he wouldn't have cared; he would have skidded all the way to the shop, making a mess in the ice and snow, turning parts of it to slush. The cold stung his face, making his eyes water. At least that's what he told himself: it was just the cold and not the memory of Sam, who would have loved Christmas and this snow and would have made a monster snowman for Izzie and helped him with his R2-D2 figure.

'Really? What did you guys talk about?' Eli asked. It didn't sound to Noah like he was genuinely interested but that he was making small talk, like some adults did, trying to get children on their side.

'Lot of things, but mostly *Star Wars*.'

They were halfway through the park before he could make out the figure he'd been building yesterday because it had become totally misshapen with fresh falls of snow. 'Oh no,' he said impulsively, coming to a halt. 'It's ruined. I spent ages on it yesterday, trying to get it right.' Immediately, Noah was raging he'd spoken aloud and shown his annoyance in front of Eli.

'Looks like a funny snowman to me,' Eli asked.

'It's an R2-D2,' Noah said.

'A *what*?'

'A *Star Wars* character. Luke Skywalker's best helper.'

'Why don't you just make one of those droid things instead, might be easier?'

Noah was about to correct him and point out that R2-D2 *was* a droid. Practically everyone knew that, even Tigi, and she wasn't into *Star Wars* like him, but he changed his mind. Instead he asked, 'What was your favourite *Star Wars* movie?'

'Um – hard to say,' Eli said. 'Probably *Return of the Jedi*.'

Noah aimed a kick at a small hillock of snow. That wasn't

what Sam had said. According to Sam, his and Eli's firm favourite of all was *The Empire Strikes Back*. Which had made Noah decide it was his favourite as well.

'What about *The Phantom Menace*?' he asked.

'What about it?'

Noah sneaked a glance at Eli. He looked bored. Which was odd. Sam had told him that Eli and he had been the best lucky suckers in the world to get seats for the premier in New York. Sam had won them in a competition. Wouldn't Eli have remembered that?

'I thought Kylo Ren was great in that movie,' Noah said, as casually as he could, daring himself to catch Eli out.

'Yeah, I guess he was.'

This guy had a short memory or else he was a plonker, Noah decided. The character of Kylo Ren hadn't appeared in any movie until *The Force Awakens* in 2015. Noah was about to correct Eli but he stopped himself in time. It would sound like he'd been trying to trip him up on purpose, and while Sam might have laughed and given him a high five, because trying to outdo each other with *Star Wars* quizzes had been a running joke between them, he sensed this guy would do no such thing.

'I've even been to see Skellig Michael,' Noah said, wondering what his reaction would be. 'Just from the boat, though. I didn't get to go on the landing tour yet – maybe next summer.'

Eli didn't even comment, which was weird. Sam had been delighted for Noah when he'd come home from his summer holidays and told him that his grandad had arranged the boat trip off the Kerry coast so that Noah could see the wonderful place that featured in the two most recent movies.

They were through the park now, and they crossed the road and walked up to the junction.

'Have you been to see the latest yet?' Noah asked. His dad had brought him the previous week, the full IMAX experience, and he'd sorely missed not having Sam around to chat to afterwards.

'No,' Eli said, without even asking Noah if he'd been. A big let-down. 'Is that the main road, straight up there?' he asked outside the mini-market.

'Yep – why?'

'As soon as I have Izzie's shopping, I'm going looking for a taxi. If I make enough noise at the airport, I might just get a seat to New York when flights are back up and running.'

Noah's heart soared at this thought. 'Serious?'

'Well, son, I'm sure not going to get a seat home if I'm stuck in Izzie's.'

'No, you're not.' He almost didn't mind Eli calling him 'son', this time. He didn't care if he sounded happy at the prospect of Eli going. 'May the force ...' he began. It had been his *Star Wars* catchphrase with Sam – whenever they were saying goodbye, Sam would always have answered '... be with you.' But Eli ignored him and marched on into the store.

Noah put milk and eggs into the basket and even though there was a massive queue for the till, he hung around the aisle, watching Eli do some shopping, and, afterwards, watched him head up to the main road. Something about him was really souring his gut, and not just his being with Izzie. He sounded like he didn't know anything about *Star Wars* at all.

Which for Sam's best mate was totally weird.

CHAPTER TWENTY-FOUR

'Hey, thought you were awake,' Kian said.

Gemma forced her eyes open. She'd been awake for a few moments, trying to come to terms with the abject humiliation of this situation, wondering frantically if there was any way of extricating herself with a scrap of dignity. She was pathetic. Totally and utterly pathetic. Kian stood beside the bed. He was wearing a T-shirt over a pair of boxer shorts. He had a glass of water in one hand and a foil strip of paracetamol in another.

'Hope you're okay, but you could probably do with these,' he said, putting down the glass and tablets on the bedside table.

'Thanks,' she said, her voice thick.

She sat up, her head groggy, ensuring the duvet came with her up as far as her chin. A wave of panic set in. She didn't recall anything from the night before and was afraid to ask what had happened. She did a mental checklist: her underwear was still intact; her clothes were in a neat pile on a chair close to the bed – she couldn't recall taking them off but they looked as though they'd been placed there carefully as opposed to having been wrenched off in the heat of passion. Her phone was on her bedside locker and her bag was under the chair.

Kian sat down at the end of the bed. 'Don't worry,' he said, as if sensing her panic. 'We're in my friend's apartment and nothing happened.'

'I know that,' she fibbed, hiding her relief. She saw that the room had an en suite and was pleasantly decorated. It could have been a comfortable hotel room and was far superior to the sofas and floors of the dingy student accommodation she'd woken up to in the past. 'Is your friend here?'

'Nah. The jammy bastard is gone skiing for Christmas. This is his spare room and he rents it out, but he's between lodgers right now until the new year. We're in Smithfield, so it's close to the city centre. He gave me a spare key in case I needed to crash over the Christmas and we were able to walk here last night.'

'Yeah, I remember,' Gemma said, vaguely recalling a crazy walk home through the snow. She wanted to cry inside. It could have been amazing, it could have been magical, coming up through Christmassy city-centre streets with Kian and all the snow-covered paths reflecting glittery lights. She'd ruined it for herself by drinking too much.

Ruined everything.

'Would you like some tea and toast?'

'Yeah, that would be nice.' She didn't want anything to eat. She wanted to get out of bed and into the bathroom without him around. As soon as he went through to the kitchen, she swallowed three tablets with a long drink of water, then grabbed her clothes and hauled herself across to the en suite.

The sight of her face reflecting back from the mirror almost sent her into shock again. She wanted to cry with the shame of it, only her eyes were bleary-looking enough. All the time she spent perfecting her make-up before she appeared in work, the time devoted to her clothes, making sure she looked her best, and now this – she looked totally wrecked. It was a wonder Kian had even offered to make tea and toast and hadn't tried to get rid of her immediately. She splashed water on her face and used toilet tissue to wipe off some of her streaked mascara. She ran her fingers through her hair, teasing out tangles. She splashed water under her arms. There was a tube of toothpaste on the shelf so she squeezed some onto her fingers and gave her mouth a haphazard rinse. Then she pulled on her crumpled clothes and went out to sit on the edge of the bed.

It was only when Kian came back in with a mug of tea and a plate of toast, putting them down on the bedside locker, that she remembered something else. 'Jesus. I thought it was Saturday. It's Friday. Shouldn't we be at work?'

He laughed and shook his head. 'Gemma, you're gas. No one is expecting us in. There'll be nothing happening, and anyone who managed to show up this morning has gone home by now.'

'Why, what time is it?' A clutch in her stomach.

'Half past twelve,' Kian said. 'We got back here about midnight last night. You slept the clock around.'

'I did, didn't I?' She fell silent, mortified and embarrassed by turns. 'What's the weather like today?' The weather. Holy crap. This time yesterday she'd never have envisaged this scene in a million years. The creeping mortification of it.

'Much the same,' he said. 'Still snowing.'

'I'll have to think about getting home.'

He looked at her for a long moment, warmth in his hazel eyes. 'There's no rush out of here, Gemma,' he said softly. 'You can stay for as long as you like. I'm not going anywhere for now. But hey – no worries if you want to head home as soon as possible.'

His meaning was clear, and somewhere inside her, a warning bell went off. She was still drunk from the night before. Drunk on his attention, on the feeling of having a job, albeit an internship, and just starting out in life. But mainly drunk on all the alcohol she'd swigged the day and the evening before, and it meant her guard was down and her brain had flown out the window. She was able to grasp all this in a corner of her head but it made no difference. Kian hadn't been put off by her. He'd said she could stay as long as she liked. She knew she was allowing herself to act impulsively, but it felt wonderful and free, and she didn't care about being impulsive as she smiled at him.

'I don't need to be anywhere at the moment,' she said. 'Except – God – I need to let my family know I'm alive and well.'

'You texted them last night,' Kian said.

'Oh, yes, that's right,' she said. *Shite*. Something else she didn't remember.

'I'm going to have a shower,' Kian said. 'I'll use the one in the bathroom down the hall in case you need to use the en suite. But Gemma, seriously, it's up to you what you want to do. If you're gone when I come back, I hope you get home safe, have a smashing Christmas and I'll see you in the office in the new year.'

'Same to you,' she said.

'And if you're not gone … well, that would be lovely.' He looked at her, a hopeful smile in his eyes.

She drank the tea and chewed on the toast, feeling marginally better. He'd been so *nice* to her, as though it wasn't her fault at all that she'd got so drunk. The paracetamol kicked in and the worst of her headache began to ease. She wasn't gone when Kian came back in, dressed in jeans and a tracksuit top. She was still sitting on the edge of the bed.

'I think I'll have a shower as well,' she said, an edgy excitement building inside her.

He grinned. 'Hey, that's great. There are plenty of towels and shower stuff.'

When she came out of the shower, swathed in a big fluffy towel, her hair formed damp tendrils around her head and her face glowed with excitement. He was sitting on the bed, waiting for her. It didn't take him long to whip the towel from her body, but he took ages to graze his mouth and hands across her skin, and an even longer time to press kisses down past the swell of her stomach, going down to where desire inside her swelled to a hot, delicious ache.

He told her she was magnificent and that he loved her gorgeous body like this, all dewy and scented from the shower. He loved the way she moaned at his touch. He hadn't even begun. That was just a warmer-upper. He shed his clothes with a speed that thrilled her, and she still couldn't believe this was actually happening. Hot Kian, fully aroused, in bed with curvy Gemma Nugent. Oh, wow.

Then everything went out of her head, except the feeling of being magnificent.

CHAPTER TWENTY-FIVE

When her intercom buzzed and Eli said he had a taxi waiting by the kerb, the relief that surged through Izzie surprised her, considering nothing had touched her emotions for months.

'That's good,' she said, pressing the button to release the hall door. She waited in her hallway, eyeing his case and backpack, seeing them as the equivalent of an alien invasion. Just like he'd been. She knew it would take him less than a minute to come up two flights of stairs but for a wild moment she was tempted to check the side pockets of his backpack to see if there was anything there to tell her more about Sam's friend. On impulse, she pushed back a zip with the tip of her finger.

It didn't open onto a side pocket: it opened onto a padded compartment that was designed to hold a laptop. She patted the compartment with her hands. Eli had a small laptop secreted away. He had lied to her.

She stood immobile for a moment. Then Eli's knock at the door sent her heart ricocheting around. She closed the zip hurriedly and took a couple of deep breaths before she opened the door. He stepped into the hall, the bulk of him almost overpowering her. He was carrying a supermarket bag with some groceries and juggling a bottle of wine and a carry-out pack of beer.

'I got you some groceries and a couple of extras just in case,' he said, walking through to her kitchen, emptying the bag and putting the drink on the counter top and food into her fridge.

'There was no need.'

'There was every need,' he said. 'The store shelves are emptying fast. And thank you for putting me up,' he went on. 'You've been a lifesaver.'

Out in the hall he picked up his backpack and then he put it down again. Her breath stuck in her throat. 'Hey, I'm forgetting something,' he said, smiling easily. A ripple of unease ran across her stomach. He reached out for her, enveloping her in a big bear hug. Sam's best friend, she reminded herself as she went rigid in his arms. She sensed the strength of the man. If he hugged her much tighter she would snap in two.

'Thanks so much,' he said, releasing her and holding her by the shoulders. 'You've been great.'

'No bother.'

He swung his bag easily onto his shoulders. 'Fingers

crossed I get sorted in the next day or two. I don't relish spending Christmas sleeping on the airport floor. That's if I can find a free spot. The best of luck with your own travels.'

He looked so innocent as he said this that an alarm bell rang inside her and she became flustered.

'I don't know what I'm doing,' she said, weary to her bones. Everything just seemed like a massive mountain to climb and her head was sore and fuzzy. The only thing she felt certain of was that she wanted him gone.

'Whatever you decide to do, best wishes and I sincerely hope the new year brings you some peace and consolation.'

'Thank you.'

Izzie couldn't resist going to the living-room window to watch his departure, to make sure he was actually going. Right enough, there was a taxi waiting by the kerb, starkly black against the white snow. He put his bag into the boot and opened the passenger door, glancing up towards the top floor as though he sensed her eyes on him before he jumped into the car. She shrank back, annoyed that he'd caught her doing just that – why hadn't she simply waved at him?

She made coffee and, too distracted to leaf through a magazine or settle down to a book, she slumped in front of the television, the volume muted, staring unseeingly at a Christmas movie. It was far too early for wine. Even in her befuddled state, and no matter how much she'd planned to drink her way into a Christmas coma, she knew that. She looked around the apartment and felt the walls closing in on her. Breathe, she told herself, swinging her feet up on the sofa and relaxing into the cushions. One minute at a time. Even though he was gone, Eli's visit and his behaviour had agitated her and left a ripple of disquiet in the atmosphere, like a bad taste in her mouth.

She wondered how he and Sam had become such good friends.

CHAPTER TWENTY-SIX

Dublin,
thirteen months ago

When you ask me to marry you I say yes.

I know what I'm taking on, you've made sure I do, but any other answer is inconceivable. Love is not defined by its length or its ending. It resonates forever in your heart, whether you've been with the loved one for a day, a year or a lifetime.

It's mid-November. I've been back to New York twice since we first met and now it's your second time to come to Dublin to visit me in my small apartment in Sandyford, which is south of the city, close to the mountains. The early Sunday-morning landscape is glittering under the first crystalline frost of winter. Yesterday I brought you down to Wicklow to meet my mother, and I showed you around my childhood home close to the Vale of Avoca. We also popped in to see Paul, Audrey, and their two gorgeous daughters who live near Mum. At first, Tara and Emily, age five and six, hung back shyly, clinging to their dad. By degrees, and under the spell of your jokey warmth, my nieces were soon chattering and singing and dragging you out into the back garden to show off their beloved pet rabbits and guinea pigs. They fell in love with you when you held their pets carefully in your arms and asked them loads of questions as though they were the most precious beings in the world.

You were silent as we drove home up through a beautiful glen, and I know you were thinking of what might never be. I stayed silent myself, reaching out when it was safe to do so to touch your hand. A light touch and calm stillness can sometimes be the best form of love.

This morning you are your usual happy and upbeat self. 'Is there a beach near here?' you ask.

'Yeah, why – do you fancy a swim?' I joke.

'Not quite. A walk and some fresh air would be good.'

'Sure. We could get to a lovely beach in no time.'

Forty minutes later we have climbed down a series of steps cut into a hillside, and muffled up in jackets, gloves and scarves, we are on White Rock beach, a hidden jewel tucked into the northern end of Killiney. The air is sharp and bracing, the sea a ruffled expanse of sparkly grey. You ask me to sit in the shelter of the bluff for a while.

'What are you up to?' I ask.

'Trust me.' You grin.

I trust you with my life. I trust you with my love. I listen to the rhythmic crump of the tide, the hiss of the waves, and watch as you go down, close to the water's edge, where the sand is hard, picking up pebbles and shells on the way. You place them at intervals along the compact stretch of sand and after a while you call me over.

Using the pebbles and shells, you have written a message in the sand.

'Izzie, I love you, marry me? S XXX'

I don't know how we will manage the practicalities of this, or how long our marriage might last, but that doesn't matter. Out here with you, in cold, bright sunlight that's bouncing off a shimmering sea, where waves crash on the beach with a life force that's contagious, we're both invincible. I pick up some pebbles and write my own message.

'Sam, yes, I love you too. I XXX'

We hug and kiss and I taste the salt on your lips and the chilly breeze whips my hair into your face and you laugh. Afterwards we walk back up the steps to the top of the hill, the world around us opening up from this vantage point, and it seems right that I can follow the curve of the beach for miles and see all the way south to the mountains and valleys of Wicklow, all the way back to the days of my childhood; to the young, carefree girl with messy hair who free-wheeled down the lanes on her first bike, to the shy girl getting the bus to school at the start of her secondary education, the sixteen-year-old going to her first dance in a state of nervous excitement, all dressed up and feeling like an impostor of sorts, forging a path into adulthood and work and a shared flat with Ruth, to the woman I am now. Everything that has happened in my life seems to have been leading me to you and building towards this wonderful, life-affirming moment.

Getting married to you is love in action. Hope is the

diamond-hard force that unites us, binds us and makes us soar so that the two of us together are bigger and shinier than the sum of our parts.

As we walk back to the car, I have one small seashell taken from your message and a pebble from mine tucked into my jacket pocket. Any more and I'd be guilty of disturbing the eco system. The pebble is cream and grey and white, flecked with silvery filaments and smoothed from aeons of shifting sands and tides. You tell me afterwards that you chose a beach and picked these deliberately: the sea meets the sky and stretches to infinity; the pebble and shell have been around for thousands of years and will last for thousands more, just like the spark of us.

CHAPTER TWENTY-SEVEN

Tom was surprised when Florence knocked on his door just before lunch. She rarely ventured up to the first floor, as befitting her inclination to keep herself to herself.

'I hope I'm not disturbing you,' she said. She was wearing a Christmas jumper and black jeans that showed off her trim figure. Her short, layered hair was different, boasting slightly red tones. Christmassy, he thought, fair dues to Florence for getting into the spirit of it.

'You're not disturbing me at all,' he said, opening the door wider. 'Come in. I have something for you under the tree and was about to drop it down to you, so your timing is perfect.'

Her face lit up as though she was surprised, even though Tom had had 'something under the tree' for her every

Christmas since he'd moved in to Henrietta Square. 'Thank you,' she said. 'That's kind of you.'

In the living room, she admired the Christmas tree he'd decorated with Noah.

'It's the same year on year,' he said. 'Everything we've ever had gets put on it, including decorations Noah made in junior school.'

'Old traditions are the best.' She glanced around at the other decorations festooning the room. 'And you have it lovely for a—' She paused.

He knew she'd been about to say for an unattached man but had stopped herself in time.

She gazed at the framed photographs on the sideboard. Besides the one of Cathy, Noah and himself, taken on Noah's fourth birthday, there was another of Noah starting school and one of himself and Noah when they were on holidays in Cork. 'You must still miss Cathy,' she said. 'Both you and Noah. She was beautiful.'

'To be sure, we always will. I can't believe Cathy's gone now the same length of time we were married. We've had to learn different ways of living without her. It took time. A lot. You're great with Noah. I really appreciate the time you spend with him. I've already said this to you, Florence, but don't be afraid to shoo him out if he ever gets under your feet too much.'

Florence shook her head. 'He never would. I enjoy Noah – he brings a bit of life to the house. He's a great kid. Where is he now?'

'Back out in the park, making more snowmen. I don't know how he can stay out in that freezing cold.'

'It's great to be young.' Florence smiled. 'At that age the

snow is just one big exciting event. Anyway, the reason I called up is to invite you both to my snow-themed get-together later this afternoon – say around five-ish?'

Tom tried to keep the surprise off his face. He'd lived here for over two years and it was the first time Florence had issued an invitation to her apartment. Even when he'd dropped down with his customary Christmas gift in previous years, she'd thanked him so effusively and with such an air of fluster that he hadn't felt in the least bit snubbed when she hadn't invited him in. He sensed she was a private lady, apart from her fondness for Noah.

'A snow-themed get-together?' he asked, wondering what this was in aid of. He had a silly vision of needing to turn up dressed as a snowman or something on-theme like that.

'I've been remiss when it comes to entertaining at home. For various reasons, I haven't bothered in a long time,' she said, sounding as though she'd practised those words until they sounded just right. Tom sensed there was a lot going on behind the 'various reasons' that she wasn't about to reveal.

'This weather has us all over the place,' she went on. 'Normal life is suspended, we're all a bit marooned and I, for one, am in severe danger of getting cabin fever. I thought having a get-together would be a bit of diversion for us all, just the residents of number sixteen, me, you, Noah and Izzie. Some drinks and music, snow-themed of course.'

'Hasn't Izzie a visitor staying?' Tom asked.

'You mean Eli. He's left,' Florence said.

'Left? So he's not here for Christmas?' Not here offering Izzie comfort and consolation in Sam's absence?

'No, he was a good friend of Sam's and was stranded in Dublin airport yesterday afternoon – that's why he threw himself on Izzie's mercy. I saw him heading off with his luggage before lunch, so he's gone, wherever he's bound for. I presume it was the airport. Mind you, he'd be lucky. I don't think there'll be much flight activity today. All transport is in a proper mess.'

'So Izzie's coming to your party too?' Tom asked.

'I hope so, although I haven't asked her yet. I don't like her being all alone for Christmas. It's not good for the soul.'

'Isn't she going to family?' he asked tentatively.

'Apparently not, from what she told me,' Florence said, without elaborating.

'Maybe that's what she wants right now.'

'I know.' Florence sighed. 'That's the problem. There are times when you need your own space but I don't think it's good to be alone at Christmas.'

Florence sounded like she was speaking from personal experience, and Tom recalled other Christmases when he'd asked what she was doing out of politeness as he proffered a gift of wine. Without divulging any details, she seemed to be always busy on Christmas Day. He realised how little he knew about her life. Had she ever been married? Or thwarted in love? Not questions you would ask out of courtesy.

'Will the weather affect your Christmas plans?' he asked her in a roundabout way, not wanting to appear too inquisitive.

'It had better not,' she said spiritedly. 'I'm doing my usual stint, helping to serve dinners at the Brooke Street centre, along with Wendy and Jean.'

'Wendy and …?'

'Jean. My friends,' she said. 'I met them at the local bridge club soon after I moved to Henrietta Square. We help out every year.'

The Brooke Street centre was in the news regularly for the large number of breakfasts and dinners it served to the poor and homeless, never mind the increasing number of food parcels it handed out, particularly in the run-up to Christmas.

'Good for you, Florence. I'd say it's very rewarding.'

'It can be,' she said, giving him her usual all-well-with-the-world bright smile. 'I can stay for a couple of hours and have my own dinner there if I wish. It can be a hectic day.'

So, no family. No one inviting Florence for dinner, unless she'd turned them down for reasons of her own. And Izzie – instead of spending a wonderfully warm and cosy Christmas with Sam, as she'd no doubt anticipated, from what she'd told Florence she'd chosen to be alone.

'So you'll come this evening?' she asked.

'Of course, I'll look forward to that.'

'It's more than time I had a little soirée at Christmas,' she said. 'Not that I'm a hermit altogether. I see my friends at bridge and aqua aerobics, and we try and get away for our birthdays and make weekend celebrations of them.'

'Sounds a bit like what my father, Sean, gets up to.'

'I've never met him, but I know Noah is close to him.'

'He is, which is lovely to see. Dad rarely comes to Dublin – he prefers the craic in Cork. Mum died years ago, but he makes the most of every opportunity and heads off on regular weekends with friends.'

Tom gave her Christmas gifts of wine and chocolates before she left. 'And Noah has something for you,' he said, 'but he wants to give it to you himself.'

'He's a dote,' Florence said. 'You're not to bring anything down this evening,' she cautioned. 'If you want to contribute you can sing a song.'

'That would be one way of bringing everything to a close. Just give me the nod, Florence, and I'll clear the room for you.'

Her laughter echoed as she went down the stairs. He closed the door slowly, wondering if Izzie would turn up.

CHAPTER TWENTY-EIGHT

He got the taxi to drop him off at the corner of Merrion Row. He'd no intentions of heading back out to a crazy airport. This was far enough from Henrietta Square, yet not so far that he couldn't make it back if conditions worsened. Snow was falling again, pelting into his face, and he pulled up the hood of his jacket as he stepped onto the kerb. He shouldered his backpack and grabbed his case from the boot. Oblongs of light glimmering out onto the street brought home the sombreness of the dark day.

He ducked into the nearest pub. Even though it was barely lunch hour it was already bursting with office workers, and to judge by the number of glasses littering the table-tops, the shrieks of forced festive laughter and clumps of mistletoe being fired around, they were already hard at work celebrating the Christmas break. The air was stale and clogged with the fug of alcohol and damp clothes, and the aroma of food filtered up from the back of the pub where they had begun serving lunch. He was starving. The bitch had had nothing decent in her fridge until he'd gone to the store and bought some food. He tucked that away as a useful piece of information.

He pushed his way through the crowds, heedless of whether his backpack cannoned into anyone. He dropped his case by a table set for four, grabbed a tray and went along the counter, choosing roast beef and all the vegetables. Back at the table, he slid off his backpack and took off his cumbersome jacket, hanging it over the back of another chair. He took out his cell phones, the American one that the bitch had seen and the Irish phone she wasn't aware of. Any more than she was aware of the software he'd had installed on it that was linked to her phone and monitored her every move.

He began to wolf down his food and sip chilled water. He needed a clear head to work out a way to get what he wanted from that bitch without anyone suspecting. That was the key. Stealthy and undetected. The hand he'd played all along. Otherwise he stood to lose everything.

If she'd realised how close he'd come to smacking her in the face, she might have co-operated. He'd had to get away from her before he did something stupid, like hit her where it would show. He'd been tempted to shake her – she had to know that password. Getting into Sam's laptop was the key to everything. A bit of help from her and he'd have been sorted for life. He'd had a nasty moment when she'd asked him about money, but he'd covered it okay.

As for that little brat who told him he'd been best buddies with Sam. Yeah, right. Sam who could do no wrong, even with a kid. Everybody had loved Sam, the gifted student with the white-hot career, the intelligent and charismatic asshole. He experienced a long moment of emptiness. He'd never expected his life to turn out like this – sitting alone in an Irish bar at Christmas time, having a solitary meal, all washed up at thirty-seven years of age, trying to work out a strategy to save his life and prop up his future.

He'd move on to the next pub after a couple of hours – no point in bringing undue attention to himself by hanging around here for too long. He'd have to work out the finer points of Plan B now that he had an idea of what he was up against, as well as the logistics of Henrietta Square and the occupants. Nothing like the pressure of a gun to his temple to sharpen his wits.

He'd resort to Plan C if he had to. It would be messy for both of them, but especially the bitch.

CHAPTER TWENTY-NINE

It had been one thing to talk to Noah and Tom about her little get-together but inviting Izzie was a far bigger mountain to climb. Florence tried to shake off the feeling that she was invading her space when she arrived on the second landing.

All was cool and silent up here at the top of the house. Henrietta Square wasn't like modern apartment blocks where thin walls allowed every sound to penetrate. It had been built solid and square and had been renovated soon after she arrived here, almost ten years ago, with triple-glazed windows designed to maintain sensitivity to the original architecture. She couldn't help imagining Sam and Izzie coming up these stairs, happy in their togetherness.

Now all that had vanished. A sense of loss resonated inside her, in a place she never wanted to revisit.

She knocked twice and was almost about to go back downstairs, mission abandoned, when Izzie opened the door, slowly and cautiously, her dark eyes glazed as though she'd just awoken from a deep sleep.

'Sorry if I disturbed you, Izzie,' she said.

'I'm glad you did,' Izzie replied, her voice husky. 'I fell into a doze, and that's not good at this hour in the day.'

'It's the weather,' Florence said. 'It has us all at sixes and sevens.' She could have bitten her tongue. Surely Christmas, the snow and the general chaos it had brought barely registered on Izzie's radar.

'Come in, Florence, I've forgotten my manners,' Izzie said.

'I don't want to be in the way,' Florence said. 'I called to let you know I'm having a get-together this afternoon, say five-ish, for the residents of number sixteen. You can get a bit of cabin fever with this snow, can't you? Although, strictly speaking, compared to the rest of the country we're not really all that snowbound,' she gabbled on. 'Still, the disruption makes you uneasy, and everything is kind of up in the air, isn't it?'

'I know what you mean,' Izzie said. 'I think that's what's wrong with me. Cabin fever has set in.'

'Are you okay?' A stupid question, Florence chided herself.

Izzie smiled faintly. 'Just groggy, that's all.'

'A change of scene might do you good,' Florence said. 'I'm not having anything fancy. It would just be you, me, Noah and Tom, a snow-themed get-together. That's if you want to come. I'll understand if you want to stay put. Your friend has gone?'

'Yes, he's headed back to the airport. But Eli's not my friend

– he was Sam's.' Izzie's voice sounded constricted, as though she had difficulty in saying the words, in uttering Sam's name, and Florence had an urge to give her a big hug.

She smiled gently at Izzie. 'So he said. He pressed my bell first and asked which apartment was yours, but I vetted him before I told him or let him in and he seemed okay. Then again, any friend of Sam's is sure to be kosher – isn't that the word?'

Izzie's eyes narrowed a fraction and her pale face whitened further. She looked, Florence thought, like a thin, fragile shell of her former self.

'Did I say something wrong?' Florence asked.

Izzie shook her head, but Florence could see it was an effort, as though the simple movement pained her. 'You're grand, Florence,' she said. 'And you're right – any friend of Sam's is sure to be kosher.'

'Well, you know where to find us if you want to join us for a drink,' Florence said as gently as she could manage. 'You can stay as long or as short as you like. You don't need to bring anything except yourself. And if you don't feel like coming, that's okay too. No worries. I know what it's like to want to spend time alone.'

She patted Izzie on her forearm in a gesture of empathy and turned to leave. She was out on the landing and about to go downstairs when instinct made her look back. Izzie was standing there unmoving, her arms hugging herself, her dark eyes big pools of anxiety.

'Izzie, are you sure you're all right?' she asked, perturbed.

'Yes – no. Florence, actually – would you like to come in and have a tea or coffee?' The words came out in a rush, Izzie's voice thin and wavery, like a weak SOS of sorts.

'Of course, tea would be lovely,' Florence said, as matter-of-fact as if she had tea with Izzie every day of the week. She retraced her steps. Even if she'd had a pressing commitment somewhere, she would have made it wait. Even if tea was the last thing in the world she wanted right now, she was determined to accept Izzie's invitation. There was something about the young woman that put her on edge, partly because memories stirred of the time Florence had felt as fragile as spun glass, only then she'd slipped and fallen and had shattered, and even to this day the scars and jagged edges that were left had never fully healed.

The contrast between Izzie's undecorated apartment and Tom's, one floor below, tore at her heart.

'Milk or sugar, Florence?' Izzie asked.

'Just milk, thanks.'

Florence sat down on the sofa and waited until Izzie brought the tea over. There was a box of luxury chocolates on the low table, which Izzie pushed towards her, but she declined. 'There'll be more than enough sweet things in the next few days,' she said.

Izzie sat, staring into space, her tea cooling.

Florence leaned forward. 'Do you mind me asking, is everything all right? Apart from, well, I know it's your first Christmas without Sam, so that's bound to be tough. But you seem to me ...'

'Seem what?'

'As though – you're not ill, are you?'

Izzie shook her head. 'My head is full of cotton wool after I fell asleep that time. I didn't realise how tired I was.'

'You're bound to be tired. At the risk of being personal, it's an exhausting thing, going back to work and keeping your act together when you're coming through the kind of trauma that you are. Tell me to butt out and mind my own business, but, Izzie, dear, you need to be kind and gentle with yourself.'

Izzie gave her a wan smile and Florence knew her words were not registering at all. She summoned the best of her school-teacher authority, pulling it out of the thick layers she'd encased it in when she'd retired from that profession.

'I mean it, Izzie. You need to go softly with yourself, treat yourself as a precious thing or you'll end up …' Florence didn't continue. What worse could happen, after all, now that Sam was gone? And what right had she to impose her ideas on someone who was held fast in those first, crazy stages of mind-numbing grief?

Only that she knew that mad sense of gut-wrenching panic, the moments you felt unable to breathe for fear of the pain slicing you in two. But she also knew that the worst of the pain would pass. Eventually. She knew also what it was like not to want to talk of these things. In her case, it had been for fear and shame. She'd bottled it all up, remaining silent, and the words had hardened within her, turning turgid and cankerous. So long as the tragedy of Sam's death didn't leave Izzie sour and embittered for the rest of her life. It would be such a waste. She was still young, she was beautiful and she had so much to give and experience. Like Florence had been once upon a time. But thanks to adopting the role of her own worst enemy, sourness and bitterness had prevented her from appreciating that until it was too late.

'Look, Izzie,' she began, 'although things seem hopeless right now, and there is no magic cure-all, some day you'll feel the sunshine on your face again. I'm saying this to you because I've been somewhere dark too, but I made the mistake of letting it spoil the rest of my life. Please don't do that. Sorry if I'm intruding – that's my speech done. You can tell me to leave and I won't take offence.'

'It's all right, Florence, I'm not taking offence. I know Sam was fond of you.'

'He was?' Florence's eyes suddenly prickled with tears.

'Yes, he thought you were a lovely Irish lady.'

Sam had thought that. He'd even said it to Izzie. Sam, the gorgeous young American who'd brightened up the hallways of number sixteen with his cheerful presence.

'He said you reminded him of Elena, his mother,' Izzie went on. 'Her parents were Irish, from Limerick. They emigrated to America in the fifties.'

'Oh gosh.' Florence swallowed. 'It's a long time since anyone paid me a compliment like that. I'm really touched to think I reminded Sam of his mother.'

Somewhere inside her, something cracked. There had been many days when she'd lifted her chin and squared her shoulders and gritted her way through the hours, the armour she'd encased herself in so secure that no one could get through; the interested men she'd given short shrift to, not letting anyone get close, hardening herself against the prospects of anything but the most casual friendship, so that it became a way of life for her and, in time, the interested men had ceased to be. Here, in Izzie's cheerless apartment, thoughts of that lovely young man and the heart-warming idea that she'd reminded him of his mother was like a balm to her soul.

'Just remind yourself of one thing, Izzie,' she said gently. 'You will survive this. You'll always have Sam's love in your heart. You will go on. You're doing just fine.'

Izzie smiled, albeit shakily. 'Thank you. Sometimes it feels strange that I'm still alive. Other days go by without me noticing.'

'That's perfectly normal. But don't shut others out too much.'

'In other words, come to your snow get-together.'

'Only if you want to,' Florence said, touching her arm briefly in a comforting gesture.

CHAPTER THIRTY

Noah had almost given up on Izzie appearing at Florence's snow party. He and his dad had arrived soon after five. Florence seemed a bit flustered when they got there, asking over and over if they were comfortable, until his dad said it was really cosy, like a home from home, and Florence smiled and said she should have invited him in before now. She said she hoped Izzie would come down, but not, Noah guessed, as fervently as he did. Weirdo had left all right, earlier that day. Noah wasn't long back from the shops when he saw him leaving in a black taxi. Hurray! He'd built a brilliant R2-D2 snowman after that. Even Tigi was impressed.

In Florence's living room, the lamps were switched on,

music played softly and there were lots of sparkly lights – around her Christmas tree, over the mantelpiece and in big glass jars on her table. She had star-shaped cookies and snow blob cakes, marshmallows and sweets. Noah sipped white lemonade from a frosted glass with lots of ice and a dollop of ice-cream.

'It's slushy, a bit like the snow,' Florence had said.

And after a while there was a soft knock on the door and there she was: Izzie, her face nearly as white as the snowy park outside. Noah thought her eyes looked a bit funny, as though she'd just woken up from a deep sleep.

'Izzie!' Florence gave her a hug. Noah hoped his dad might give her a hug as well, but Florence drew her into the room, plumped up a cushion on her sofa and told her to sit down. And then his dad actually moved up along the sofa, so that he was nearer to Izzie.

Result.

Florence got her a drink, a tall glass of clear liquid with lots of ice, the glass frosted around the rim. 'Glad you decided to come,' she added in a low voice that only Izzie was supposed to hear.

Izzie smiled without saying anything. She took a sip of her drink and made a funny face. 'More tonic, please, Florence, or I'll be on my ear.'

Florence handed Izzie a bottle of tonic water. 'Sorry, I'm not used to pouring gin, but I thought it most resembled ice and snow. For our snow theme. Anyhow, you only have to go up the stairs afterwards. There's just Tom and Noah here, so you're with friends,' Florence said, a firm note in her voice. 'Even if we sometimes pass like ships in the night, we're all under the one roof, and in the time we've all lived here, there have been no altercations between us at all. There's a lot to be said for that.'

Izzie's soft smile included both Noah and his dad.

His dad tipped his glass to Izzie's. 'Good to see you,' he said.

'I thought it was practical to get us all together in view of the weather,' Florence said. 'We might need some help or support from each other or to pool our resources if we're stuck. One of the good things to come out of the big snow is neighbours getting together and helping neighbours. Thanks for clearing the snow off the steps and the footpath, Tom – you did us all a favour. Are your plans disrupted?'

'I'm not sure yet,' his dad said.

'Are you off to family?' Izzie asked.

'I'm waiting until tomorrow to call it,' his dad said. 'Cathy's mother in Kilkenny is expecting us for Christmas Day. She'll be disappointed if we can't make it, but she doesn't want us to take any risks either. We usually go to my dad on Stephen's Day but unless things improve drastically I'd say a trip to west Cork is out until closer to the new year.'

For a moment, when Florence had spoken, Noah had imagined them all sitting down to Christmas dinner together because they were unable to travel. That was hardly going to happen. Still, there was no harm in hoping. Izzie and his dad looked right together. Almost as right as Izzie and Sam had been. They were even talking. People said his father was handsome but he didn't know: he was just Dad to him. He'd heard it muttered at get-togethers and the occasional party they'd gone to, other women wondering why such an attractive man was still unattached. He was a little taller than Izzie and they both had dark hair and brown eyes. Although, while Izzie's eyes reminded him of chocolate buttons, his dad's eyes were more of a greeny-brown. And his dark hair was starting to grey at the sides. A slice of terror cut through his tummy; his dad wasn't going to live forever. After what happened to his mum – and then look at Sam.

He wasn't supposed to be feeling like this. It was a snow party and he wanted his dad and Izzie to be happy. Look at Florence – she was fine and she'd already told him her skin and hair might be over seventy years of age but on the inside, where her heart was, she was just seventeen and that was where it counted the most. Sam had been a bit like that. Noah knew he'd been thirty-six years of age, he'd told him, but he'd talked to Noah as though he was an older brother. He wondered if his dad and Izzie felt like that. Younger on the inside than they looked on the outside. His dad had turned forty earlier that year, but he didn't know how old Izzie was. Certainly younger than his dad, though.

'What about you, Florence?' Izzie asked.

'I'm helping with the Christmas dinner in the Brooke Street centre with some friends. I hope we make it. We're part of the Ents team as well.'

'Ents?' Izzie asked.

'Entertainment,' Florence said. 'We're on first because my friends will go back to their families for their dinner but I'll stay on until I feel like coming home. It's great fun. I just hope the snow doesn't stop us.'

'I'm sure it won't – it's local enough,' Izzie said. 'Sounds good. And it must be rewarding to be involved in the community effort.'

'It is,' Florence said.

It was the opening Noah had been waiting for. 'Izzie, would

you like to come to my carol service?' he asked. 'My school choir is singing in the local parish church tomorrow night. I'm even doing a solo, 'Walking in the Air'.'

Izzie looked at him as though she hadn't registered a word he'd said.

'Izzie could be busy,' his dad said, giving Noah a look that told him not to push it. 'People usually have a lot on around Christmas. And what if the weather is still bad?'

'If Izzie is free she could come with us,' Noah said. 'We could all walk together.'

'Thanks for your invitation, Noah, it's very kind of you,' Izzie said at last. 'I didn't intend going to any carol services this year but in your case I might make an exception. Tomorrow night?'

'Yeah, at half past seven. We could meet in the hall at seven o'clock. It'll be over soon after nine.'

'Noah, I could do with some help with the finger food in the oven,' Florence said.

'Yeah, sure,' he said, following her down to the kitchen.

It left his dad talking to Izzie.

Mega result.

CHAPTER THIRTY-ONE

There were times after Cathy had died when Tom had found it hard to breathe, such had been his feeling of paralysis. Life going on around him had seemed garish and noisy and out of reach, as if it were taking place behind an impenetrable sheet of glass. Tonight he sensed that Izzie was caught fast behind that opaque glass, because her presence on the sofa beside him was so brittle.

This evening was the first opportunity he'd had to spend any appreciable length of time in her company since Sam was gone, and Florence's apartment was safe and non-threatening, with her soft lighting and aroma of baking mingling pleasantly with the Christmassy scent coming from her pine garland. But to his annoyance, he didn't know what to say to Izzie for the best. Surely he, of all people, who had been in a similar situation himself, would know? He took a sip of wine and racked his brains.

He'd cringed big time when Noah had asked her to the carol service. In her circumstances, an evocative carol service was surely the last place Izzie wanted to be.

Tom watched Noah heading down to the kitchen with Florence, and when he was out of earshot he turned to Izzie and said, 'I'm sorry if Noah annoyed you. I know you mightn't feel up to being at a carol service so please ignore his request.'

Izzie looked at him for a long moment. When she eventually answered, he sensed that she had dropped any kind of front and was speaking to him honestly. 'Don't worry about Noah,' she said, her voice edged with hoarseness. 'I think he's great and I love that he talks to me without weighing up every word, without putting a label on me or seeing me as a … victim of some sort, never mind a bashed-up piece of humanity.'

'You're not in the least bit bashed up,' he said, knowing how it had felt to be treated like a crock by well-meaning acquaintances. He'd resented it hugely. 'You're still a vital, card-carrying member of the human race.'

'Thank you,' she said, one of her hands playing unconsciously with the ends of her hair. 'I'm still at the stage where everything is a muzzy fog. Going to a carol concert would make no difference to how I feel. Nothing I do makes any difference in the slightest.'

There was a small beat of silence. Tom said, 'I'm sorry everything is muzzy right now. I'm sorry for what happened to Sam. It was cruel. I wish there was more I could do. If you ever want to talk, anytime, about anything, I'm happy to listen.'

'Thank you. Mostly I'm just …' she paused, gave him a quick, hesitant smile, 'totally frozen. Disconnected. I suppose I should be more in tune with myself and more engaged in the world. I hope I might begin to pick up the pieces in the new year.'

'There's no time limit on anything,' Tom said, giving her a small smile back. 'Grief can ebb and flow when you least expect it. So don't think you have to be in tune with yourself by a certain number of months. Or years. It takes time to absorb the loss of a loved one, never mind adjusting to a new day-to-day reality. The thing is—' He paused for a moment, having second thoughts about this whole conversation. Who was he to talk? To give advice? He deliberately calmed his mind and made himself take slow, easy breaths.

'Yes?' she prompted.

'However you feel is perfectly right for you at that moment – angry, sad, mad, a mixture of all these or even nothing at all. Some things can never be fixed, but you find ways of carrying them. I thought Sam was a really lovely guy, and he was great with Noah. When you lose someone you love from your life, you need to give yourself time out and permission to mourn the loss properly in a world that's busier than ever and always seems to be in an endless rush, where everything has to be picture perfect. And sorry if I'm intruding.'

'It's okay,' Izzie said. 'I wanted to talk to you.'

'You did?'

'I know you've been through something similar in losing your wife. I know now I should have acknowledged it better, but I was one of those people who found it too awkward. I was one of those,' her voice dropped, 'who was too embarrassed to … bring it up. I was all wrapped up in my own bubble of happiness and I didn't want anything to spoil that in any way. I didn't want to acknowledge that life could be so cruel.'

'That's perfectly understandable,' he said. 'In the early days after Cathy, I didn't want people to talk about her. *I* didn't want to talk about her – I wanted to keep her still alive, all wrapped up and tucked away safely. It's frightening to know that life can be brutal, that these things *do* happen to couples. It makes people uneasy.'

'It was more than that with us, with me,' she said. 'I had good reason for ignoring it.'

He waited, sensing there was more.

'You see, the thing is … me and Sam … we were …' Her voice grew thinner and thinner until he could hardly hear her. She took a long gulp of her drink. She was wearing a red jumper and dark jeans, and in the soft light of Florence's living room, her face was pale, almost transparent. He noticed her hand was shaking as she put down her glass. He wondered what she had been about to say. He knew people had avoided him in the aftermath of Cathy's death, as though he had a contagious disease, but Izzie seemed to have a different kind of problem.

Still, he thought he might have been mistaken when the words came, as soft as thistledown. 'Sam and I … and I haven't told this to anyone else apart from my immediate family …'

She paused. She took a shaky breath and looked at him with perfect honesty in her eyes.

He waited.

'Well, Sam and I knew from the beginning that our time together would be limited,' she murmured with a gulp. 'Although we didn't realise how short it was actually going to be.'

CHAPTER THIRTY-TWO

Tom froze. Had he heard her right? Had she really said that? What had she meant exactly, their time would be limited?

Florence had told him that Sam died in an accident in Galway, that he'd been in the wrong place at the wrong time. He risked a glance at Izzie and saw her eyes were bright with unshed tears. She was sitting rigidly, except for her hand, which was still shaking. He put his hand over it. She didn't move away so he held it in his. It was freezing cold so he reached out his other hand and enclosed hers within both of his. She didn't slide her hand away, but sat there quietly. She bit her lip and glanced sideways at him, as if for reassurance.

He smiled at her with all the warmth he could muster, and the curious intimacy of the moment held him transfixed.

Florence noticed. He caught her startled expression when he glanced down to the kitchen area. He shook his head slightly and Florence kept Noah up at that end of the room, asking him to help her with the sausage rolls, suggesting that he sample one to make sure they were tasty enough. He sat in calm silence with Izzie for several moments and then he sensed her relaxing a little.

'Thank you,' she said, flexing her fingers slightly. Gradually, she slid her hand out of his joined ones.

'Any time,' he said. 'How are you now? Although you don't have to answer that, or even talk to me if you don't want to.'

'I'm here,' she said.

'Here is as good a place as any,' he said. 'If you ever want to talk, or just sit and not talk, I'm here for you. And don't forget, if you need anything practical done, I'm around for that as well.'

They sat in silence for a short while, and the next time Florence looked over, Tom gave her a nod. Sensing the moment had passed, she asked Noah to help her hand out napkins and finger food.

He was happy to see Izzie eat some sausage rolls and follow them up with a mince pie, and that a little colour returned to her cheeks.

'How about all of us going for coffee in the morning?' he heard himself say. 'The Italian nearby does great coffee and pastries. We should have no problem getting around there.'

'I'd like that,' Florence said.

He jumped when Florence's intercom buzzed, far louder than the ringtone in his apartment.

'That's to make sure I hear it,' Florence said, catching his surprised glance. 'Sometimes I have the music up too loud to hear the bell. But I'm not expecting anyone, and I don't know who could be out at this hour of the evening and in this snow.'

She pressed the button on the intercom and called out. 'Yes?'

In the infinitesimal second before the person answered, Tom knew instinctively who it was, and knew he was powerless to prevent the next few moments unfolding as they did.

'It's me, Florence. Sam's friend, Eli,' he said. 'I've been trying Izzie's apartment but she's not answering. Do you know where she is? She seemed a bit low when I left this morning so I'm worried about her.'

Florence gave Izzie a questioning glance, raising her eyebrows. Izzie nodded.

'So you're not waiting on a flight in the airport,' Florence said, 'because you're worried about Izzie?'

'Partly that. I think it must be fate that I couldn't get on a flight, and there's hardly space to breathe on the airport floor.'

'Oh dear,' Florence said. 'I suppose you'd better come in. And you needn't worry about Izzie – she's here with me, and Tom and Noah. We're having a residents' snow party.' Another questioning glance at Izzie that Izzie nodded at. 'You're welcome to join us.' She pressed the release button for the main door and went across to the door to the hallway, throwing it open.

Eli marched into the room with a big smile on his face, the combined bulk of him and his jacket seeming to take up a lot of space. 'This is lovely,' he said, looking around at the group. 'All very cosy compared to the horrors of the airport. Sorry to intrude, Izzie, but I couldn't stick it out there anymore. They're hoping to schedule some additional flights out late tomorrow afternoon so fingers crossed I get going then. I couldn't find any space to rest my head, no matter how much charm I dispensed.'

'So you've been out to the airport *and* back?' Florence said. 'How did you manage that? There's very little moving outside.'

'I had to come back, even though I practically had to arm-wrestle a cab driver. Driving conditions are rough on the side roads and we went at a snail's pace. But I got here. I hope that's okay with you, Izzie?'

Izzie's face, when she looked at Eli, was perfectly smooth, much like her voice. 'That's fine with me.'

He smiled at her. 'At least the delay means I'm still here to support you in these difficult days.'

Something sour twisted in Tom's stomach. With a sense of mild shock, he realised he was envious of Eli. Surely he, Tom, was far better placed to support Izzie? He thought they'd reached a special understanding this evening and he'd been happy about that. There had been a moment of vulnerable honesty between them that transcended barriers. Foolishly, he'd hoped it had been the beginning of some kind of breakthrough with Izzie.

Now Eli had burst that bubble, but he was Sam's friend, and Tom couldn't compete with that.

CHAPTER THIRTY-THREE

The minute Izzie saw Eli walking into Florence's apartment, the walls shrunk around her and her throat closed over. To all outward appearances he was Sam's best mate, stranded in Dublin at Christmas, needing a bed for the night. Here to offer her any necessary support at this difficult time. He'd known Sam better than anyone else.

But after the sneaky way he'd tried to access Sam's laptop, and the way he'd lied to her about his, the thoughts of putting up with him for another few hours filled her with unease. She was trapped. What could she say, for example to Florence, without sounding off the wall? *I don't like this man. I'd rather he wasn't here? Pity there's no room for him on the airport floor. Sorry that it's Christmas – I don't really care.*

And what kind of insult would that be to the memory of Sam? Sam, who would have given the shirt off his back to anyone. Especially to a stranded, jet-lagged Eli. He had overstepped the mark, but in the circumstances surely Sam would have expected her to overlook an error of judgement and a little deception on Eli's part and give him another chance?

She heard Florence say brightly, 'Eli, can I offer you a drink?'

'You're too kind, Florence,' Eli said, his smooth American tones beginning to grate on her. 'I'd really appreciate that. A beer would be great, if you have it. Otherwise some wine, whatever's open. And thanks for allowing me to join your party.'

He lowered himself into the armchair nearest Izzie. His pale-blue eyes scanned her face. 'Thank you so much for your hospitality,' he said. 'You're one in a million, but then I knew that already from what Sam told me. I don't know how to thank you, and I'll be forever in your debt.' He spoke in a voice just loud enough for everyone else to hear.

To her surprise, Izzie caught Noah making a face behind Eli's back, not realising she was able to observe him. No one else seemed to have noticed. Eli might be impressing Florence and Tom with his impeccable manners, but for some reason Noah wasn't amused. Then again, Eli had been unfriendly to him the other night.

'There you go.' Florence handed Eli a beer. 'I've seen the airport on the news, all those people upset at being unable to get home for Christmas.'

'It's all a matter of perspective,' Eli said. 'There are far more tragic stories being beamed into our living rooms every night of the week from different corners of the world. I count myself fortunate to be among friends. Isn't that right?'

Friends? Again he fixed her with a smile. It was like a net tightening around her, but what could she do except smile in return? Tom was giving her an odd look, as though he was trying to figure out what kind of connection she had with Eli.

None whatsoever, she wanted to say.

'You're more than welcome to the party,' Florence said, offering some of her snow buns. 'It's good to be able to do our bit for at least one inconvenienced traveller. Small acts of kindness oil the wheels that help to make the world go around. But what am I thinking? These tiny little cakes aren't enough for you. When is the last time you had a decent meal?'

'I got something in the airport. I'm fine for now, thanks.'

'You did? I wouldn't say it was anything much, to judge by what I'm hearing,' Florence said. 'They're saying even catering supplies are becoming thin on the ground. Are you sure you won't have something more substantial?'

'I'm okay. We eat far too much food in the west anyhow, but if I get peckish later, I'll cook something for me and Izzie. I stocked up her fridge this morning to make sure she wouldn't be stuck for meals over Christmas. She had practically nothing at all in it.' He turned to her and gave her an indulgent smile. 'Isn't that right? I don't know what you were thinking, my dear. A package of past-its-sell-by-date cheese and a few soft tomatoes. Were you planning on not eating at all over Christmas and making do with your stockpile of alcohol?' He'd already commented on the contents of her fridge; she didn't know why he was making a point of highlighting it, as well as her artillery of wine and gin, in front of everyone.

'You've forgotten,' she replied. 'I'd been planning on doing a yoga boot camp.'

'Had you really?' Eli said, smiling indulgently at her as though he knew full well it had only been a smoke screen.

'You sound as if you don't believe me,' she said, putting it up to him.

'I think, my dear girl, that you were being very brave and independent, telling people you were going away so that your family could enjoy their Christmas and no one would feel obligated to try and comfort you over the festive season.' He spoke in a quiet voice, as though he didn't want anyone else to overhear, but Izzie knew it was loud enough for Tom to hear every word. He threw her a glance she was unable to interpret.

'You must think you know me better than I know myself,' Izzie countered. She wanted to yell at him that she wasn't his 'dear girl'.

'I know what Sam said about you, how much he adored you. But I'm not sure you should be on your own over Christmas, never mind drinking so much gin, in your fragile state.'

'Who cares? I don't, for one.'

'In that case, don't mind me and drink up all you like,' Eli said. 'I can understand that it's a crutch for you right now. And sometimes we need those as a temporary measure. It's understandable that you're in a lot of pain, especially for your first Christmas without Sam.'

Some friend of Sam's he was turning out to be, Izzie decided in a black moment. He couldn't be saying or doing any more to try and upset her. She tried to clear the fog in her brain to understand why Eli might have a reason to behave like this, fishing for recollections of the last time Sam had spoken of him.

'I'd trust Eli with my life,' he'd said. 'If anything happens to me, he's the one guy I'd want in my corner.'

She thought of the lovely email he'd sent after Sam had died and tried to equate that email with the Eli who was here now, showing up on her doorstep unexpectedly. *Oh, Sam. Your friend is nothing at all like I'd expected. He's not the Eli I'd imagined from the way you spoke of him.*

Not the Eli?

Up beyond the foggy cloud taking up space in Izzie's brain, there was a clear spot, like the bright-blue vault of the sky you find when you're flying and you burst through the grey bank of cloud. In this limitless space her thoughts scattered in all directions. She tried to make connections as well as go back over everything Eli had said, a lot of which had barely registered with her. There was something Florence had said about Eli earlier that afternoon; it had struck a wrong note with Izzie. Another remark he'd made after Noah's visit had jarred with her. She searched through her head, unable to recall what they were, thanks to the opaque cloud in her brain.

She'd never actually met Eli, had she? He hadn't even been at their wedding. It had been a small affair, and Sam had only emailed him about it after the event, not wanting to drag him back from his expedition in the depths of the Amazon.

Of course he wasn't a different person. He had to be Sam's Eli. She was still all over the place in the absence of Sam. So much so she couldn't think straight. And she'd been drinking far too much in recent days, on top of which they were now in the thick of the most emotionally charged days of the year. She watched him talking to Florence – he was busy admiring the results of her baking, and he was perfectly polite and charming. He must have sensed her looking at him because he caught her glance and his pale-blue eyes stared at her shrewdly before he switched on a smile. It was like he'd put a false front back in place.

Jesus. Izzie gripped her glass. She would have to cut back on the booze, get rid of her crazy thoughts. They were so way out that they scared her.

CHAPTER THIRTY-FOUR

One of the things Izzie and Sam had loved about their apartment was its being situated on the top floor. As soon as they came up past Tom's apartment and reached the return in the staircase, it was as if they were in their own exclusive space, and it had given them a certain privacy. The whole top floor belonged to them. There was no need for anyone to come up this way unless they were visiting, and visitors to Henrietta Square were few and far between. Now, with Eli following her up the stairs, Izzie was suddenly conscious of how eerily quiet it was. The thick, well-constructed walls and heavy panelled doors that were a feature of the building meant that little sound carried between the apartments.

Calm down, she told herself. Don't let your imagination

go galloping in all directions. She was hardly inviting Jack the Ripper home. He had to be Eli. He was hardly a strange guy who'd wandered in off the street, taking his chances. She unlocked the door to her apartment and waited in the small hallway until Eli followed her in with his luggage. He stood behind her as she locked the door again, realising she was effectively securing both of them in behind a deadlock.

'You are okay with this, aren't you?' he asked, so close behind her that she felt his breath on her neck and she jumped.

'It's exactly what Sam would have wanted me to do,' she said, resisting the attempt to shiver. 'I can't see his best mate stranded.' She went into the living room, Eli so close on her heels that she could scent his aftershave and her scalp began to tingle. Sam's best mate, she reminded herself, whom he would have trusted with his life.

'Are you sure you won't have something to eat?' she asked, standing in the middle of the floor, hugging herself. 'Thanks to you there's stuff in the fridge. Or I can make some coffee.'

'No, thanks, I never drink coffee after lunchtime,' he said. He'd left his case in the hall, and now he sat down on the sofa, in the same place he'd sat the previous evening, his backpack on the floor beside him.

'Don't you?' she said, as casually as she could.

'It plays havoc with the sleep process,' he said.

Not something she would have imagined Eli having problems with, the Eli who had trekked India *and* kayaked down the Amazon, never mind herding elephants in Africa.

Somehow Izzie managed to keep her voice bland. 'Funny, that's exactly what Sam used to say too,' she said casually, visions of him pouring through her memory bank: Sam, bringing coffee across to her while they relaxed on the sofa after their evening meal; Sam helping himself to just one more cup while he finished up a program on his laptop; Sam grinning at her as he lobbed a squashed-up chocolate wrapper in her direction, telling her that a ton of caffeine and chocolate was obligatory when it came to fixing awkward glitches in systems at ten o'clock at night, and especially when he had to take a conference call from New York.

Coffee after lunchtime had never interfered with Sam's sleep. He had thrived on it.

'Yeah, I remember that,' Eli said. 'We must have been the only Americans who swore off the stuff beyond the morning.'

She stared at him. He looked perfectly relaxed. What he had said didn't actually mean anything, did it? He could have been simply going along with her for the sake of good relations, humouring her instead of disagreeing flatly. Or else, the dark thought nudged, he wasn't fully acquainted with Sam's coffee habits. Which Eli should have been.

Izzie pulled herself up sharply. She was only having freaky ideas given her circumstances and the amount of alcohol in her system.

'A beer?' she said, the crazy notion that he'd known this morning he'd be coming back here sidling into her head.

'Yes, thank you, but only if you're having one. It was good of Florence to have a party and invite me in, then you allowed me a place to rest my head for the night. I'd heard loads about Irish hospitality, but this is the first time I've personally experienced it. It's even more wonderful than I'd been told. Lucky Sam,' he added in a quieter voice.

'*Lucky?*' she said.

'Well ...' He slapped the side of his head. 'Apologies – I phrased that badly. I hope you know what I meant by that –

married to a beautiful woman such as yourself, living in this splendid apartment, at close hand to the city, *working* in this beautiful space as well. He had it all. I'm sorry, but everything in his life was going so well it makes what happened seem all the crueller.'

She ignored him, busy fixing her drink, too much gin to be sensible when she needed to keep a cool head, drowning it with loads of tonic, taking beer out of the fridge and searching for the bottle opener … the bottle opener usually kept in the drawer along with the cutlery. It eluded her. Her hands scrabbled, picking up knives and forks, making a clatter as she replaced them, digging deeper into the drawer, searching for it.

Eli was somehow behind her. She sensed him between her shoulder blades. She froze. She didn't want to turn around because she'd be far too close for comfort to his bulk.

'Are you looking for this?' he said. His arm appeared, curving around in front of her, the bottle opener gripped in his brawny hand, directly in front of her face. It was one of those gadgets with a lid opener as well as a corkscrew, and the corkscrew was extended, ready for action. The thought flashed that it would only take a couple of seconds for him to injure her with this.

'Where was that?' she asked, staying absolutely still.

'On the counter, right beside the wine.'

She could have sworn it hadn't been there a few seconds ago. 'Strange I didn't see it.'

'I don't think you're quite yourself,' he said. 'I'm glad I'm here to keep an eye on you.'

She sensed him stepping away from her and she turned around. 'I don't think any of us are quite ourselves,' she said, looking at him from under her lashes.

'Oh?'

She noticed the soft glitter in his eyes as he stared at her. There was something hypnotic in them, as though he could see right through to her thoughts, and she willed her mind to go blank, finding it hard to break the connection. She waved a hand dismissively. 'With the snow,' she said. 'The way it's impacting on everything, it suspends normal life.'

'But regardless of the snow, you must feel like that already,' he said, picking up the beer and flipping off the lid in a quick, easy movement. 'In a kind of suspension.' He took a long slug, his eyes not leaving hers. 'With Sam gone, I mean.'

She shrugged. 'Well, of course I am – surely that's obvious?'

'You were with him during his last year,' he said. 'I know he was very happy, although I never thought he'd leave New York. I can't believe he won't be around when I head back. There's so much I don't know about his life in Ireland.'

'Like what?'

'How did he find it in general? What did you guys get up to in your spare time? Your wedding day – was it fantastic?'

'You ask a lot of questions,' Izzie said. She wished she was still downstairs, sitting in the comfort of Florence's apartment, in the circle that included the dear, ingenuous Noah and empathetic Tom and Florence herself, putting on a good face and striving to keep everyone happy. She realised with a sense of shock that it was the first time since Sam had died that she would have opted voluntarily to be in the company of other people and that in the moments before Eli had reappeared she had felt safe, even though she'd spoken to Tom with an honesty that had surprised her. She went across and switched on the television, anything to add some distraction to the evening and dilute the presence of this man in her apartment. There was yet another Christmas movie on, and she purposely increased the volume.

Eli sat on the sofa, his legs stretched out in front of him, his arm slung along the back.

Izzie sat as far away from him as possible. 'We were beyond happy,' she said. 'He loved it here. That sums it up.'

'I can't help wanting to know more about him,' Eli persisted. 'Like, did it suit him to work remotely instead of going into the office? Did he ever talk to you about the projects he was involved with?'

'No,' she said, her gut reaction telling her that, in front of Eli, the less she knew, the better.

'Strange. You'd expect, if he was working from home, that he would have mentioned his job from time to time.'

'Sometimes he worked in the evenings to match the New York clock. But once he closed the laptop, that was it. There was a clear division between his working life and our life together.'

'But you must have had some idea of what his job entailed?'

'Very little,' Izzie said, as nonchalantly as possible.

He gave her a lopsided smile. 'I think we were fated to meet like this.'

'Fated? I don't believe in fate.'

'Don't you think you were fated to meet Sam when you did?'

She ignored his question.

'Sam would have liked that we met. I guess we were the people he was closest to. Wouldn't you agree?'

'I can't agree or disagree. I don't know how close you actually were to Sam.'

'Very close,' he said. He watched her appraisingly for a while before he continued. 'I don't suppose …'

She waited, not attempting to fill the pause.

'You told me you knew nothing about his work,' Eli said.

'That's right,' she said blandly.

'Okay, but is there any chance you might have remembered his passwords?'

Beneath the layers of booze-induced cotton wool in her brain, an alarm sounded. 'I can't remember something I didn't know in the first place.'

'I'm surprised. If you were all that close I thought you'd know. I thought you'd know everything about him.'

She shook her head.

'Had Sam any other devices that he saved his work on?'

'Devices?' She feigned ignorance.

'Yeah, memory sticks, external hard drives, CDs, whatever.'

'I never actually watched him at work,' she said, deliberately sounding vague. 'I gave him space to get on with it.'

'You must have come across something after he … after he passed on?'

Her head was light and she was glad she was sitting down. From somewhere she summoned the energy to reply. 'I don't know because I haven't gone through all of his stuff yet.'

He gave her a long, measured look before his face softened a fraction. 'Of course, and here I am, stomping my big feet over everything.'

'I don't understand why you're interested in his laptop and stuff.'

'I need to send some emails.'

'And you need Sam's laptop for that?' She couldn't help it. She was tired and out of sorts. Too tired to prevent her eyes from darting to where he'd placed his backpack, within his easy reach.

He intercepted her glance and his face tightened. 'Yes, as it happens I need to access Sam's laptop.'

'For what, Eli? What's the real reason?'

'I was hoping not to tell you,' he said. 'I was hoping to spare you this.'

'Spare me what?'

He leaned forward, as though he was about to impart something confidential. 'The thing is, I'm taking over Sam's position in Stanley Trust.'

'His *job*?'

'I didn't want to mention it in case it bothers you that I'm stepping into his shoes. That I'm replacing him. He'll be a hard act to follow, but the company contacted me about three weeks ago. Sam was finalising a program as part of their new systems, but it needs further adjustment. Having worked with him for years on those particular systems, they knew I'd be the perfect man for the role. It suited me because I'd already been considering putting a stop to my adventures and becoming a more useful member of society. My aunts won't live forever and it seemed like the right time to come home.'

'Yes, but …' she tried to grasp what he was saying, 'surely the work will wait until you get to New York?' *And what about the laptop hidden in your backpack*, she wanted to say but couldn't bring herself to voice. She sensed he'd be furious with her for going through his things and catching him out in the lie.

'That's the problem. I should have been there by now only for the travel disruption, and the program needs further refinement before the new systems go live at the end of the year. If I had access to Sam's notes and stuff it would make my job a helluva lot easier. I've lost two or three days as it is. You mightn't know much about his work but I'm sure you appreciate how intricate and pressurised these programs can be, how the time frames can be critical. It would be a fantastic advantage for me if I could get started on some work while I'm stranded here.'

'I'm sure it would,' Izzie said. 'I'm sorry I can't help.'

'He must have had stuff saved elsewhere,' Eli said. 'I know the way he operated. He wrote down passwords, heavily disguised. He had back-up plans for everything. His work was so important that he would go beyond even tight security to make sure there was a fail-safe factor somewhere. All of us in Stanley Trust had to ensure we had back-up data stored externally but safely. So he would have had stuff saved on other devices, like an external hard drive or a memory stick.'

'If I had something like that, which I don't, what use would it be if you can't access his laptop?'

'I might be able to access the information on another device if I plugged it into your laptop. As an old friend of Sam's, I'm sure you'd oblige.'

Izzie shrugged. 'I don't know of any devices Sam might have had for work, so I can't help you with that either,' she said, speaking as casually as she could, praying the deliberate lie wouldn't show on her face.

'You can't help me with anything, can you?' He gave her a wintry smile. 'Forget it,' he said, getting to his feet. 'It's my problem, not ours. Let me fix you another drink,' he said, picking up her glass and going over to the kitchen area before she had a chance to protest.

'Lots of tonic,' she said.

'Lots of tonic coming up,' he said.

Izzie stayed in the living area, tidying around, trying to ignore him making himself useful in her kitchen, doing things Sam should have been around to do. Her eyes were closing before she got to bed. Eli offered to switch off and unplug everything. Izzie was barely able to clean her teeth let alone remove her make-up. It seemed far too much of an effort. Her arms and hands were too heavy and her face seemed to be coming and going in the mirror as she swayed against the basin in the en suite. She opened the wall press and made a grab for the bottle of mouthwash that was jumping in front of her. It fell against the basin, bounced off the bin and skittered across the floor.

'Izzie?'

She froze. Eli's voice. He seemed to be right outside the door. In her bedroom.

'What is it?' she asked

'Are you okay?'

'Of course I'm okay,' she said crossly.

'I thought I heard something falling.'

She opened the door and stuck her head out. Eli was at her bedroom door, leaning in. Had she forgotten to lock it? She couldn't remember. Did she *need* to lock it? Surely not.

'I'm fine,' she said crossly, knowing she was anything but fine.

'Okay, sorry, just making sure.' He put up his hands, backed out onto the hallway and closed her bedroom door quietly behind him.

Izzie staggered across the room, turning the key in the lock as quietly as possible. She undressed, pulled on a pair of fleecy PJs, crawled into bed, her energy at such low ebb that it took monumental effort to drag the duvet up around her. She fell into a deep, unguarded sleep, the defenceless place where her dreams softened with memories of Sam.

CHAPTER THIRTY-FIVE

Wicklow,
nine months ago

I fix everything about our wedding day in the corner of my heart. No matter what happens or what the future might bring, nothing will ever take away this day. It shimmers inside me as pure as a beach pebble or a perfect seashell right from the moment I walk up the short aisle of the country church on my mother's arm, coloured sunshine frizzing in the reflection of the stained-glass window on the ivory wall, and the look on your face when you turn around and see me will stay with me forever.

The room where we hold the reception for close family and friends is conservatory style, decorated in white and silver, wall-to-wall windows on one side looking out onto a beautiful garden, and beyond that the breath-taking glory of a Wicklow valley, trees fuzzed with the arrival of spring.

I have a quiet moment with Elena, your mother. She hugs me and wipes away a discreet tear. 'Thank you for loving my son and making him so happy. You are very brave.'

'So is Sam,' I say quietly. 'I couldn't not love him.'

'Izzie, you are an inspiration. You look so beautiful today.'

'Being married to Sam makes me feel beautiful.'

Very few of the small gathering in the country church realised the full import of the wedding vows we exchanged: 'For better or worse … in sickness and in health.' Right now, together we are unbreakable. You smile, you laugh and you toast me as your new wife as if you haven't a care in the world. As the sun is setting, and dusk spreads a violet glow across the valleys and hills outside, you sweep me out onto the floor for our first dance under a ceiling glittering with hundreds of tiny lights, like a galaxy full of stars.

'Happy now, Mrs Mallon?' you ask, as we slowly move around the floor to the sound of John Lennon's 'Oh My Love', face to face, foreheads barely tipping.

'Not happy,' I say.

You make a mock sad face. 'You reckon you're not cut out for married life after all?'

'Nah, I just wanted a trip up the aisle, the chance to wear a wedding dress and get a ring on my finger. Oh, and see you in your best clobber.'

'Did I pass the test?'

I tilt my head sideways. 'I guess you scrub up well.'

'That'll do for now.'

I press closer to you. 'I feel blessed,' I murmur. 'I will always remember this day.'

For a nano-second, a shadow passes across your face. You too, like me, are thinking of what lies ahead – a short honeymoon in Donegal, our new home in Henrietta Square, but after that the unknown. I raise my arms and wind them around your neck, clasping my hands behind your head. Someone has opened a door out to the garden where pathways are edged with the soft glow of candles in lanterns, and you dance me out there.

'I'll always remember how good it feels to love and be loved,' I say.

'That's what you have to keep on doing,' you say. 'Right to the end of your life. It's the only thing that matters. Promise me?'

'I promise.'

'Cross your heart?'

'Cross my heart.'

Then you link your fingers with mine and, raising our joined hands into the air, you twirl me around. I see the flash of a camera and we are freeze-framed like that for the rest of time, silhouetted against the softly glowing lanterns and the purple countryside beyond.

SATURDAY, 23 DECEMBER

CHAPTER THIRTY-SIX

Sam was there when she awoke, stirring her senses. Fragments of her dream came back to her. She heard music playing and relaxed immediately. The songs he sometimes played on repeat washed over her, soothing her tired mind, easing out any remaining knots in her limbs, relaxing every pore in her skin so that she drifted on a soft cloud and every part of her body lay suspended in the bed as though she was free and weightless. He could have been right beside her because she could sense him, feel the heat of him in bed, taste him on her lips and inhale the sleepy scent of him.

Elizabeth ...

She strained to move into his embrace, to burrow her body

into his, have his limbs come around her and wrap her up in a place of love and safekeeping.

When she stretched out her hand, his side of the bed was empty. Reality ripped through her, tearing her apart like shrapnel from a bomb. Her whole body tensed in shock and her eyes flew open. She was in her bedroom in Henrietta Square. The worst had happened and Sam was gone forever. She bit back a scream.

Yet the music continued. Coming at her in waves, flowing through her veins and pinpricking every inch of her scalp. Almost too weak and exhausted to move, she forced herself to get out of bed, breathing deeply to push back her dizziness, pulling on her dressing gown and pushing her feet into her slippers. She padded over to her bedroom door on legs that were like water but was unable to open it. It was locked. Why had she locked it? She couldn't remember. She turned the key and was out onto the corridor, moving across to the living room, catching the drift of a smell that nauseated her. She stretched out her hand, the door swung open and the music increased in volume.

John Lennon's 'Happy Xmas'. Sam's favourite Christmas song that he'd played constantly when she'd visited New York just before Christmas last year. Pain sliced across her stomach. The cadences swirled around her, and her throat closed over. A man was standing over by the record player, a record sleeve in his hand. Eli. She remembered now. She found the scent of his aftershave repugnant and she had locked her bedroom door because of something to do with him. Hadn't she?

'What are you doing?' Her voice was a whisper.

'Good morning,' Eli said. 'Isn't this a lovely way to wake

up?' He looked across at her and smiled happily as though he was doing her a huge favour. He was dressed head to toe in a black tracksuit and he made her think of a large, powerful panther.

Izzie went over to the turntable and lifted the arm. The music stopped instantly. 'What were you thinking of?' she repeated.

'What does it look like?'

'You're playing his song—' She couldn't continue, her throat was closing over and her legs were too weak. She groped for the nearest armchair and sank into it heavily.

'I was looking through Sam's vinyl,' Eli said. 'He had quite a collection. Did he bring it over from New York?'

A memory sprang up of the two of them painstakingly packing his precious albums between layers of bubble wrap, prior to shipping to Ireland. One of the last afternoons they'd spent in his New York apartment. It had been almost stripped bare by then.

'But—' *you had no right …* She tried to voice an objection but she could hardly speak. She was still absorbing the shock of being plunged right back in time, especially on top of her vivid dream, traces of which were still clinging to the corners of her mind.

Eli said, 'I'm a bit tired of all those mawkish Christmas songs. This is a decent one. I miss Sam too, you know. I thought playing his albums would be a nice way to honour him at this time of the year.'

'Are you crazy?' she said unthinkingly, her voice thick.

It was the wrong thing to say. 'Who's calling me crazy?' His eyes bored into hers. The cords in his thick neck bulged. She was unable to look away. Then his face changed. 'Hey, we're friends, chill, relax, whatever you say in this part of the world. Let me make you some coffee.' He went across to the kitchen area and she heard the clink of him taking mugs out of the press. The drapes were still drawn but light seeped in to the room. She sank back into the armchair, weak and helpless, as though her veins and limbs consisted of nothing but water, like they'd been in those first few days after Sam.

'What time is it?' she asked. She hadn't thought to check the time on her phone before she'd got out of bed. Come to think of it, she couldn't remember the last time she'd seen her phone or recall where she'd left it. She'd switched it off and put it away before Eli had arrived, then she'd taken it out to check the latest news and transport information – and then what?

'It's just gone ten o'clock,' Eli said, putting a cup of coffee on the low table in front of her.

'I can't think of where my phone is,' she said. 'Have you seen it?'

'Don't worry about that now. Have your coffee, and as soon as you're up to it, I'll fix some breakfast.'

'There's no need,' she began to object. She didn't want him fussing over her. She didn't want anyone fussing over her – she just wanted to be left alone. How had she allowed this to happen? How had she allowed this guy into her space?

'Yes, there is,' he said. 'I can see I gave you a shock, playing Sam's albums. I didn't mean to upset you like that.'

'You must have had some idea,' she said. 'You've lost loved ones yourself. You must know how it felt – or do you?' She tossed the question out to him.

'What makes you say that? Are you doubting me?'

She sipped her coffee. It tasted slightly off. Last night's alcohol was still in her mouth, and her head was thick. 'I don't get you, Eli. You're not what I expected.'

'In what way?'

'I just – I dunno. You're different to what I would have thought.'

In answer to that he opened the drapes. The room flooded with brightness and she blinked. The sky wasn't as dark as it had been on previous days and the snow in the park reflected light into the room.

'How different?' He wasn't laughing her away. He wasn't apologising for any shortcoming. He looked at her steadily, annoyance in his eyes, like she was a nuisance to him. She felt vulnerable and at a complete disadvantage in her dressing gown and slippers. She tried to get her head around appropriate words, tried to formulate them with her tongue.

'Sam was funny, and he made me feel wonderful, but above all, he was a kind and gentle person. I find you unkind at times and I'm surprised that Sam would have seen you as his best mate.'

'Unkind? Oh dear, I don't have the likeability factor. How annoying. What can I do to fix this, I wonder?'

She didn't like the look of the challenge in his eyes. 'Forget it,' she said lamely, swirling the dregs of the coffee around in her cup.

'How can I forget that? You don't like me. I feel I've failed a test of some sort.'

'Did you say you were getting a flight out today?' she asked, changing the subject.

'That all depends.'

'On what?'

'On you, actually.'

'*Me?*'

'I have work to do,' he said. 'It's critical. I need access to Sam's files but you're not helping me.'

'I told you I don't know his password. If it's really that important to you I'm sure you can figure out a way. Get on to the firm, I'm sure they can help.'

'Maybe I don't want to get on to the firm.'

She didn't like the way he was looking at her, as if he was assessing her.

'Why not?' she asked.

'Then again, maybe I shouldn't be protecting you, hiding the truth from you.'

'What truth?'

'I bet you don't know. I bet Sam never told you.'

'Told me what?'

He took a long, slow breath before he started, watching her reaction carefully as he spoke. 'I hate to say this, to ruin your perfect memory of Sam, but he'd screwed up big time. He'd made a big fuck-up with the security of a program for the Share a Wish Foundation and I'm trying to fix it.'

'I find that hard to believe.'

'I'm sure you do. Naturally he didn't tell you. Knowing Sam, he wouldn't have wanted to disappoint you or let himself down in your eyes. So, you see, you should be helping me because I'm trying to salvage things before it gets any worse. The new program has to go live on New Year's Eve and I need to apply some fixes before then. If you helped me you'd be helping Sam, or rather his legacy with Stanley Trust and the foundation. I'm sure you don't want to see it tarnished.'

'What you're saying makes no sense to me at all,' Izzie said.

'I'm trying to fix his work and restore his reputation. Is that clear enough? I don't want to see him left with a black mark striking out all the good in his career. Do you? I bet he worked hard. He doesn't deserve this. It matters to me, and as soon as I have the access to the information and get the glitch fixed, I'll be on my way to the airport and leave you in peace. But not until then.'

His tone of voice sounded more like a threat. There was no spark of friendship in his eyes, no trace of anything except animosity. Nothing he'd said about Sam added up. He was bound to have noticed she'd been drinking steadily since he'd arrived. Maybe he'd thought she'd be easily swayed and he'd get away with this ridiculous story. Right enough, she was hardly able to move. Her limbs were liquid and her brain was too hazy to even figure out where she'd left her phone. She knew she'd been overdoing the booze, but this seemed worse than a normal hangover.

And this was far from a normal situation.

'Eli,' she said, 'what you're saying about Sam – I find it hard to believe. It sounds like bullshit to me. What are you really looking for and why?'

CHAPTER THIRTY-SEVEN

He didn't answer her at first. He went across to the window and looked out, blocking the light with his big frame, his posture ramrod straight as though he was a general surveying his army on the battlefield. Then he wheeled around. 'Not much moving out there,' he said. 'But at least it's not getting any worse.'

'I asked you a question,' she said, lethargy making her slur her words. 'The least you can do is answer me.'

'Oh dear, you sound angry,' he said in a sing-song voice that chilled her. 'This won't do at all. I much preferred it when we were friends. Can we still be friends?'

'What do you want?' she asked. 'Why are you here? *Tell*

me.' She tried to breathe slowly and collect her scattered wits. She'd have to keep him talking until she gathered some strength.

He let out a long sigh. He clasped his hands behind his head and paced the floor for several seconds, before stopping and looking at her sorrowfully. 'Bullshit? That's not nice of you, is it? I was really hoping it wouldn't come to this. I was really hoping I could just get what I wanted and disappear out of your life before you were any the wiser. It would have been easier all around.'

She tried to ignore the alarm bell shrieking in her head. The sooner she got out of here the better, but she needed to think. Would she manage to get down the stairs and shout for Tom before Eli caught up with her? A slim chance but worth taking. Her heart sank when she realised that the apartment door was locked. She'd secured it last night, thinking in a funny way that she'd been locking herself in with him. Where had she left that key? There was also a spare key somewhere. *Think*, Izzie.

'I haven't a clue what you're talking about,' she said, playing for time.

'I hoped you'd never find out. Honestly I did. I hoped it could all be sorted – the less people have to know, the less complicated it is. And everything was going great, the snow was perfect – beautiful, even – but you wouldn't play ball, even though I said Sam's reputation was at stake.' He tilted his head to one side and looked at her quizzically. 'I expected you to be different.'

'In what way?'

'I thought you'd want to help me, but you don't, do you? You're being stubborn.'

'What do you mean "the snow was perfect"?' she asked, ignoring his remarks about her stubbornness.

'Perfect for my cover. You hardly think I was genuinely snowbound,' he said.

'Weren't you?' She thought back to when he'd first arrived on her doorstep and then last night, when he'd reappeared, of his talk of flights and airport chaos and sleeping on the floor. Of the chat with Florence and Tom about airport food and taxis.

'The snow was a big help,' he said, sounding as if he was boasting. 'It seemed like fate. I had a few different calling cards ready to impose on your hospitality, but I didn't have to use them. Being snowbound gave me a cast-iron excuse for turning up here. And you had little or no good reason to turn me away without being totally heartless, which I knew you weren't.'

'So this was planned,' she said. 'You weren't really stranded.'

'Not at all,' he said. 'I'd already been in Dublin for over a week, but I went out to the airport to soak up the vibes before I called here, the better to appear authentic.'

'Then you haven't come from deepest Africa.'

'Clever girl.'

'You came here for something.'

'I did. A little matter of saving my skin.'

She finished the last of her coffee. She didn't want to know what he meant by saving his skin. 'Supposing I hadn't been here when you called?' she said. 'I could have been going away for Christmas. That would have spoiled your plan.'

'It would have altered it, that's all. I've been planning this little operation for a while, ready to move at the most opportune moment. When I figured out you intended hibernating here to avoid all festivities ...' He stared at her, as if challenging her to question how he'd known that. She stared back defiantly, a twist of fear uncurling in her stomach. Then, as if the fright had somehow sharpened her sensibilities, she remembered the spare key. It was under the carpet runner in the hall, kept there in case she ever needed to get out of the apartment in a hurry.

'It was perfect for my needs, like the snow,' he went on. 'Only now you've gone and spoiled it all by not helping me. Plan A, I would have got what I came for without you being any the wiser. It's not working, though, is it? I'm going to have to move to Plan B.'

'I need the bathroom,' she said, getting to her feet.

He seemed unconcerned. 'Go ahead,' he said, leaning back against the table, his arms crossed.

Her legs were unsteady and everything swam around her as she left the room and shuffled out into the hallway. Nausea soured her stomach as she bent down and lifted the carpet runner.

There was no sign of the spare key.

She heard a noise behind her and looked around. Eli was standing there, waggling something in his fingers. 'Is this what you're looking for?' He held up a key.

It took an effort, but she straightened up, biting on her lip against another wave of nausea.

'Give me that key,' Izzie said.

'Nope.' He pocketed it.

'I want you to get out of my apartment,' she said as forcefully as she could.

'Nope to that as well.'

She tried to scream when he lifted her easily, but her voice came out hoarse and squeaky. He pinioned her against him as he propelled her back into the living room. She tried ineffectually to pummel his shoulders and chest. He threw her on the sofa. Bending down, he reached out and extended his arms either side of her, balancing himself by holding onto the back of the sofa so that his body was looming over hers. He lowered his face until it was level with hers, his eyes bulging, and a stab of fear flashed through her.

'You're making this hard on yourself,' he said.

She tried to move, to kick out at him, to knock away his hefty arms, but by now her whole body was lethargic, every limb liquefied. Once more she tried to yell but her voice came out hoarse and raw and all she could manage was a thin, baby-like cry. This was more than the after-effects of too much alcohol. It reminded her of the time she'd had her appendix out and the way the anaesthetic had floored her for several hours afterwards, rendering her almost immobile.

'What have you done?' she asked, fighting back panic. 'What have you given me? What was in that coffee?'

He grinned. 'Your coffee this morning, your gin and tonic last night and a small trace in your wine the first night I was here.'

'You didn't.'

'It's not permanent,' he said. 'Enough to keep you under control but conscious for now. Bitch.'

CHAPTER THIRTY-EIGHT

'I need to get to the shops,' Kian said. 'I'm starving. I could murder a decent fry-up – all that screwing has made me hungry.' He winked at her. 'But there's nothing here in the way of food. We're nearly out of milk and we need more booze as well.'

Sitting at the table in a borrowed navy bathrobe, Gemma cradled her coffee mug in her hands and smiled at him over the rim. 'I need to go shopping myself.'

They'd spent most of yesterday in bed. They hadn't even bothered with lunch in the first flush of sex. Later, Kian had got dressed and gone out for a takeaway, bringing back cartons of Thai food along with beer and wine. That morning, after he'd woken her up in the nicest way possible, he'd suggested she stay one more night. She'd readily agreed and she'd texted home again to say she was staying in town with a friend from the office.

Her mum had replied to say she was delighted Gemma was making new friends and she was in the best place given the weather, but she was to make sure she was home for Christmas Eve. Gemma had experienced a sliver of remorse when she read it. What her mum considered to be making new friends differed greatly from what Gemma was actually doing.

'We're not too far from Mary Street,' Kian said. 'I'll head to M&S.'

'I might run down to Penneys,' she said. At the least, she needed fresh underwear and some toiletries. Even her Christmas jumper was a bit stale, although she'd hardly worn any clothes since she'd arrived in the apartment.

'Run? In that snow?' he teased, reaching across the table and lacing his fingers in hers.

'Yeah, well, I feel a bit powerful at the moment.'

'Good. So do I. Let's be powerful together,' he said, standing up and coming around to her. He lifted her to her feet and stood behind her, hitching up her bathrobe and sliding down her pants; she undid the belt, let the bathrobe fall open and turned her face sideways to him so he could kiss her mouth.

Gemma closed her eyes. She guessed Kian was about thirty years of age, and he was someone who knew exactly what he was doing with his hands and mouth, a change from the student fumblings she'd mostly experienced up to now. He knew just where to touch and how to bring her right to fever pitch and make her wait there for long, excruciatingly delicious moments, before she exploded with pleasure. He also had enough confidence to show her exactly how to please him. He'd suggested things they could do to each other that had never crossed her mind and her heart glowed at the thoughts of another night with him and the fact that he'd chosen her to bring back to the apartment, when he could have had his pick of some of the other girls in the office.

She liked to think that the aftermath of her first ever office Christmas party had turned to lessons in love, with Kian, in their own special love nest. She was in no hurry to go home. It was an hour later before they headed out into the raw, wintry day and up towards a city centre thronged with crowds and buzzy with Christmas cheer. They did a food shop in the M&S supermarket, and then Gemma went across to Penneys.

'I'll follow you back,' she said to Kian, not wanting him to see what she was buying, as well as needing to have some breathing space before round two.

'Make sure you do come back,' he said, his eyes gleaming.

'Oh, don't worry, I will.'

He took out his phone. 'What's your number? I'll send you a text so you have my number in case you get lost.'

She gave him her number. 'I won't get lost and I'll be back,' she promised him. He'd bought microwave dinners and wine, along with strawberries and whipped cream. Her legs had almost buckled when he'd put them into the shopping basket, leaned in close to her and whispered what he planned to do to her with them. Taking his time. As they'd edged along the queue, he'd said she was to wear her Kris Kindle mask and he might try out the handcuffs. If she was good, he'd said, he might even let her use the whip. She'd tried not to giggle too much, hoping he hadn't been overheard.

In Penneys, she picked up some toiletries, make-up wipes, fresh underwear that was far more frothy than the kind she usually wore and a pink velvet Christmassy top. When she was paying for her purchases, she put her hand into the spare compartment of her tote bag, where she kept an emergency fifty euro note, and found Izzie's small sequinned purse. It had been tucked down there since Thursday lunchtime.

She was supposed to have texted Izzie on Thursday. Now it was Saturday. *Damn.* She knew how much that purse meant to her. How could she have been so careless? After the way she'd looked after the bereaved Izzie as you might a defenceless baby, she'd been thoughtless with something that was important to her. Caught up in her sex-fest with Kian, she'd completely forgotten about Izzie, who was probably lonely as hell and crying into her pillow, sad that it was her first Christmas without Sam.

Gemma paid for her purchases and came away from the counter completely flustered. She went into a nearby coffee shop and used the bathroom to fix her face. Then she sat down at a table with a large cappuccino, took out her phone, and fired off a text.

CHAPTER THIRTY-NINE

'You have an interesting text in from Gemma,' Eli said. He was sitting at the table, feet stretched out, scrolling through his phone. He looked and sounded so casual about it they could have been a couple relaxing on a Saturday morning, with Izzie lounging on the sofa. Except she could scarcely move, her legs and arms were like blobs of jelly and she knew if she tried to stand up she'd fall back down again as quickly.

'Give me my phone,' she said.

'Ah, but it's not your phone, it's mine.'

'It can't be.'

He smiled and held up the phone, waggling it from side to side. It wasn't hers. Something cold slithered through her veins. How was he able to see her texts?

'Did you know that phones can do great things nowadays?' he said conversationally. 'It's amazing the information you can find out about people, like tracking their movements, seeing their texts and emails. If you can get your hands on one for a while, you can make it supply lots of information.'

The fact that he was looking at his phone, rather than her own, brought it scarily home to her. She'd mislaid her phone in a pub about a month ago. She thought she'd been careless and had left it behind.

'You stole my phone?'

'I borrowed it to improve the functionality. I happened to be in the same pub as you and I managed to lift it out of your pocket as you squeezed through the crowds. It was careless of you to leave it in your jacket. The following day I went back and handed it in to the barman, telling him I'd found it wedged into the banquette.'

'But that was a month ago …' She faltered, trying to get her head around facts that were too alarming to grasp fully.

'Yeah, I came over to check you out and do a kind of surveillance. You never noticed me hanging around. Clever, huh?'

Her blood turned to water at the thoughts of him brushing up close enough to rob her phone as well as stalking her. Whatever he wanted, the guy meant business. And whatever he wanted, it was serious stuff.

'So you've been checking on me for weeks,' she said, hoping he wouldn't realise her stomach was contracting with fear.

'I guess I have. Then I just had to figure out an easy way to get in here.'

'Weren't you afraid I'd recognise you from the pub? That would have blown your story.'

'Nah, I had a beard and a different hairstyle then.'

She strove for calm. 'Didn't you see my emails telling my family I'm off to a yoga retreat?'

'I did, and I saw the one you sent your brother.' His soft voice and indulgent smile was alarming. 'I knew then I was in. Even if I'd missed something, I guessed I'd catch you here either side of those dates. Once I was in a few days before midnight on New Year's Eve, I figured I'd have enough time.'

Silence fell. He continued to look at her, sizing her up with the same calculated interest a cat might grant a mouse that's caught in his grip, and her chest tightened.

'I'd let you read Gemma's text for yourself,' he said. 'But I'm afraid you might try something silly.'

'Where's my phone now?'

'I'm looking after it. Listen closely while I read out the text: "Izzie, hope I'm not intruding on your Christmas, letting u know I have your special purse & contents left behind on your desk. I know it's important so I'll keep it safe till we're back in the office but if you need it before then, I can put it in an envelope and pop it into your letter box." She signs off with some kisses and hearts,' he said. 'Aww, isn't that nice, Izzie? I wonder what's in this purse. This special purse that's so important. Did you leave it deliberately in the office? You already have a purse with your credit cards and cash, I've seen it, so I wonder what contents Gemma is talking about.'

'It's nothing,' Izzie said hastily. 'It's not that important. And it's not what you think it is. I don't need it until after Christmas.'

'I don't agree. You look agitated,' Eli said. He stared at her intently and she couldn't help a blush from creeping into her face.

'Hmm,' he said. 'Agitation and alarm. I think you don't want me to find out what's in your purse. I wonder why.'

'It's nothing of any relevance to you.'

'I don't believe you and there's only one way to find out.'

Izzie could do nothing but look on helplessly as Eli plucked her phone out of a pocket in his backpack, entered a PIN number and scrolled through to her texts. She had no way of preventing him from replying to Gemma.

'What can I say that sounds like Izzie-speak?' he said. 'How best do I get her to deliver the goods?' He smiled thinly at her before tapping the screen and sending a message back to Gemma.

Izzie hoped that Gemma was too busy, too snowbound, too far away to do anything but hold onto the purse until the new year. But naturally, the dedicated Gemma wanted to help Izzie as much as possible.

'Ah,' Eli said, 'Gemma has replied. "Will do, I know how important this is to you. I'm in the city centre but should be with you in 30 mins. What's the house number again?"

'I can tell her that myself,' he said, tapping the screen swiftly. He sent another couple of texts to Gemma before putting Izzie's phone on the table. 'Now we just have to wait until the lovely Gemma arrives to see what she's going to bring to the party.'

'I told you, it's nothing you'd be interested in, and certainly not what you seem to be after.' Izzie tried to think clearly, but the stress of it all was sending her brain skittering in a million different directions. Surely there was a way of alerting Gemma? How could she let the young woman know that all was not as it seemed?

'But you don't know exactly what I'm after – or do you?' he

said, looking at her with such a chill in his eyes that it scared her.

She mustered a false bravado. 'Who cares? I don't.'

'Is that all you have to say?'

She shrugged. 'I don't see that it has anything to do with me,' she went on. What did anything matter anymore? The worst had happened and Sam's life was over. Who cared what this impostor wanted? She knew by now he couldn't be who he said he was.

'That's not very helpful,' he said. 'That attitude won't do at all. After all the effort I went to to set this up. I hope Gemma is more helpful than you've been. Otherwise you're in trouble.'

'Who are you?' she asked, not caring if the question antagonised him further. 'I know you're not Eli Sanders.'

He narrowed his eyes until they were slits and twisted his face until it was a grimace. 'Does this look more like him?' he asked, before dissolving into a fit of giggles.

Right then, Izzie would have given anything to be out in the Italian café having coffee and pastries with Florence, Tom and Noah. She was acutely aware that the house was unoccupied at the moment and she was alone on the top floor with this man, this impostor.

CHAPTER FORTY

After she fired off the text to Izzie, Gemma sipped her coffee and scrolled through her phone. She had a number of messages waiting to be read, texts she'd barely looked at – she hadn't wanted to waste any time on her phone while she'd been making the most of everything with Kian.

There were texts from both Katy and Rachel, wondering if she'd survived the party and got home all right. Katy had texted her twice, sounding more worried the second time. She had a sudden memory of their concerned faces swimming in front of her in the ladies' bathroom of the pub on Thursday evening and, as if from far away, she heard herself telling them – had she really said this? – to get lost, she was a big girl now, she wanted to make the most of her first office party, and what was *wrong* with them? Shrugging off an arm – Katy's arm? – saying she was well able to take care of herself, that growing up in St Finnian's Gardens had prepared her for life.

Something burnt through her stomach. Embarrassment, guilt and regret. *Jesus.* She'd made a show of herself. After all her conquer-the-world plans, never mind her pride in the job, she'd fallen at the first fence. How was she going to face them in the office? How would she make up for her drunken behaviour? It was beyond mortifying. She'd let herself down, big time.

Only she was in a public place, Gemma would have sunk her head into her hands and howled. She sat there, her mind whirling, then she plucked up the courage to text them both, thanking them for their kind concern, telling them she'd had a lovely night, although maybe one or two glasses too many, and wishing them all the best for Christmas.

She had just sent the texts when she had a reply from Izzie: 'Thanks, Gemma. I need that purse. Will you be anywhere near the city centre in the next day or two? It would be great if you could bring it over.'

Prompted by her guilty conscience and attempting to somewhat assuage it, she replied immediately, offering to bring the purse to Izzie, asking for her house number, remembering just in time to keep up the charade of Izzie being on a yoga retreat.

'You didn't manage to get away? No surprises in this weather!' Gemma texted back.

'Change of plan. I'd really appreciate it if you could deliver the purse. I'll owe you one.'

Gemma thought swiftly. Izzie lived about a twenty-minute

walk from here. After she delivered the purse, it would be another thirty-minute walk back to Smithfield, where Kian was waiting. After spending so much time in bed, the brisk air and exercise would clear her head. And doing a kindness for Izzie could atone in some way for her rudeness to Katy and Rachel. Besides, there was no harm in letting Kian wait for her. She tried not to think of how easily she'd fallen into his arms. How drunk she'd been. How willing to go along with his suggestions.

She replied: 'C u soon.' She rang Kian, getting through to his voicemail, leaving a message to say she'd been asked by a friend to do a favour for them and she'd be back to Smithfield later in the afternoon.

Then she tucked her scarf tighter around her neck, pulled on her gloves and set out for Henrietta Square.

CHAPTER FORTY-ONE

Noah had never been in the Italian with his dad *and* Florence. Florence said she knew just what he'd like and she ordered him a hot chocolate drink with chocolate sprinkles and mini marshmallows. He wished she was his granny. She'd stopped him being nervous of his Irish homework, and there was always a lovely smell of baking in her apartment.

He had too many wishes: that was the problem. He was being greedy, expecting too much. He'd forgo all his wishes, including his Santa present of Lego *Star Wars* BB-8, if Izzie and his dad became friends. Things had been great the other night until Weirdo had come back. After that, his father and Izzie hadn't said a single word to each other. His dad had barely looked at Izzie when she said goodbye before going upstairs with Weirdo, and Noah's heart had sunk right down to his feet.

'We're going to have to give Cathy's mother a miss,' his dad said. 'I was talking to her this morning – the motorway is passable, but her village is cut off at the moment so she said to stay put and stay safe. She doesn't want us travelling in those circumstances.'

'I hope she's okay herself,' Florence said.

'She's fine. After Cathy died she moved to Kilkenny to be nearer her son and his family – they live close by, and they're always prepared for bad weather in the winter so she has company and they're not short of anything. The other thing is, Noah, I know you'll be disappointed, but we won't get down to west Cork. Grandad also told us to stay put for the next few days.'

'I bet Grandad is disappointed as well,' he said.

'Will he be on his own?' Florence asked.

'I dunno,' his dad said. 'He was a bit vague about his plans. He's in Cork city at the moment, visiting friends, so at least he has the option of staying on there instead of attempting to make it home. So I'll be going turkey shopping, if I can get my hands on one at this late stage.'

'Have you seen Izzie this morning?' Florence asked.

'No, but I don't think she has any need to leave the apartment,' his dad said. 'That guy Eli did some shopping for her, didn't he? She's probably okay for everything.'

His voice sounded funny, kind of light and careful, like when he wanted to talk to Noah about something he was unhappy with. He wondered if his dad was unhappy with something Izzie had said or done, and the chocolate in his stomach turned sour. Florence's face didn't show if she noticed anything about his dad's tone of voice.

'I hope she comes to my concert tonight,' Noah said.

'It's hard to know if she'll feel like it,' Florence said kindly. 'Could I come?'

'Certainly,' his dad said.

'I'd love to hear Noah singing,' Florence said, smiling at him. 'If Izzie doesn't make it, it'll be because she has a visitor, not because she doesn't want to hear you sing.'

'I don't like Weir— Eli,' Noah said, risking a look at her, hoping she wouldn't break his confidence. And that she wouldn't think he was spoiling their outing. He was reassured when she winked briefly at him, unnoticed by his dad.

His dad ignored him; he was staring into his coffee.

'I dunno how he was Sam's friend,' Noah went on. 'He's not one bit like him.'

'No two people are alike,' Florence said gently, her face soft with empathy for Noah. 'And isn't it just as well? Imagine how boring it would be if everyone was the same.'

'We know how much you looked up to Sam,' his dad said. 'I don't think anyone could replace him.'

His dad sounded as though he was rightly fed up with Noah and something in his tummy rebelled. He wasn't sure how to get his message across without sounding like a spoiled child, unhappy because he wasn't getting his heart's desire.

'Yeah, I know all that,' he said. 'But with your friends, you'd have to have some things you'd share, games or football or movies. Like me with Alfie in school: we're good mates, we're on the same team, we both like the same kind of things, we talk about the same football teams and games. But I'm not friends with Ryan or Joe: we wouldn't have anything to talk about or do together. They'd never be on my team. From what Sam told me, I thought Eli would be different. I can't see him and Sam together at all, either talking, or watching a football match, or anything even …'

It was no use. He sounded like he was whining. He knew by Florence's face that she thought he had a grudge against Weirdo for turning up on Izzie's doorstop. His dad was staring into space as he slowly sipped his coffee. He didn't look like he was even listening to him, which upset Noah further.

'I'd bet he isn't even the real Eli,' Noah went on, wondering if he'd get a reaction from his dad.

'I'm sure Izzie wouldn't have let him in if she didn't think he was who he said,' Florence said.

He couldn't blame Florence. Even he knew how ridiculous he sounded. Of course Izzie would have recognised Sam's good friend. Or would she? Something Sam had told him during their many chats slowly rose to the surface.

'I don't know if Izzie even met him until now,' Noah said grumpily. 'Sam said his friend was an adventurer and he hadn't seen him for a couple of years. That meant Izzie couldn't have seen him. She only met Sam last year in New York.'

'I'd say that was all the more reason for Eli to call on Izzie,' Florence said. 'So that he could express his sympathies in person. Maybe share good memories of Sam.'

His dad made a funny noise, turning it into a cough, and grabbed a napkin. 'Excuse me. Noah, I think it's best to keep your thoughts to yourself. Eli is a guest of Izzie's at the moment and we have to respect that.'

'I wish he'd respect *me* and not pretend to know about *Star Wars* when he hasn't a clue.'

'We can't all be experts,' his dad said. 'I don't know half as much as you.'

'Weir – Eli hadn't a clue of even basic stuff, but according to Sam, he and Eli had seen some of the movies three times.'

'Yes, according to Sam,' his dad pointed out, his voice a bit gruff. 'Maybe Sam was just being friendly to you. That's the type of guy he was, all around friendly and kind.'

'I'm not stupid, Dad, I know when someone is talking down to me because I'm a kid. Sam wasn't like that. We had really cool chats about what it was like in New York when he went to one of the premieres with Eli – I mean, that must have been mega for them – but Eli didn't even remember. I think he sucks. Big time.'

His dad folded his arms tightly across his chest. 'Noah, that's quite enough.'

He knew he'd gone too far. Even the sympathy on Florence's face was hard to take.

'Sorry, Dad,' he said, staring down into the remnants of his hot chocolate. He gave it a desultory stir with his spoon.

Maybe he was doing this all wrong. Maybe he should have tried talking to Sam. Like the way his dad said that Mum would always be listening out for him, that she was a star so high in the galaxy that he couldn't see her, but she could hear him whenever he spoke to her. Supposing Sam was the same? Sam would want Izzie to be happy. Noah knew that beyond the shadow of a doubt. Maybe he should stop his selfish ideas about what *he* wanted, and ask Sam and his mum for whatever they thought was best to make Izzie happy, and his dad …

CHAPTER FORTY-TWO

The man who called himself Eli Sanders sat down on the sofa and smiled at Izzie as though she was a fractious child. 'What makes you think I'm not who I say I am?'

'You've said things that don't ring true with me.' She was tiptoeing through a minefield, knowing she couldn't go back once the words were said. 'Small things about Sam, and the kind of person you are.'

He shook his head, his smile indulgent. It was clear he had decided to humour her, rather than take offence. He had never seemed more dangerous.

'Like what?' he asked, his tone amused.

'For instance, Sam was a coffee addict – even after his evening meal. He didn't stop his caffeine intake after midday. Yet you agreed with me when I said he was the same as you in that regard.'

'Maybe I was confusing him with someone else.'

'How come, when you arrived, you had to ask Florence what floor I was on? I remember it seemed odd when she mentioned it to me, but I was in a different zone. Then when I began to figure you out, I realised Eli knew we were living on the top floor. I saw one of the emails Sam sent him, boasting about our penthouse apartment.'

'So? I could have forgotten.' He still had that grin on his face that unnerved her. 'Anything else on your mind?'

'Your story about Sam and his job is a load of crap,' Izzie said. 'Sam was meticulous about his work, especially anything to do with the foundation. If he'd been careless, he'd have been so annoyed with himself that I'd have known about it. '

'Maybe he hid it well.'

'I think you're lying. Another thing that bothered me was the way you treated Noah.'

'I told you I'm not good around kids.'

'Says the guy who was supposed to have spent six months volunteering in Zambia with Sam? Engaging with young kids who, according to Sam, were wonderful kids and all over you both? That doesn't add up.'

'Maybe I'm not good around nosy kids like Noah,' he countered.

Izzie shook her head. 'Noah's a pet. What was it really like out there, renovating schools and community centres? Go on, tell me,' she pushed. 'I bet you haven't a clue, because you were never there with Sam in the first place.'

'Hey, what's all this?' he asked, speaking lightly, as though he hadn't a care in the world. It didn't seem to bother him that she had blown his cover. 'Are you trying to catch me out on purpose?' he asked in a silky voice. 'Planting little traps for me to fall into?'

'I've no reason to plant anything – why should I do that? You set yourself up, Eli – or whoever the hell you are.'

'That's not very nice.' A mock-sad face.

'It's not nice to blag your way into someone's home, pretending to be someone else.'

'Ouch. You think I've done that?'

'Yes, you have. I know you can't be who you say you are. Weren't you concerned I might have met Eli already?' Even as she asked the question, she knew the answer. It was clear from Eli's email to her after Sam's death, an email he would have been able to access, that they hadn't yet met.

He got up off the sofa and swaggered across to her. He sat down beside her and gripped her chin with his hand. His scent overpowered her and she tried to hide the revulsion in her eyes.

'It's best for your sake if you forget what you've just said,' he snapped, tightening his hold. 'As far as you're concerned, I'm Eli, right?'

'Whoever you are,' she said defiantly, 'weren't you concerned about me getting a text or a call from Eli? Or maybe an email? That would have blown you out of the water.'

'Not really, I covered as many eventualities as I could. His calls, texts and emails have been blocked from your phone. Anyhow, he's not really chasing elephants in Africa. I've been keeping close tabs on him and he has satisfied his wild side. He was headhunted for his skills and he's currently out in the hellhole of the Middle East, undercover and incognito, helping with intelligence and humanitarian efforts. So he has other things on his mind. But as far as you're concerned, he's here and you're looking at him. So what's my name?'

She stayed silent.

'Repeat after me, it's Eli.'

'I hear you,' she said. Humanitarian efforts sounded more in keeping with the Eli Sam had spoken fondly of and it sickened her that this guy was impersonating him. He released her chin and she tried to stay calm.

'If anyone is to blame for the mess I'm in, it's Sam,' he said, 'so you owe me. Do you know what he did?' he asked.

She shook her head.

He got up off the sofa and began to pace the floor. 'I'm sure you do. I'm sure he was boasting about it. I hated his guts. Even in college. He was bright and smart, always ahead of me. He'd no time for me whatsoever. I was always on the outside looking in. But he was so bloody mother-fucking meticulous about his work that he's gone and ruined my life.'

He stared over at her. Panic surged inside her. 'He must have told you what he was up to? The sonofabitch. I had a sweet little scheme set up only he rumbled it.'

'I don't know what you're talking about,' she said.

'Let me enlighten you. I want you to understand that I'm not just a crazy monster. I'm normally a good, upstanding American citizen. I have a very valid reason for my actions.'

Izzie stayed silent.

'Earlier this year, as part of his work for the Share a Wish Foundation, Sam identified and isolated program activity that he found questionable. He alerted the foundation's CEO and the heads of Stanley. It was all kept hush-hush.'

'What kind of activity?' She didn't want to know, but maybe the more she found out about this man and his motivations, the better.

'I was clever. I had a program set up to direct a tiny percentage of financial transactions into a private bank account on a monthly basis. It helped me to pay off my debts. See, I wasn't as privileged as Sam. I couldn't keep up with him, so I borrowed some money from friends to help me fund a luxury lifestyle, much better than his, but then I found I couldn't pay it back and now my friends in New York are unhappy with me.'

'Do you work for the foundation?' she asked, trying to think of any names Sam might have mentioned.

'Do I *what*? No, thanks.'

'Their accountancy partners?' she guessed. Something Finance, Sam had said. He had been fixing a glitch in the interface during the summer.

'Never mind,' he snapped. 'The individual amounts were negligible, a little rounding down instead of rounding up, but the cumulative effect was significant. It was buried deeply but Sam managed to find it. Sam created a program to close this off, and the first I knew of it was when the funds due at the end of September failed to come through and I couldn't pay my debts.'

His words sent a chill right through her. 'I don't understand what this is all about,' she said. 'And if it was kept hush-hush, what makes you think it was Sam?'

He grinned. 'I did a little digging around and, with the help of champagne and a night in a plush hotel room, one of the private secretaries who was upset when Sam met his accident was only too glad to cry in my arms about the brilliance of the guy and all he'd done. So put it like this,' he went on, his voice strident, 'that asshole robbed me of my future and put my life at stake. I was doing fine until he put his nose in the way. It's the second time one of my little interventions has failed, thanks to him, and—' He paused.

Izzie guessed he'd been about to say Eli. 'This has happened before?' she said. She recalled Sam telling her about cyber-attacks that he and Eli had contained in their early days at Stanley Trust and Eli being intimidated as a result. They hadn't known where the attack had originated, but now she knew. Someone had to be on to him, hadn't they? Even if Sam had sorted it for now, what this guy had done was criminal.

'And now I need the money,' he said. 'I'm in trouble with my friends in New York. Big trouble. Do you know what it feels like to have a gun stuck to the side of your head?' He raised his hand and, extending his index finger, came over and pushed it into her temple. 'I'm running out of time and my debts have been called in. I need to escape somewhere they'll never find me and that takes funds.'

'I'm sure the police have been alerted about the fraud,' she said.

'The police?' He smiled. 'Can you imagine the bad publicity that would create for the foundation? What would happen to Stanley's reputation? Or Cannon Finance?'

Cannon Finance. That must be where this guy worked.

'Lots of corporations pay handsomely to prevent security blunders from being made public,' he said. 'They fork out hefty ransoms to hackers who steal their files and databases. Then they bury what happened and hope it never sees the light of day. It's a big, booming business. Neither Sam nor the CEO knew the identity of the person behind the activity. I covered those tracks. They might have guessed the source all right but they'd have to call in experts to unravel that particular money trail and it's not something they want to draw attention to.'

'How do you know?' she asked. 'Maybe that's happening as we speak. Perhaps your CEO has someone on the job, someone who can be trusted to be discreet.'

Her question didn't faze him.

'Maybe so,' he said. 'But they wouldn't be able to take the matter any further without involving the police, and that would blow it all wide open, including the fact that they weren't transparent in the first place. Word gets around like wildfire in those cases and reputations are shot overnight.'

She stayed silent.

'I've been a busy man. I've been working on my strategy ever since Sam met his unfortunate accident. After he died I realised I had a chance to recoup some of my losses. I need to reverse Sam's program for a short window to allow some final and more substantial funds to be derailed, so to speak, then close it up again before the end-of-December accounts are balanced and the system is upgraded. I plan to disappear into a golden sunset, never to be heard of again. I was hoping to get this done without alerting you – the less people know, the less complicated it all is. Only that's not going to happen now that I've had to move to Plan B. I hope for your sake I don't have to implement Plan C.'

He could forget about getting any co-operation from her as far as reversing Sam's program was concerned, Izzie decided. It had been his final project for the children's charity, into which he'd poured a lot of his precious time, commitment and dedication, and she wasn't about to jeopardise that.

But from the glitter in Eli's eyes, she also hoped he didn't have to go to Plan C, whatever that entailed.

CHAPTER FORTY-THREE

The south of France,
five months ago

Our lives start to slip sideways in July.

You're still working remotely for Stanley Trust. Your work for the foundation has suddenly become extra busy. You don't need to tell me there are fresh problems – I see by your face and the extra hours you are spending at the laptop. You go to New York for a long weekend, and although I usually go with you, I don't go this time. Staff on summer leave and appointments in the office mean I can't take Friday and Monday off like I usually would.

When you come back to Henrietta Square, you suggest a week away in the south of France. I have leave booked for later that month. We could go then.

'Why the south of France?' I ask.

'We might as well go to one of your all-time favourite holiday places,' you say. 'I'd love to see that part of the world with you.'

'How did you get on in New York?' I ask, slightly uneasy at your surprise suggestion. I had assumed we'd go to Kerry or Donegal, which were just a drive away, for a mini break. I hadn't been planning on going further afield. The monthly trips to New York are tiring enough for you, what with your busy agenda added to jet lag. It's relaxation you need, not more airport queues.

'There are problems with the foundation interface that I need to fix,' you say, talking about your job and ignoring everything else. 'The work is at a critical stage. I'd have to bring the laptop to France. I can't be gone AWOL for even a week. It'd be just for an hour a day, following up on any urgent emails and crisis issues.'

'Why not save France until your project is finished?'

'No, that could take months,' you say.

Months. And you don't want to wait. Why not? Silence swells and strains between us. I feel choked. I swallow hard and ask you, 'How did you really get on in New York?'

You know exactly what I'm referring to.

'Everything is fine,' you tell me, meeting my stare with a clear gaze.

A shiver scuttles down my spine like freezing-cold fingers on my back. I go along with you because I want to, because I want everything to be fine. I don't want to acknowledge that it might not be fine or allow anything else to taint our conversation.

*

I have the odd sensation that our holiday in France is something we are stealing out of time, like children robbing an orchard while the owner's back is turned. No matter how much we like to pretend, we're not destined to be a couple whose lives are coloured with annual carefree holidays, as well as other things.

We fly into Nice airport and head east. We're staying in a cottage on the edge of a small hilltop village, which is quaint with cobblestone streets, ancient honey-coloured stone walls overhung with splashes of scarlet bougainvillea and riots of white and pink oleander. The area possesses a rustic charm of its own, and we take that charm and absorb it into ourselves, so that we are glinting and glowing from the calm rhythm of our days.

In the early morning we throw back the shutters and welcome the warm orange slice of sunshine, as well as the silvery glitter of the Mediterranean in the near distance. We stroll along the path to the nearby shop, buying crusty bread warm from the oven, breaking off pieces of it and exploding our mouths with taste all the way back to our cottage. There is fragrant coffee out on a tiny terrace tucked to the side of the cottage, where lavender flowing out of big terracotta pots infuses the air around us. We get the rattling bus down the hill to the sea, where there are other couples and families enjoying the warm sunshine, or we spend the morning mingling with relaxed tourists sauntering around the medieval quarter of the village. We have a siesta then, followed by an afternoon relaxing with books or music under the canopy on the terrace.

The evenings darken suddenly, twilight descending like a soft blanket, heralding the balmy night. After you spend an hour on the laptop, we stroll hand in hand to the small village restaurant for food and wine, sitting outside in the mellow evening, surrounded by other families and couples, watching the stars coming out, listening to heart-tugging cadences of French love songs, the air fragrant with aromatic scents, the overhead lamps throwing your profile into relief.

I drink in everything about you so that it fills up my senses to overflowing.

I don't want this week to end, I decide, as we lie in bed together one warm midday, about halfway through the holiday; we have come in for a little respite from a hot sun that is dazzling off whitewashed walls. Even though we have the shutters open, there is no breeze. Nothing moves. Everything is held fast in the grip of midday heat. I have the sense that time itself stands still, holding its breath for a long, glorious moment. I lie still, not even breathing, and I don't want the future to come beckoning. But then I have to take air into my lungs, and time marches on once more, thrusting us forward like the ceaseless tide. I feel cross that there is so much I can't control.

'I wish I could stop time for a while,' I say, lying on my back and staring at the ceiling. 'Like you can pause a television programme.'

'So do I,' you say.

'I don't want this week to be over,' I say. 'I hate the thoughts of going home.'

I know I sound petulant and silly, but I can't seem to help it. Are we tempting fate by taking this time out? In the last two weeks, and especially out here in the luminescent Riviera sun, I think your face is a little thinner, your eyes more tired. I know every tiny crease fanning out from your eyes, the laughter lines framing the sides of your mouth, and I think there are more creases and lines. The distant thunder I'd heard one autumn afternoon in New York is galloping closer. A breath-stopping wave crests inside me at the thought of you being gone.

'We'll have to make sure we shine,' you say.

'What do you mean?'

'In our lives. Nothing can stop time moving on. Month on month, year on year. We're not going to be favoured any more than previous generations were. In the breadth of time, we're just small, insignificant dots. While we're here, we must take big gulps of life, grab it with both hands and squeeze it dry.'

'Other lovers, other families are more favoured than we are,' I say.

I know I am crossing a line. You laid down a marker months ago in New York, just after we met, and I'm ignoring it. I know my words will make you unhappy, but I can't help envying the carefree lovers and happy families we saw on the beach and in the restaurant, knowing we will never be like them. I can't help thinking of what lies ahead for us and it fills me with anger.

You don't say anything at all. You are lying quietly beside me.

Even that is making me cross. I slide out of bed and slip on a white cotton robe over my underwear. I go across to the window and stare out beyond terracotta roofs to the rim of the glistening sea. I wonder how many hundreds of people before me have stared at this sight, how many more will stand here in the future, next month, next year. Your words about being insignificant roar in my head. The impermanence of life shakes me.

I turn around. 'It was a bad idea to come here,' I say. 'It

only brings home to me how beautiful and carefree life can be. But it's not that way for us, is it? It never will be.'

You're lying inert on the bed, wearing a pair of faded denim shorts, your flip-flops on the tiled floor beside the bed. They are cheap flip-flops that you picked up in a village tourist shop, having forgotten to pack a pair. I realise with utter helplessness that these pieces of rubber have the power to outlive both of us.

'Is this why you asked to come here?' I prod. 'To show how far removed we are from the average holidaymaker? Is this what you wanted?' I'm furious with myself and I know my outburst is totally unfair, but I'm unable to contain my frustration, my hidden anxiety, and need to lash out, somehow.

You get up off the bed. 'Hey, what brought this on?' Your eyes lock on mine. It's the first time I have seen you annoyed with me. You stride towards me, as furious as I am.

'Maybe you're better off not knowing what you're missing,' I snap. 'It's frustrating to get a glimpse of a different kind of life, a sunny, carefree life, and know that you'll only have a tiny crumb of that. It's cruel to get a taste of how things might have been and to have that morsel whipped away from your mouth.'

'If that's how you feel, you don't have to go back to Henrietta Square after this week,' you say.

'Oh, yeah? Hey, Mallon, pull the other one.'

'I can go back to New York and you can go wherever you like. You could even stay here. You do have choices.'

The silent words scream between us: whereas your choices are limited.

I don't want our life together to be like this. But no matter what I do, I can't escape the fact that it is, and this is all it will ever be.

I pick up one of your flip-flops and throw it against the wall.

'What's that all about?' you ask.

'I hate it because it'll last longer than both of us added together.'

'Good God,' you say, throwing your arms out in surrender.

I look at you, and there is something so honest and vulnerable and scarily translucent about you that it catches me in the gut and I start to cry. Your arms go around me. I snuggle into your embrace. You hold me for a long time and shush me, rubbing my back while I shake and sob. When I eventually stop, you cup the curve of my cheek in your hand.

'I was wrong to say we're insignificant,' you say. 'We're anything but insignificant, no matter how long or short we're together. We're the meaning of life, you and me.'

'I hope so.'

Hope. Our mission statement in a single word. It underpins our time together.

You kiss me and I open my mouth to yours and as the kiss deepens I strain towards you, wanting to press as close to you as I can so that we dissolve into each other. We move towards the bed and fall across it, me aching to feel your bare skin sliding against mine, to touch the span of your ribs under my fingertips.

'*Elizabeth* ...'

You fold your limbs around me and the slow heat rises inside me. You turn me to liquid quicksilver and I'm dizzy for the joy of it. Then afterwards, you hold me in the tight, safe cocoon that always quietens my mind.

'I want you to remember what I said about tasting life to the full and taking big gulps of it. Promise me?' Your eyes search my face, looking for affirmation.

I rest my head on your chest and soak up the thrum of your heartbeat. 'I promise. But I hope you're not going anywhere just yet.'

'I'm not. But when later comes—'

I stay silent. There are no words.

'I will always be there for you,' you say, stroking my hair. 'Talk to me of the good times we've had and remember only them.'

CHAPTER FORTY-FOUR

Izzie's intercom buzzed. She saw Eli tense as Gemma's voice wafted into Izzie's apartment.

'I'm here, Izzie,' she said, 'with your purse. I completely forgot to get an envelope. Is it okay to push it through the letter box? If it's that important to you I can bring it up.'

'Fuck. What happens to the post here?' Eli asked Izzie in a quiet voice.

'We have separate boxes in the hallway, but sometimes it's left on the hall table by whoever sees it first,' she fibbed, deciding to make it awkward for him. 'No-one's going to know who owns that purse. If you go down for it and leave me here I'll scream my head off. If you bring me with you, I'll scream my head off as well.'

'That's not going to happen,' Eli said. He pressed the door release and spoke into the intercom. 'Gemma, this is Eli, I'm with Izzie and she wants you to come on up.'

While he was talking, he slid a small, scalpel-like knife from his tracksuit pocket and slashed the air with it. Izzie froze. He must have had it there all along. He leaned in close to her and rested the blade between her eyes, saying in a quiet voice, 'This is an introduction to Plan C. Don't try anything funny. One wrong move and I'll rearrange every piece of Gemma's lovely face. I know how to use this and I won't hesitate. Got it?'

'Got it.'

They were in a different territory now.

'That must be the lovely Gemma,' Eli said. 'We'll let her in and see what she has.'

When Gemma knocked at her apartment door a few moments later, Izzie could only sit helplessly while Eli went out into the hallway.

Their voices floated through to the living room.

'Hi, you must be Gemma,' she heard him say. 'I'm Eli. I was a friend of Sam's in New York and I'm staying with Izzie at the moment. You're very kind to come all this way with Izzie's purse, especially in this weather.'

'Is she there? Could I speak to her?' Gemma's voice was young and fresh, and Izzie heard the wanting-to-please tone in every inflection.

'She is here, but she's a little, ah, indisposed right now.'

'Oh,' Gemma said, sounding deflated. 'I'd like to hand this to her in person. I know it's important to Izzie.'

'Of course it is and it's good of you to be so careful with it, but she's – look, it was one of those late nights followed by a long lie-in.' Eli sounded friendly and conspiratorial. His meaning was clear.

'I can go off for a coffee and come back later,' Gemma said.

Bless her. Izzie closed her eyes and tried to think of some way she could warn Gemma about the set-up without alerting Eli. She managed to move off the sofa but fell in a heavy heap on the floor. *Shite*.

'Would you wait a minute?' Eli said. 'I'll see if I can get her to make herself decent. We can't have you being delayed in this weather.'

He came back into the living room and scooped Izzie up effortlessly, sitting her back down on the sofa, propping her feet up.

'Izzie, darling,' he said, loud enough for his voice to carry, 'Gemma is here at the door. Would you mind putting on some clothes? She'd like to see you.'

Then, in a quiet voice, he said, 'You behave, or else', catching her hand and putting the knife to the inside of her wrist.

Eli went back out to the hallway and called Gemma in, locking the door after her. 'Izzie has just made herself respectable, haven't you, darling?' he went on, as he ushered Gemma into the living room. He went over to the back of the sofa and squeezed Izzie's shoulders. 'She was a naughty girl last night, or should I say we both were. It must have been four in the morning by the time we got some sleep. Or was it five?'

'Hi, Izzie,' Gemma said.

With her pale face and sketchy make-up, Gemma looked as though she'd been partying since Thursday lunchtime. It had been a long time since Izzie had experienced that madcap Christmas-party mania, and she was a million miles more jaded than that younger, innocent self. Still, never had the sight of wholesome, helpful Gemma seemed more welcome. Problem was, Izzie knew by the expression in her rounded eyes exactly what kind of impression Eli had given her.

'Gemma! You're too good to have come all this way,' she said brightly, conscious that Eli had moved around so that he was standing close to Gemma. 'I'm sorry to have dragged you across town, never mind leaving you standing in the doorway.'

'It's okay – sorry if I'm disturbing you. It's such a pity you didn't get going to your yoga retreat.'

'I had every intention of going and my bags were practically packed when this guy here turned up in need of a bed for the night. I couldn't leave him stranded.'

Gemma frowned and Izzie smiled fixedly back at her.

'The snow,' Izzie went on. 'No flights. He was stranded – weren't you, Eli?' she continued. 'The airport is crazy and the hotels are full, I couldn't turn away Sam's friend.'

'No, I guess you couldn't.' Gemma's eyes were taking everything in, including her attire.

'Would you like some coffee, Gemma?' Eli asked smoothly.

'No, thanks,' Gemma said, looking as though she couldn't wait to escape. 'Here you go.' She rummaged in her bag and took out Izzie's glittery purse, handing it to her.

'Thank you,' Izzie said. 'I don't know how I was so careless as to leave that behind. You've been so good at looking after me. I hope I haven't disrupted your Christmas plans, hauling you over here.'

Gemma began to walk back towards the door.

'And could you do me a huge favour, please?' Izzie asked.

'What favour do you need?' Eli stared at her pointedly, his hand darting to the pocket of his tracksuit top.

'Let me give Gemma the Christmas gift for Noah,' Izzie said, forcing herself to sound nonchalant.

'What gift?' Eli asked, his eyes narrowing.

'The *Star Wars* DVDs, remember?' Izzie said, her heart hammering. 'I said he could keep them and that I'd wrap them for Christmas. It'll save me a trip downstairs,' she said.

'Okay, then.'

'I left them on the mantelpiece,' she said, nodding her head in that direction.

If the situation hadn't been so fraught with tension, Izzie would have laughed at Eli's efforts to get his hands on the DVDs as quickly as possible and give them to Gemma, lest Izzie get up to something while he was distracted.

'They're for Noah, the boy who lives on the middle floor,' Izzie said to Gemma, trying to control the tremor in her voice as she visualised the gleam of the knife in Eli's pocket. 'I promised them to him for Christmas, but I don't have any wrapping paper. You'd be doing me a huge favour if you could knock in at the ground-floor apartment on your way out – a lady called Florence lives there. Could you ask her to wrap them for me and put them under Noah's Christmas tree? He's not to open it until Christmas Day.'

'Yeah, sure, Izzie.' Gemma looked slightly puzzled. 'Will I bring them back up if Florence isn't in?'

'If there's no answer from Florence's apartment just leave them on the table in the hall downstairs. Noah will know they're for him. Thanks a million, Gemma – it'll save me a journey.'

Gemma put the DVDs in her bag and turned to go.

'I'll see you out,' Eli said, walking towards the door.

'Oh, and by the way,' Izzie called out.

Gemma turned back, Eli watching Izzie carefully.

'Thanks for all your help with the Conways' house purchase,' Izzie said.

'The Conways,' Gemma echoed, her face blank.

'Yeah, it was good of you to double check that solicitor's signature. I appreciate it and it saved a lot of problems. Have a lovely Christmas.'

'Oh. Right. Thank you, Izzie, same to you.'

It didn't escape Izzie that Gemma ignored Eli completely as she sailed out the door. God knows what she thought of the carry-on, but the most important thing was that she got out, safe and unharmed, bearing Noah's precious gift.

CHAPTER FORTY-FIVE

What the hell was all that about? Gemma stood on the landing outside Izzie's door, flustered and let down. There were no meeting points between the Izzie she'd seen this afternoon and the Izzie she'd worked with in O'Sullivan Pearse. She'd had to struggle to hide her surprise at the sight of Izzie in her dressing gown, lounging on the sofa in the early afternoon, with Eli standing behind her. The overpowering sense that she'd interrupted something didn't compute whatsoever with an Izzie too heartbroken at having lost Sam to get through the day without making loads of silly errors. Even the favour she'd asked Gemma to do rankled. Surely Izzie could have popped downstairs herself? It was clear that she didn't want to leave her apartment, not even for a minute.

The only thing that had been remotely in character with that heartbroken Izzie was her confusion over the Conway case and the crooked solicitor. Gemma had never even worked on that case, let alone discovered the falsified document.

Eli had clearly turned her head.

It hadn't taken her long to get over Sam. No wonder she'd wanted to be on her own for Christmas – some yoga retreat it was turning out to be. It seemed more like she was enjoying a Christmas love-in with Sam's mate. It could even have been planned in advance. Her stomach soured when she thought of how much she'd tried to help Izzie over the last few weeks, covering up for her silly errors, smoothing her path in the office, buying her flowers week after week and overall keeping an eye on her. Even the way she'd abandoned Kian temporarily to come over here with Izzie's purse. He'd sent her a text, telling her the white wine was chilling in the fridge along with the strawberries and cream, and he'd be ready and waiting for her.

Gemma came down the stairs slowly. At least Izzie had had the decency to look a bit embarrassed. She probably guessed that Gemma was gobsmacked at seeing her with another man, considering the mess she'd been in after Sam. Although who was she to talk, Gemma asked herself. Look at the way she'd fallen into bed with Kian. She'd spent most of yesterday sliding her naked body against his, throwing on a borrowed bathrobe the few times she'd got up.

She paused on the return, taking in her surroundings. This house was the house of her dreams, Gemma decided. Lucky Izzie to be able to live here. Even the bannisters were beautiful, the wood carved and mellow, and the stair carpet was thick and luxurious underfoot. The house had a spacious feel to it, wonderful proportions and original features that had never graced any of the shoe-box apartments of her college mates. She took her time going down the stairs, pretending she lived here and the whole house was hers. She decided that Noah was very lucky indeed to live in the apartment on the first floor, and then she was down in the wide, elegant hall, with the tiled floor and beautiful fan light, reluctant to go back out into the snow and the cold and leave this house with all its relaxed grandeur. She paused for a moment to check her reflection in the ornate gilt-framed mirror, resting her arms on the marble-topped table in front of it as she spoke to her reflection, pretending she was a lady of the manor.

On her way out, Gemma knocked at the door to the ground-floor apartment but there was no answer. She knocked again and waited a few moments, and was just about to take the DVDs out of her bag and leave them on the hall table when a small group came bustling in through the door, bringing in a wave of cold air, stamping their feet on the mat, shrugging off scarves and gloves. A pre-adolescent boy, a man whom she guessed to be his father and an older, diminutive lady, who could have been the grandmother.

'Are you okay?' the lady asked. 'Can I help you with anything?'

'I'm fine, thanks,' Gemma said brightly. The lady seemed friendly enough but Gemma couldn't help imagining she was trespassing. 'I was upstairs visiting my friend, Izzie, and she asked me to give a message to the lady who lives here, Florence.'

'Oh, so you're a friend of Izzie's?' The lady's face brightened with a smile, showing classical cheekbones. 'That's nice. She needs friends. And I'm Florence,' she said.

'This is Tom and Noah, who live upstairs.' Tom smiled and nodded and Noah looked at her with curiosity. Noah – the gift was intended for him, Gemma realised, but there was no point in handing it to him now because Izzie wanted Florence to wrap it first.

'Gemma, lovely to meet you,' Tom said, pulling off a thick glove to shake her hand. 'Are you on your way up to Izzie?'

'No, I've been up there already. I'm heading home now.'

'I hope you haven't got far to go in this weather,' Tom said.

'I'm staying with a friend in the city for a night or two,' Gemma told him.

'Good idea. We'll see you later, Florence,' he added before heading for the stairs with Noah in tow.

'Don't I know you?' Gemma said, recognition dawning as she looked at the small, neat stature of the lady and a memory stirred.

'Know me? How?' Florence's hand flew to her throat in a peculiar defensive gesture as though Gemma's words had startled her.

Gemma hastened to reassure her. 'Yeah, you're Hawkeye – em, sorry, Miss Hawkins, MacBride Secondary School?'

Hawkeye. Had she really said that? Gemma reddened with embarrassment. After meeting Izzie, she hadn't been thinking straight.

'Oh. That's right,' Florence said with a grimace. 'That was me. It's over ten years since I've heard it,' she said, examining Gemma's face with puzzlement.

'You didn't teach me,' Gemma said. 'It was Janet, my older sister. I'm Gemma. I was in first year when she was in sixth year, and that was your last year in the school. Actually, Hawk— Miss Hawkins, she still talks about you.'

'She *does*? Really? And please call me Florence,' she said gently. 'It's a little kinder than Hawkeye.'

'Sorry,' Gemma said. 'It was really a fond nickname – the girls loved you. Well, some of them. Cos they knew you tried to get the best out of them.'

'I don't know about that,' Florence said. 'I'm under no illusions. I know I appeared to be a bit of a slave driver. I *was* a slave driver.'

'Yes, but they really appreciated that. In the end. You turned Janet's life around. And some of her mates' as well.'

'Good gracious, did I? Are you sure you're not mixing me up with someone else?'

'I doubt it. English and Irish, fifth and sixth years.'

'That's right.'

'I can't believe I'm talking to you,' Gemma said. 'Wait till I tell Janet – you're a legend. I'm glad Izzie gave me that message for you now.' She took the DVDs out of her bag and handed them to Florence. 'These are for Noah, a Christmas gift, not to be opened until Christmas Day. Izzie has no wrapping paper so she was hoping you might do her a favour by wrapping them and leaving them under Noah's tree?'

'Of course I will,' Florence said warmly. 'I don't suppose …' The older lady seemed to be wavering and then she said, 'It's quite snowy out. Would you like to come in for a Christmas drink? Maybe a glass of wine? Although,' to Gemma's surprise, Florence's face lit up with a big, mischievous grin, 'as a former teacher I probably shouldn't be advocating alcohol in the early afternoon. Still, we'll blame it on the weather – a lot of people are doing things they wouldn't normally do, thanks to the circumstances.'

'That would be lovely, thank you,' Gemma said. And

much to her surprise, she meant it. She was in no huge rush back to Kian – it would do him good to wait a bit – and she was curious about this house and its inhabitants. And a glass of wine with Florence might help to take away the sour taste of seeing Izzie cosying up so comfortably with another man.

CHAPTER FORTY-SIX

As soon as Gemma left, Eli locked the door and came back into the living room, striding across to where Izzie was half-sitting, half-lying on the sofa. He plucked the small purse out of her clasped hands, opened the zipper and pulled out a memory stick. He threw the purse back to her, ignoring the seashell and beach pebble.

'A-ha.'

'It's not what you think it is,' Izzie said. 'It's got nothing to do with what you're looking for.'

He ignored her. 'You bitch. After all the efforts I've made to get my hands on this – you knew all along you had left it in the office. I bet you did that on purpose just to make my life more difficult.'

'Why would I have done that?' Izzie asked, managing to rise somewhat above the dullness in her head. 'You hardly think I visualised your arrival like some kind of psychic? What's on that stick is personal – it has absolutely nothing to do with Sam's work.'

In answer to that, he took out his knife and flattened the blade against her cheek. 'Oh yeah? I don't believe you. One shout or scream or move in the wrong direction and it will be your turn to have your face rearranged so fast you won't know what happened and you'll never recover. Understood?'

'Understood,' she said.

He waved the knife under her nose. 'I mean it. No one is going to interfere with my plans. You just don't get it. I'm in urgent need of saving my skin. Even if that means ruining yours.'

'You're going to be disappointed.'

He ignored her. He went over and got her laptop, sitting down with it on the sofa beside her. The ease with which he opened it and accessed her desktop alarmed her.

'You've been in that already,' she stated.

'Clever you,' he said, speaking as though she was a five-year-old child. 'I checked it out the first night I was here. I thought Sam might have sent some files over to you, but I couldn't find anything on your hard drive.'

Izzie watched him slotting in the memory stick. She knew exactly what was coming next and she braced herself. There was just one file on it, titled 'Sam and Izzie'. It was a video file that wasn't even password protected and it opened immediately on Eli's click. She had tried to watch it, just the once, bolstered by so much vodka she was technically beyond drunk, but she had only lasted a few seconds before she had closed the video and ejected the memory stick. Now, watching it would be marred by the threatening presence of this man beside her.

Sam appeared on the screen, sitting on the same sofa she was sitting on now, casually dressed in jeans and a white T-shirt. He was strumming the guitar and he began to sing John Lennon's 'Oh My Love', picking out the simple melody with ease.

It had been Sam's signature song and their wedding song. Izzie knew the words off by heart. Despite the situation she was in, the sound of his voice soothed her senses. When the song was finished, Sam put down his guitar and leaned forward. He could have been there, right beside her.

'Hi, Izzie,' he began, his voice soft and loving.

CHAPTER FORTY-SEVEN

Izzie only had eyes for the man on the laptop screen in front of her. Beside her, Eli sat up straighter, on the alert. Izzie somehow managed to blank out his presence as she absorbed Sam and everything he was saying.

'Darling Izzie, this is the story of our first year,' Sam said. 'If you're watching this it means I'm no longer around and that our worst fears are realised. I said I'd find some way of saving my smile for you and this is it. I'm not sure how much time we'll have together. It's all in the lap of the gods, but that's like everything in life, isn't it? We can be dealt a lucky hand or not. Then again, you might decide not to bother looking at my mug.' He laughed gently. 'You might say that ol' guy is part of the past, over and out, I've moved on. Good riddance.

I'll be glad in one sense if you do, because that means you're out there living your life.'

Sam picked up his guitar and began to sing again, another John Lennon song, 'Imagine'. The screen changed from his image to a succession of photographs following seamlessly one after the other, colour, black and white, flowing to sepia, a temporary fadeout and back to colour again; it was a montage of Izzie's face against a New York City skyline, lying under a tree in Central Park, leaning against a wall along by the glinting Hudson river, prancing up 5th Avenue, smiling at the camera, laughing at the camera, turning sideways to it, making faces at it, arms flung out in exultation, the landscape in the images moving from autumn to winter to spring. Then Sam in the same locations, the photographs taken by Izzie. There were images of both of them together, some selfies, others taken by co-operative bystanders.

There were photographs of their wedding day, Sam and Izzie strolling together along a curved cobblestone path, the borders edged with paper lanterns that glow softly. Both of them in silhouette under the stained-glass window of a small grey-stone church. Izzie in profile, her veil spread out behind her, the curve of her face beautiful in the soft lighting. Sam and Izzie on the dance floor under a ceiling of hundreds of tiny soft lights, a circle of family and friends around them.

The music stopped and Sam spoke again. 'That was the best day of my life. I walked in some kind of magic space. But there were more brilliant days, more perfect days, when I walked in the light of your love and they filled me up completely so that I wanted for nothing.'

Lastly, a sequence of photos shot in Henrietta Square: Izzie, unpacking a box in the kitchen, smoothing out a tangled-up duvet, a series of stills showing her dancing across the living-room floor with a bottle of bubbly in her hand, sitting at the table on a Saturday morning, cradling a mug of coffee, her face bare of make-up.

'Thank you for making my life so happy and full of love. Remember to grab your brief time in the sun and live your life to the full. I will never leave you because I will always be in your heart. Talk to me whenever you like and tell me how you're doing, but remember that you promised to go out there and open your heart to the possibility of other love. It's all that matters in the end.'

Sam picked up his guitar again and played out the end of the video segment with a rendition of 'Bless You'.

CHAPTER FORTY-EIGHT

Florence couldn't believe that, in the space of less than twenty-four hours, she was entertaining in her apartment once more, that this young woman, whom she didn't know at all, was making herself comfortable on her small sofa over by the fireside. Gemma, she reminded herself, not exactly a stranger, a sister of Janet, who had been one of her pupils in her final year in MacBride. Gemma looked around the room like Tom and Izzie had the previous evening, but like them, it was in appreciation and not as if she found Florence's apartment in any way wanting.

'This is a fabulous house,' Gemma said. 'And your apartment is lovely and cosy. Are you living here long?'

'Since I retired,' Florence said, without elaborating. 'White or red?'

'White, please,' Gemma said. 'Gosh, this is mad, Janet won't believe me. Me having a Christmas drink with Hawkeye – oops, sorry. But, look, it really was a pet name for you.'

'Pet? I was far from being my students' pet. I think most of them feared rather than respected me.'

'Well, your reputation preceded you all right. But whatever you said to Janet and her circle of friends during English lessons struck home.'

'English lessons.' Florence smiled. 'I think it was *Macbeth* that year, and *Wuthering Heights*. I loved the poetry, Kavanagh and Yeats and Robert Frost. I did my best to bring it all alive for the class.' She had tried, time and time again, not knowing if she was truly connecting with anyone.

'Janet used to hate poetry,' Gemma said. 'Then whatever you said got her really interested, and it turned things around for her. There were lots of problems in our neighbourhood – drugs, crime, low expectations of kids in school. Janet nearly got in with the wrong crowd and was ready to leave school at sixteen, then a couple of months before that birthday she started back in the autumn term and had you as her teacher, and that's when everything started to change for her.'

'Really?'

'She got serious about school. After a few weeks she told us all she didn't want to leave. She wanted to stay on, work as hard as she could and maybe even go to college. Mum was thrilled and encouraged her as well. Janet was the first in our family to go to college and now she's working for an American firm in Silicon Docks. She even writes some songs and poetry in her spare time.'

Florence found she was holding her breath. 'I didn't know any of this. I didn't even stay around that year to find out how everyone had done. I thought I was just a pain in the ass for most of the girls.'

All she could remember was row upon row of disinterested faces. The occasional mouthful of abuse. She had mainly taken examination years, preparing recalcitrant pupils for the state examinations, and her reputation for strictness in the classroom preceded her, but facing thirty-odd teenagers, most of whom didn't want to be there, was not for the faint-hearted. Any sign of weakness and she'd be walked all over.

There had been a few bright sparks in among the crowd, but after twenty years in MacBride, she'd been tired by then, ground down by thankless years of dragging mostly bored and uninterested pupils through the system, never mind angry parents berating her for handing out too much homework to their children and putting them under pressure.

She'd been ground down too by the soreness in her heart, which had lurked there for most of her adult life.

'I don't know about most of the class,' Gemma said. 'I only know about Janet and her friends. There were four of them altogether, and they all went to college. Janet was lucky she turned things around and didn't fall in with the gang that hung around the neighbourhood, because a couple of them didn't even see their twenties.'

'That's very sad,' Florence said.

'It is. And it could have been Janet's story, only for your influence. Mum did her best to encourage her to do well, but Janet had to want it for herself, to be committed enough to work and study. Thanks to you, she did. I'm sure Janet and her friends weren't the only ones you influenced. My big sister blazed a trail for me to follow.'

'This is lovely to hear and you seem like a fine young lady,'

Florence said. Maybe her years in MacBride hadn't been fruitless after all. Pupils left in her hands were now young women taking their rightful place in the world, thanks to her. Maybe that part of her life had, in fact, fulfilled a good purpose.

'Are you on Facebook, Florence?'

'*Face*book? No, not me.'

'Why not? It would be good for you. Janet and her friends have set up a group of interested schoolmates, and some of the teachers are on it as well – you'd enjoy it. It would be a way of finding out how everyone is doing. Some old pupils are doing very well for themselves. They're living all over the world now, Australia, America, Japan. I'm sure they'd love to hear from you. '

'I'm on WhatsApp,' Florence said. 'And I have internet and an email address,' she went on, keen to show she had joined the digital community.

'Well then, Facebook would be a cinch and you'd enjoy it – that's if you want to connect with people, of course.' Gemma looked at her questioningly.

'Let me think about it,' Florence said.

'I'd help you set it up if you like,' Gemma offered. 'It would open a new world for you. I know Janet will be delighted I met you. It's funny how small Dublin is, me working with Izzie and she living above you.'

'Ah, Izzie. How did she seem?'

'Okay-ish,' Gemma said.

'I was broken-hearted when Sam died,' Florence said. 'I can't imagine what Izzie is going through.'

'I never met Sam. I'm only working with Izzie a few weeks, so I didn't know her beforehand.'

'Oh, he was absolutely gorgeous and terribly attractive – I don't mean like someone who's stepped out of an aftershave advertisement, but there was something incredibly kind, even beautiful, about him. He seemed to have great patience and time for everyone. And such a warm smile. My heart went out to Izzie afterwards. I still can't get my head around it and I still feel helpless in front of her, not knowing what to say or do. And her first Christmas on her own – it'll be tough for her not being with her family.'

'I don't think she's quite alone,' Gemma said.

'You must mean Eli, Sam's friend. He got stranded in Dublin on his way home to New York, so it was great that he was able to come to Izzie instead of sleeping on an airport floor. Did you see him?'

'Yes, he's upstairs with her. I thought he had planned to spend the holiday with her.'

'No, she wasn't expecting him at all.'

'Seems strange, then …'

'What does?' Florence asked, alerted by something in Gemma's face.

'Oh, nothing, don't mind me,' Gemma said. 'Except she seems to be quite happy up there. With Eli. So I wouldn't worry about her too much.'

'I see. And there was me wondering if I should be a bit more hospitable.'

'Umm, I got the distinct impression that they didn't want to be disturbed.'

'Are you saying what I think you're saying?' Florence frowned. 'Because if you are, I won't go near them. Izzie deserves some happiness and a bit of tender loving care. Although no one could be a substitute for Sam, I'd rather see

Izzie with another man than being on her own. What are we like?' Florence pulled herself up. 'We shouldn't be gossiping about her like this, but I've been so concerned about her ...'

'So have I,' Gemma said. 'Her head has been elsewhere these weeks. There was something vulnerable about her in work. She was always forgetting things and making silly mistakes. I used to check her stuff without her knowing. She'd leave keys behind, she left her phone in a pub when she went out for lunch one day ... So I hope this guy is good to her.'

'I'm sure Izzie appreciated your help,' Florence said. MacBride Secondary School had been good for something, all right, if it had turned out decent people like Gemma. 'She was lucky to have you looking after her like that. If this guy is a true friend of Sam's, he'll be extra kind to her. How did she seem to you today? Did she look happy and relaxed?'

'I've never seen Izzie looking happy or relaxed,' Gemma said. 'Even today, she looked – not so much embarrassed, but kind of odd. Probably because I saw her with another man. I've only ever known her in grieving mode in the office. She always seemed to be just going through the motions but not really there. Sometimes the look on her face – God, it made me want to wrap her up in a big, soft blanket. So it was a surprise to me to see her with someone else. Still, you know what they say, none of us really knows what goes on behind the scenes.'

'I can agree one hundred and ten per cent with that,' Florence said.

'I'd better get going,' Gemma said. 'Can I take your phone number? I'll call you after Christmas, and maybe you'd be happy to meet up with Janet? We could go for coffee or something?'

Florence gave Gemma her number, and Gemma keyed it into her phone, sending Florence a text immediately.

'Now you have mine,' Gemma said. 'I'll call you after Christmas, when this snow has gone and life has got back to normal. Lovely to see you, Florence.'

She stood up, put on her coat and scarf and gave Florence a hug.

Florence was a bit surprised at first, but her heart lifted a little with the younger woman's embrace.

'Your visit has meant a lot to me,' Florence found herself admitting. 'My life didn't turn out exactly as I had thought it would, but I'm glad to hear I made such a positive difference to other people's lives, and helped young women to go out and take their place in the world. Things were different when I was growing up, Gemma, and sometimes I battled against this, other times I didn't, but everything changes all the time. You're in your early twenties, I'd guess, just at the start of it all. Who knows what changes you'll see in your lifetime – hopefully they'll be positive ones. If I had my—' Florence paused.

'If you had what?' Gemma asked, fixing the strap of her bag across her shoulder.

Florence gave a half-laugh. 'I nearly came out with my mantra of the moment.'

'And what's that?'

'If I had my life to live over … the things I'd do …'

'Like what?' Gemma asked, with nothing in her face but friendly curiosity.

'Ah, Gemma, I'd only bore you. Your life is still ahead of you – you don't need to know other people's regrets …'

'Well, no, actually,' Gemma said slowly. 'Because it's ahead of me, it's exciting but scary as well. How do I know I won't take the wrong turn or end up with my own regrets?'

'Oh gosh, that can be a hard one to call.' Florence hesitated. She veered away from her most painful regrets and went on. 'We could talk all day on this topic. You have to do ultimately what's best for you, but for me, if I was doing it all again, I guess I'd put a higher value on me, warts and all. I'd honour my own needs and I wouldn't short-change myself for anyone. Coming from that place of empowerment, I would have made different choices in life. And this is too heavy a conversation for today.' Florence smiled.

'If you'd made different choices, Janet and I might have lost out,' Gemma said. 'And anyway, I'd say there's plenty of life and choices left ahead of you yet.'

'We'll see,' Florence said.

'We'll talk again, me, you and Janet.'

'I'd like that,' Florence said. 'Don't forget your shopping,' she went on, indicating Gemma's carrier bag.

'No, I'd better not,' Gemma said, her face pinking a little as she picked it up.

Florence went out to the main door with her. 'Safe home,' she said, opening the door. 'And a happy Christmas to you.'

'You too, Florence.'

CHAPTER FORTY-NINE

zzie braced herself as the last notes of 'Bless You' faded and the video clip of Sam came to an end.

Eli wrenched the memory stick out of her laptop and flung it across the room. 'And what the flying fuck was that all about? Was Sam speaking in some kind of code?'

'There are no hidden meanings,' Izzie said. 'It's exactly what it is, a message from Sam to me.'

'Bullshit. There's a helluva lot more to this. Why go to the trouble of putting that all together?' His eyes narrowed. 'And what did he mean, his worst fears were realised? Did he know something about himself?' he said, softening his voice without losing any of the menace. 'For instance, that he wasn't going to be around in the future? Because if so, I know you're holding out on me.'

Izzie fought to keep her voice steady. 'Sam was thirty-six years of age. He died in a car accident. Do you really think he was able to anticipate that?'

'Sam wasn't the kind of person who sensed things. He had a logical brain. He only dealt with facts. From what he said, there's more to this than you're letting on.'

'Why shouldn't Sam have made a record of our first year together?'

'Don't fuck with me, you bitch. What was he afraid of? What did he think might happen? Maybe he didn't foresee a car accident, but there was something else behind his comments. Something that made him think he might run out of time. Was he ill?'

Izzie didn't reply.

'Knowing Sam, he would have covered all options. If he had time to put together this shit, he would have safeguarded his work. He would have made sure you knew how to access his laptop, and he would have backed up his files elsewhere. What else are you hiding from me?'

'Nothing.'

'You're lying.'

'I didn't need to know about Sam's work. The office in New York was continually updated. Everything he did was encrypted and sent over. They have everything. Sam didn't need a back-up.'

'Don't be so naïve, you stupid bitch. Of course he did, like any consultant with a brain between his ears, especially if he thought he mightn't be around. And who would Sam trust most of all, only you? You had to have been his safety net in the event of something unforeseen …' He stared at her speculatively. 'Did he tell you about me?'

'I thought you said you hadn't been identified?'

'So you have been paying attention. In spite of your dopey head. You're cleverer than I thought you were.'

She ignored the comment.

'He mightn't have personally identified me, but he must have known the threat existed. For all I know he probably boasted about how brilliant he was at his job and the fantastic work he was doing.'

'We rarely discussed work. We were busy with our wedding, our honeymoon, him moving to Ireland. Outside the essentials of his job, these are the things that took up our time and attention. You can look all you like but you'll find nothing here.'

'I'm going to have a damned good try. Don't you understand? I need to get this job done – and fast.'

Izzie was also going to make a damned good try, she decided. Some strength was coming back into her bones and she waited until Eli was in the kitchen area, with his back momentarily turned to her. He was helping himself to an apple, washing it and slicing it up. She used every ounce of energy she could gather to raise herself from the sofa, her legs like lead blocks. She forced herself to put one in front of the other, attempting to inch across the short space to where the daylight beckoned. What she hoped to achieve she didn't know, but it was worth a try. When Eli spotted what she was up to, she lunged across, grabbing hold of the drapes, cannoning against the window.

He yanked her back and pressed his fingers into the hollow at the side of her neck, bringing tears to her eyes before throwing her onto the sofa. Marching over to the window, he pulled the drapes across, blotting out the afternoon and thrusting the room into shadow.

'Stupid bitch,' he said. 'Don't try any more tricks like that. Don't forget what I have in my pocket, and don't take me for a fool either.' He took out the small razor-sharp knife, and she felt its coldness as he pressed the blade flat against her cheek. 'I don't want to do this. I need to make it look like a personal tragedy. But I'll use it if I have to, no problem.'

CHAPTER FIFTY

New York,
fifteen months ago

There are certain things in life that are non-negotiable: we are born, we will die. But in between the dance of life and death there are other things that we take for granted will happen: we will find love, passion, commitment, have a family, have a career, take holidays, enjoy celebrations.

Take away those assumptions, and we can be left floundering, a life unravelled.

But the day you tell me you have a terminal illness and your time ahead is limited, you are not floundering or raging at fate. You are not frayed in any way. You are calm and composed as if you are aware of a secret I haven't yet fathomed. I find out as you speak that indeed you are. It's the absolute preciousness of being fully alive to each moment. That life is not lived in the future or the past, but rather in the here and now.

It's two days since we first met. We spent all of yesterday together, and although I've always known the sense of you in my bones, talking to you, seeing your face light up with a smile and hearing your laughter is a kind of validation, a confirmation that something – or rather someone – who would hugely enrich my life has finally arrived in it.

You have phoned me and said you needed to see me, to talk to me. And when I meet you outside a café close to Central Park, something in your face sends a shard of alarm dropping down through my body. I cast my mind back to see if I'd said anything wrong, or done anything silly or stupid to offend you, but I can't think straight.

At your suggestion, we get coffees to bring across to the park.

It's the kind of day New York is made for. Skyscrapers dazzling in sunshine reach up like fingertips touching crystal-blue heavens. Sidewalks teem with people; the hum of traffic and hooting horns is a constant and lively background. It's a city full of heart and spirit, but my heart is full of nameless dread. We stroll through the park, my whole body prickling with the nearness of you, and for a few sweet, blissful moments I pretend nothing is wrong: we are simply going for a walk in this beautiful place. We sit down on a bench near the John Lennon memorial, where the sun flickers through the canopy of sweeping trees.

You put your coffee down on the bench and take my hand. 'Am I right to think there's something extraordinary happening with you and me?'

Your eyes search my face. I can't look away. I nod my head.

'Well, then, I don't know how to put this,' you say, 'but I have to tell you, today.'

'You mean it was nice knowing you and all that, but …' I joke, painting a fake smile on my face, hoping my eyes don't look too stricken. I sip coffee, almost gagging on the taste.

'This isn't a "but", it's a full stop,' you say.

My gut twists. 'Oh gosh, Mallon, well, thanks for telling me. I've never had that kind of brush-off before.'

'Hell – there's no easy way to say it.'

It's when you curve your free arm around my shoulders and draw me close that I start to shiver.

You stare straight ahead. 'I'm afraid you and I don't have much of a future.'

'There's a bit of a distance between our lives,' I say through a constricted throat. 'For example, an ocean. How many miles is that? Probably about five thousand or so.'

'That's not it. I'd leap oceans for you. Cross planets if I had to. It's me. You need to know something about me before anything else happens between us.' A long silence.

Then you hold me tightly as you break the news and every piece of my heart explodes. You've been living with pancreatic cancer for the past few months. Coming from an inherited gene mutation. One of those shitty calling cards that fate can hurl at people from time to time. Your grandfather died of it soon after diagnosis but you are lucky to live in an era when gigantic strides are being made in cancer medicine. You had chemotherapy earlier this year and had responded well. It could never be cured completely but managed with oral therapy, and you are currently trialling a new type of drug.

'I'm fine, most of the time,' you say. 'I report to the team every month. There are no guarantees that it won't flare up again and no guarantees that I'll be around in, say, two or four years' time. Or even this time next year.'

I'm cold with shock. I don't know how I find the words, considering everything inside me has crashed down into smithereens. From the scintillating high of meeting you to the picture you are painting with your implacable words is a long drop. I speak on autopilot. 'There are no guarantees in life whatsoever.'

Some things are sure-fire. Yin and yang. Light and darkness. Deep love can come with deep pain.

'I'm not letting it stop me from doing whatever I want to do, as far as possible,' you say. 'But it does concentrate the mind somewhat.' I sense you smiling at me and I turn to smile back, and in that moment there are no barriers, no secrets between us and no going back.

'I'm thankful for each day,' you say. 'I try to live it to the full. I still work, trying to keep up a normal life for now. I love the work I'm doing for the foundation, it's worthwhile and important, but I'm not putting in anything like the hours I used to, and it's good that I can work remotely. I like to think I'm being productive, using my skills, living a life for the greater good, but maybe next year I'll have a rethink about that. Although I won't be trekking through India or kayaking up the Amazon. See, Izzie, you're a new complication.' You squeeze my hand.

'How?'

'I don't want to put you in a situation where you might get hurt, or be sad, when any commitment I can give is tempered with the unknown.'

'It's far too late for that.' I manage to grin, hiding my heartbreak. 'Besides, life is full of unknowns. It can change in a split second. That's what makes it mad and beautiful and terrible and exciting. Being with you will be all of that.'

I lean in closer to you. I don't tell you that I'm freezing cold or that a door to the shiny new future I envisaged has slammed closed. Or that being with you in this moment is more precious to me than anything else in the world. Instead I say, 'Sam, whatever is behind you or in front of you, I'm so glad I met you and we are now here, together. I wouldn't change this moment for anything. Every single day with you will be a gift. I can no more walk away from you than stop breathing. I'm in this for the wild rollercoaster ride. So fasten your safety belt.'

'Have a think about it first,' you say. 'It'll be a leap into the unknown.'

'Good. How exciting is that.'

'And, Izzie, very few people know about me. Just my immediate family, my immediate boss, the hospital consultants and now you.'

'Any particular reason?'

'I'm not going to be defined by this, to have my condition take over,' you say. 'I want to enjoy the life I have now. I don't want whatever time I have left being calculated and measured out by friends and acquaintances, or watching them studying me to see if I look fractionally worse or better. And when I fall apart, eventually, I don't want to become a showpiece for my condition, an object of curiosity or drama.'

I can't say you haven't spelled out the stark reality of it all with the images you put in my head.

We go back to your apartment because time has become precious, every moment distilled to its absolute essence. In your room, where sunshine fizzles sideways along the wall, we stand, holding each other, at first as silent and motionless as stone. My heart is thumping in my throat. Then your hands cradle the sides of my face, your forehead tips against mine and, in the long moment before we kiss, our breaths mingle.

It is the most urgent kiss I have ever savoured, ever given; unwilling to break the seal of our mouths, we grapple with clothes that are in the way. We slide out of things, move legs and arms, crash across the room, topple over the bed, still kissing deeply like we never want to be apart again. Our limbs lock around each other; you finally move your lips from my mouth down to my breast and the tug on my nipple sends a flame shooting through me.

'Elizabeth,' you whisper, lingering over every syllable so that your voice is soft velvet sliding against my skin.

But I am not the person I used to be. You have turned me into a warrior woman, hungry to give and receive as much love as I can. My skin is melting into yours as I press myself against the hardness of your body and weave my fingers through your hair. You in turn are melting into me, and we are hard and soft fusing together until we are both liquid gold.

I don't ever want to let go of you. But afterwards there is a need to rest, and as we lie together in tangled sheets, you smooth the messed-up hair from my face and smile.

I wish I could wrap up that beautiful smile in glittery paper and tuck it in my jeans pocket, so that I can take it out and savour the glow of it enfolding me whenever I want. Instead of keeping quiet about my wishes, I speak them aloud. Because this is no time for holding back; this is time to go out there all love blazing, and whether it is going to be six weeks, six months or even – if a miracle happened – six years, I'm going to tell you every single day that I love you.

You take my hand and kiss my fingertips. 'I'll make sure there's some way of saving my smile for you.'

CHAPTER FIFTY-ONE

After she said goodbye to Florence, Gemma crossed the road and went in through the gates of the park, drawn irresistibly by the incandescent light of the thick snow covering the grass and hedging. It was a beautiful square, down at heel in some areas, like a gracious lady fallen on hard times, tastefully restored in others, but all the buildings were underpinned by an elegant Georgian beauty that shone like splendid bone structure beneath aged skin.

Safe home, Florence had said. Nothing could be further from what Gemma had in mind for the rest of the afternoon.

She had the strange sensation that she was being watched

and she glanced back at the façade of number sixteen, picking out Florence's window, the Christmas lights faint now against the stark whiteness of the day outside, another colourful tree in the window of the apartment on the floor above and then on the top floor, Izzie's apartment – no Christmas cheer in this window.

Hang on – no wonder she'd felt a prickle on her neck. She thought she could make out the shape of Izzie's pale face at the window, looking out at her. Then she disappeared. It seemed to Gemma that she jerked away from the window as if embarrassed by being caught staring out. Or maybe that Eli guy had pulled her back to bed for another hot session. It all happened so swiftly she wondered if she'd imagined it, but as Gemma stood there, Eli appeared briefly at the window, pulling the drapes across in a swift movement, and now the window was blank.

As if anyone was going to be able to see in to that top floor. Still, whatever they were getting up to in the privacy of Izzie's apartment was none of her business.

A voice broke into her thoughts. 'Hey, you're Izzie's friend, aren't you?'

Gemma stared at the boy for a few seconds before realising it was Noah, whom she'd met in the hall. The hood of his jacket was pulled up, and she could barely see his face as he angled it towards her. He had a shovel in his gloved hands and had been making some kind of snow shape.

'Hi, yes, I am,' she said.

'Were you up talking to her?'

'I was.'

'What do you think of that guy, Eli?' he asked, aiming a kick at the snow.

'I dunno, I hardly met him,' she said.

Noah screwed up his face. 'Do you think he's really Sam's best mate? Cos I don't think he is.'

'He has to be some kind of friend if he's staying with Izzie,' Gemma said, wondering what was bugging Noah.

'Did Izzie ever talk about him?' Noah asked, his eyes clear and guileless.

Gemma shook her head. 'No – then again, she never talked about Sam either.'

Noah looked surprised. 'She must have said something about him to you.'

'Sorry, Noah, I'm not exactly that kind of friend, I work with Izzie, and I only started there after Sam died, so—'

'Yeah, I get it.'

He sounded so downcast that Gemma was compelled to ask him, 'Why, what's the problem?'

'I don't think he's Sam's friend at all,' Noah said. 'I think that guy is a fake, pretending to be Eli.'

She didn't understand where Noah was coming from. Even though Izzie had been in a bad place, with her head scattered, she was hardly that confused.

'I really liked Sam,' Noah went on. 'He was cool. But I don't understand how Eli could be his best mate. He's a – well, I can't say it out loud, only in my head.'

In a flash of inspiration, Gemma realised that Noah was more than likely as disillusioned as she was. After the near-perfect image she'd held in her head of the lovely Izzie and Sam, it was hard to see Eli replacing him so quickly before Izzie had waited a decent interval.

'Well, at least he's company for Izzie over Christmas,' she said, knowing it wasn't what he wanted to hear.

'I'd rather have no company than that weird dude,' Noah said, turning away to dig his shovel into the snow.

*

Gemma stomped her way through the snow-covered grass and crossed the square to the other side, spotting the mini-market that she'd passed on the way to Izzie's. The lights inside were blazing, illuminating the small seating area to one side, and there was a faint but inviting aroma of coffee when someone opened the door just as she passed by. On impulse, she retraced her steps and went in, wiping her feet on the damp mat, helping herself to a latte at the self-service counter and sitting down on a plastic chair by the window, tucking her carrier bag under the table.

The moment, in Florence's, when she'd picked up the bag and handed it to Gemma had sent a rush of embarrassment through her. Just as well her frilly froth had been packed underneath her pink velour top, otherwise Florence might have had an eyeful. Now, even recalling what she'd bought, and how she'd visualised parading around in it, gave Gemma a lurch in her tummy.

Was this what she wanted? Buying barely-there underwear in an attempt to titillate a guy she scarcely knew? It was cool to put it on for a guy so they'd have some fun, but getting so drunk at a Christmas party that she'd fallen into bed with the first guy out of the office who'd hit on her hadn't been in her grand, conquer-the-world plan.

Talking to Florence had reminded her about all the ambitions she'd had when she'd left MacBride, thrilled to get to college, thanks to her hard work and committed teachers, over the moon to get her degree, looking forward to following in Janet's footsteps, basking in the glow of her mother's pride on graduation day, her two sisters' excitement, even how thrilled she'd been about her first foray into the big wide world.

How determined she'd been to make her first internship a success.

Gemma sat at the plastic table, sipping her tasteless coffee, her spirits low. Surely she was worth far more than a Christmas-party aftermath with a guy from the office who'd more than likely forget all about her as soon as it was over? Cross her off his bonk list, maybe even talk about her afterwards, comparing her performance to others? It didn't matter how hot Kian was, she knew deep inside she was only someone to amuse him, a kind of compensation in advance of being immured at home in the 'numbingly boring' – his words – Christmas traditions. She didn't feel like that about Christmas at all. She thought of her mother making a huge celebration out of carving the turkey, saying the same things year after year about a wonderful dinner for her beautiful daughters, and a cold chill ran down her spine. The troubled neighbourhood might have had a bad name, but the warmth of the sitting room in St Finnian's Gardens, hung with far too many decorations, a cosy log fire in the grate, her mother staunchly at the heart of the family, more than made up for that.

Gemma picked up her phone and called home. Her mother answered immediately. 'Gemma! How are you, love? Where are you?'

'I'm fine, Mum, I'm still in town.'

'That's grand, Gemma. I'm delighted to hear your voice

and that you're making new friends. Will you be home this evening or tomorrow?'

'I'm not sure yet,' Gemma hedged.

'That's okay, it's just Janet and Amy want to put on *Ghost* this evening. They've already opened the sweets. I've asked them to hold off but they can't wait to start Christmas and get in the mood.'

Ghost. Her mum had seen the movie just before Janet had been born and it was one of her all-time favourites. She had two copies of it at home. Watching it every Christmas, while passing around a tin of sweets and munching on crisps, had turned into a comforting family tradition.

'They'd better not scoff all the caramels,' Gemma said, wanting to weep at the image of her sisters tucked up in front of the television in their fleeces and fluffy socks, watching the movie in the glow of the Christmas lights and candles without her.

'Ah, there's more than one tub of sweets – knowing you lot, I have another hidden away. But don't tell your sisters.'

'Sure we know that already, Mum, including where it's hidden.'

Another silly, year-on-year family tradition: Mum acting surprised when the first tub was demolished before Christmas Eve and coming to the rescue with a 'spare one she'd bought just in case this exact thing happened'.

'See you whenever, love, and mind yourself coming home.'

'I will.'

Mind yourself. Her mother's standard catchphrase at all times. Said so often it went in one ear and out the other. Somehow, today it hit home. In what way was she minding herself? She wanted to have fun, of course she did, and there would be lots of it. But maybe not like this. Florence's words came back to her about short-changing herself, and she wondered what Janet would have done in her circumstances. Then again, she couldn't visualise Janet getting wasted at her first ever office Christmas party.

Although this wasn't about Florence or Janet. This was about Gemma Nugent and what she wanted, or didn't want. And she knew the answer to that straightaway.

She called Kian, wanting to get this over with, glad that he answered and she didn't have to resort to leaving a message or sending a text.

'Sorry, Kian,' she said, 'I won't be back this afternoon after all. I need to get home.'

'Oh.' He sounded surprised. There was a silence.

Her heart was thumping. 'Yeah, look, it's been great, we had fun, but—'

'But?' A snappy retort. He wasn't happy.

'The Christmas party has started at home and I want to be there for it.'

Another silence. 'How exciting,' he said in a tone of voice that implied the opposite. So what if he thought she was sad for opting for the traditions of family instead of the delights of his body. It was best to be honest, wasn't it?

'Not so much exciting, just homely and relaxing and everyone together …' Her voice faded away. His pride was probably far more dented at being passed over in favour of something 'homely and relaxing'.

'Good luck with that,' he said. 'I thought you would've been up for more fun.'

'Christmas is only once a year,' she said, annoyed at sounding defensive.

She thought she heard him mutter that once a year was way too often for him, as he ended the call. She picked up her shopping and got to her feet. She didn't know what it would be like facing Kian in the office but she'd deal with that, just like she'd apologise to Katy and Rachel.

It was time to go home.

She went out into the cold, crisp day, the air scented with snow, and couldn't help recalling the image of Izzie at the window, before the curtains had been pulled, shutting out the light. All the time Gemma had been sitting there, it had played at the back of her mind. It was none of her business, though, and whatever about looking out for Izzie in the office, she'd no right to be concerning herself with her private affairs. Mindful of the slushy pavement, she walked around the corner towards the city centre and the warmth and cosiness of St Finnian's Gardens.

CHAPTER FIFTY-TWO

'You can make this easy or hard on yourself,' Eli said. 'I'm not leaving until I get what I want. You're not leaving here either.'

'Surprise, surprise,' Izzie said.

She'd fallen back asleep. Whatever he'd put in her coffee and drink last night was still in her system. After she'd woken up, he'd made sandwiches, so he didn't intend for them to starve. There was a little more strength coming into her limbs, but she couldn't make a dash for it. Apart from the threat of him using his knife, she was locked in and he had the key. He'd already escorted her to use the en suite, having checked it first to make sure there was nothing she could use against him, and she'd pretended to be weaker than she was. Now she was back on the sofa and, with the drapes still pulled and the lamps lighting, she had no idea of the time, guessing that it was late afternoon.

'Why didn't you just take Sam's laptop and fuck off with it?' she said. 'Why didn't you swing by here weeks ago? You would have had plenty of time to crack the passwords. I don't understand all this last-minute stuff. You weren't all that well prepared.'

'Are you kidding? I'm prepared for all eventualities, including you.' The confident smile he gave her chilled her. 'What's the first thing you would have done if your apartment had been burgled and Sam's laptop robbed?'

'I would have notified the police, and New York.'

'See? I didn't want to alert New York and give them a chance to close me down or run another fix. I need to get in and get out of the systems as quickly as I can without forewarning anyone. If you'd been co-operative with the passwords, that would have worked just nicely. Unfortunately you weren't. You've messed that part up and I've already had to adjust some of my plans. But I'm ready for all contingencies, no matter what they are.'

Listening to what he had to say, it all began to feel surreal to Izzie.

'Thanks to your refusal to co-operate,' he went on, 'I'm going to have to do this the hard way. I'm going to trash this room and every room until I find what I'm looking for.'

'You won't find anything,' she said.

He came across the room and lowered himself until his face was inches from hers. 'You're lying. Sam never left anything to chance. That program was too critical for him not to have stashed his password somewhere or have some back-ups.

Especially if he thought he might not be around. I just have to find them. With or without your help.'

'It'll be without my help,' she said.

He went over to the bookshelves and began to take the books out one at a time, holding the covers apart and shaking them, flicking through the pages from start to finish before throwing them to the floor.

'What do you think you'll find there?' she asked.

'Passwords,' he said. 'Anything in writing. Scribbled in the margins. Sentences underlined. A Post-it. I told you, I know the way Sam operated. He had ways of hiding his passwords in the most ordinary places. If it's here, I'll find it; failing that, I'll find the back-up. I should have just about enough time to get what I want.'

'I told Noah I'd go to his carol concert – they'll all be wondering when I don't show.'

'No, they won't,' he said. 'Not with me here, taking such excellent care of you. They'll think we're in the middle of a love fest. It was a good idea to have Gemma call to Florence on her way out – she seemed quite chatty and I'm sure she's telling Florence all about us, plus the fact that you were reluctant to leave this apartment. No one is going to disturb us, you can be sure of that.'

'Noah might come up, just to check if I'm ready,' she said.

In answer to that he went into the hallway and switched off the light. Coming back into the sitting room, he stood behind her and pressed something cold and metallic against the back of her neck. She froze.

'In that case we'll ignore him,' he said. 'And you had better not try anything funny.'

CHAPTER FIFTY-THREE

When Noah arrived at the turn in the landing that evening, he saw straight away that Izzie wasn't down in the hall, waiting to come to his concert. Florence was, however, muffled up in a black chunky coat, with a knitted bobble hat on her head and matching scarf.

'Are you sure about coming out in this weather?' his dad asked, going ahead of him down the stairs and reaching the hall first. 'We won't be offended if you want to change your mind.'

Noah came downstairs deliberately slowly, hoping he'd hear Izzie behind him.

'No way,' Florence said. 'I'm all set. I even have my snow grips on my feet.' She extended a leg to show something metal attached to the underside of her boot. 'I got these during the last big snow,' she said. 'I had to do a good search for them but I managed to find them.'

'Good.' His dad smiled. Then, as Noah reached them, he said, 'No sign of Izzie?'

He was glad his father asked the question on the tip of his tongue. This was the evening he'd been looking forward to for ages. He'd desperately wanted Izzie to be there. Thanks to Eli, it wouldn't be happening now.

'I haven't seen her all day,' Florence said. 'She's in hibernation mode.'

'Yeah, obviously.'

They were about to leave.

'I'll just call up and let her know we're leaving,' Noah said, fighting back sick disappointment. 'She might have got the time wrong.'

Florence gave him a small smile. It didn't help. If anything it made him feel more wretched.

'Right,' his dad said. 'You have two minutes. The sooner we leave, the more time we'll have to get around in the snow.'

Noah retraced his steps up to the first-floor landing, and then went on up to the next floor. All was silent. There was no sound at all coming from Izzie's apartment. He knocked on the door, crossing his fingers, but there was no reply. He knocked a second time, for good luck, he told himself, but all remained still and silent. She couldn't have been hibernating completely, because there was a gift-wrapped package under his tree that looked suspiciously like the DVDs she'd promised him, so she must have called down at some stage today. Not only had he missed it, but his dad hadn't even mentioned it. He hoped, by some miracle, that Izzie might have left for the concert already, and that Eli might have cleared back off to New York. Even as he thought it, he knew he was being silly. He had no option but to go back downstairs to where the others waited in the hall.

'Well?' his father asked.

He shrugged. 'No answer.'

To his surprise, his father slung his arm over his shoulder. 'No worries, son – let's go to a concert.'

Florence opened the door to a blast of arctic air. The spill of light coming from the hallway illuminated a man standing outside, peering at the row of doorbells. He was muffled up in a heavy padded jacket, with a Russian-type hat on his head.

'Dad?' his father said. 'What the—? Come in!'

The man outside lifted his head and, to Noah's surprise, his grandad Sean's face beamed out at him from under the rim of his hat. He stepped into the hall, lugging a big sports bag. He dropped the bag and enveloped Noah in his arms.

'How did you get here?' his dad asked, as both men then embraced.

'Think mountain and Muhammed,' his grandad said. 'Or something like that. I've come straight from Cork city. The roads back home to west Cork are in a terrible state and a friend of a friend was coming to Dublin in his jeep so I hitched a lift. The motorway was scary at times and took hours but we got here. Am I still in time for the concert?'

'Yeah, just about,' his father said, looking pleased and puzzled. 'We're on the way out to it now.'

'Great. I can't miss my grandson singing my all-time favourite Christmas song. We can talk on the way.'

'I'll throw your bag upstairs first,' his dad said.

'No need to go all the way back upstairs,' said Florence,

taking her keys out of her pocket. 'You can put your bag in here.' She opened her apartment door.

'You must be Florence,' his grandad said. He hefted his bag past Florence.

'I am. And you must be Sean.'

'I am.'

'And we had better get going,' his dad said. 'We won't be able to leg it around on this ice.'

'Sure we will,' his grandad said, winking at Florence. 'If I've skated up from Cork, we can all skate around to the concert.'

Everyone laughed and Noah thought how perfect it would have been to have Izzie here, sharing in the laughter. They left the house, securing the hall door after them, and as they crossed through the park Noah looked back, but the curtains were drawn across Izzie's windows and everything looked blank. Maybe, just maybe, she'd already left for the concert. As they stepped carefully up the far side of Henrietta Square, his grandad telling his father and Florence about his journey up, there was a gap in the clouds, finally, and he saw the glimmer of some distant stars high up in the dark heavens. It made him think of his mother and Sam, and the words of the Christmas song he was going to sing swelled up in his throat. He thought he was going to cry for a minute so he stared really hard at the whiteness of his puffs of breath in front of his face.

But any last hope he'd had that Izzie might have gone ahead to the parish church disappeared when there was no sign of her. His dad, grandad and Florence took their seats and he went to meet his classmates and warm up by practising his scales. The choir sang some carols, and then it was his turn for the solo. He stood in the spotlit pool in the centre of the small altar, took a breath and began to sing. He pictured his mother and Sam, floating up high somewhere, looking down at all of them from a moonlit sky. He imagined wrapping up his wishes in silvery foil and throwing them up into the sky so that Sam caught them with a grin and gave him a high five.

The arrival of his grandad was a lovely and unexpected surprise. He hoped it meant there'd be more unexpected surprises. He'd heard it said that bad things happened in threes; maybe good things could happen in threes also. Especially at Christmas.

CHAPTER FIFTY-FOUR

Sitting in the church, sandwiched between Tom and Sean, Florence gave up trying to halt the tears from trickling out of her eyes and sliding down her cheeks. Christmas carols – sung by children in particular, with their high, thin, innocent, voices – always possessed the power to move her. But here, this evening, listening to Noah had shaken her to the core.

It was a combination of everything: the purity of his voice, soaring out into a softly lit church, the atmosphere created by a gathering of people who had crunched through the glittery snow and a freezing-cold starlit evening to come out in support, the suppressed air of excitement that the Christmas season inevitably intensified the closer you got to the big day. At this time of the year it was harder to prevent her thoughts from veering down her dark and gloomy personal rabbit hole.

Tonight, she was rudderless, all over the place, unable to gather any remnants of herself together. Where was her sparky Girl-Power image? The one she liked to hide behind as she faced the world at large? It seemed to have deserted her in her hour of need.

And she knew when it had dissolved – she could pinpoint the exact second: the moment Sean Brady had walked into the hallway in Henrietta Square and smiled at her with those warm brown eyes and spoken to her in a voice equally warm and rich. And then the considerate way he had held out his arm for her to hold as they made their way around the snow-covered pavements to the church.

All of a sudden she felt seventeen again, but in the next moment, every one of her seventy-two years.

She'd thought to herself from time to time that Tom was the kind of man she would have been attracted to had she been thirty years younger. It had been safe enough to indulge in such casual thoughts because, most assuredly, nothing was going to happen. Well, quite unexpectedly, fate had called her bluff, because an older version of Tom had arrived on her doorstep. Approximately thirty years older. She knew, beyond a shadow of a doubt, that if she'd had her life to live over, Sean Brady was the kind of man she could have married and shared a life and family with. A powerful pull of regret swept through her at the missed opportunities and the long, lonely years she'd spent without someone like him in her life.

Florence grew cross with herself and told herself to cop on – she sat up straighter, reminding herself that there was no going back and it was a total waste of time to have any kind of regrets. That didn't stop the tears from slipping down her face as Noah came to the final chorus of his song. She lifted her bag and tried to remove a tissue from a small cellophane packet without making any noise, only to have the packet slip from her grasp and skitter across the linoleum floor, coming to a stop just out of her reach.

Sean Brady came to her aid. He reached down easily under the pew in front and picked up the packet, handing it to her with a smile. She noticed that his eyes, too, were bright with unshed tears, and on impulse she offered him a tissue, which he accepted readily.

'I'm getting soft in my golden years,' he murmured. 'It's the innocence of it all that catches me and the world they're going into. Plus it's a nostalgic time of year.'

'I know,' she whispered. 'Me too.'

There was a moment of shared understanding between them, and she settled back in her seat for the finale of the concert, a little less alone, conscious of his proximity.

Sean surely had his own dark moments, Florence realised. He'd lost his wife several years ago, and then his lovely daughter-in-law. Two people who should have been sitting with them this evening, listening to Noah sing his heart out and watching him cast a spell over the gathering. Christmas, with all its poignancy, could be wonderful yet gut-wrenching at the same time.

When they arrived back in Henrietta Square, there was a moment of awkwardness in the hall.

'I'll get your bag,' Florence said to Sean, opening the door to her apartment.

'Allow me,' Sean said. 'Don't attempt to lift that.'

'Thanks again,' Florence said, turning to Tom while Sean got his bag. 'It was lovely, and it was a joy to hear Noah sing, so thanks for asking me along. Enjoy the rest of your evening,' she said, nodding at Sean as he joined Tom and Noah in the hallway.

'Don't tell me you're breaking up the party?' Sean said, looking from Florence to his son. 'Surely that's not allowed?'

'Yes, Florence,' Tom said. 'You have to join us for a drink. I'll need some help keeping this man out of mischief. Besides, I think it's my turn to have a snow party. Florence had a party last night,' he explained to his father, 'just to take our minds off the snow and because we were beginning to get cabin fever.'

Sean looked at her with interest. 'I'm sorry I missed that. I bet you had a good evening. And there was I thinking I was having the craic in Cork. Seems like Henrietta Square is party central.'

'It was lovely,' Florence said. 'And it's kind of Tom to return the hospitality, although I doubt I'm qualified to keep you out of mischief,' she went on, giddy at the realisation that her cheeks had flushed a little. 'But I'll certainly join you for a drink. Give me half an hour or so and I'll be up.'

She spent the next half an hour in a flurry of fixing her hair and her make-up, taking off her black denims and changing into her leather jeans – so what, she thought, squaring up to herself in the mirror – squirting a dose of her favourite perfume and throwing an eye around her already tidy apartment, plumping up cushions, a hazy and equally crazy notion beginning to form at the back of her mind and run through her veins like quicksilver.

Noah answered the door. 'Hey, Florence,' he said, stalling

her in the hallway, his eyes anxious. 'D'you think I should ask Dad to invite Izzie, seeing as we're having a party?'

Her heart faltered. Why was life so shitty at times? This child had the voice of an angel and had just held a full church spellbound with his rendition. He should be happy with himself and his performance, yet here he was, full of little worries and anxieties, and there was little she could say to smooth them over.

'Probably not,' she said gently. 'Your dad wouldn't mind in the least, but do you really think it's a good idea? Eli would have to be asked as well.'

Noah made a face.

'Anyhow, I don't think they're in,' Florence said. 'Izzie didn't answer the door to you earlier on and I didn't see any of her lights on when we were coming back, so they must have ventured out somewhere local.' Earlier that afternoon, when Noah had been in the park, she'd gift-wrapped the DVDs and brought them up to Tom. Glancing on up the staircase as she stopped at Tom's door, there had been no sign of life or any kind of activity coming from the top floor. It could have been deserted. The landing light wasn't on and, even in the afternoon, the stairwell was in shadows.

'They didn't. There's someone in cos I heard footsteps coming from her apartment. Earlier tonight and just now.'

'Well, then,' Florence said, 'it seems Izzie doesn't want to be disturbed, so I'd leave it if I were you.' She was surprised at the way Izzie had ignored Noah that evening. Given the way Noah looked up to her and had adored Sam, a quick trip to the concert wouldn't have hurt, Eli or no Eli.

But then she went inside, into the warmth of Tom's living room, and there was Sean, getting up from an armchair and smiling at her. He was wearing jeans and a navy jumper and his figure was trim and youthful.

'Ah, Florence, I'm glad you came.' His warm brown eyes looked at her appreciatively. 'Thanks for rescuing me from my family.'

She couldn't turn back time, never, ever, but she was here now, and she was just seventeen on the inside with the way he was looking at her.

'So long as you don't expect your family to rescue you from me,' she attempted a joke.

'There you are, Dad,' Tom said. 'I told you Florence would well and truly give you a run for your money. You won't get much past this lovely lady.'

'Good,' Sean said. 'I like being kept on my toes.'

'What will you have, Florence?' Tom asked. 'We have beer, wine, gin, brandy …'

'Wine would be lovely, thanks,' she said.

Tom organised drinks and nibbles and mince pies. He flicked on to a Christmas movie on the television, the volume low, to give an atmosphere more than anything else. He had plugged in the Christmas-tree lights and another set running along the top of the mantelpiece, so that the room was softly lit with the glow, and Florence relaxed. They talked about the concert and compared their favourite Christmas songs and carols and after a while Tom confirmed that they were having Christmas in Henrietta Square and going to his mother-in-law's closer to the new year.

'And the weather means this crew here will have to put up with me for a couple of days,' Sean said.

'I'm sure that will be a terrible hardship,' Florence said.

Tom smiled. 'I don't know how I'll cope.'

Noah turned around from the television. 'Are you really staying here, Grandad? That's ace,' he said.

'So long as you don't mind me stretched out along the sofa, snoring my brains out.'

'You can have my room and I'll bunk in with Dad,' Noah offered immediately.

'Actually, I have a suggestion,' Florence said, suddenly emboldened. It was something that had been playing in a corner of her mind ever since Sean had lugged his bag through her door earlier that evening. She hadn't been sure if she'd have enough nerve to suggest it, to take such a vast leap out of her military-strength comfort zone, and then the words were out of her mouth.

Three pairs of eyes looked at her and she had to take a slow breath to continue. 'I have a spare bedroom – you're welcome to it, Sean. It means nobody will be turfed out anywhere and we'll all have a comfortable night's sleep.'

'I couldn't put you to that trouble,' Sean said.

'The room is lying empty, so you won't be putting me to any trouble,' Florence said, her heartbeat skittering slightly. 'It's just a bed for the night, no big deal,' she heard herself say with forced nonchalance, as though she invited men home on a regular basis. 'It can be my contribution to the snow effort. It'll make me less guilty when I hear all about the people who have been inconvenienced. So you'll be doing me a favour.'

'Are you sure about this?' Sean asked.

'Absolutely,' Florence told him.

Florence saw Tom's keen gaze move slowly from his father to her. Whatever he saw seemed to satisfy him because he said, 'That could work out all right, Dad. You could come straight up here for your breakfast in the morning and not be bothering Florence.'

'You never know, I might be able to stretch to a cup of coffee,' Florence said.

'Sounds good to me ...' Sean smiled at her as though she'd given him a particularly nice gift. She wanted to sit in the glow of that smile and never move.

'That's settled then,' Florence said, wondering what was coming over her. First snow parties and now an overnight guest, and not just any guest but a man who made her feel young and foolish all over again. She pulled herself up sharply. Correction: he made her feel strong enough to step out of her comfort zone and wise enough to know that she had to grab any and every opportunity that came her way. Opportunity for what? She didn't know yet. All she knew was that the evening had changed thanks to this man, the prospect of Christmas had changed now that he'd be on the radar; something shimmered in the air, an expectation, a ripple of excitement that swirled around her.

CHAPTER FIFTY-FIVE

It seemed to take forever for Eli to go through the books on Izzie's shelf to his satisfaction. He checked each page and inside the covers, and eventually, when they were all lying in a pile on the floor, he gave them a savage kick.

'It's a pity you decided to screw things up,' he said. 'You could have made this so much easier for both of us.'

'I can't because there's nothing here,' she said.

'Let me see, what's up next?' He ran his fingers over Sam's collection of vinyl, watching her face as he began to pull out the albums. She reminded herself that they were just inanimate things and, no matter what he did, he could never destroy the music or the warm memories it evoked.

'Quite the two lovebirds you were, listening to this crap.'

He put a record on the turntable, increasing the volume so that Dire Straits' 'Brothers in Arms' flowed out across the room. 'Your nosy neighbours will think we're having a party of our own.'

One by one he slid the records out of their sleeves, letting them drop to the floor among the pile of books. He checked the inside of each sleeve and, when he was finished that, he picked up the records one by one and began whirling them across the room. She forced herself to sit impassively as they landed on the table, on the fireplace, and hit off furniture, the kitchen cabinets.

He yanked the record off the turntable, sending it sailing in a high arc through the air. 'Wheeee,' he said, watching as it hit the ceiling chandelier and came down on the coffee table right in front of Izzie. 'Pity you can't join in the game and see who can throw these the furthest.'

He turned his attention to the top shelf where there were three framed photographs: one of her and Sam on their wedding day, another one of them standing on a beach in the south of France and a third taken of them in New York last Christmas against the backdrop of the Rockefeller Center Christmas tree. He picked them up one at a time, using his knife to lever the frame apart, checking inside it, casting the frame to the ground and tearing the photographs into strips. She told herself that these too were replaceable.

'Oh dear, no luck here either,' he said.

He pulled down the few ornaments, discarding them when they proved fruitless, reaching up to brush his hands across the empty shelves. The low press that held the television was next. He pulled out movie DVDs and box sets, checking everything, turning the discs around in his hands, angling them in different directions and holding them up to the light before throwing them on the floor.

'Nope. Not even Sam could overwrite one of these.'

'How do you know?' Izzie said. 'Maybe he was cleverer than you think. You might just have to play them all to be sure.'

Eli looked at the pile of discs and slammed his foot into them. 'You'd better watch what you're saying. Unless you know something I don't.'

She shrugged her shoulders.

'Fuck you,' he said, going across to the kitchen, where he systematically pulled everything out of the presses, looking inside boxes and containers and upending drawers.

'Even if you manage to get what you came for, you won't get away with it,' Izzie said as spiritedly as she could. 'The minute you leave here I'm calling the police.'

'Oh, brave you.' The look he gave her sent a chill down her spine. 'Surely you realise I've got that covered.'

'Oh yeah?' she said.

'By the time you manage to surface from the alcohol I'll make sure you drink and the sleeping tablets I'll have you ingest, it'll be too late. I'll be on the other side of the world and the funds will have transferred to my account.'

'Ha. You're forgetting one thing – there are no flights.'

'Not right now, but I expect there will be tomorrow. And there are still ferries running, if I'm stuck, that will get me the hell out of this country. I'll be seeing in the new year in a far-away part of the world while you'll still be recovering from the motherfucker of all hangovers.'

'I'll still have time to raise the alarm,' Izzie said. 'I'm sure some of the New York techies could disable your program.'

'It'll be too late. Besides, how reliable would your word be in your befuddled state, especially when you don't even know who I am? Once I've done my thing and the money is gone, the damage is done. Stanley Trust and Cannon Finance will be too embarrassed to follow this up with the authorities. They'll want to wash their hands of this, discreetly. Bad enough being duped before but to be careless enough to have it happen to them again? Disaster. It would implode their credibility and the future of the firm and damage the public's trust in the foundation as well.'

'You don't have much time left,' Izzie said. 'You told Florence and Tom you'd be leaving on Christmas Eve – it must be nearly that now.'

'As I said, I've prepared for all contingencies. I might or might not be leaving – it all depends. Anyway, it's time for more medicine, Izzie, and after that you're going to sleep like a baby while I continue my search. You're beginning to annoy the hell out of me with your stupid remarks. You'd want to be careful you don't make me too angry.'

'I'm not swallowing anything,' she said.

'Oh yes, you are,' he said, slashing his knife in criss-cross motions through the air.

CHAPTER FIFTY-SIX

Florence almost floated down the stairs at the end of the evening with Sean behind her. She showed him around her apartment, finding it strange to be ushering him in to her spare bedroom, watching him stow his bag on the floor.

'The heating has been on most of the day, so you should be comfortable,' she babbled, suddenly nervous. 'I'll get some fresh towels for you.' She nipped out of the room and returned with the towels, placing them on a chair near the bed. 'There's not much of a view from your window,' she went on, wondering why it seemed so imperative to talk. 'It's to the back of the house.'

A short silence fell between them. Florence was sure her erratic heart was firing out awkward vibes in all directions.

Sean was perfectly composed. 'I appreciate this, thank you,' he said.

'I'm glad of the opportunity to do a good deed,' she said. 'Even Izzie upstairs has an unexpected guest thanks to the weather.'

'Actually, Florence, you're quite trusting to take me in.'

'If you're Tom's father you have to be kosher.'

'You never know,' he said. 'Tom and I could have cooked this up between us.'

'Yeah, so you could murder me in my bed?' Florence said, pushing her doubts aside and recovering some of her spirit. 'Or help yourself to all my worldly goods? You happen to be the image of Tom, so you have to be his dad, but you won't find much worth robbing here. Unless you're here to seduce me.'

Sean laughed, and the sound of it bounced around the walls of Florence's apartment, walls that had been silent for far too long. His eyes, bright with intelligence and amusement, gazed into hers, lighting up the dark of the long black tunnel that sat in the back of her head and stretched all the way down to her private heartache.

'It was worth hauling my ass up to Dublin for that fascinating offer,' he said, his eyes sparkling with merriment. 'I've heard a lot about you from Noah, but I know I'm going to enjoy getting to know you even better.'

She led the way back to her living room. 'A nightcap?' she asked. 'I have brandy.'

'I can't think of anything more perfect.'

When they were settled at either end of the sofa in front of the dying embers of the fire, he asked her where she was from.

'I could be wrong, but I don't think you're an original Dub,' he said.

'No,' Florence said, 'I'm not. I was born in a far corner of Donegal and lived there until I was eighteen.'

'Opposite ends of the country, so,' he said smiling. 'It's a wonder we've met at all.'

She asked him about his wife.

'Mairead was a wonderful person,' he said. 'We lived in Cork city for most of our lives, and we moved to west Cork and had a total change of life direction when Tom and Cathy settled in Clane. I took early retirement and we set up home on the outskirts of a small village. Mairead followed her dream and set up a café business in the main street. Unfortunately our idyll didn't last too long. We had three years. Then Mairead had a heart attack one morning and was gone, just like that. I'm just glad she managed to meet Noah – he was about six weeks old or thereabouts.'

'So it's been ten years.'

'Yes.'

'What a shock.'

'In the beginning it was a nightmare, but that has softened now. I'm grateful for the good times we had. I try to stay positive.'

'And you've continued to live there?'

'I love it. Home is a bungalow up on an elevated site with fantastic views, I do a lot of photography and the landscape is astounding, both winter and summer. There's a thriving community around and I have friends. I go into Cork regularly too – it's a lively city and there's always something on.'

'Sounds like a great kind of life.'

'It is – you should come down some time with Tom and

Noah. I have some spare rooms, so you wouldn't all be squished together. I can even stretch to a good cup of coffee. And maybe a nightcap.'

'Well,' she laughed, taken aback and equally thrilled at the whole idea of it, 'that's kind of you, and it's a lovely offer, but I could be anybody ...'

'You're a friend of Noah's, aren't you? I've heard all about you from Noah himself, and any friend of his is a friend of mine. I adore everything about that child, from the tiniest hair on his head right down to his smallest toenail. We go out for nature walks when he comes down to visit and that's when we chat. You know he thinks of you as his third granny?'

For a long time, Florence was so moved she was unable to reply.

'I've said something wrong?' Sean asked, his voice warm with concern.

'On the contrary,' she said, anxious to reassure him. 'You haven't said anything wrong. But what you've said is far too nice and complimentary for the likes of me. I don't deserve to be Noah's third granny.'

'I don't think so.'

'You don't know me, Sean,' she said carefully. 'You don't know what I've done.'

'I know how Noah speaks of you and that's enough for me. Tom, also, thinks very highly of you.'

'I suggest we leave it at that, before I disillusion you.'

He looked at her astutely. 'For an intelligent woman, I'm disappointed to hear you talking like that. I'd be interested to know what happened to make you think anything you've done would disillusion me.'

'You'd be surprised.'

'Would I? Florence,' he said gently, 'neither of us has got to this stage of our lives with blemish-free existences. I've no doubt we've both been through lots of ups and downs. We've both imagined how we might have changed things if we'd had a second chance or – the favourite of all – regretted the things we didn't do. Am I right?'

She nodded. 'But in my case it's regretting something I did.'

'It's the nature of life and living to make a balls of it from time to time,' he said. 'It's what puts the empathy in our smile, the light of understanding in our eyes. It gives us our ability to connect more deeply with another human being. And I hope it helps us to appreciate more fully the good things in life when they come along, like kindness and friendship and,' he smiled at her, 'the pleasure of sharing an unexpected nightcap at the end of the evening with a like-minded contemporary who might have been through the wars but hasn't let it take away her energy or zest for life. They're not called the golden years for nothing,' he said. 'It can be a golden age for those of us who are privileged enough to be able to enjoy it. If we so choose.'

Florence had to swallow hard as she met his bright, keen gaze.

'A toast to us, for having survived this wonderful and chaotic life thus far,' Sean said, lifting his glass and tipping it to hers.

'To us,' she said, moved in a way she'd never been before. The urge to speak swept through her. She wanted to tell him about herself, to get rid of the barriers she'd erected between herself and the world and to heal her spirit by pouring some light into the dark part of her heart. She sensed by his gentle tone that he would understand and not sit in judgement.

'Actually,' she began, 'there's one regret I have, one thing I wouldn't do if I had my life to live over.'

'And what is that, Florence?'

'I would never have let them take away my baby,' she said.

*

They were just a few words but they freed her. Once they were said, sliding out into the calm, accepting air between them and barely causing any ripples, except a soothing acknowledgement, her spirits lightened.

Of course Sean understood. He, too, had lived through life in Ireland in the late fifties and early sixties. He had witnessed the stigma of unmarried pregnancy, the spectacle of condemned teenage girls being disowned by their families and sent away in shame, to either England or a mother and baby home, where only the so-called lucky few were given permission to return home afterwards, permanently scarred from their experience.

She sketched out that terrifying time briefly, feeling as though she was talking about a stranger and not someone who had carried her shame for years, trying to bury it deep only to find it surfacing every so often: pregnant at eighteen to the horror and shock of her parents, banished to a midlands mother and baby home, the trauma of that along with the guilt and shame, the emotional abuse, emerging shattered, without her baby, after it all.

'I never got over losing my baby girl,' she said. 'She was beautiful. She was mine for just a week, and they took her one night when I was asleep. I never got to say goodbye. I was too numbed, too cowed by the whole experience to kick up any fuss. Yet I was considered one of the lucky ones – I went back home and completed my education, I went to university in Dublin and even joined all the women's rights marches, shouting as loudly as everyone else, but deep down inside I regarded myself as a two-faced fraud because I'd allowed myself to be manipulated on one of the most important issues affecting my life: the right to be a loving mother to my child. Then again, I hadn't had the guts to stand up for myself. I hadn't had the courage to demand my baby back and be her mother.'

'Florence, you were eighteen,' Sean said gently. 'Things were different then. There were no supports like there are nowadays. You should have more compassion for yourself.'

'I took up a teaching position in Dublin and the rest was history,' she said. 'But I was never at peace. My family could have supported me, but they pretended nothing had ever happened. My brothers emigrated to Canada, my father died when I was forty, my mother lingered on and moved in with her sister. We never had a good relationship and she spent her final years in a nursing home. When she died, just over ten years ago, I had a huge wake-up call and decided to look for my daughter. It had always been a dream of mine to find her. But then—' Florence bit back a sob. Her hands shaking, she rummaged for a tissue.

Sean went over to the counter and came back with some kitchen roll.

'You don't have to talk if you don't want to,' he said.

She shuddered. 'I want to finish this. I want you to know.'

'Okay. Thank you for taking me into your confidence. I'm honoured.'

'There's not much more to add.' She gave him a strained smile. 'When I went looking, I hit a blank wall. There were no records of my baby at all. There was no co-operation, no information in the mother and baby home. It was as though she'd never existed. And there was no empathy whatsoever forthcoming, as though it had served me bloody well right. Even though it was years later and I was in my early sixties and these were supposed to be more enlightened times, all those old feelings I'd had at eighteen came back to me and swamped me completely: the humiliation, the shame, the stigma of it all. What's worse, I have no idea if my daughter is dead and buried here somewhere, or still alive in another country, England or America. And I've no way of finding out anything.'

There was silence. Sean didn't try to dilute her grief with patronising comments or advise her that she was foolish to have harboured such feelings all her life. He simply opened his arms. 'Come here,' he said, enclosing her in his warm embrace.

*

Afterwards she lay sleepless in bed, thinking of Sean asleep in the room next door. Fragments of their conversation drifted through her head, including something she'd said earlier ... *I could be anybody.*

She could be anybody, couldn't she? She could choose to be the retired school teacher who'd shut herself away from life, held prisoner by decisions she'd made in her youth and a long-held dream that had turned sour; she could choose to be the retired, inspirational school teacher who'd helped other young women turn their lives around with her dedication and commitment. She could choose to be Noah's third granny and Sean's like-minded, empathetic contemporary.

Everything ran around in her head as she lay in the dark until something sparked inside her – whatever she chose, she didn't have to be who she'd always been. There was no age limit on rising like a phoenix from the ashes of what might have been and creating a brand new future.

CHAPTER FIFTY-SEVEN

Galway,
three months ago

We almost don't go to Galway. It's the end of September, and you haven't been quite yourself for a week or two. I have the instinctive sense that something has changed between us. There is a tiny, almost imperceptible gap opening up in the rhythm of our life together, like a longer pause than normal in the break between one breath and the next.

'Is everything all right?' I ask you. You are sitting at the table and, framed in the window, Henrietta Square outside is showing signs of autumn. I'm looking forward to experiencing it with you, walking through the park with crispy leaves underfoot, new woody scents in the air, that last blast of colour and glory before the square is transformed with the stark beauty of winter. A year since I first met you. We've come full circle.

'Sure, yeah, why do you ask?'

I shrug. 'No real reason.' I can't put it into words because I'm too afraid to, and I don't have the words to pinpoint the ephemeral change I sense in you. A slight withdrawal. Something inward in your eyes, something beautiful in the way they rest on me and follow me around, as though you are imprinting every image of us, here, together, indelibly on your brain. As though you are storing it all up for future reference, banking these Henrietta Square days in your mind for when they might no longer be possible. We were back in New York at the end of August and you told me everything was fine. They were happy that your treatment was working. You went to a business meeting while I went shopping, going as far as to buy some Christmas decorations for our tree in Henrietta Square, as though the purchase of these was putting down some kind of definitive marker that I fully expected us to be celebrating Christmas together.

But now, three weeks later, I sense something has altered. Behind my calm front, an icy terror grips me. I knew that if your medication was beginning to fail, we could be looking at the beginning of the end.

We'd planned the weekend in Galway because we had a gift voucher for a three-night stay in a luxury hotel in the city. It had been a wedding present. You'd never been to Galway, and September seemed a good time. The city would still be buzzy and lively with visitors, although the crowds that flocked during the summer months would have dissipated a little.

'We don't have to go to Galway this weekend – we can postpone,' I say.

'There's no reason to postpone,' you say, giving me a determined look. 'I'm looking forward to it.'

*

You don't believe the song about the sunsets falling into Galway Bay until you see it for yourself. Sharing it with you, it becomes the most glorious and beautiful sight.

'Next stop America,' I say, watching the crimson ball slowly slip down into the infinity where the sea meets the sky. The horizon blazes with the radiant hues of a long, lingering sunset and the surface of the sea carries a crumpled reflection.

'Over there on the other side of the sea it's the early afternoon and that exact same sun is a bright yellow disc. The world is amazing, isn't it?' You smile at me, the vivid sunset lighting the planes on your face.

I breathe in the moment – it is perfect.

The following afternoon, the world is not so amazing at all.

Life changes in a split second. Words I'd spoken blithely to you in a New York park come back to haunt me. We are on our way up from Claddagh Basin, back to the hotel through quaint narrow streets, when it happens. A car mounts the pavement at the junction where the pedestrian area begins. I think at first it's an errant driver going the wrong way, and he or she will realise the mistake in a minute.

Then I realise the car is out of control.

I freeze. You are slightly ahead of me, lured across the laneway by the sight of guitars lined up in a music-shop window, but you sense something, hear something, because you jerk around and—

There is a child in the path of the car, a child who has run ahead of his mother.

You stare right into my eyes, a gaze of diamond-hard love that I meet with split-second understanding. There will be no slow falling apart for you.

You run to the child, pushing him to safety, taking the brunt of the impact. There is a crumping sound and you are lifted into the air, and you … and you …

I see the horror of it sliced into a bystander's face but I don't feel anything at all because I am encased head to toe in frozen numbness.

In the next few hours I am sucked under a deep arctic ocean full of ambulance sirens, hospital smells, my constricted throat gagging on hot, watery tea, chairs scraping across grey linoleum floors, my breath caught in my chest, a transfer across to a hospital in Dublin that specialises in head injuries, flying into my mother's arms, my brother's embrace, an endless jigsaw of bright lights, sterile smells, concerned faces refracting in front of me, mixed up with a cold sludge of knowledge pushing at the icy barrier in my heart. I see the approach of dawn light cracking against a stippled window pane when I take a bathroom break. How could the sun rise again? I read the sombre faces of the doctors and nurses. I want to rewind time to the moment we came up from the Claddagh. You try to hold on until your family arrive from America, but twenty-four hours after we were on our way back to the hotel, you are gone forever.

I don't want to look at you. I don't want to know you have left me. My brother holds me tight and tells me it's okay. I peek out from the shelter of his arms. You have no fear on your face. You look young and peaceful. It is impossible to think you will not talk to me again, kiss me and hold me. So I don't think at all.

I find out afterwards that the driver suffered a heart attack at the wheel. You saved the small child's life but the car caught you at the last moment, sending you into a dizzy spin so that you fell backwards, smashing the back of your skull against the kerb, causing irreversible brain damage.

I also find out that the therapy you were trialling had begun to fail, something you must have known but had chosen to keep from me.

Two or three months max, they estimated, is all the time you would have had left on this earth.

*

Your family are with me, as are mine, the day we bring your remains to a crematorium in Dublin. They agree with me that you are of the sunlight, the stars and constellations, and not the cold, dark earth. Three days later we travel back to Galway and we release you into an orange and ruby autumn sunset, into the air above the crimson-speckled ocean that goes all the way to America.

I see you borne up on wind thermals, whirling around in the cosmos like glittering stardust.

CHRISTMAS EVE

CHAPTER FIFTY-EIGHT

Florence had always found Christmas Eve bitter-sweet, but this morning it was different. As soon as she awoke, she remembered Sean and the warmth of sharing a nightcap with him. Then she remembered their conversation of the night before, and instead of thinking about what might have been, the default mindset that had bogged down her Christmas Eves for years, she let those thoughts go and lay for several moments in the cosiness of her bed, thinking of the lovely man in the room adjacent to hers and his warm understanding.

Sean had a coffee with her, before going upstairs to Tom's for a cooked breakfast.

'You're welcome to join us,' he said to Florence, looking

better than ever in the morning light, his face fresh and relaxed, wearing jeans and a thick grey jumper, his brown eyes calm and friendly.

'No, I'm fine, thank you,' she said, annoyed that her voice sounded so prim. She'd loved to have joined Sean for breakfast up in Tom's, but right then, she felt too shy. 'Besides,' she said, softening her reply with a smile, 'I have a few things to sort out for tomorrow.'

There was a short pause.

'Thank you for last night,' he said. 'For your hospitality, for our chat and for trusting me enough to confide in me.'

'Thank you,' she said. 'It was a great help to me.'

'Good. We can talk about it again, any time you want. There might be other avenues you can try – I'd be happy to help, and if you're ever in need of a hug, I'm happy to supply that as well,' he said, smiling at her.

'Thanks for that too.'

'I hope you're up to joining me in my snowman-making?' he asked just before he went upstairs. 'I promised Noah I'd build him the biggest one ever, over in the park, and I might need your help.'

'I haven't made a snowman in a long time.'

'I'm sure it's like riding a bike, something you never forget. We'll call for you in about an hour,' he said, taking her acceptance for granted.

'Okay,' she said, something warm running through her veins. She chided herself in the next breath for her adolescent reaction. She busied herself contacting Wendy and Jean, finalising the arrangements for Christmas Day dinner and planning last-minute baking. Her pulse began acting up again when Sean knocked on her door later, just as she saw Noah through the front window, rushing across to the snowy park.

Together they strolled out into the cold, crisp day in Noah's wake, Florence bundled up in the black parka she'd put on the night before. The thick, threatening clouds of previous days had finally cleared away and the world about her seemed to be gleaming. The low winter sun glinted through the trees, sending buttery yellow columns across the snow, the beautiful tracery of the bare tree branches etched against a clear blue sky. She breathed deeply of the cold, crispy air, letting it seep all the way into her bones, getting rid of anything stale and fusty. Sean and Noah's laughter echoed in the still air, and in the Christmas Eve morning, Henrietta Square looked wonderful. She had a sensation of being at one with the calm beauty of the day and she remembered how easily she and Sean had chatted the night before and how the words she said had freed and cleansed her.

She glanced up at Izzie's windows but the drapes were still drawn. She'd meant to knock up that morning, but it had slipped her mind. She wondered what time Eli was leaving at, surprised they still appeared to be sleeping in.

Then, as she rolled a ball of snow, something from last night snagged in her brain. *If you're Tom's father you have to be kosher*. Similar words she'd applied to Eli, visiting Izzie upstairs. Only Noah thought he was a fake and it seemed Izzie had never actually met Eli before now. Even Gemma had been concerned about Izzie's behaviour being at odds with the woman she'd known in the office.

She'd put her mind at rest later that morning. She'd go up to the second floor and check Izzie out for herself.

'I'm putting you on notice that we're expecting you for dinner tomorrow,' Sean said later, when they came back into the hallway and stamped the snow off their feet.

She shook her head. 'I don't want to intrude on your family Christmas.'

'That's an order, it's not an invitation,' he said. 'I know you help out with dinners for the homeless, Tom explained all that to me, so we're timing our food to make sure you're back home for it. In fact, I'm going to go with you to lend a hand and escort you across and back through the snow. To make sure you do come back.' His eyes twinkled roguishly. 'Tom and Noah will be cooking the dinner for us. It's all arranged.'

'Oh gosh,' she said faintly.

'Don't ask me what we'll be having – it all depends on whatever Tom manages to get his hands on at this short notice. He headed out to the shops straight after breakfast.'

'That's what I need to do,' she said. 'If I'm going to dinner tomorrow I want to bring something decent with me to contribute to the party.'

'You don't have to do that.'

'I know I don't have to, but I want to.'

'Right, then. We'll head out together, I'll pick up something too and maybe we could fit in a visit to the Italian for lunch – is that an idea?'

Her heart quailed at the image of the two of them sitting at a small table. This was ridiculous. Hadn't they shared a nightcap last night? Hadn't he slept in a bed just a room away from her? Hadn't she shown him the depths of her pain and regret? And it had meant more to her than she could ever have thought. Where was her Girl Power when she most needed it? She forced herself to meet his eyes. His smile was warm and gentle. There was nothing to be afraid of. Except her palpitating heart.

'Yes, Sean, I'd like that,' she said.

'Good. One o'clock-ish?'

'Perfect.'

CHAPTER FIFTY-NINE

Later, as it approached lunchtime, Florence remembered Izzie. Glancing at the clock, she saw she'd have enough time to pop up for a minute and make sure she was okay before she went to lunch with Sean. She had got as far as the hall when she saw Noah coming down the stairs, looking dejected.

'Noah? Are you okay?'

It was Christmas Eve. A child like Noah should be bubbling with excitement.

'Yeah,' Noah said, looking anything but happy.

'What's wrong with you?' Florence asked.

'It's Izzie – she won't open the door,' he said.

'Were you up there knocking again?' Florence asked as kindly as she could.

'Yeah, but she won't answer. Maybe she didn't hear the knock. I thought if I called her through the intercom I'd get her that way. It's important.'

'What do you want to see her for?'

'It's one of the DVDs.'

'Your Christmas present? That's sitting under the tree? Waiting until tomorrow morning to be opened?' Florence tried to keep a broad smile from breaking across her face.

Noah shifted from one foot to the other. 'Yeah, well, I know I wasn't supposed to open the present until tomorrow, but I figured I've already seen them, so it's not as if it was going to be a surprise ...' He paused, clearly discomfited. 'I just thought I'd have a quick look.'

'I can understand that,' Florence said. 'Did you want to thank Izzie?'

'Not exactly ... she sent down two discs I didn't have before and I put one of them on, but it's not *Star Wars* at all. It's one of Sam.'

'*Sam?*'

'Yeah, I got a fright when I saw his face. He's playing music and talking. I just played it for a couple of minutes before I took it out. It looks like Sam recorded himself talking to Izzie, but I don't want to hear him being all lovey-dovey.' Noah made a funny face and put his eyes up to heaven. 'I didn't play the other disc in case it's Sam as well.

'Say that again – it's a DVD of Sam talking to Izzie?'

'Well, I guess he is. He starts off with 'my darling', and you can see their apartment window in the background so he recorded it up there, sometime during the summer. Before he—' Noah gulped.

'Oh dear, it sounds as if it's personal. I'm sure Izzie didn't mean you to have that. She must have given it to you by mistake, or else Sam put it away in the wrong box.'

'Sam would never do that,' Noah said, his tone scoffing. 'He'd never get his precious *Star Wars* discs mixed up. I think Izzie put the discs in the wrong box by accident when she gave them back to me and she might be missing them!'

'It might be best to leave her alone for the moment – she has Eli looking after her so it's probably not a good time to give the discs back.' What else could she say? She remembered Gemma's story of Izzie in her dressing gown in the early afternoon. They were obviously still in bed. Some attraction Eli was turning out to be.

'That's exactly why I wanted to give them back to her. They'll remind her of Sam, and she'll see that Eli is—'

'Yes?' Florence told herself to go carefully. Noah was going to be hurt if he still expected some Christmas magic to happen between his father and Izzie.

'Eli has to be a fake. He doesn't know anything about *Star Wars* – he's only pretending to know.'

'But why would he do that?'

Noah shrugged. 'I dunno. I guess he's trying to make Izzie like him more by pretending to be the same as Sam, but he's not. He's not even a quarter as nice as Sam, or my dad.'

Florence sighed. Noah clearly saw Eli as the biggest threat to his impossible Christmas wish. 'Look, Noah, leave it for the moment,' she suggested. 'We're all a bit upside down with the snow. Normal life has been thrown up in the air and that's without Christmas on top of us. Put the discs away safely for now. Does your dad know?'

'No, I had it on the player in my bedroom.'

'Well, tell your dad as well, in case he puts it on by mistake.

If I see Izzie I'll mention it to her.' She could have asked Noah to give her the discs for safekeeping, but she trusted him to look after them and it was better if Izzie didn't think her discs were going all around the house.

'I'm going to try her intercom first,' Noah said.

'I think Izzie is lucky she has someone like you looking out for her,' Florence said.

Noah's face brightened a little, but not enough for a child on Christmas Eve. And from what he had told her, Florence knew there was no point in her venturing up to the second floor. Izzie was otherwise engaged.

CHAPTER SIXTY

The shrill of the intercom bell roused Izzie. She reached out of thick layers of sleep. She was lying on her sofa, cramped, her neck stiff, her head throbbing, all of her insides aching. The room was in semi-shade thanks to the closed drapes, but daylight pressed at the edges, telling her it was morning.

And it was Christmas Eve. One of the most sentimental days of the year.

The bell rang again. Eli came into her line of vision, striding across the room, the sight of him in his black tracksuit making her stomach churn. She closed her eyes and pretended to be asleep. He pressed the answer button on the intercom and she heard Noah's young voice.

'Izzie,' he said, 'I went up and knocked at your door but

I got no answer – maybe you didn't know it was me and I'm sorry if I'm disturbing you but I need to talk to you.'

There was a silence. Izzie held her breath.

'It's the *Star Wars* DVDs you gave me for Christmas,' Noah said. 'There's a bit of a problem and I need to see you to explain.'

Fuck. Izzie froze and willed Noah not to speak. She should have guessed he'd be unable to resist opening the gift before Christmas Day. It had been a foolish ploy on her part. She'd hoped the package would have stayed put under Noah's tree until Eli had left, the package that contained another copy of Sam's farewell message to her, and a disc containing a backup copy of everything Eli was looking for.

'Why don't you come on up, son?' Eli said.

She heard him marching out into the hall and she strained to listen, holding her breath. Presently there was a knock at the door and Eli opened it.

'Hi, is Izzie—?'

Go away, Noah. But that was as far as Noah got before Eli interrupted.

'Izzie doesn't want to be disturbed,' Eli said. 'So no more coming up here.'

'It's just—'

'Didn't you get the message, you stupid little jerk? Why don't you fuck off and wait for Santa Claus to arrive like a good little boy.'

There was silence. Izzie willed Noah to go back downstairs. She imagined him staring at Eli, stunned by the words coming out of his mouth.

After a minute Eli spoke again. 'Izzie wants to be left alone. She doesn't want to see anyone. Least of all you.'

The door slammed shut and Eli locked it.

Izzie heard him walking back into the living room and after a minute she felt her hair being pulled.

'Wake up,' he said.

Izzie sat up slowly, pretending to be far drowsier than she was. 'What time is it?'

'It's Christmas Eve. That's all you need to know.'

'Aren't you supposed to be gone?'

'Are you trying to be funny? We have a problem on our hands.'

'What kind of problem?'

'So far I haven't found what I need.'

'I told you there's nothing here.'

'That's a shame for both our sakes. Worst-case scenario, if I don't get what I want I'll have to go back to New York and try something different. I can't leave you around as a witness. It'll ruin my game plan.'

'You're mad,' she said, unable to prevent the words from coming out of her mouth, although she knew it was best not to antagonise him.

'So look on this as your last chance,' he said. 'Give me what I want, let me sort out what I have to and I'm gone. You'll be gone as well. Into the land of Nod for a few days. I'm not running the risk of having you blab and reverse all my hard work at the eleventh hour.'

Eli picked up Sam's guitar. He stroked the wood, ran his fingers across the strings, pulling them one at a time, making plinking sounds. 'Seems a shame to destroy this,' he said, raising the guitar in the air and bringing it down hard on a dining chair, damaging the body. 'If I don't get sorted, I've no option but to go to Plan C. Do you want to know what that is?'

'No.'

'It's not a nice story. It doesn't have a happy ending and it means permanent land of Nod for you. Poor Izzie,' he said, his voice suddenly softer. 'Left all alone on Christmas Eve night and for Christmas Day, the most emotional time of the year. So upset she can't bear to see anyone. So broken-hearted she won't even answer the door to any of her nosy neighbours. And by the time your family realise there's something wrong and come running, I'll be long gone. And it'll be too late for you.'

'What do you mean?'

'What does a combination of too much alcohol and sleeping tables do?' he said, in a sing-song voice. 'And the beauty of it is, you have your end all set up perfectly. I didn't have to do too much – it fell into my hands. Look at the amount of alcohol you have stacked up, just for one person, the lack of food in your fridge. The way you insisted on being alone. It will come as no surprise to anyone that you've spent Christmas in a drunken stupor and were feeling so blue you OD'd yourself. Permanently. Ha, ha. Am I clever or not?'

'Florence and Tom – they'll wonder about me.'

'Why? I'm the old friend you invited into your apartment. Of your own free will. The good news is the airport is fully operational today, and additional flights are planned so that they can clear some of the backlog. Pity you felt so alone after I left. They've already seen you fuzzy from alcohol. They know you didn't bother to stock up on food. What does that add up to?'

'You're forgetting something – the mess you've made in the apartment.'

'I don't have to explain that, but you will, in your goodbye message to your family,' he said. 'Poor Izzie. Everything got too much for you. You apologise for the mess you left behind but the sight of everything you shared with Sam and all the memories they created got on top of you. You hoped that by trashing the place you might have felt better, but it only made you more depressed.'

She let his words fall around her without reacting. Maybe if all this had happened two months ago, she would have welcomed oblivion. Back then, there had been dark moments when she hadn't seen the point in living after Sam. There had been times when it could have been easy to take whatever she could to send her spiralling into something she never had to wake up from. Wherever Sam had gone, she would be with him. All the pain would have vanished.

But even though there were times when it seemed impossible to get through the next hour, let alone the day, and everything she did was on some kind of frozen autopilot, she *was* getting through the days. She *had* survived one of the worst things life could have thrown at her. She *was* getting up and showing up each day, alive and breathing, moving around in this world, engaging with it in some shape or form.

She'd gone back to the office. Not quite easing into it as though she'd never been away, like after a holiday, it seemed a strange fit, a microcosm of the awkward shape her life felt around her. Gemma had helped. In the middle of those days when Izzie felt she was sliding helplessly around on thin ice, she just had to pause, look at the fresh flowers on her desk and inhale gently as she focused on their perfect beauty. Before she knew it, the worst of the dark moment had passed.

'I'll be doing you a big favour, Izzie, taking you out of your misery,' Eli said. 'It'll be easy and gentle. You'll hardly know what has happened.'

Was he serious? He couldn't be. She couldn't let this happen. She tried to knit the edges of her dulled head together. *Focus*, Izzie.

She thought of Noah, Tom and Florence, going about their business, moving around beside gaily lit Christmas trees, tucked up from the snow, cosy fires in the grate, oblivious to what was happening on the top floor. Noah must have been disappointed at her no-show for his concert the previous evening. And she knew Tom would never forgive himself for being so close yet so oblivious to what was happening just up the stairs from him. If anything happened to her, thoughts of their unhappy faces shook her more deeply than she would have expected.

She couldn't bear to think of her family, gathered in her brother's house for Christmas. How traumatised they'd be if anything happened to her. Why had it seemed like such a good idea to keep away from them for Christmas? Why had it been so necessary not to inflict herself and her wounded heart upon them? They all loved her, so even in her absence, they were surely feeling helpless. She pictured her mother sitting by a Christmas tree, a glass of something in her hand, her thoughts turning constantly to Izzie. Worrying, fretting about her. An Izzie she had been asked not to contact. Her brother, Paul, knowing she'd preferred to stay in Dublin alone rather than spend time in his lovely, inviting home. How could Izzie have done that to her family? To herself?

'We're going in here now, bitch,' Eli said.

She didn't offer any resistance when he half-dragged, half-carried her into her bedroom. While she'd been in a drugged sleep on the sofa, he'd gone through her wardrobe and dressing table, and all the contents were dumped in a heap on the floor. She pretended to be limp when he lifted her and threw her down on the bed. So far he'd forgotten to drug her that morning. If she put up a fight, he'd only pour more stuff down her throat and she needed to gather some remnants of her wits about her.

'It's not too late to make it easy for me,' he said. 'I'm sure you know where the back-up is. Or the passwords. Come on, tell me – stop dragging this out.'

'Go to hell,' she muttered.

He laughed. 'I won't be going there any time soon. I have a lot of living to do. You don't, however. You'll soon be joining Sam.'

CHAPTER SIXTY-ONE

Tom went through kitchen cupboards, searching for crystal champagne flutes. He knew he had half a dozen stashed away somewhere – they had been a wedding present, but they hadn't been used in so long that they'd need a wash.

He'd been falling down on Cathy's legacy. She'd been a firm believer in not keeping anything for a special occasion, that every day in their lives together was a special occasion. She'd lived her life according to that belief and had used the beautiful glasses as often as she could, even if it was just for bargain-bin Prosecco. She'd put out the best cutlery, the good plates; she'd lavished her special perfume, worn her jewellery and pretty underwear.

For the first time in years there would be proper champagne

on Christmas Day, because Sean had decreed it. Right now he was out with Florence, hunting down a bottle in the locality, even though Tom had warned him about the ridiculous queues he was bound to face. Sean had just laughed, saying it would allow him and Florence to spend time together, soaking up the Christmas vibe. Noah was in his bedroom, playing a game on his console. The television was on, tuned to a carol service.

He didn't feel like listening to a rendition of 'O Holy Night', no matter how beautiful it was, simply because it was almost too lovely to listen to without being moved. The choir, coming from some cathedral or other, sounded heavenly, but the concert last night had been bad enough; every note, every beautiful cadence, melting his heart strings, memories of Cathy and previous Christmases exploding in his head. Even earlier Christmases ran through his mind, before Noah, although he could hardly remember a time without his son in his life. But there had been days where he and Cathy had stood in the midst of Grafton Street sing-songs under a shower of glitter, wrapped up in warm coats and scarves. Then, after Noah arrived, he'd been deeply grateful to have a baby at Christmas, then a toddler, to watch the lights reflected in his innocent eyes, the house in Clane redolent with the tender warmth and peace that symbolised the best of Christmas Eve.

He found the glasses, filled the basin with warm, sudsy water and set to work. He was glad his father was out with Florence, giving him some quiet space. And what a turn-up that was – his father and Florence striking up a friendship.

Tom knew he'd be fine once Christmas Day arrived – there was just something evocative about the immediate lead-up to it that seemed to heighten the sentimental nostalgia of the date. This year, overlaid with missing Cathy, was the sourness in his gut because of what was happening on the second floor. If Eli hadn't turned up, there was a chance Izzie might have joined the group for dinner and he would have liked that. He would have told her she didn't have to talk to anyone if she didn't feel up to it, that Sean and Florence would be doing enough talking for the whole table, to judge by last night, that she didn't have to pretend to be cheerful: all she had to do was be there.

'Dad, can I put on something else?' Noah asked, coming out of his bedroom and heading across to the television.

'Sure, whatever.'

Noah pressed a few buttons on the remote and brought up a movie. 'This will do.' He threw himself back into the sofa, looking a little too glum for Tom's liking.

'Okay, whatever is bugging you, spit it out,' Tom said, slinging a tea towel onto the counter top and sitting down beside him.

'It's nothing, I'm fine.'

'Are you missing your mum?' Tom asked gently. 'I know it's a hard time of the year when you've lost someone you love, especially someone like your mum, so I understand if it makes you sad.'

'No, that's not it,' Noah said. 'And that's the big problem.' He sat forward, his elbows on his knees. He bent his head and rubbed his eyes, and then he sat there, his chin in his hands.

'What big problem?' Tom said, alarmed.

Silence. He couldn't believe how unhappy his son's face was. 'Noah, please tell me what's the matter. I promise I won't be cross no matter what you say.'

Noah sighed heavily. 'It *is* Mum.'

'What about Mum?'

'This might sound awful, Dad, but I don't miss her at all. I can hardly remember her.'

'That's okay,' Tom said, glad to wipe away the awful scenarios he'd begun conjuring in his head at Noah's unhappy face. 'That's allowed. You were very young when she died. Is that what's bugging you?'

'Sort of. I can hardly remember her face or what it was like to hug her. It makes me feel guilty that I'm forgetting her bit by bit.'

Tom ruffled his hair. 'Don't feel guilty,' he said. 'How could you remember much? Of course the picture you hold in your head will fade, but in your heart you'll always know that Cathy was your mother and she loved you very much.'

'Yeah.'

Noah's face still looked haunted. Tom said, 'Is there anything else bothering you?'

'Apart from weirdo upstairs?'

'Weirdo? You don't mean Izzie?'

'No way. I love Izzie to bits.' Noah clamped his hand over his mouth after this frank admission, as though he'd said something wrong.

'You do?' Tom asked.

Noah let his hands fall and stared at him. Then he obviously decided there was no point in pretending. 'Yeah. After Mum, I think she's – great.'

'Really?'

'Don't you like her?' Noah asked.

There was something in his eyes, an appeal, a kind of entreaty that surprised Tom and made him pause. He searched for the correct words to say to Noah, and then he knew there were no correct words: there was just the truth in his heart.

'I like Izzie very much,' he said. 'I think she's kind and gentle and lovely. I think what happened with Sam is the biggest load of – awfulness, and I'd love to help Izzie if there was any way I could.'

Noah slanted him a glance. 'And you don't think I'm forgetting about Mum if I say I kinda love Izzie?'

'Nah.' Tom smiled. 'Your heart is bigger than that, Noah. It has enough room for lots of people. That's what your mother would have wanted.'

'How about you, Dad?' Noah asked. 'If you like Izzie a lot does that mean you'd have room for her in your heart?'

Room in his heart? Tom wavered, shaken by a surge of tenderness in his chest as the image of Izzie's face swam in front of him. He thought of how beautifully she'd glowed when Sam had been around – the way her mouth curved when she smiled, the way her laughter sounded like a musical riff. He thought of the way he'd often found himself deliberately catching up with her in the park as he came home from work, or checking for post in the hallway at the same time she did, the kind attention in her eyes when she looked at him, the warmth emanating from her. The whole essence of Izzie – surely it was still there underneath the fog? He thought of the way there had been no awkwardness between them in Florence's the other evening, but instead moments of unflinching honesty and shared connection. Had Izzie already found a niche in his heart? And if so, had he the courage to open himself up to the possibility of loving someone else with no thought of being loved for now, given her current circumstances?

What would Cathy have wanted for him, his wonderful live-life wife? She would have given him a kick up the ass for putting his heart out of reach of anyone else, leaving it tucked away in a box like a pristine, unused champagne glass. She would have wanted him to spread more love around instead of using her absence as an excuse to avoid passion and commitment.

Even his father – Sean Brady's world had been pulled from under him, yet he'd become master of the art of embracing life to the full in honour of his beloved wife.

And what did he want? He'd been in bits after Cathy had died, just as Izzie was in bits with the loss of Sam, but he'd been wrong to think that love sucked; love had given him many happy years with Cathy, some wonderful memories and the joy of Noah – it was the absence of love that sucked.

Still, there was Noah to consider.

'What would you think if I said I had room for Izzie in my heart?' Tom asked tentatively. 'Would you think I'm forgetting about your mum?'

Noah smiled. 'Not if it's Izzie.'

'Well then, that's good to know. I'm glad we talked about this, but it might be best if we kept it between us for now.'

'Duh – I've already said something to Florence.'

'Florence?' Tom was bemused. 'What have you said?'

'I told her how much I hoped you and Izzie would become good friends. That would have been the best Christmas present.'

'And what did Florence have to say?'

Noah's face clouded. 'She told me not to be expecting too much, that Izzie was still hurting after Sam.'

'Florence is right,' Tom said. 'The best we can do is look out for her, let her know we're here if she wants anything and be kind and gentle and loving around her. She needs time to get used to life without Sam. Who knows, she might decide to move out of here, but while she is around, you and I can keep an eye on her and let her know we're both in her corner.'

'That's why I don't like that weirdo guy, Eli. He's not a kind person, like Sam was. Or you.'

Tom's heart ached. 'I know why you resent him now.'

'It's more than that, Dad. Something else happened.' Noah hung his head.

'What else happened?' Tom asked, swallowing back more alarm.

'It's to do with Eli.'

'Eli.'

'Look, Dad, I know I wasn't supposed to, but I opened Izzie's present, cos I already knew what was in it and I'd seen them all. I just wanted to look at them now that Izzie gave them to me for keeps, but she made a mistake and put in two DVDs that weren't *Star Wars*. One of them was of Sam playing the guitar and talking and it seemed personal.'

'She has been a bit forgetful all right.'

'I went upstairs to give it back, but I didn't even have a chance to explain, or even see Izzie. Eli opened the door and used the F word and called me a jerk.'

'When was this?' Tom asked, gripped with an overpowering urge to punch out Eli's lights.

'Today, when you were out at the shops.'

'Do your best to ignore him, Noah,' Tom said, forcing himself to dismiss his fury and sound calm and reassuring. 'He was way out of order to speak to you like that. Hopefully he'll be gone soon.'

'Yeah, I hope so too. He must have seen the shock on my face because he switched back to being the smiley Eli we saw the other night and told me Izzie wanted to be left alone, that she didn't want to see anyone, least of all me.'

It sounded most unlike the Izzie he thought he knew, Tom decided hollowly.

'I don't like him, Dad. Not one bit,' Noah went on. 'I think he's weird. I can't believe Sam would have had a best mate like him.'

'I don't care for him myself, Noah, as far as I'm concerned the sooner he's on his way home, the better.' Tom didn't confide that privately he couldn't believe Izzie was entertaining such a crass, insensitive guy. Then Sean Brady chose that moment to arrive home after his lunch with Florence, bursting through the door brandishing a bottle of bubbly and a tin of sweets, sparking the air around him with a barrage of Christmas cheer.

Quite the opposite to Tom's dark thoughts.

CHAPTER SIXTY-TWO

Gemma strolled slowly through the park in Henrietta Square. The clouds had all cleared, washing the sky a bright azure blue, and sunshine dazzled on the snow. The walk from St Finnian's Gardens had taken almost forty minutes, and she'd tried to get her thoughts in some kind of order as she'd come through slushy city-centre streets fizzing with crowds and carol singers and the excitement of Christmas Eve. Now her pace slowed and every so often as she drew closer to number sixteen, she glanced up at the top-floor windows. Everything looked exactly as it had the previous day. The drapes were still drawn even though it was after lunch. Another late night for Izzie and Eli?

Instead of pressing the bell for the second floor, she rang Florence's bell. She didn't realise she'd been holding her breath until Florence answered and she sagged with relief.

'Hi, Florence, Gemma here. I'm back again.'

'Gemma! You must have pressed the wrong button – Izzie's is the top one.'

'No, it's you I'm looking for.'

Florence didn't just buzz her in. She came out to the hall door immediately and opened it wide. 'Hello again. Have you something else for Izzie?'

Gemma hesitated. Now that she was here, Florence looked so nicely normal, happy even, that she told herself she must have been imagining everything.

'Are you on your way out?' she asked, noting that Florence was wearing a black padded coat.

'I'm just back this minute,' Florence said, opening her coat and freeing her scarf. 'I've been out to lunch with – a friend.'

'I'm not sure what I'm doing here,' Gemma said, 'but something Izzie said … it bothered me.'

'Sorry, Gemma, what am I like! Don't just stand there, come in,' Florence said.

Gemma stepped into the hall, wiping her slush-encrusted boots on the mat. 'This hall is beautiful. Everything about this house is so lovely and normal that I'm beginning to think I'm probably imagining stupid things …'

She found herself being ushered warmly into Florence's apartment. 'Sit down,' Florence said. 'You don't seem like a stupid person to me. What is it?'

'Is Izzie still here?'

'Well, yes, I think so.'

'Have you seen her, yesterday or today?'

360

'No, but I didn't expect to. I think she plans to hibernate in her apartment for now.'

'How about Eli? Is he still here?'

'As far as I know he is. I haven't seen him leaving.'

'I hope Izzie's okay with that,' Gemma said slowly. 'With Eli being here, I mean.'

'Why, do you think she mightn't be?'

'I dunno, it's just a gut feeling I had from yesterday that something wasn't quite right. It's not any one thing, more a combination of everything.'

'Like what?'

Florence sat down slowly in an armchair, fully attentive.

'I saw Izzie day in, day out after Sam,' Gemma said. 'The blank expression in her eyes. The way she walked around like a robot, how she spoke to people on autopilot. I know what she was like in the office – I shadowed her. She was there, but not there, right up to the time she left last Thursday. Seeing her with Eli yesterday ... and the carry-on, it didn't make sense to me. How could everything have changed? Almost in an instant? That Izzie had someone to take Sam's place, even if it's just for Christmas? She said something when I was leaving that didn't make sense either. I thought she was confused. And then the young boy, Noah, he was talking to me in the park. He had a few things to say about Eli that weren't complimentary.'

Florence smiled. 'Noah doesn't like Eli at all.'

Neither do I, Gemma said silently. 'I wonder why?' she said aloud. 'Everything was floating around in my head and when I was at home last night – we were all sitting around in our comfy PJs watching the telly. It was fun, it was cosy and I had a couple of glasses of wine, but I couldn't relax ...

You see, we were watching *Ghost*, my mum, my sisters and me. Mum loves that movie – it's our family tradition to put it on at Christmas, break open the sweets and have a girlie night …' She paused.

'That sounds lovely, Gemma,' Florence said. 'I have to say I'm quite jealous.'

'It's fun,' Gemma said. 'But last night – you see, Florence, the guy's name in the movie is Sam as well, and watching Sam and Molly in *Ghost*, it just hit me – Izzie and Sam must have been like that, so close, so much in love. I saw their wedding photograph. I saw what Izzie was like in the office after he died. I can't understand how she could have turned to Eli so quickly, no way … I'm concerned, too, that Izzie could be especially vulnerable right now.'

Florence was silent for several moments, as if she was absorbing Gemma's words. 'So what exactly are you worried about?'

'I could be mad, but when you add what Noah said to everything else, I think it's all a bit odd with Izzie and Eli,' Gemma said slowly. 'I had to come back to talk to you. Izzie doesn't know I'm here, by the way.'

'I know how Noah feels and why,' Florence said. 'Did he worry you? Noah has a vested interest in disliking Eli.'

'He told me he thinks Eli is not who he says he is.'

'I know. He's already said that to me. But does that make any difference? Eli told me he was Sam's friend, and I let him into the house. It was up to Izzie to allow him into her apartment, which she did. Twice. Even if he's not Sam's actual mate, maybe Izzie knows that? Maybe she and Eli are in a relationship and don't want us to know their business.'

'I dunno,' Gemma said. 'I can't believe Izzie's happy to hook up with someone else so soon after Sam.'

'To be honest, neither can I,' Florence said.

'And there are other things that bothered me.'

'Like what?'

'When I was leaving yesterday, I thought I saw Izzie at the window, then she disappeared in a hurry. I couldn't make out whether she ducked because I caught her watching me or she was pulled back.'

'Pulled back?'

'That's what it looked like. Then that guy closed the curtains, even though it was the afternoon. They're still closed. And if you add what Noah said to what Izzie said to me when I was leaving ...'

'What did she say?'

'I was on my way out the door,' Gemma said slowly. 'Izzie made a point of bringing it up. She mentioned a case we had in the office, thanking me for my help – she actually said it was good of me to have checked the solicitor's paperwork. Thing is, Florence, I'd nothing at all to do with that case, and at first I put it down to Izzie's general confusion. The case involved a solicitor who faked a signature ... I didn't think too much of it yesterday – I was too gobsmacked at the sight of Izzie, half-dressed, with another man. It was last night, when I was thinking of her and Sam and added everything up, that I thought it was peculiar. Why did she say that? Was there a particular reason?'

'What kind of reason?'

'Maybe there's something fake going on with Eli. Even when I think of the way Izzie didn't even bother getting up off the sofa yesterday afternoon – she looked like she was stuck to it. And I don't know why she couldn't have popped down herself with the present for Noah.'

'So you think there's something odd going on.'

'Yes, I do', Gemma said. 'It's not just one single thing. It's when you put everything together. It's even odd that the curtains are still closed even though it's the afternoon on Christmas Eve.'

'They could be just having a major lie-in. How do we know, Gemma? Maybe Izzie is all over the place, and especially vulnerable right now, but more than happy to have Eli there as a friend because she's missing Sam so much.'

Gemma stared at Florence. 'Is there any chance Eli could be taking advantage of her, knowing she'd be low at a time like this?'

'I see where you're coming from,' Florence said slowly. 'Eli invited himself here. Maybe Izzie was too frail to refuse him. To set our minds at rest, why don't I go up and invite both of them down for Christmas Eve drinks? We'll see what happens then. I don't want to risk embarrassing Izzie. I hope we're wrong and that for her sake we're adding up two and two and making twenty. She's been through enough.'

'But what if we're right?' Gemma said.

There was a moment of taut silence as she and Florence stared at each other, imagining the worst.

Florence said, 'If we are, I'm sure we can summon the best of our Girl Power to come up with a plan.'

Gemma grinned. 'Hey, Florence, you're my kind of woman.'

CHAPTER SIXTY-THREE

Izzie lay on her bed, hearing the knock on her door, her mind screaming for help through some kind of fog. Most likely it was Tom or Florence – anyone outside would have rung the intercom bell first. It was unlikely to be Noah, back up again after the way Eli had sent him off.

Eli marched into the room. 'Who the fuck is that now? Don't they know we're not to be disturbed?'

Izzie forced herself to talk, grappling with the words. 'It's probably Tom or Florence. You can't get rid of them the way you did Noah. Maybe Tom's annoyed at the way you spoke to him.'

Eli went out to the door and returned a moment later. 'It's that nosy pig, Florence.' He went to lift Izzie off the bed but she flopped against him, pretending to be weaker than she was.

'You can't show me off like this, like you did with Gemma.'

'Can't I?'

'If anyone sees me like this they'll know there's something wrong. Go on, I dare you. I've nothing to lose, have I?' she challenged him.

'Izzie, it's me,' she heard Florence call through the door. 'I just wanted to ask you to Christmas Eve drinks,' she said, raising her voice further. 'If Eli is still with you, both of you are welcome. No problem if it doesn't suit. I hope you're keeping okay.'

Eli pressed the point of the blade to Izzie's throat.

'Not one word,' he said.

Despite her bravado, the pressure of the knife at her throat kept Izzie silent.

'If you can't come down, Izzie,' Florence called out, 'I'd like to drop up later with a bottle of wine, just to wish you a happy Christmas.'

After a short silence, Eli grasped Izzie's hair and angled her head backwards. 'Just as well that nosy bitch is gone,' he said. 'I hope you haven't done anything to alert her.'

'How could I?' Izzie said in a strangled voice. 'Florence was just asking us down for a drink, that's all. It's Christmas. We do celebrate it in Ireland.'

'She'd better not come knocking again. Or anybody else, for that matter.'

'My family might.'

'Even though you've told them you'll be away?'

'They might guess I didn't get going with this weather.'

'You texted them to say you'd arrived and that you'd be switching off your phone for a few days.'

The pressure on her scalp hurt. Izzie tried to ignore darts of pain. 'My brother knows I'm here,' she said.

'And you made it clear you wanted to be left alone.'

'Florence might be back with that bottle of wine,' Izzie said.

'You won't know because you'll be out of it, I promise you that. And it's beginning to look like I might have to arrange a permanent solution.'

CHAPTER SIXTY-FOUR

Sam, I need to get out of here. Do something. Fast. You said you'd always be with me, you said you'd love me forever – well, come on, now's your chance to prove it. And I'm sorry, but the main thing I've found out with this Eli guy and his attempts to hurt me is that even though I still feel all-round cold and empty, and much as I will always love you, I'm not ready to join you just yet. When I felt the cold knife at my throat everything crystallised inside me, and just when I was in danger of losing it, my life became infinitely precious in a way it never was before.

So I'm not ready for my bones to become glittering stardust floating around the universe, no matter how beautiful that may look. I'm not ready to join incandescent constellations just yet. I want to go on living and relish the ordinary yet wonderful joys that are part of this world – read books, listen to music, go to concerts, walk barefoot on a beach, eat ice-cream and chocolate and drink champagne, watch the sunrise and sunset. Most of all I want to love and be loved, to be wrapped in the glow of a hug, luxuriate in the tenderness of a hand holding mine, share a deep, meaningful kiss and a total togetherness with someone special. I want to make love and celebrate passion. I want to bring new life into this crazy, mixed-up yet beautiful world, something precious and momentous that eluded you and me.

In the meantime, there's just a little problem. I need to get out of here. Somehow. Soon. I'll do my bit if you do yours. Fifty-fifty.

*

Izzie lay on the bed, her eyes closed to slits as she watched Eli go through the chest of drawers, and she cast her mind over anything and everything that might be possible for her to do to save herself. The main door of the apartment was locked and Eli had both her keys and the spare key tucked into his pocket so that was a non-runner.

If she could get to the front windows and throw something out? The triple-glazed sash windows were also secured with window locks, and she tried to think where those keys were kept. The mantelpiece. Of course. They were sitting in a bowl she and Sam had brought back from France. She tried to visualise how it might be possible to get her hands on the keys, open a window and throw something out that might alert Florence – or Noah if he was going over to the park to play. There was no point in throwing anything out her bedroom window, which overlooked the laneway. It might lie unnoticed until tomorrow or the next day.

Then she remembered that Eli had found those keys when he'd trashed the room.

She remembered that she had a couple of spare sleeping tablets in a small travel bag in the bathroom. It held some essentials for when she spent a night away from home. If she got her hands on them, there might be a chance to slip them into Eli's drink. She could ask him to make tea and distract him somehow. It was a slim chance but worth a try.

'I need to use the bathroom,' she said.

'No.'

'It's a woman's thing. Do I have to spell it out?'

He looked at her through narrowed eyes. 'How come I think you're trying to fool me?'

'What's the point in that? You're in control, but it's my time of the month and I need, um, protection.'

'What do you want exactly?'

'Tampons. I'm all out of them in the en suite but I have some spare supplies in an overnight bag in the bathroom.'

'Show me.'

He pulled her off the bed and half-dragged, half-carried her to the bathroom. She stumbled over to the cabinet and, grabbing onto the basin for support, took out the vanity bag. She opened the zip and held it out for his inspection. 'Look, see?'

'I'll give you two minutes.' He closed the door and left her alone.

Precious minutes alone, Izzie sagged with relief. But her relief was short-lived. She took out two tampons and a mini-tube of toothpaste, underneath which there should have been a bubble of foil with two sleeping tablets. There was no sign of them. When she stumbled out of the bathroom a few minutes later, Eli was waiting outside the door, a big grin on his face.

'I hope you weren't looking for these,' he said, taking the foil-wrapped tablets out of his pocket and holding them up. 'Naughty, naughty. I checked everything,' he said. 'I'm taking no chances with you. Problem is,' he went on in a silky voice, 'it's almost time for me to leave, I don't have what I need and you know what that means. Plan C.'

'Wait!' she said. He'd been so caught up with searching the apartment that he still didn't realise he'd forgotten to drug her up that morning. Another dose, force fed by Eli with a knife at her throat, and she'd be out for hours, longer – forever, maybe, if he followed up on the worst of his threats. She was tired of fending him off. She'd come to a dead end and couldn't see a way out. She'd everything to lose and she wanted to *live*.

Buy time. Somehow. String him along and hope for the best. It was her only chance.

'Okay,' she said, leaning against the doorpost for support. 'You win. I can't take any more. I'll tell you where everything is.'

CHAPTER SIXTY-FIVE

'No luck, Gemma,' Florence said when she arrived back in her apartment, a little defeated.

'No answer?'

'No response at all. I don't know if Izzie's there and just not bothered to answer the door. She could be gone out,' Florence said, voicing all the things she'd said silently to herself as she'd come back downstairs, trying to ignore the peculiar sensation she'd had standing outside Izzie's apartment: that the top floor had been hushed, as if it were holding its breath, that unseen eyes were watching her, and a shiver had gone down her back as she'd looked at Izzie's spyhole and wondered if someone was staring out.

'Sorry,' Gemma said, getting up to go, 'I'm wasting your time. I'll leave you in peace.'

'You have me worried now,' Florence said. 'The more I think about what you said …' She went across to the window and looked out onto the square, niggles of anxiety darting through her stomach, thinking how good it would be to see Izzie coming through the park on her way back from the shops, and wishing she could somehow conjure this up.

'It could all be my imagination getting the better of me,' Gemma said.

Florence turned away from the window. 'Then again it might not be. I'll talk to Tom,' she suggested. 'See what he thinks.' She picked up her phone and Tom answered immediately.

'I'd like to see you for a moment,' Florence said. 'It's kind of awkward so could you pop down to me, but leave your father and Noah where they are?'

This was swiftly turning out to be a Christmas Eve with a difference. She'd been kept busy from the get-go. No time to dwell on what might have been and, for the first time in fifty-four years, no time to agonise achingly over absent loved ones or whether they might be in this world or the next. Moments later, she opened the door to Tom.

'You're on your own?' she asked.

'Yeah, Noah and Sean are stuck into *Home Alone* for at least the next hour. Gemma! Hi, I didn't see you there for a minute.'

Florence watched Tom's relaxed face grow taut as he registered the concerned expression on both her and Gemma's faces. 'What's up?' he asked. 'Is there something wrong with Izzie?'

'That's the thing – we don't know,' Florence said. She turned to Gemma. 'Why don't you tell Tom exactly what you've told me?'

Tom listened without interrupting while Gemma went through everything, wincing when she commented about Izzie being in her dressing gown and Eli's pointed remarks about the late night and a long lie-in, his brow furrowed with disquiet by the time she had finished.

Florence then recounted her fruitless trip up to the top floor. 'There's nothing concrete that I could put my finger on,' she said. 'It's more that we both think something doesn't feel right about all of this.'

'That guy is a piece of work all right,' Tom said. 'Noah had a run-in with him earlier today.'

'Did he talk to him? When I spoke to Noah he told me they weren't answering the door.'

'He rang the intercom. There seems to be a problem with the DVDs Izzie gave him, but Eli sent him off with a flea in his ear – he called him a jerk and said they weren't to be disturbed.'

'Did Noah talk to Izzie at all?' Florence asked.

'He wasn't in the apartment. This all happened at the door.'

'So he didn't see Izzie?'

'No. Eli asked him to come up only to bawl him out of it. It's not like Izzie to ignore him.'

'So either Izzie is totally into this guy, to the point of ignoring everything going on here, including Noah, or ... he's somehow preventing her from talking to anyone.'

'Why, though?' Tom asked. 'He's here because he's Sam's friend and happens to be stranded, like hundreds of others. How could that add up to someone who's now intent on stopping Izzie from seeing us?'

'I don't believe that Izzie could be into this guy,' Gemma

said. 'And Noah has good reason to believe he's not Sam's friend.'

'I know exactly what Noah believes,' Tom said. He shot Florence a meaningful glance that spoke volumes. He took out his phone. 'There's no point in me going upstairs if they're not answering the door. But the least I can do is text her.'

'Do you have her number?' Florence asked.

'Yes,' Tom said. 'And she has mine. After Sam died I insisted we exchange numbers in case she needed my help at any time or had any emergencies. She hasn't texted me yet, though.'

'Not even now?' Gemma asked.

'No,' Tom said. 'That's why I assume everything is okay. If there was any kind of problem surely she would have got on to me?'

'Unless …' Florence said, hesitating. 'Is there a chance she can't get to her phone any more than she can get to the door? I'm trying to decide where the boundary lies between being a nosy neighbour, the last thing that Izzie needs, and being a friend who's looking out for her.'

Tom looked at her steadily. 'Can't get to her phone? You're talking serious stuff here, Florence.'

'I know. And if that's the case, Gemma and I are both prepared.'

CHAPTER SIXTY-SIX

'Are you trying to make a fool out of me?' Eli said, glaring at Izzie. He grabbed her arm and bent it up behind her back, hurting her.

'Let go of me,' she spat. He let go of her so suddenly that she fell back into the bathroom and had to grab onto the door for balance.

'Are you telling me that all the time I've been searching you knew everything I needed was on a disc? And yet you went and handed it out to that little fuckwit?'

'Yes,' Izzie said. 'And Noah's not a fuckwit.'

'You stupid bitch. I can't believe you did that.'

'I didn't want you to get your hands on it,' Izzie said. 'How could I stand by and let you cream off funds meant for a children's charity? And it was Sam's work. I know how much it meant to him. He put a lot of commitment and passion into that project. It was his last ever job, and I didn't want you pulling it apart.'

'Aw, shucks,' he sneered. 'Sam, the good guy. Well, say hello to the bad guy. You'd better find a way of getting it back, hadn't you?'

'You mean *you'd* better find a way. *I* can't see anyone considering the state I'm in – they'd know something was wrong. And it's all thanks to you.'

He stared at her through narrowed eyes for several moments. 'I hope there's no chance you're fooling me. Or sending me on a wild goose chase. Let me think for a minute. In here, where I can keep an eye on you,' he said, taking her arm and propelling her into the living room where he pushed her onto the sofa.

She watched him pacing the floor, sensing the energy exuding from him, an energy she was unwilling and unable to confront. Presently his phone bleeped and he took it out of his pocket.

'Well, what do you know.' He grinned at Izzie. 'I guess it is my lucky day after all. I told you I deserved a break. It's Tom, your good friend from the floor below, sending you a text. He wants to wish you a happy Christmas Eve, and if you need anything to let him know. Isn't that cute! So now, what do we do?'

CHAPTER SIXTY-SEVEN

Tom looked at the text coming through.

'Izzie seems to be fine,' he said. 'Although I'm surprised by her text.'

Surprised? He was being polite for the benefit of Florence and Gemma. As he'd read Izzie's message, he'd got a hollow sensation in his chest.

'What does she say?' Gemma asked.

'She wants me to return the DVDs she gave to Noah. She made some kind of mistake and wants to check them again.'

'That's not too surprising,' Gemma said. 'It wouldn't be the first time Izzie has been absent-minded.'

'I know,' Tom said. 'Noah already went up to return them, but got the lash off Eli.'

He didn't bother to explain that the text also asked him not to open the discs, but to return everything to Izzie as soon as possible. If he dropped up to the apartment, Izzie's text said, he could hand them in to Eli because she wasn't up to visitors at the moment.

Visitors? Was that how Izzie saw him? It was like a slap in the face, especially after the night in Florence's and the way she'd trusted him enough to talk to him. He'd welcomed the idea that for a sweet, precious moment they were kindred souls sharing the same quiet space. He'd been fooling himself. Big time.

'At least it'll give you an opportunity to see Izzie,' Gemma said.

'Yes, Tom,' Florence agreed. 'You can set all our minds at rest.'

'I can't, actually,' Tom found himself admitting. 'I've been asked to hand them in to Eli because Izzie's not up to visitors.'

'What?' Gemma said. 'For fuck's sake – excuse the French, but she's asked you to return a pressie she's gifted to Noah, and you won't even get to see her? That's not the Izzie I know.'

Florence stayed silent.

'What are you thinking, Florence?' Tom asked. It wasn't the Izzie he knew either.

'I don't know what to think,' she said. 'Izzie has answered your text so she's using her phone. If there was anything wrong, she would have let you know, wouldn't she? But I agree with Gemma – it does seem a bit out of character for her.'

Prickles of indecision ran down his back. To hell with it – he'd never forgive himself if Izzie was in trouble and he hadn't come to her rescue. And if he ended up making a fool of himself, so what? Her safety was all that mattered.

'Why don't we all go up?' Tom suggested. 'We'll be friendly and polite. We can say we're just bringing up some Christmas gifts, okay? You'll have to loan Gemma a box of chocolates or something, Florence, so she's not empty-handed. We can say that we fully understand Izzie doesn't want to see us and that we've no intentions of disturbing her. We'll see how Eli reacts, and if we think there's the slightest problem, or smell a rat with him, well then there'll be three of us to sort it out.'

'So,' Florence grinned, 'in other words we're going in? As in taking him out?'

'If we have to, absolutely,' Tom said.

'Gemma and I have a sort-of plan,' Florence said.

'Let me at him,' Gemma said.

*

'You'll be glad to hear Tom is on the way up,' Eli said.

'What happens next?' Izzie asked.

'I'll do what I have to do and get the hell out of here,' Eli said. 'Once I know I have the program in the bag, it shouldn't take too long. You don't have to concern yourself with any of that.' He grinned at her. 'You won't know. As soon as I've checked the disc to make sure it has what I need, you're going to have a nice long sleep. You really should have just handed it over in the first place. Being noble about Sam's work didn't get you anywhere. It made no difference to Sam and you could have prevented all this trouble.'

'I hope you rot in hell, you low-life bastard,' Izzie said.

He giggled as though she'd cracked a great joke.

'The disc will be encrypted,' she said.

'Well, naturally,' he replied, taking a small laptop out of

his bag. 'I've enough tools on this to make short work of any encrypted disc.'

'You've had that all along,' she said.

'Surprise, surprise.'

She heard the knock at the door, signalling Tom's arrival. Eli got to his feet, smiled at her as though she was his best friend and reminded her that he had a knife.

Izzie concentrated hard on wiggling her toes and flexing her legs, her chest tightening with panic.

*

Tom had had to be discreet as he'd slid the DVDs from under the tree and re-sealed the gift; there had been no point in involving Noah. Standing outside Izzie's door, he knew he'd never forgive himself if Noah had been right about Eli and he hadn't taken his son seriously. Then again, he'd never forgive himself if Izzie was annoyed that they'd ignored her request not to disturb her – 'they' included Gemma and Florence, who were waiting either side of the door, out of the line of sight of the spyhole.

'The element of surprise,' Gemma had said.

The door opened several inches, just enough for Tom to see Eli standing inside.

'Is that all of them?' Eli asked brusquely, holding out his hand.

'Yes, but I'd like to see Izzie,' Tom said, not relinquishing his grip.

'That's not possible,' Eli said. 'She asked not to be disturbed.'

The urge to punch Eli in the guts returned with full force. 'I know, but I have a Christmas gift I'd like to give her in person.'

'Didn't you hear me? Izzie doesn't want to see anyone.'

'Funnily enough, Eli, even if she's annoyed with me, I'd rather she said that to my face.'

Eli opened the door a little wider and squared up to Tom, his polite veneer ripped away. 'Why don't you just get lost, give me those discs and leave us in peace.'

Tom sensed the suppressed rage coming from the man. He stepped back, still holding onto the discs. 'Hey, man, cool it. We're Izzie's friends – we come in peace.'

'We?' Eli said, moving forward to thrust his head out the door.

'I've a gift for Izzie,' Gemma said, waving a box of chocolates.

'So have I,' Florence said, holding up a bottle of wine.

Eli's face darkened with annoyance.

'We all want to give her these in person and wish her a happy Christmas,' Tom said. 'Surely she can spare a few moments?'

'Don't you get it? Get the fuck out of here, all of you. Izzie wants to be left alone.'

At that moment Tom saw a figure sidling out of the sitting room, into the hallway behind Eli. He froze. Izzie – a white-faced, dressing-gowned Izzie. Slumping against the wall, as if needing it for balance, she inched towards him. In the same moment, the expression in Eli's eyes hardened, as if registering the change in Tom's face. Any second now, Eli would turn and see her.

Tom wasn't the only one who had spotted Izzie. Florence had.

She began to sing. As loudly as she could. Holding the bottle of wine as if it were a microphone, she jived across the top-floor landing shouting out a Beatles melody about being just seventeen, catching Eli off guard.

Tom was lifted with a rush of love for Florence and her feisty spirit. The sight of her antics transfixed Eli long enough to enable Tom to push past him and reach Izzie, taking her into the safety of his arms.

'He has a knife,' Izzie whispered.

One arm supporting Izzie, Tom whirled around to Gemma and Florence. 'He has a knife,' he called out, at the same time as Eli flicked something small, silver and deadly out of his pocket.

'Come and get me,' Gemma roared, standing back, her arms raised in combat, totally unfazed.

'Here's to Girl Power,' Florence called out, launching forward with her bottle of wine and bashing it off the side of Eli's head. He lunged for Gemma, the knife in his hand. She let out a half-cry, half-scream and went in for the attack, kicking her booted foot into his groin and moving closer to jab her elbow into his throat.

Tom was just about to come to Gemma's aid when she took him by surprise. 'You dirty bastard,' she yelled at Eli. In a neat movement she grabbed the bottle of wine from Florence and brought it down heavily on Eli's wrist, causing him to relax his grip on the knife. It dropped to the ground and Gemma kicked it away. Then she made short work of wrestling Eli to the ground, whereupon she sat on him, fingers digging into his windpipe. Sitting on Eli's legs, Florence grabbed the knife and held it against Eli's crotch.

'Not one move, you skunk,' she said. 'Or I'll inflict a life-changing injury.'

'Gemma! How the hell did you do that?' Tom asked,

grateful that his arms encircled Izzie, who was clinging to him.

'My mum sent me and my sisters to self-defence and karate classes,' Gemma said. 'One of the perks of living in St Finnian's Gardens. Although mind you,' she glared down at Eli, 'I've never have to use those skills until this gobshite came along.'

Alerted by the commotion, Sean Brady and Noah had come up the stairs, Sean taking in the situation in a single glance. His phone out, he was calling the guards before he reached the second landing.

'Nice one,' Noah said. 'I told you that dude was a weirdo.'

CHAPTER SIXTY-EIGHT

It was turning out to be the best ever Christmas Eve, Noah decided that evening.

Weirdo was gone. Not only gone but arrested, taken away in an actual squad car with flashing blue lights. Noah had stood at the first-floor window and watched, pinching himself to make sure he wasn't just imagining all this. He'd a great view of the car outside, the lights firing blue strobes across the snow in the hazy evening, just like Rey's blue lightsabre in the finale of *Star Wars: The Force Awakens*. But best of all was weirdo dude being sandwiched in the back seat between two guards. He hoped Tigi had seen it all too. Then he reminded himself not to hope for too much, in case there was a limit on his wishes.

He'd felt very important when the guards had talked to him, a woman and a man, the man writing down everything Noah said in a notebook, his dad having to leave Izzie's side for a few moments and sit beside Noah because of his age. His dad had even told the guards that Noah had had his suspicions about 'Eli' from the beginning and he was sorry he hadn't listened to him. Noah didn't feel any glow in being right. He'd hated seeing Izzie in bits. He was glad that a doctor had been called and said she'd be fine.

The guards were still in her apartment and she wasn't allowed up. Florence and Sean were going around to everyone with tea and drinks and Gemma was passing around some of Florence's cakes and biscuits but, for once, Noah wasn't hungry, even for Florence's cakes. His dad was now back on the sofa beside Izzie, and Noah decided it was okay to have a warm feeling in his tummy because of the way his dad had his arm around her shoulders and Izzie seemed fine with that.

It turned out that weirdo dude was Todd Wilson, a cousin of Eli's who looked very like him. He'd been to college with Eli and Sam and had worked in a company they had lots of dealings with. He seemed to be in some kind of trouble in New York and he'd been stalking Izzie and planning some kind of cyber-robbery on a children's charity. He heard his dad call him lowdown scum. He didn't even give out when Noah called him a bollocks to his face. He'd loved that moment, but not as much as he loved seeing his dad and Izzie sitting close together.

Then just when Noah was allowing himself to feel a fuzzy kind of glow, like the Christmas-tree fairy lights were shining inside him, the intercom rang. Sean answered it.

'Hi, I'm sorry to bother you, but I'm looking for Izzie,

Izzie Mallon.' It was a man's voice. 'She's not answering her intercom.'

'Oh dear,' Florence said. 'Another man looking for you, Izzie – this is exactly how it all started.'

'No, it's okay,' Izzie said, sounding happy. 'That's Paul. You can let him in and tell him I'm here.'

In the space of an instant, Noah couldn't believe how low his heart sank, never mind how quickly his father's face changed. It was like someone had wiped off his smile with a wet dishcloth. Moments later, a cool-looking guy walked into their living room and Izzie got up and went into his arms, laughing and crying as though she knew him well.

Bollocks.

'Did you seriously think I was going to leave you home alone for Christmas?' the guy said. 'I have a borrowed jeep outside and there's a tractor ready at the other end, if you don't mind a bumpy ride.'

Izzie leaned in and hugged him tighter.

Then everything changed again when Izzie turned around to his dad.

'I forgot, you two have never met,' she said. 'Tom, this is Paul, my brother.'

'Ah, Tom,' Paul said. 'I've heard about you. Thanks for keeping an eye out for my little sis.'

'You don't know the half of it,' said Izzie, as his dad stood up to shake Paul's hand.

'Yeah, what's going on with the police?'

Then Izzie and his dad sat down together and his dad put his arm back around her shoulders as they began to talk to Paul.

Ace.

CHAPTER SIXTY-NINE

Hi Sam.

It's five o'clock in the evening on Christmas Eve and I'm in Tom's apartment. Things went a little crazy in the last few days, but good things happened as well.

Seriously? I can imagine you laughing. How could that be, you ask, considering I'm sitting here in my dressing gown, the guards are still in the apartment and it could be sealed off until after Christmas? Well, you see, over the last few days, and for the first time since you died, I've been thinking about you again, talking to you just as you asked me to, reconnecting with all the lovely filaments of you that are engrained in my heart, remembering how joyful it was to be with you. Up to then I'd bleached out everything about you and me from the fabric of my life as though you had never existed, as though our love had never breathed and fired us up and made us molten gold. Remembering you and talking to you has given me a strength I didn't know I had, and the courage to face the future, to think that I might *have* one. There is great joy in knowing the spark of us will always be there in the infinity of time – your death will never reduce that. There is hope – our touchstone – in recalling the promise I made to you to love again.

Thank you for that.

I'm also following your example of being fully alive to the moment and this is as good as they come. I'm sitting between Tom and Noah on a sofa that's drawn up to the warmth of a glowing fire. Tom's mantelpiece is decorated with soft white lights and candles, and Christmas-tree lights are sparkling away, reflecting off baubles, a cosy and comforting sight as the evening draws in. Henrietta Square is framed in the other window. The street lights have come on and the park is now a silent yellowy-white under its blanket of snow. You'd love it.

For once Noah's usual chatter is a little subdued. He keeps glancing at me as if to reassure himself that I am really here, and I find myself winking at him. It turns out he never played the second of the discs that I hid in the *Star Wars* box for safekeeping. It was the disc with all your back-up files, encrypted of course, but with a cautionary opening message you'd put there as to the sensitive Stanley Trust material it contained and the immediate need to return it to them. The evening my visitor arrived back in Florence's, I tucked it away as soon as he went to the bathroom and was relieved I'd done that when he began to ask about your devices. But it's just as well Noah didn't see it. He probably would have blurted it out on the intercom message when he tried to return them, whereas he'd been too embarrassed to mention the private contents of the disc he'd started to view.

Florence is making herself at home in Tom's apartment, pouring tea and organising drinks and nibbles, aided and abetted by Sean. Her face is flushed and I know it's not just the wine – I don't think I've ever seen her so vital and vivacious. Florence and Sean are sparking off each other, the banter between them infectious and drawing everyone in. I think we all know from the way they are looking at each other that this is the beginning of a wonderful friendship. They are talking about spending New Year's Eve together in Cork city and heading out to west Cork on New Year's Day. Sean says the January countryside is starkly beautiful. The way he talks about it makes me long to see it for myself and inhale the absolute gorgeousness of it, which is a good thing. Watching them together makes me realise there are many different aspects to life and love; mostly that love comes in many forms, life is fluid, it keeps going on, twisting and turning, shifting and reforming, bringing you around unexpected corners, and all of them can be enriching, if you allow them to be.

It'll soon be the new year, and no matter what has happened, it's a chance to start afresh. The months and years that are ahead of me are still a blank canvas, waiting to be filled. How richly they are coloured depends on me. I'm the girl who once free-wheeled down Wicklow laneways and saw life as a big huge escapade. I'm the woman who went on a rollercoaster adventure with you, loving you to the limits. I can still be the passionate warrior woman that you inspired me to be once again.

First there is Christmas to celebrate in Paul's house with

my family. Tom is going to visit Cathy's mother in Kilkenny as soon as the weather permits in the days after Christmas, and on his way home, he has offered to make a detour to Paul's to bring me back to Henrietta Square.

'That's if you're still going to call this home,' he says, a question in his eyes.

'Yes, I will,' I tell him. 'Sam and I chose to live here, on purpose, because we knew there would come a time I'd be without him. Henrietta Square seemed like a good place to be. It still is.'

Tom looks away, trying to hide it, but I see the private smile breaking out across his face.

'I'll tell you all about it sometime soon,' I say, knowing he will understand more than anyone else.

Henrietta Square is a good place to be mostly because of Tom and his smile. It lights up his face and it is so profoundly kind it settles around me like a blessing. Together with the memory of us, it touches a part of me that has been frozen for months, like a warm spring breeze breathing gently across the solid winter ice, dissolving it slowly so that the water flows and ripples again, like my life and my love.

ACKNOWLEDGEMENTS

Writing a book and getting it out there is a team effort.

Huge acknowledgement is due to the indispensable champions behind the scenes, my team of family, friends and cheerleaders – wonderful people who have my back, who supply coffee, a glass of wine, a listening ear, a friendly nudge, words of encouragement, inspiring messages, and who offer unconditional love and friendship. You keep me going through the hours I spend in solitary splendour, so a big thank you from the bottom of my heart is due to each and every one of you.

To my agent, the brilliant Sheila Crowley and the team in Curtis Brown, London, thank you for your unstinting support, enthusiasm and energy.

Another part of the team is the fantastic Hachette Books Ireland. Thank you to my talented and insightful editor, Ciara Doorley who reads my drafts and enables me to bring out the best in them – also warm congratulations to Ciara on the birth of her new baby daughter. Big appreciation is due to Joanna Smyth for tireless help and in particular the gentle but diligent way she took care of this manuscript at the copy-editing stage. Thank you to everyone in Castleknock – Breda, Jim, Bernard, Siobhan, and big hugs to Ruth. I am grateful to Emma Farrell, the copy-editor, and Aonghus Meaney the proofreader, whose skills helped to put the final polish on my words.

Book bloggers and bookstore staff are another vital part of the team. I wouldn't be able to enjoy this wonderful career as much as I do without your passionate support and commitment, so thank you for everything.

And to my loyal troupe of readers, thank you so much for your uplifting messages and for keeping me in a job that I love.

I hope you all enjoy *The Visitor*.

Zoë xx

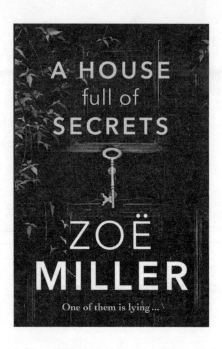

A HOUSE FULL OF SECRETS

All she sees is the perfect man – but what is he hiding?

An invitation to visit Niall's childhood home is too good an opportunity for Vikki to pass up. This is the chance she's been waiting for to get closer to her friend, and to meet the family he's always been so cryptic about.

But when Vikki arrives at the beautiful but remote Lynes Glen on Ireland's west coast, and finally meets Niall's estranged brother Alex and his overbearing sister Lainey, she realises that this reunion will be far from heart-warming.

As Vikki fails to convince any of them that she saw a mysterious woman at the lake – off-limits since a tragic accident – strange and sinister incidents begin to happen at the Blake family home. What secrets are they keeping? And why exactly did Niall ask Vikki to join him for the weekend?

Also available as an ebook